"Wyatt!" Remy shouted. *"Wyatt!"*

He didn't bother to look back, but moved more quickly now, easing backward, shoving the branch at the spitting jaguar. The feline swiped a massive paw at the branch, jolting it in his grip and snapping several more branches. There was hope that when the zombies arrived, the cat would become their target or at least be distracted by them . . . but then again, he'd never seen an animal attacked by a zombie.

They preferred human flesh.

"Wyatt!" Remy cried again, and he finally looked over at her, a furious retort at the ready, but then he stopped.

She was brandishing a blazing torch, and gesticulating wildly with it.

"Get back in the damned truck," he snarled, grabbing the torch from her.

The zombies were in full view, but the jaguar didn't seem to notice. She was intent on the man who'd infuriated her, and in one breathtaking move, launched herself in a long, sleek pounce . . .

Romances by Joss Ware

JOSS WARE

NIGHT RESURRECTED

AVON
An Imprint of HarperCollins*Publishers*

This is a work of fiction. Names, characters, places, and incidents are products of the author's imagination or are used fictitiously and are not to be construed as real. Any resemblance to actual events, locales, organizations, or persons, living or dead, is entirely coincidental.

AVON BOOKS
An Imprint of HarperCollins*Publishers*
10 East 53rd Street
New York, New York 10022-5299

Copyright © 2013 by Joss Ware
ISBN 978-0-06-201867-0
www.avonromance.com

First Avon Books mass market printing: March 2013

Avon Trademark Reg. U.S. Pat. Off. and in Other Countries, Marca Registrada, Hecho en U.S.A.
HarperCollins® is a registered trademark of HarperCollins Publishers.

Printed in the U.S.A.

10 9 8 7 6 5 4 3 2 1

*This book is dedicated to the memory of Nora Ephron,
who wrote one of my all-time favorite screenplays.*

NIGHT RESURRECTED

PROLOGUE

June 2010
A suburb of Denver, Colorado

Wyatt adjusted his facemask as the black wall of smoke surrounded him. The sounds of his breathing, forced through the regulator he clamped between his teeth, were barely audible beneath the loud roar from the fire. Glowing flames rose in a hot, angry blaze and cast eerie shadows that danced on the ceiling and along the top of a long sofa. His protective gear helped shield him from the heat and smoke, but once inside an inferno, it was impossible to see.

Yet, with the aid of his TIC, Wyatt could use the thermal imaging device to make out vague shapes in the living room. No sign of the woman here. Her husband waited in the front yard of their blazing home, hysterical and half dead from smoke inhalation himself. If his wife was closed up in one of the rooms—a bedroom, or better yet, a bathroom—there was a chance she'd come out alive.

The loud crash behind him had Wyatt dodging as a chunk of ceiling fell in a flaming mass. A new wave of heat shimmered in the eerie blue light of the camera lens. He felt his helmet jolt and then the skim of hot pain over his back as a second piece fell.

Fuck. *Got me.*

Wyatt grabbed Handlemann and gestured toward the dark hall, relieved the flames hadn't spread here yet.

Cheech McDermott hadn't wanted his boss to go in after the woman. He'd planted himself in front of Wyatt in a wide stance as he adjusted his helmet. "It's too damn late for her, Chief. You know it is."

But Wyatt and Handlemann went in anyway. If there was a chance, and even if there wasn't, he'd go in. Just like if there was any chance of dragging a member of his platoon out of the remnants of an explosion in Iraq, he'd take it.

He'd want someone to do the same for any member of his family.

Love you, Cath. Love you, Abby. Love you, David.

Take care of them for me if I don't make it out.

Only moments ago he'd sent up this silent prayer as he stepped onto the porch of the burning house, Handlemann behind him.

Now he started down the hall, moving as quickly as possible in the dark. The smoke was thick and his breath rasped in his ears, but it was half a degree cooler over here at least. Sweat trickled down his spine and cheeks. A noise-dulled shout from behind had him spinning in time to see a chunk of flaming wall collapse.

Handlemann ducked out of the way, but now there was burning drywall and wood flaring between them. Flames skipped in a riotous orange fence. Wyatt pressed the button on the mic clipped to his collar and said, "H, I'm going on."

He took two more steps and the floor gave out. *Christ.* Pain shot up his leg and he knew he'd scraped the shit out of it, probably burned it too. He was up to his hips, one foot dangling into the basement below, the other miraculously stopped against a ceiling beam. Now the flames were coming along the hallway fast, and he had to pull himself out.

But it was like dragging yourself out of a broken patch of ice . . . the floor kept shattering every time he put any pressure on it.

This could be it.

No, not yet. Not yet by a long shot.

Wyatt forced himself to ignore the throb in his leg and the same ache in his back. Focus. He needed leverage. *There.* The underside of a closed bedroom door.

His fingers curling up beneath the bottom of the door, he gripped the wood, and leveraging with his one stable foot, pushed up and pulled with his hands. With one hard, sharp movement, he launched himself out of the hole and tumbled onto the ground.

Christ.

He staggered to his feet, a flash of panic whipping through him. The hall was choked with flames behind him and in front loomed darkness . . . but not for long.

He still had his TIC strapped around him and he lifted it as he felt for the knob of the door that had just saved his life. The brass knob was warm even through his gloves, and Wyatt knew he had less than a couple minutes to get the hell out, woman or no woman. Or his wife would be a widow and his children would grow up without a father.

But not this day. No, not this damned day.

He twisted the knob and stumbled through the door as yet another chunk of something crashed to the floor. The bedroom was filled with smoke, and he looked through the viewer of the imaging device, searching for the shape of a human body. Then he saw it—the lump on the floor by the window.

A window. With fresh air on the other side, and a streetlight streaming through. Flashing red and blue lights from the trucks strobed in the darkness. Hot damn.

Wyatt staggered over, his leg still screaming with pain, his back scraped and already blistering, and scooped up the body. She moved weakly and he felt a blast of relief.

He smashed the window with his axe and didn't even have to wait; his crew was outside. Ready.

Curling his arm around the woman, he climbed out the window.

Three hours later Wyatt wandered into the kitchen at the fire station. His back was bandaged up, the first degree burn medicated and protected. His leg, the skin peeled off in a three-inch wide swath, was not burned and had been attended to by the paramedics on-site. He kept his limp to a minimum, practicing for when he got home.

"Yo, Chief, you about done being a hero and want some chili now?" Cheech looked up from the pot he was stirring.

"If it's Bev's chili, you're damn right I want some."
Wyatt settled gingerly onto a chair, careful not to
press his tender back against it. He could have gone
home, but the injuries were mild, relatively speaking. And he only had two more hours on his twenty-
four-hour shift. He'd be home for a day, then take
off for the weekend to Arizona with his buddies. Elliott and Quent were two of his closest friends, their
bond forged when they met doing hurricane relief
in Haiti a decade ago. This was going to be a fun
trip, though—an all-guy getaway, where the only
danger was running out of beer or hiking too long
and too hard and having to sleep on tough ground.
He couldn't wait.

Besides, if he went home early, Cathy would be all
upset and probably make even more of a fuss about
him going away this weekend if he was injured. Better
to power through it. This was nothing compared to
the time he ended up beneath half a car in Iraq. Or
nearly fried in the fire at a dry cleaner's. And then
there was the time he fell on his ass into an iced-over
lake, trying to extricate a hunting dog . . .

The chili was damn good. Spicy as hell and filled
with chunks of tender beef, and accompanied by a
hunk of corn bread. The only thing that would make
it better was a cold one to go with it—but not while
on duty.

"The wife tonight—she gonna be all right?"
Cheech asked, settling at the table with his own bowl.
He scooped up a bite before his ass even touched the
chair. "Damn, this is good."

"Your Bev makes the best," Wyatt agreed, shovel-
ing in another bite. "And yeah, the wife's gonna live.
Close one, that."

"You're telling me. Handlemann thought you weren't going to make it out."

"*I* thought I wasn't going to make it out. But I did. I sure as hell wasn't going to miss this weekend," he added with a grin. "First all-guy getaway in three years. We're going on an extreme hiking trip deep in the Sedona caves in Arizona. Just us and the outdoors. Think you can hold the fort while I'm gone?"

Cheech snorted. He was the assistant chief, and because their department was so small, both of them worked normal twenty-four-hour shifts at the fire station while managing the department. Wyatt liked it that way; it kept him close to the work, reminded him why he did it. "We all can't wait for you to get your tight ass out of here. You need some time off."

"That's the truth." Wyatt grinned, feeling about as happy as he'd felt the day he and Cathy got married. The only other times he'd felt so full of himself, so beyond happy, was on the days his children were born. And the day he stepped off the plane, Stateside, after his last tour in Iraq.

He loved his children, his wife, and his life—but there was nothing like being able to just be with his friends and have no responsibility but to enjoy himself. Every so often a guy needed a getaway.

He gulped down a big glass of milk and looked at Cheech. "Just so long as Cath doesn't hear how bad it was tonight, okay? Tell everyone to keep it under the hood." He knew how close he'd come to biting it tonight. But it was best to keep that stuff to himself. His wife didn't need anything else to fuss over. She understood why he did what he did, but she didn't like the long hours and the danger that came with it.

"You got it, brother." Cheech nodded.

The next day, Wyatt kissed his wife Catherine good-bye. He bear-hugged his eight-year-old son David and smooched his ten-year-old daughter Abby. Then he got on a plane and flew to Sedona.

CHAPTER 1

May 2061
Somewhere in the former State of Nevada

"What are you doing here?"

Wyatt looked at Remington Truth, who was pointing her gun at him, and thought, *Christ, sweetheart, I've been asking myself that for a damn year.*

If I'd never gotten on that damned plane to Sedona . . .

Instead of answering, he walked over to the fire she'd built for her overnight camp in the woods. She wouldn't shoot him. Not yet anyway.

Not that she hadn't already tried.

"How the hell did you find me?" Remy asked, lowering the gun. Even in the dim light, he could see the fury in her eyes. "Dantès showed up early yesterday, so I know you didn't follow him."

He hadn't expected a particularly warm welcome. After all, it was almost butting up to midnight. He was surprised she wasn't sleeping, and even more surprised she was camping out in the open like this. Damn good thing he'd decided to track her down and make sure wherever she was going, she got there in one piece.

But Dantès was glad to see him. Wyatt crouched by the fire as Remy's large dog, a German shepherd/wolf mix, greeted him with soft, ecstatic whines and crazy licking kisses.

"Hey there, bud," he said, shoving his hands into the thick, warm fur around the dog's neck and massaging. The dog was so enthusiastic, there was a danger he'd knock Wyatt into the fire, so he shifted from his haunches onto his ass. "Glad to see you again too." It was true. Dantès was one of the few things that made his new life somewhat bearable.

He glanced over at Remy, then around the small encampment. "You're a sitting duck for zombies here—or worse. I thought you'd know better than to be outside and on the ground at night."

Remy shot eye-daggers at him. She had the most incredible blue-violet eyes, but right now he imagined they were black with ire. He couldn't see for certain in the dark.

"It was only a temporary stop. I've gotten pretty damn good at avoiding getting myself killed, in case you haven't noticed. Besides, Dantès will smell or hear any threat long before it gets close enough to me. Although," she said, jabbing the fire with a violent stick, "he didn't see fit to warn me about you."

Wyatt held back on the obvious comment. Instead, he unhooked the pack he was wearing and let it flop to the ground behind him. "Did you eat yet? I—"

"I don't want you here; I'm certainly not going to feed you," she informed him. "I don't know why you followed me."

He stretched out one long leg as he untied the boot on the other. "I have food. I was offering it to you," he said mildly, pulling off his shoe. *Ahhh*. He wiggled his toes, then went on to yank off the other boot and sock.

At first he'd been on and off horseback while tracking her from the small settlement she'd left nearly a week ago. But when Dantès took off after finding his mistress's scent yesterday afternoon, Wyatt set the wild mustang free so he could better follow the trail on foot. He suspected once Dantès was with Remy, she wouldn't allow her dog to go back and bring Wyatt to her, so he'd moved as quickly and expediently as he could before the trail went cold.

It had taken him a little more than twenty-eight hours to catch up to her, even though he could tell she'd increased her pace. He had to give her credit: she moved along at a good clip, leaving only hints of her trail.

"What are you doing here, Wyatt?" she asked again. This time her voice wasn't as strident. It was weary.

It's complicated.

And even that was an understatement. Fifty-one years ago he'd boarded that goddamn plane from Denver to Arizona. He'd met up with his buddies Elliott and Quent for what the latter called an extreme camping trip, exploring some mountain caves in Sedona.

While they were deep in the caves with their guides Fence and Lenny, all hell broke loose. Some major earthquakes caused falling rubble and cave-ins, released poison gases, and knocked them all out . . . or something. When they woke up again and stumbled out of the cave, they discovered that the inconceivable had happened.

The earth had been changed. Most of civilization was destroyed—people, buildings, infrastructure.

And it was *fifty years in the future*. The year twenty-fucking-*sixty*.

And he—none of them—had aged a bit. They looked exactly the same.

But they'd lost everything.

Wyatt reached for Dantès, who'd settled halfway between his two human companions. Scratching near the dog's tail, he tried not to remember how devastating and paralyzing the realization had been. And still was. It was a year since he'd walked out of that cave, grateful and jubilant to be alive . . . only to find himself in something worse than hell.

He, Elliott, Quent, and the two others who were in the cave had been trying to accept this changed world ever since then . . . a world populated by dangerous crystal-wearing immortal Strangers, zombies, and lacking anything resembling infrastructure. This new environment was a strange mixture of simple, almost third-world settlements in overgrown buildings and empty towns combined with glimpses of twenty-first century America. Cell phones and the Internet didn't exist anymore, but there were lights and washing machines running on solar or wind power, carefully maintained televisions, and disc players for whatever DVDs survived—or had been scavenged—along with random books, clothing, and even furnishings that lasted fifty years for a variety of reasons. It was a strange juxtaposition, almost like the Old West meshed with a world filled with superhero pop culture and synthetic fabric.

Wyatt and Remy had been crossing paths for months—she wearing her distrust of him and everyone else on her figurative sleeve by being secretive and running away whenever she could. But this time he'd followed her, because he knew she was in danger—from the zombies as well as the Strangers. They'd been searching for someone named Remington Truth ever since the devastating events of the Change.

So far, he didn't think the Strangers knew that the woman sitting in front of him was the granddaughter—and namesake—of the deceased Remington Truth. But when and if they did, they'd be after her just as desperately.

"Do you have a destination in mind, or are you just running away again?" Wyatt asked.

"It's none of—" To his surprise, she stopped. Clamped her lips shut and looked at him through the fire. "I have a destination," she said after a minute.

"Good. I like to have my missions closed-ended."

"I'm not your mission, Wyatt."

He shrugged. "Dantès is. I can't believe you left him behind." *With me.* The dog was her most prized possession . . . except for the thumbnail-sized crystal she wore beneath her shirt. His gaze couldn't help but drop to her midriff, mostly obscured by the flames dancing between them.

She looked away, and might have intended to respond. But whatever she'd have said was cut short as Dantès's ears snapped up and he froze, completely at attention.

They both stilled, listening while looking into the darkness along with the canine. Dantès gave a low growl and got to his feet. And then Wyatt heard it. The low moans, rumbling in the distance.

Ruuu-uuuuthhhhh. Ruuuuthhhhh.

Zombies.

Searching for Remington Truth.

He didn't need to say a thing; Remy was already up, kicking dirt onto the small fire. He jammed his sockless feet back into his boots and snatched up his pack. She grabbed the one next to her, shoving her gun into the waistband of her jeans as he said, "Let's go."

He pointed north as she started to head east, but he was faster and grabbed her by the arm. "This way," he said, and propelled her toward the forest. "From the shadows, looks like there's high ground in the distance."

Damned if she refrained from arguing, setting off at a good pace instead with Dantès at her side. If they got to the base of the hill before the zombies found them, they could climb up the other side, leaving the clumsy creatures behind them. Zombies—or gangas, as they were also called—couldn't climb stairs or anything steep. But despite their awkward movements the bastards covered ground quickly, especially when they smelled human flesh. They were strong. And they were violent.

Remy moved along rapidly and with more confidence than Wyatt expected, being in the dark and in an unfamiliar place. Maybe Dantès helped. Nevertheless, he stayed close behind her, pausing occasionally to look back and listen, then easily catching up.

They were hiking through a junglelike forest, but threaded through it were remnants of the world Wyatt had left behind. Cracked and overgrown slabs of concrete that once could have been parking lots, building foundations, or even roads. They passed rusted-out cars, often sprouting the eerie shapes of trees or bushes growing through the windows. By the dearth of buildings, he figured they were on an old two-lane highway in the middle of nowhere. Fifty years ago this had probably all been desert. But since the Change, the climate and environment had been altered, turning Nevada into a tropical jungle. He wouldn't have believed it if he weren't living it.

And there wasn't a day went by he wished he weren't.

Wyatt kept an eye out for a possible hiding place, but the problem with charging into an old building in a hurry was a question of safety. They didn't have time to determine whether the floors were stable and could hold weight, or if the roof would come crashing down at the slightest jolt or vibration. Aside from that, any structure that was a potential sanctuary from the zombies would have to have access to a second level—and then again, there was the problem of stairs and whether they'd hold his 190-some pounds.

All at once Dantès stopped and began barking. His attention was fixed on something in the darkness.

Crap.

"What is it, Dantès?" Remy stopped, looking into the darkness. His ears were up at full triangulation, and his barking became a threatening growl. An animal threat, then, not human.

Wyatt automatically moved in front of Remy, thrusting an arm out to shield her. He had a Glock tucked in the back of his waistband, courtesy of the dead bounty hunter named Seattle. But he had only a little ammunition, and a handgun was of little use against the large predators that roamed this wild, overgrown world. Liberated from zoos and circuses during the catastrophic events of the Change, all sorts of non-native wildlife were threats to humans. A handgun bullet wouldn't stop a lion or tiger if it attacked. The pain would just make them angrier.

Dantès's growling became more intense, verging on barking. His ears were angled forward, and from the shape of his silhouette, Wyatt could tell his scruff was standing upright. Not good.

Remy bumped against him. She had her gun in hand now and had eased up to stand next to him. He didn't waste his breath explaining why that wasn't a good idea. The damn zombies were coming up from behind, and whatever it was in the brush was coming from the left. They didn't have many options. He scanned the area with new purpose, his eyes recognizing familiar shapes, calculating options.

"This way, slowly," he said, pulling her to the right. "Into that truck there. And for God's sake, don't make any sudden movements."

She muttered something that sounded like *duh!* and disengaged her arm from his grip. Dantès stayed in place, guarding the area, as Wyatt nudged Remy toward the only thing that looked like a safe bet. It was an old semi-truck cab. High enough to dissuade the zombies or a pouncing cat, strong enough to withstand a battering rhino or elephant. He hoped.

Still eyeing the shadowy forest, Wyatt reached for the metal handle of the truck cab's door. It was too much to hope it wouldn't be rusted into place. It was, but the window was missing most of its glass. "I'm going to have to lift you up through there," he said, glancing back at the dog. "Watch the glass." Dantès had backed away from whatever he saw in the shadows and stopped growling. Bad sign.

Ruuuu-uuuthhhh . . . ruuuu-thhhhhh.

"They're getting closer," Remy said, and he wasn't certain whether she meant the zombies, whatever was in the woods, or both. To his surprise, she actually sounded nervous.

Suddenly, Dantès erupted into a frenzy of chaotic barking and Wyatt saw a long, low figure slinking from the shadows. The moonlight dappled over its face, spots, and triangular cat ears. A jaguar. Just fucking great.

Without another word, he scooped up Remy by the waist and launched her at the cab's window, just above his head. He couldn't worry about pieces of glass stuck in the frame; that was her problem if she wanted her ass saved.

She muttered something rude as she slammed up into the steel, but caught an edge of the window anyway. Still watching the frenzied Dantès, Wyatt gave Remy another good boost, neatly avoiding grabbing her ass by levering her off a foot instead, just as the cat pounced. Dantès's barking choked off into a snarl as he met the jaguar in a ball of fury.

"Dantès!" Remy screamed, her head popping out of the open window.

Wyatt was already looking around for a big stick. Between that and his Glock, he might be able to help before the dog was injured too seriously. He was a good-sized canine and a match for the jag, but Wyatt was taking no chances.

He'd lost enough of what he loved.

Ruuuthhh . . . ruuuuthhhh . . .

"Stay there, dammit," he shouted at Remy, who was actually trying to climb back out of the damn truck cab.

The animalistic snarling was now interspersed with squeals and whines. *Something . . . need something.* Wyatt saw shiny blood in the mix of two frenzied animals, and, suddenly terrified he would be too late or ineffective, he whipped the Glock from his jeans. He wasn't going to stand there and let Dantès die while protecting them.

But as he was about to flick off the handgun's safety, the sounds of zombie moans rumbling ever nearer, Wyatt saw a large, fallen branch illuminated by the moonlight. He lunged for it, shoving the gun back into his pants, and swung it up.

As thick as his biceps, eight feet long, the branch was actually a dead sapling. It still had its countless branches and dried leaves, and without hesitation he charged toward the chaotic mess of snarling teeth and sharp claws. He slammed the heavy branch onto the back of the jaguar as hard as he could. The cat yowled as Wyatt jumped back, ready to protect himself. He could see too much blood.

"Dantès, *come!*" Remy shouted, fear pitching her voice high.

He didn't spare a glance to see if she was still in the truck or if the daft woman had climbed out after all, for the cat had separated from her victim and now faced him, snarling and spitting.

Dantès growled, but the sound was more feeble than before. He was still on four feet, his hackles up, but Wyatt could see him trembling.

The jag spared the dog a glance, then turned to the new threat of Wyatt, who still brandished the small tree. He was ready, holding it in front of him to keep the cat at a distance like a lion tamer with a chair. After a moment's hesitation the cat turned and dove toward Dantès.

"Oh no you don't!" Wyatt growled, using both hands to thrust the heavy tree at the cat again.

The jag hissed and twisted toward him in a breath-taking midair snap, but Wyatt didn't have the luxury of admiring it. He was now the target and the beast was pissed. He rammed the tree toward the furious cat, angling himself around so he and his weapon were between the jaguar and Dantès.

Ruuuuuuuthhhhh . . .

Surely the zombies were close enough by now to smell him and Remy. Damn it. Now they were really screwed.

He heard a creak and metallic thuds behind him and suspected Remy was clambering out of the truck. He wanted to shout at her but dared not let his guard down with the jag. The cat fixed him with green-yellow eyes that glowed in the moonlight, bisected by a vertical black iris. Her tail twitched like an angry whip. Along with streaks of blood, he could see the outline of her shoulder muscles in a stripe of moon-light. Damn. He'd be appreciating her sleek beauty and strength if he wasn't half certain he'd be dead in a few minutes.

"Get back in the damn truck," he shouted over his shoulder as he lunged toward the cat, catching her in mid-leap with the widespread branches of the tree. It connected with solid muscle and furious fur, and he grunted with effort from the force, then shoved it back as hard as he could. A few branches snapped but there was still plenty of brush between him and the cat as she tumbled backward, landing on four paws. As long as he could hold her off . . .

"Dantès!" Remy called behind him. "Come, Dantès! *Wyatt!*"

A little out of breath, still hefting the thick branch, Wyatt looked over at the panting dog, who still snarled and growled, ready to leap back into the fray. "Go, Dantès. Go!" He edged backward, urging the dog to move with him, still using the tree as a shield against the cat.

Ruuuuuthhhhhh. Ruuuu-uuuuthhhhh.

Something crackled in the bushes and Wyatt whipped around to look. He saw heavy, clumsy figures outlined in black against the dark gray of night, staggering through the trees. Their orange eyes glowed eerily.

"Wyatt!" Remy shouted, as if he didn't notice the damn creatures. *"Wyatt!"*

He didn't bother to look back, but moved more quickly now, easing backward, shoving the branch at the spitting jaguar. The feline swiped a massive paw at the branch, jolting it in his grip and snapping several more branches. There was hope that when the zombies arrived, the cat would become their target or at least be distracted by them . . . but then again, he'd never seen an animal attacked by a zombie.

They preferred human flesh.

"Wyatt!" Remy cried again, and he finally looked over at her, a furious retort at the ready, but then stopped.

Damned if the woman hadn't lit a fire from something *and* gotten the truck door open. She was brandishing a blazing torch and gesticulating wildly with it. Her meaning was clear, but he was already moving toward her while holding off the jag and didn't need her explanation.

"Get back in the damned truck," he snarled, grabbing the torch from her and nearly tripping over Dantès as he spun back. Fire in one hand, hefting the branch in the other, he rammed toward the wild cat once more, trying to give Remy the time and space to get her injured dog up into safety.

Then he had an idea. If he could set the branches and leaves of his branch on fire . . .

The zombies were in full view, but the jaguar didn't seem to notice. She was intent on the man who'd infuriated her, and in one breathtaking move launched herself in a long, sleek pounce from atop a fallen tree. This put her higher and sent her farther than before, and she would have landed on top of his branch if Wyatt hadn't dodged away. He tripped and nearly lost his balance, dropping the torch as he caught himself. It rolled out of reach. *Damn*.

Heart pounding, he swung quickly and connected with the cat, then realized his error was an opportunity. Distance gave him the chance. He jammed the dead tree and its dry leaves at the flaming torch, still circling around, keeping it between him and the jag until suddenly it burst into flames.

Now he had a massive torch, and in the breadth of a moment it was blazing wildly.

The sight terrified the cat, and she backed away, still hissing and spitting as Wyatt charged after her. Heat from the flames radiated toward him and he could feel the trunk beginning to warm. But he had two threats to attend to. No sooner had he chased off the cat than, trying to avoid inhaling the smoke, he turned to the zombies. They, too, were afraid of fire, and it took him only a few well-aimed thrusts in their direction to run them off. They lumbered awkwardly into the darkness.

By then, sweat trickled down his temples and chest and his hands were uncomfortably warm from the flaming tree's heat, not to mention cut and scraped up like hell. Most of the branches had burned off and the fire was eating at the trunk, making its way toward him. He looked around for somewhere safe to put it, knowing how quickly a whole forest could go up in flames from one small fire.

Had he seen any water? Had they passed anything . . . ?

He tried to think, then remembered seeing the gleam of a shallow pool in the indentation of a car's hood. But where?

He heard Remy shout after him—something obvious like *Where are you going?*—and ignored it, running off with the ever-flaming branch. Water or concrete or something that could contain the fire . . . He peered, hard to see in the dark, and not more than ten yards from the truck cab found a pool of water. Dropped the branch in, rolled the fucker around as it sizzled into nothing, and then, dusting off his abused hands, headed back to Remy.

"How is he?" Wyatt asked, hoisting himself up into the truck cab. He slammed the door behind him and turned to Remy. He had a moment to realize that this was a full sleeper cab, with what had been bucket seats in the front of the rig and in the back a compact living space.

But then he saw Dantès, lying on a pile of something, and Remy crouched over the dog's head. Blood gleamed in the low light, but Dantès moved, giving a whine of greeting and lifting his face as soon as he saw Wyatt.

"This," Remy said, looking up at him, tears glistening in her eyes, "is precisely why I left him behind—where he'd be *safe*!"

"Don't be a fool," he snapped. "If he hadn't been here, this would have been *you*. And then what would have happened to that damn crystal of yours?"

CHAPTER 2

Remy jolted, her hand going automatically to her navel. Of course he knew she had the crystal, that she wore it. But he didn't know what it was or why it was so important. How could he, when she didn't even know?

"Let me see him," Wyatt was saying, his attention refocused on Dantès. "I need light," he added in that commanding way of his that made her want to box his ears.

No thank-you for giving him the torch that saved their butts, no appreciation for forcing open the truck door so he could climb his sorry, stick-up-his-ass *ass* up into it, no concern for whether she'd cut or scraped herself when he shoved her up into this messy place (which she had, thank you very much) . . . all after showing up unexpectedly and uninvited, calling her a fool and snarling at her . . . and now he was ordering her around asking for a light.

He really was a dickhead.

Do it for Dantès, she reminded herself. And dug out a small, manual-powered flashlight from her pack, ignoring the streaks of her own blood that made it

slippery. She wiped her hand on her pants near another bloodstain, then, with three quick cranks, pro-
duced enough energy for a decent beam of light. She
shone it onto her beloved pet.

It wasn't as if she hadn't thought of the light before
Wyatt demanded it, but she didn't have the chance
to get to it. It wasn't an easy task helping an injured,
ninety-five-pound dog up into a door five feet off the
ground . . . especially when she was only five-foot-
eight and 135 pounds herself. It was the cut along her
thigh, deep enough to slice through her cargo pants,
that protested the most and gushed a little harder.
Damn. She'd have to sew up the tear too.

Remy looked down at Dantès, watching Wyatt's
large hands moving gently over the dog as the canine
rested his head in her lap. She knew one thing: the
ever-angry Wyatt might despise her, but he loved
her pet as if it were his own. He'd do anything for
Dantès, as evidenced by his actions tonight and the
tension emanating through him as he examined the
dog. At least she had that.

But there was a lot of blood. Her insides tightened and fear burned inside her. He couldn't die. He
couldn't.

"Well?" she asked when the silence had stretched
for too long. Her fingers clasped tightly over the
flashlight while her other hand stroked Dantès's soft
head as she waited for her companion's diagnosis.
She'd done a thorough examination before Wyatt appeared, but she was too upset to be confident in her
estimation in this case. She wanted someone else to
tell her what she thought she knew.

"He's going to be fine," Wyatt said. She saw his
tension relax, and so did she. "Aren't you, bud?" His

fingers spread wide, he gently stroked his hand along the length of Dantès's torso. "Just need a little fixing up and some rest." He looked up at Remy, meeting her eyes for the first time. "He's hurt, there's a lot of blood, but I didn't find anything serious. Nothing that shouldn't heal up."

She nodded, relief shuttling through her. "That's what I thought, but . . ."

"There is a lot of blood," he said, reading her mind. "But it looks worse than it is. He's a good fighter."

So are you. She looked back down at the dog before those words slipped out. She guessed that deep-seated anger he always carried was good for something. From her safe perch in the truck, she'd watched him with a combination of horror and admiration, saw him swinging a small tree as if it were a sword, dodging and feinting and jumping, always a step ahead of the snarling jaguar, then going back for more.

Wyatt's accusation rang in her memory: *Don't be a fool. If Dantès hadn't been here, this would have been* you.

But he'd misspoken. If *he* hadn't been here, this would have been *both* her and Dantès.

"By the way, nice job with the torch," he said, and rose to his feet. The ceiling wasn't quite tall enough for him to stand fully upright, but he only had to bend his head a little.

Remy felt a wave of guilt for her earlier irritation; after all, he had clearly been distracted by worry for Dantès. She was about to thank him for saving them when Wyatt added, "Next time, don't keep screaming my name. It's distracting."

"Next time?" she retorted, her blood racing again.

"God forbid there should be a next time." The sooner she could ditch him, the better.

She thought she heard a muffled snort, but he'd turned away and was examining the contents of the room or space they were in. She couldn't figure out exactly what this thing was. It looked like the front of a huge truck, like a larger size of the Humvees driven by the Strangers and bounty hunters, but behind the two seats in front was something like a small room. Almost like a tiny house or bedroom.

There might have been a mattress once, but the years and animals had done a number on it, and all that was left were the frame and springs. Cupboards, two small chairs, and a table were made from some woodlike material that was still fairly intact. They took up about half the space behind the driver's seat and its partner.

The only windows were in the front of the truck-like thing: one on each side, and the big one over the front. The glass was only gone from the one side, though, and although it was shattered, the front window was still intact. Both windows were filthy with mildew and dirt. Nevertheless, it was a safe place to hole up for the rest of the night. The zombies couldn't get up there, and it would be nearly impossible for the jaguar or any other animal to launch itself through the window. She guessed it was well past midnight and moving on toward dawn by now, though the night was still dark as pitch.

Dantès was going to be all right. She was safe. She could relax.

Except for *him*.

Remy shifted out of the way, arranging her flashlight as a general illuminator as Wyatt inched around the room, half bent, digging through the contents. He made one satisfied grunt and many disappointed noises, dropping things into piles that seemed to be useful versus nonuseful—the latter pile much larger and including gnawed away upholstery and other trash. While he did that, she moved up to the front of the truck and opened her pack. She had an extra shirt that could be used to wash up some of the blood, maybe even bandage Dantès's worst injuries. Eventually, she'd need to get more clean water, but she had some in her canteen. And so she'd be less one shirt, but in the grand scheme of things . . . At least the slice alongside her wrist had stopped bleeding, for the most part.

Despite what Wyatt might think about her being a fool, she'd planned her departure from the settlement of Yellow Mountain carefully, packing a good number of supplies. It wasn't the first time she'd had to make a quick escape. She was used to it.

And when Dantès showed up yesterday, she suspected Wyatt wouldn't be far behind. Which was why she'd altered her route, going in random directions. Trying to lose the man.

Unfortunately, it hadn't worked.

Casting a glower at him, Remy extricated the shirt and a small blanket from her bag and crawled back to Dantès. He was no longer lying on his side but was half upright and panting with interest at all the activity. That had to be a good sign. She poured a small dish of water for him and he drank noisily and sloppily, splashing all over as he was wont to do. Then she fed him a few pieces of cheese and some dried meat she'd gotten from Vonnie, the lady who cooked at Yellow Mountain.

Just then Wyatt sucked in his breath in an audible, delighted sound. She turned to see him pulling out a plastic tub from one of the cupboards.

"Oh, baby—airtight and clean as a whistle even fifty years later," he murmured like a man to his lover.

She couldn't help it, she had to investigate, even though it meant acknowledging his existence again. "What's in it?"

He had pulled off the top and was taking things out. "Hot *damn*. A first aid kit. Matches. A screwdriver set. Some emergency glow sticks, even. And *duct tape!*" He rustled through several other items, pulling out a blanket four times larger than the one she had, a pair of scissors, and some other things Remy didn't see.

She didn't wait for an invitation but took the first aid kit and dug through it. "Antibacterial ointment," she read, aiming her flashlight onto a small tube in order to see. "Hmm." It sounded important, but it was awfully old. And she wasn't sure what it was.

"Can't hurt to try it," Wyatt said, holding a ring of silvery tape in his hand. "It's been locked up airtight. Put it on the deepest cuts and then bandage them up."

Remy glanced at him, then back at the tube. All right. She set about doing just that, using the scissors to cut away some of Dantès's fur. Then she squirted out the tube's contents and gently rubbed it on her pet's leg, his shoulder, and the worst bite mark, which was on the left flank. He whined softly and licked at her in gratitude as she ministered to him.

"Christ. I meant on *you*," Wyatt said, suddenly looming over her. That anger bristled all over him again.

She looked up. "What?"

"Put the ointment on *your* cuts," he said impatiently. "Especially the one on your leg. Dantès doesn't need it as much as you do. He'll clean his own wounds. Dogs are built that way to heal themselves. You, on the other hand . . . you don't want to get an infection from that filthy glass." Shaking his head, he turned away, pushing past her in the small space to move to the front of the truck.

Remy looked down at her hands, at the gash oozing along the side of her right wrist and the blood seeping around the tear of her pant leg. Then she glared at the back of Wyatt's head as he knelt next to the driver's seat, doing something under it. Why did he always have to be so angry?

Having attended to Dantès, she cranked the dimming flashlight back to full brightness, then turned her attention to herself. She knew the dangers of infection, but hopefully she'd bled freely enough to wash away any serious germs. And she did have a small bottle of alcohol in her pack for just such an emergency, but there wasn't that much of it. This ointment could help, if it didn't kill her from being so old.

She glared at Wyatt again, ignoring the fact that his shoulders were so broad they hardly fit between the two bucket seats in the front. He was still scrabbling around in there at the base of them, grunting and muttering under his breath with effort. She refused to ask what he was doing, even when there was an ominous thud. She hoped he'd dropped something on his foot.

"Don't turn around," she said, aiming her words to the front of the truck. "I have to take off my pants."

Wyatt didn't deign to respond, but she knew he heard her. Turning so her back was to him, she stood and undid her cargo pants. The blood had dried, plastering the lightweight material to her leg and its wound, and it stuck as she tried to pull them off. Gritting her teeth against the pain, she peeled them down, dragging away the newly formed scab.

"Sweet . . . *Jesus* . . . *Christ*," Wyatt breathed in a worshipful voice.

Enraged—and yet, oddly delighted by his reaction—Remy whirled so fast that, still tangled in her pants, she nearly lost her balance. But he wasn't looking at her. The driver's seat was flipped up toward the steering wheel, revealing a storage space beneath it, and he was gazing down at something he held in his hands.

"Jameson's. A whole damned bottle, unopened. The paper's still on the cap." He sounded as if he were about to cry.

"What is it?" she was compelled to ask as she wrapped the small blanket around her waist and tucked it in tightly. No need to flash him, especially since her panties had seen better days. Good underwear was hard to come by.

Wyatt looked over, holding up a dark glass bottle. "Irish whiskey. *Good* Irish whiskey. Sonofabitch, I can't hardly believe it."

"Alcohol? That's great for cleaning wounds," she said, understanding his delight. "It'll sting, but—"

"Are you crazy? I'm not pouring this stuff anywhere but down my throat. There are alcohol pads in the first aid kit. Use them. *I*," he said, clambering back toward her, "am going to open this right about now." He barely glanced at her as he settled onto the floor next to Dantès. "It's been a hell of a long day."

Remy considered pointing out that it was his own fault for being here—and thus creating his "long day"—but decided her best course was not to engage. There was hardly enough room in the small space for both of them plus the massive chip on his shoulder, so she pointedly ignored him as she finished tending to her cuts. She kept the blanket close around her waist, opening it just enough to see to the slice on her thigh. The cut was ugly and crusting over, and, with a twinge of concern, she slathered it with a good amount of the antibacterial ointment. She also used some of the alcohol pads—little cloths wrapped up in foil packets, still damp and smelling of astringent even after half a century—and cleaned the cut.

"Does it need stitches?"

She was startled when he broke the silence. Sitting against the wall as far from her as possible, he was little more than a shadowy silhouette. As she watched, he lifted the bottle and drank, then settled it back between his long, jeans-clad legs. They were extended into the small room, and she could see his bare feet nearly brushing the opposite wall.

"No," she replied immediately. There was no way she was letting him near her to stitch anything up, especially after the last time he had to help her. She reached beneath her shirt to touch the crystal, back in its place at her navel. Only days ago, at Yellow Mountain, it had started to glow and heat, burning her skin unbearably. Wyatt had been the only one around, and he'd had to use those long, elegant fingers to help her unfasten it from its piercings.

And how had he seen the cut on her leg anyway? He hadn't given her the barest of glances since climbing into the truck. She frowned and shifted subtly so her back was to him.

Silence reigned again, broken only by an occasional *whuffle* from the sleeping Dantès or Remy's own rustling through her pack. If she were alone, she'd change and try to wash up a little. But with Wyatt here . . . After a while there was the soft glug of whiskey, then the dull clink as he set the bottle back down.

"You going to tell me where we're going?" he asked. His voice was quiet, and a little smoky from the drink.

Remy's mouth flattened. She'd like to tell him where to go, that was sure. Yet, she was a realist. And, most of the time, honest with herself. She supposed it might not be a bad idea to let him tag along; it would be hard to get rid of him anyway. God knew, he kept showing up whether she wanted him around or not. She could find plenty for him to do—like deboning any fish she caught or skinning a rabbit. Not her favorite tasks, but necessary when on the run.

And he'd been handy tonight, fighting off the jaguar and zombies. Not that she wouldn't have been fine on her own. But.

"I'm going to Envy," she said finally.

"So the woman who runs away from everyone is heading for the largest settlement, the last bastion of human civilization. Interesting."

Silence again. She listened for the sound of him lifting the bottle to drink, but he didn't. She began to clear away a place to sleep, eyeing the large blanket he'd pulled from the plastic box. Hers was around her waist and it was a little too chilly to sleep without a covering.

"You still having nightmares?" he asked.

She tensed. "Don't worry," she replied. "I'm sure at the rate you're slugging that whiskey down, you'll be too passed out to hear me, even if I do."

He gave a short chuckle that sounded more bitter than amused. "You got that right, sweetheart. Nothing better than a good drunk to keep the nightmares away. Want some?"

"No. Someone's got to stay awake and aware." *Oh, God, please don't let me have nightmares tonight.*

She drew in a long, slow breath, remembering the mantra Selena had taught her to help clear her mind and to keep the ugly memories at bay.

Another sharp laugh from Wyatt. "I hate to disappoint you, but I'm a long way from drunk, and an even longer way from not being awake and aware. If it were that easy to block it away, I'd be smashed all the time."

"You ought to try meditating," she said. "It helps."

He made a sound that could have been one of derision, or simply interest . . . it was hard to tell with Wyatt.

"So does this." He lifted the bottle in a sharp, jerky motion. In the wavering light, she caught a glimpse of his throat as he tipped his head back to drink, long and slow. Then, to her surprise, he leaned forward and offered it to her. "It'll warm you up too."

The bottle was warm from where he'd tucked it between his legs. That and the fact that he'd just had his lips around the opening gave it an uncomfortably intimate feel, but she took it anyway. Maybe she should get a little drunk. It might help her sleep . . . and she really didn't want to have a nightmare with Wyatt around.

The first sip burned down her throat and immediately rushed through her in a soft wave. She took
another swallow, careful not to suck down too much
and cause a coughing fit. This one didn't burn as
sharply, but it was warm and rich. The heat pooled
in her belly then rolled through her limbs, and Remy
immediately felt more loose.

She handed the bottle back to Wyatt, noticing
he'd inched a little closer to make it easier for them
to reach. He was tall and solid and took up a lot of
space . . . but despite what Seattle had done to her,
even in this small area, being with Wyatt didn't make
her nervous. Annoyed, maybe. But, surprisingly, not
nervous.

"Take the big blanket," he said. "Might as well be
comfortable."

She didn't have to be asked twice, but she couldn't
resist a sharp retort. "Wow, aren't you nice. The next
thing I know, you'll be offering up your very own
body heat just to keep me warm." Just as Ian Marck
the bounty hunter had done when she was traveling with him. And that had, of course, led to other
things.

"Body heat? Hell, no. That's what you've got
Dantès for." Wyatt slugged back another drink, then
set the bottle between them.

She gritted her teeth at the disdain in his voice.
Then she snatched up the large blanket. It wasn't
musty at all and it was made of a light material that
was very warm. Once wrapped up, she reached for
the bottle again. He was right, it made her warm and
easy. Hopefully it would help her sleep. And keep her
from wanting to strangle him.

"Why is it so damn important for you to get to

Envy that you took off on your own? I figure I ought to know why the hell I'm risking my ass to get you there."

"I didn't ask you to risk your ass."

"Jesus, Remy. Don't you ever say anything unpredictable?" Now his words were darker, more gravelly, and slurred a bit. "That's what I do. I risk my ass. For people."

"I'll tell you when you tell me why the hell you're so damn angry all the time," she said, setting the whiskey down a lot harder than necessary.

That drew a laugh from him, a short, uncivil bark. "All right, I take it back. You aren't predictable. By the way, now I'm getting drunk."

"Great. How soon till you pass out?"

Another bark. "Not fucking soon enough." He drew in a deep breath. "Never fucking soon enough."

The light was flickering, so she turned it off. But not before she caught a brief look at him as she picked up the flash, accidentally—or maybe not—directing it his way. His head was tilted back against the wall, his too-long dark hair a wavy mess around his face and unshaven jaw. His eyes appeared to be closed, and she could see the outline of his cheekbones and strong nose.

He'd be handsome enough if he didn't have that dark, angry brood strapped to him all the time. He was built nicely, that was for sure. He wore his battered jeans well, and his shirtsleeves were rolled up to show firm, muscular forearms. And he even had attractive feet, solid, strong, and elegant. They matched his hands.

She put the flash away and settled down to sleep, her world muzzy. Hopeful she wouldn't dream.

The last thing she heard was the soft clink of the whiskey bottle.

Wyatt opened his eyes to bright, warm sunshine. He was still tilted back against the wall, the bottle of Jameson's still wedged between his legs. Damned if it wasn't even half empty.

Maybe that was a good thing. He'd have some for tonight.

He stretched, capped and put the whiskey aside, and glanced over at Remy. Wrapped in the blanket, she was curled up in a ball, and appeared to still be sleeping, tucked next to Dantès, who'd lifted his head in query.

His mouth tightened. He didn't remember dreaming. He hoped like hell he hadn't.

Wyatt gestured for the dog to come with him, and moments later he was lifting Dantès down from the high door of the truck rig so they could both do their business. To his dismay, the injured canine wasn't as confident on his feet as he'd hoped.

"You're not going to be able to travel today, are you bud?" Wyatt asked, kneeling next to him to examine the jaguar's claw marks and bites.

In the daylight, his diagnosis of a full recovery was borne out, but not without a day or two of rest first. There was no way Dantès should be hiking twenty, thirty miles a day for a while. Wyatt glanced at the truck. He hoped Remy wasn't in a hurry to get to Envy. Not only were they going to be delayed, but she'd been heading in the wrong direction for the last day and they would have to backtrack about twenty miles.

He shook his head. How the hell had she managed to evade the zombies, the Strangers, and the bounty hunters—who were all looking for Remington Truth—for so long without getting herself killed?

Of course, there was one bounty hunter she hadn't avoided. Ian Marck. They'd been partners for a while before Ian was tossed over a cliff after having the shit beat out of him by Seattle, a rival bounty hunter, who'd then abducted Remy.

He'd seen a lot of horror in his day, but Wyatt's stomach still pitched when he remembered the condition in which he'd found her. Chained beneath Seattle's Humvee, ready to be dragged off when he drove away, she'd been half dressed, beaten and raped, and God knew what else. It was a wonder she was even half sane.

If she had nightmares last night, he hadn't heard it from her. But back at Yellow Mountain, when their bedrooms were only a short distance down the hall from each other, he had. *Fucking bastard*.

"Good boy," he said, giving the dog a good, loving scrub at the neck. Dantès had been the one to pick up Remy's scent and track her down. He'd launched himself through the window of Seattle's truck and torn the man's throat out before the bounty hunter knew what happened. "Good boy," he said again. "I wouldn't have been nearly as quick and merciful about it."

"About what?"

He turned to see Remy climbing out of the cab. Her long black hair, tousled from sleep, shone in the sunlight, and he saw she'd lost the blanket around her waist and pulled on a pair of jeans instead. Damn, she had long legs. He wondered if she'd sewn up her cargo pants yet.

"Giving that fucker Seattle what he deserved," he replied.

Her steps hitched, but she recovered quickly and kept walking. "Oh. Uh, nature calls," she said, and headed for a thicker part of the woods. Dantès followed her, hobbling off at a labored pace.

When she returned, he said, "How's your leg?"

"Fine," she said.

"I hope you put a bandage on it, otherwise your jeans will rub it and get lint in—"

"Yes, I have a bandage on it." She was speaking from behind a clenched jaw.

"The other thing is . . . Dantès can't travel yet. We're going to be staying here for a day or two."

She relaxed, her shoulders literally sagging. "I'm glad you think so. I was afraid . . ." She shrugged, then said in that prim tone, "You don't have to stay."

Wyatt didn't even bother to respond. He merely shook his head and went back into the truck. He could spend his time cleaning out the place a little better since they were going to be here at least another day. Plus, the Jameson's had sidetracked him and he hadn't finished his exploration last night. Maybe he'd find another bottle.

Or, better yet, more duct tape.

Remy debated about whether to take Dantès with her. She wanted to find a place to wash herself and her clothes, and while she preferred to have him stand guard, she could see that every step he took was painful. He needed rest.

So, she asked Wyatt to hand down her pack and help her get Dantès into the truck. There weren't nearly as many threats during the daylight as at night. She'd be fine as long as she didn't go too far and had the gun in her waistband.

After all, she'd been alone since she left Yellow Mountain, and many times before. She knew how to take care of herself.

To her surprise, Wyatt didn't have one smart-ass comment about her going off alone. Nor did he give her a list of commonsense instructions she didn't need. Instead, he obliged her request for help with Dantès, then disappeared back into the truck. Moments later a wad of garbage *thwumped* out of the window and onto the ground.

Well, he was going to be busy for a while.

With all her cross-terrain travel, Remy had become adept at finding water while not losing track of where her camp was. There were plenty of landmarks to help guide her, and less than two miles from the truck cab she found a small lake.

After a quick look around, she stripped and waded in. She couldn't help one last glance toward the direction of the truck. If she were in a DVD or a novel, her bath would be interrupted—accidentally or purposely—by her handsome companion, spying on her.

She snorted. By all indication, Wyatt would rather have his hands cut off than come upon her or any female bathing. Maybe he was gay.

Then, with a rush of heat, she remembered the one time a few weeks ago when he'd looked at her without that cold, angry expression. It was right after he'd helped her remove the burning crystal from her skin.

If it were up to me, I could think of a few things to do with you, he'd said.

No. The man was not gay. Angry, rude, arrogant . . . but not gay.

The water was cool but refreshing, and it took only a moment for her to get used to it. She washed her clothes and laid them out on a bush to dry, then ducked underwater to wash her hair.

When she finished with her ablutions, Remy floated around on her back. As often happened, her fingers settled over the slight curve of her belly, covering the crystal as if to assure herself it was safe—the small gemstone her grandfather, the first Remington Truth, had given her on his deathbed, making her promise to guard with her life.

It's the key. You'll know what to do with it when the time comes.

The crystal itself was a rosy orange color and hardly bigger than her thumbnail. After he first gave it to her, she carried it in a zippered pants pocket. But then, after almost losing it when those pants were carried away down a river while she washed them, Remy realized she had to do something else with the crystal. If it was that important, she had to hide and protect it.

For a while, then, she wore it around her neck on a chain, having fashioned a setting for it. But then there was a chance it would get caught, and the chain snap and break. Or someone might see it, and ask about it or yank it off her neck.

And so, nearly fifteen years ago, she thought of a better way. She painstakingly wrought an intricate silver and gold setting for the crystal, which not only obscured most of the stone itself but also had four small wires. She had help from an old jeweler, who thought she simply meant to have an unusual belly ring, and pierced her navel in four places to hold the crystal firmly in place. It was thus hidden, protected, and always with her. She hadn't had occasion to remove the complicated ornament for years—simply flushing water behind and around it and bathing the piercings with alcohol on occasion—until a few days ago, when it started to glow and burn and she was forced to ask Wyatt to help her remove it.

His touch had been efficient and impersonal, but the memory of those long, confident fingers skating over her belly made Remy feel unsettled and warm even now. She chalked it up to the awkwardness of intimacy with a stranger and turned her thoughts firmly away, giving a powerful frog-kick in the lake. The water surged over her as she shot through the waves, still floating on her back, looking up at the blue sky from behind the filter of tree branches. Still remembering.

Hide yourself, Remy. Don't let them find you. Don't . . . let . . . them . . . find you.

She'd done what her grandfather bid, hiding from everyone, getting to know no one, disdaining long-term relationships and friendships. A lonely existence. And in the beginning it had been a frightening one. She had no idea when or if someone would be searching for her, hunting her down . . . and what they would do to her if they found her.

But after years of nomadlike behavior, Remy found herself relaxing a little. She stayed in one place for months at a time, then moved and resettled. The closest she'd come to having a permanent home was her three years in Redlo, where she'd had a small business making pottery. She'd begun to feel safe. She had Dantès. She had friends. She had a pleasant life. For a time she'd even had a boyfriend.

But that idyll had been interrupted by the arrival of Wyatt and his friends. They'd been searching for Remington Truth, and for some reason she'd never know, the words had popped from her mouth: *I'm Remington Truth.*

How many times since then had she berated herself for being so stupid? How could that have just spilled from her lips so readily, after so many years of secrecy?

Maybe it was because no one had actually said the name Remington Truth for so long? Caught off-guard, had her response been automatic?

Or maybe her grandfather was right . . . She'd know what to do when the time came. Maybe the time *had* come. Maybe somehow she sensed it. Had she somehow known she could trust Wyatt and his group of friends? That they were the ones who could help her?

Remy happened to glance over the trees lining the edge of the pond at that moment, and stopped paddling. Flipping into an upright position in the water, she shielded her eyes against the sun, squinting as she looked at the circle of birds. Large birds, like vultures. Circling. Diving.

Definitely something worth investigating—it could be someone or some animal, injured.

She splashed out of the water and dressed quickly. Her clothes were still damp, but she had clean underthings and they were dry. Stuffing everything into her pack, she put her shoes on and started off to where the birds of prey were gathered.

As she walked, she reoriented herself. The truck

cab was to her right, to the south—near an old high-way signpost that still thrust up above the trees; an excellent landmark—and the birds were ahead, to the east. By the time Remy found her way, she estimated she was no more than three miles from her camp.

When she came upon it, as she expected, the sight wasn't a pretty one. Whoever it was had been dead long enough for maggots to hatch and other insects to find their way to fresh meat. But not more than a day or two.

She chased the birds away, her stomach roiling a little as she came close enough to see the corpse. A man. What was left of his skin was pale and bloated, but his hair was dark. His feet were bare, his clothing half picked away by creatures trying to get to flesh.

Remy looked around the area. It wasn't a clearing so much as a space beneath three trees. It didn't appear to be a campsite, per se. But a pair of decrepit hiking boots sitting to the side caught her attention, and, setting her pack down, she went over to them.

As she knelt to pick them up, her breath caught. She knew these boots. One of the laces was twine, the other had no laces at all but were held closed at the top by a piece of wire. They were easy to recognize because they'd been slit over the toes on the left foot and the soles were trashed, hardly wearable any-more. He'd been complaining about them for a while.

Ian Marck's boots.

In her haste to examine the body again, Remy tripped, nearly tumbling back to the ground when she launched herself to her feet. But she righted her-self and went back over, slowing a few steps away—just as hesitant to approach this time. Her heart thudded in her chest.

She knew it wasn't her former lover's body lying there, picked away like carrion. No, but she had to assure herself of it anyway.

Because if it wasn't Ian's body, but his boots were here . . . that meant Ian was still alive. He'd somehow survived the beating from Seattle's friends, and the fall over a cliff.

He'd been here. He'd probably exchanged boots with the dead man. *He* could have killed the dead man.

He could still be around.

As if she conjured him up, there was a sharp crackle in the woods behind her. Remy whirled, grabbing for her gun.

CHAPTER 3

"This is the third time you've pointed a weapon at me," Wyatt said, stepping into view. "It's starting to get old."

Remy lowered the gun. "Then don't keep sneaking up on me."

"I didn't sneak up on you the first time. When you *shot* at me." He walked over to the dead body. "What do we have here?"

"I warned you not to move, and you did. And for the last time, I didn't shoot *at* you. I shot *above your shoulder.* Just where I aimed."

"Someday," he said, crouching next to the body, "I'm going to have you prove what a sharpshooter you claim to be."

"I'm not going to waste my ammunition in order to soothe your ruffled man feathers," she replied, tucking the gun back into her jeans.

"If you're as good as you claim, it would only be a single bullet. Right?"

Remy rolled her eyes and gestured to the body. "Any idea what killed him?" If it had been Ian, it would be something quick and efficient: a neat twist of the neck, a single bullet to the head, a well-placed slit at the neck."

"Could be that cut at the neck, but the body's too wrecked to tell for sure. And . . ." Wyatt picked up a stick and used it to move away the tatters of the man's shirt at the throat and shoulders. "No sign of a crystal."

Not a Stranger, then. Remy hadn't thought to look to see whether there was—or had been—a crystal embedded in the man's flesh. The Strangers had once been mortal humans just like her, but they'd implanted special, living crystals in their skin, just below the collarbone. The bluish gems grew, rooting themselves by spreading delicate tentacles throughout the body. Once implanted with a crystal, a Stranger would die if it was removed. But with it, he or she would live forever, never aging or growing ill. The only way to kill a Stranger, as far as she knew, was to remove the crystal. Hack it out of the flesh of which it had become a living part.

Still staring down, Remy asked, "Anyone you know?"

"No." Wyatt stood and scanned the clearing, appearing to notice the discarded boots. Then he settled his attention back on her. "You?"

"No." Remy didn't look at the boots or at Wyatt. She wasn't certain whether she wanted to tell him Ian Marck was still alive.

After all, Ian was a bounty hunter who worked for the Strangers—the people who were, according to Wyatt and his friends Theo and Elliott, the cause of the Change that had destroyed the world. Aside from that, Ian and his father, Raul, had a reputation of terror, violence, and greed. The Marcks were dangerous and hovered on the fringe between the Strangers and the rest of human civilization. But she knew another side of Ian . . . one that wasn't quite so harsh or violent. And she also knew there had been a sort of truce in the past between Ian and Wyatt's friend Elliott.

Raul was dead, but Ian had continued the family tradition, so to speak, as a ruthless bounty hunter. Working for the Strangers, he raided settlements, looking for and taking into custody anyone or anything that could be considered a threat to the control and repression they had over the mortal humans: electronic devices, communication equipment, gas-powered vehicles, or anything that could help build infrastructure.

Remy knew about the work of the bounty hunters firsthand. She'd participated in more than one raid. She wasn't proud of it. But she hadn't had a choice. And she'd never hurt anyone.

And her relationship with Ian . . . well, complicated didn't begin to describe it. Yes, they'd been lovers. But they hadn't been intimate. She'd never understood the difference until she hooked up with Ian.

She realized Wyatt was looking at her as she stared down at the body. "Let's go back," she said. "Unless you want to—uh—wash up. There's a lake that way."

"I'll meet you back at the truck rig," he said, still looking at her with speculation. "Dantès is resting. Keep him quiet."

So ready to escape his serious, sharp eyes, she took off without comment. As if she needed to be told how to take care of her own dog.

Back at the truck Remy did a little organizing of her own and made something for Dantès to eat. She had an apple and one of the last pieces of bread she'd taken from Yellow Mountain. Then she considered ideas for dinner as she sat next to him, alternately scratching her pet behind the ears and patching up the tear in her pants. Thanks to Wyatt's earlier attention, the small homelike space was clean and comfortable. She had to give him credit for that, at least, and so she figured she'd make dinner. She wasn't bad at trapping rabbits, and she knew how to find wild potatoes and strawberries . . .

Dantès sensed Wyatt's approach before Remy did, his ears snapping upright. He leapt to his paws faster than was probably healthy, too excited to see his secondary master to let pain affect him. Before she could stop him, he bounded up onto one of the bucket seats in the front of the truck and stuck his head out the window, giving a short bark.

Remy wouldn't have even acknowledged the man's return if she hadn't been worried Dantès would try and launch himself down through the window to greet him—and Wyatt would probably blame her for not keeping him quiet—so she moved to the front to hold him back just as the man appeared.

Whoa.

Wyatt came into view with long, loping strides that seemed easy but covered ground rapidly. His black hair was wet, winging every which way around his temples, ears, and jaw. It looked like he'd even shaved. As she'd noticed before, he wore the hell out of his dark blue jeans: beltless, they rode low on his hips, loose in all the right places, showing off the shape of his long legs without being too tight, bunching up a little over his sturdy boots at the ankle. But what had her mouth going dry was that he wasn't wearing a shirt. And . . . yeah.

She'd suspected he was nicely built, but seeing it in the flesh, so to speak, was a shock. A pleasant shock. Yet, knowing she had to share such a small space with him, it was a little disconcerting. He looked so very *male*. His shoulders were broad and square, his arms well-defined with large, sleek biceps and sturdy forearms. The sunlight gleamed off the droplets of water that fell from his wet head and trickled down through the expanse of dark hair on his chest and over flat, slightly ridged abs. His skin was a rich golden-bronze, and she could see the hint of a tan line as his jeans slipped with the rhythm of his steps.

Remy realized she'd gone hot and completely breathless. She ducked away, into the back of the truck, before he could look up and see her gawking. *I hope to hell he puts a shirt on before he climbs up in here.*

She heard Dantès's enthusiastic greetings, then Wyatt's reply as he helped the dog clamber down safely. Amazing how he always spoke to Dantès in such a pleasant tone, so friendly and warm . . . but to her and everyone else, it seemed as if he could hardly bear to be civil.

Remy shook her head, tying off the thread on her mended pants. It was just as well he was a jerk. With a body like that . . . She put the trousers aside—they still needed to have the blood washed out of them—and was just about to take inventory of her waning food supplies when a shadow appeared at the front of the truck.

"You *are* here."

She looked up to see Wyatt, bare-shouldered, suddenly taking up all the space in the truck as he poked his head into the back. He sounded surprised and maybe a little irritated.

"I was just going through some of the—I mean, I was sewing up my pants. Why, did you expect me to be watching for you? I have plenty of things to be doing besides waiting around for you to come back."

His lips flattened into a thin line. "No. I brought back some wild asparagus and potatoes. I was going to cook them up for dinner. For both of us. I found some cans of beans along with other canned food—I put them in one of the cupboards."

Remy took a calming breath, already regretting her sharp words. Just because he was a dick didn't mean she had to be one too. And she'd been so distracted by the sight of his bare chest, she hadn't even noticed that he was carrying anything. "That was nice of you. I'll be happy to cook."

"Deal." He climbed all the way into the truck and brushed past her so closely a droplet of water, warm from his hair, fell on her arm. "I found something you might want to see. In the woods."

"All right."

He dug through his pack, and to her relief, pulled out a shirt and shrugged into it, buttoning it quickly down the front, leaving a small vee of dark hair showing at the top. Then he emptied his pack, dug in the plastic tub and pulled out several things and shoved them into the pack.

They both thought Dantès could accompany them for what Wyatt said wasn't a difficult walk, so the three set out. Instead of going east toward the dead body, or north to the lake, Wyatt took her in a western direction. Remy realized they were traveling along an overgrown road. The concrete was hardly noticeable, though, for trees, bushes, and grass grew up through the cracks and buckles.

Part of the reason no one traveled by motorized vehicle any longer was because of the rough terrain. It was easier to ride a horse or even to walk than try and navigate the potholes and chunks of road or naked ground. Aside from that, whatever stores of gasoline might have been available in the years immediately following the Change had disappeared: used up, combusted, or leaked back into the ground. The art of auto mechanics had died out through lack of need, so there were few people familiar with running cars either. And if anyone dared try to resurrect a vehicle, they risked being found out by the Strangers or bounty hunters.

"Here," Wyatt said after they'd walked about three miles. He gestured to an oblong structure, half buried in the ground, obstructed by a clump of trees and covered by vines and moss.

"What is it?" she asked. It looked a little like a train car that had fallen into a crevice in the earth, but it had a huge tire sunk into the ground.

"It's a semi-truck trailer." When she looked at him, not quite certain what that was, he explained, "The thing we're staying in is the front part of a semi-truck. This is what would have been pulled along behind it on the highway."

"Oh," she said, and edged toward it. "Did you look inside?"

"Of course." That impatient note was back in his voice. "That's why I thought you'd like to see it. There's a lot of salvageable stuff in there. You might find something you want."

A spike of enthusiasm shot through her. She'd kill for some new underwear and socks, even if they didn't fit right. "That would be great."

"Dantès, stay. Guard," Wyatt told him, then navigated his way to the trailer, pulling a large sapling out of the way. "This is the best way in. I had to pry the door open." He climbed up onto the narrow exposed side and flung open a large metal door. It clanged against the wall, leaving half the back end open.

From where Remy stood, the inside looked dingy and deep, slanting into darkness. She glanced at the front of the trailer, noting that its nose was buried in the ground. It wasn't going to slip or slide down into an abyss.

Wyatt held out his hand. When she took it, he clasped it around her wrist then pulled her up quickly and smoothly. He lowered her just inside the doorway as if she were no heavier than a child, then slid in beside her.

"I trust you made sure there weren't going to be any surprises in here," she said, looking around the dim space. The floor tilted underfoot, angling down toward the ravine. "No snakes, no—" She bit off a shriek as something skittered over her foot, and then another herd of creatures took flight, zooming in a wave of flapping wings over her head and out. Startled and agitated, she slipped in something squishy on the slanted floor and landed on her ass.

"Sorry." His voice sounded tight, or maybe just tense. As if he were trying not to laugh. "I couldn't clear everything out. But at least the grumpy bear is gone."

"Bear?" Remy froze, then realized he was teasing her. Which was a first. Or . . . maybe he wasn't teasing her. A bear could have been living in here. And Wyatt definitely wasn't the teasing type.

She pulled herself to her feet, her hand smashing down on something soft and damp in the process. Her enthusiasm waned. It was filthy in here, with lots of rubble, rubbish, and animal leavings and remains. "This is like that scene where Luke and Leia and Han Solo are trapped in the trash compactor," she muttered.

Suddenly, she wasn't sure she wanted to start digging through the mess, and in the semidarkness. Who knew what she might put her hand into . . . or what might grab back at her, or slither out . . .

"Here." Wyatt slapped something floppy at her. "Rubber gloves. Found 'em in the first aid kit."

Remy pulled them on, stretching her fingers inside the elastic gloves. Huh. So this is what they felt like. She'd seen people wearing them in DVDs, especially shows with doctors or detectives, but never in real life. And she'd definitely never worn them. They felt odd. Hot and tight, and a little sticky. But she loved the idea of protecting herself this way. How handy.

"They'll tear easily, so watch for sharp edges," Wyatt warned, already digging through some of the rubble. "But they'll keep you clean if you're careful."

"You have any light?" she asked, feeling a lot more confident.

"You have any patience, sweetheart?" he said, and suddenly a match flared. He lit two candles and wedged them into some metal ribbing along the inside of the trailer. Now a soft glow illuminated the space, and Remy could see all sorts of lumps buried under moss, rotting debris, and even a pile of white bones in the corner. She didn't mind the bones. It was rotting flesh and animal dung she'd prefer to avoid.

"The shipping boxes will have long rotted away," Wyatt was saying, digging through some of the mess. "But anything wrapped in plastic that's still intact will be salvageable. From what I can tell, this truck was probably taking a load of orders from a warehouse or courier to the shipping company. So there could be some good stuff here."

How did he know all this? Remy shrugged and began to sift through the debris, happy to have her hands protected and hopeful that she might find some real treasures.

Wyatt was right. There were a lot of items here. Many of the plastic bags had been slit open by animal teeth or claws, so the contents were destroyed, rotted away or mildewed. But she found several that weren't, and by the candlelight, used a pair of scissors from Wyatt's pack to cut open any airtight plastic. She was particularly interested in soft bags that could contain clothing.

"We won't be able to take everything back, but we can make a few trips and store the good things in the truck," Wyatt said, rummaging deep in the bowels of the trailer. "Once I get you to Envy, I'll come back with Quent and Zoë. Oh, hot damn!"

He must have found something worthwhile. Filled with hope and delight, Remy slit open a flat plastic bag. Inside were articles of clothing wrapped in clear plastic, as pristine as the day they were packed up, fifty-some years ago.

As she carefully pulled out the contents, Remy wondered what it would have been like back then: to have clothing, whatever you wanted, delivered to your house. She couldn't imagine not to have to go to a seamstress and be fitted for something to wear—or to sew something herself. Sometimes the clothing she wore was made new, but other times it was made from scraps or refitted from original pieces. Occasionally, a peddler or salvager would come through a settlement with a cart of discovered, traded, or retailored items. About ten years ago she'd traveled with one such peddler for a few months. Everyone would rummage through the peddler's wares, looking for something that had been repaired or was otherwise usable.

She wasn't surprised that this particular treasure trove had remained unnoticed for half a century. There were stories about people finding such caches, so she knew they existed—just like the buried treasures of old. One of her friends in Redlo had found an old suitcase inside the trunk of a car and salvaged a pair of black boots and a leather coat. But she'd never come upon a collection herself, and certainly not one this large.

Remy stifled a gasp of delight as she pulled a midnight-blue lacy thing from a small plastic bag. Impractical, but lovely. *Please let it fit me. Please let it fit me.*

She held it up and saw that it was a very revealing shirt or a nightgown. Regardless, it was much too large for her frame. Damn. But she could alter it, so she set it aside. A little while later she found a package of socks and crowed with delight. Clean socks. Without holes!

The deeper she dug, the more damp and disgusting was the debris. Not a surprise, for the top layer would have disintegrated sooner over the last decades, slowly exposing the bottom items to the air and damp. But she found a thick plastic package with four tank tops

that looked as if they'd fit—and in great colors too:
sky blue, red, white, and black. And . . . she almost
cried when she found two bras that were the right
size. And panties! Pink leopard-skin design, blue dia-
monds and black and white stripes. A fourth was the
weirdest pair of panties—at least she thought they
were panties—she'd ever seen: there was no fabric
covering the butt. Just a sort of T-strap. It looked
uncomfortable, but she decided to keep it anyway
because it was black and lacy. Salvagers couldn't be
choosy, and someday there might be a reason for her
to wear something so pretty under her clothes.

"Wonder who Victoria was," she said aloud, looking at the packing slip that was inside the plastic
bag that had held these treasures. And what was her
secret? So far, that package was her best find, but she
had hardly touched the surface of the truck.

She realized Wyatt had been quiet for a long while.
No noise, no rustling, no sounds at all.

Remy looked over, toward the darkest part of the
enclosure. He was still there but he wasn't moving.
He just sat there, with something in his lap, head
bowed, his hand raised to his eyes as if pinching the
bridge of his nose.

She watched for a moment, but he still didn't move.
Had he been bitten by a hidden spider or scorpion?
Frowning, her heart thudding harder in her chest, she
rose to her feet. Her legs were sore and prickly from
being in the same position for too long, and she was
a little unsteady picking her way back toward him.

"Wyatt?" she asked as she approached, careful not
to take another awkward spill. Especially on top of
him. Or where there could be lethal spiders lurking.

He didn't move at first. He was so still and stiff, he

could have been frozen. But when she got closer, he seemed to sense her presence. All at once he erupted to his feet and the books on his lap tumbled to the ground.

"I'm going back," he said, his voice low and rough. "I'll leave Dantès here with you."

Remy gaped at him as he navigated past her with stiff, abrupt movements. She only caught a glimpse of his face, but what she saw was frightening. Stark and taut, like a horrible mask. His eyes were like dull, angry stones, his mouth compressed into a flat line.

A moment later he was gone—outside the trailer and into the daylight. Remy heard him speaking to Dantès, and she stared after his exit, uncertain how to react. What the hell?

She turned from the empty rectangle of daylight that was the doorway and looked at the books that had been in his lap. She picked them up. *Good Night, Moon. I Love You, Stinky Face. Make Way for Ducklings.*

Children's picture books? She looked down at them, thoughtful and unsettled. Had these bright-colored stories upset him, or was it something unrelated? How long should she wait before returning to the truck?

He'd looked furious. No, actually, it wasn't anger she'd seen in that momentary flash of his expression.

It was hatred. Pure, unadulterated loathing.

CHAPTER 4

Remy had her hands full, carrying back her loot from the truck trailer. She could hardly believe her good fortune, with new socks, bras, panties, tank tops, and her favorite: a short blue sundress and a pair of *sandals*, both in the same package.

Before falling into his mood, Wyatt had obviously found some things too. They were stacked neatly next to where he'd been sitting: various articles of clothing, a few pristine books, tools, and some DVDs. She gathered them up and brought them back as well, leaving the children's books behind for now.

When she and Dantès headed back to the truck rig, the sun was below the tree line. She must have been in the trailer for hours, and although it would be another hour or two until dark, she was glad she'd left when she did. She wondered if Wyatt had come out of his funk yet.

As she emerged from the thicker part of the jungle and the truck came into view, she saw Dantès standing at the base of their temporary home. He was up on his hind legs, front paws scrabbling at the metal door, yipping and barking for attention. When Wyatt didn't appear, Remy's heart began to thud nervously. How long had it been since he left her at the truck trailer? Two, three hours?

She hurried over, putting all of their treasures on a nearby tree stump, then flung the door open. She winced when Dantès leapt up by himself. He wouldn't have made it except she gave him a last second boost, then followed.

Her pounding heart slowed when she saw the figure sitting in the dark, leaning back against the wall. He was being greeted by a whining Dantès. The smell of whiskey hung thick in the air.

"Back already?" Wyatt said. His voice was rough and sandpapery.

Remy turned away, half disgusted, half unsettled. She'd come to know Wyatt during her stay at Yellow Mountain—more than a month. She'd never seen him drunk.

Actually, she'd never seen him anything but coldly competent and completely in control, albeit distant and reserved.

"I'm going to make something to eat," she mumbled, and edged back out of the dark toward the waning daylight. She wasn't certain whether Dantès would follow her, but she didn't summon him. In the faulty light, she'd seen Wyatt's arms lock around the dog's neck as he rested his forehead in the thick fur. Holding on as if for dear life.

That image made something squeeze deep inside her. He was the very picture of desolation.

She made a small fire and used her pan to cook the potatoes and asparagus he'd brought back earlier. Then she went back into the truck and found the can of tuna, opened it, and offered a plate to Wyatt.

To her surprise, he took the meal and ate. He drank some water, too, but didn't speak one word other than a short "thank you" for the food. In the dim light, his face appeared as if it had aged and gone gaunt in a matter of hours. His eyes still looked like dark, glittering pits of anger.

Remy cleaned up, brought their loot into the truck, fed Dantès, then took him into the woods to do his business as well as her own. By then the sun was setting, but the last thing she wanted to do was climb back into that truck.

Instead, she helped Dantès up inside, closed the heavy metal door with a groan, and sat on the ground. The fire had settled into a small, gentle blaze and she stared at it, hypnotized by the dancing flames.

Only twenty-four hours ago she'd been sitting in front of a similar fire. Alone, except for Dantès.

And now, here she was, with an uninvited, would-be guide in a drunken stupor. At least he'd helped her acquire a whole new wardrobe. He might be obnoxious and rude, but she didn't have to worry about Wyatt assaulting her with anything but scornful, impatient comments.

Remy squeezed her eyes closed in an immediate, desperate attempt to hold back the memory of horror. But images of her captivity by Seattle surged to the edges of her mind. Pain and terror and violation.

Think of something else. Quick—think of something else.

Ian. Think of Ian.

He's alive. How could he have survived?

She settled on that puzzle, wary because it was too close to the very thoughts Selena had helped her learn to block away, but it was a safe topic nevertheless.

She and Ian had been traveling together for almost three months when Seattle ambushed them and kidnapped her.

Ian knew she was the granddaughter of Remington Truth. He was a bounty hunter, and he knew her secret identity. The very thought should have turned her to ice, but he'd never threatened her, never tried to bring her to the Strangers. And despite the fact that they were lovers, he never even seemed to have noticed her crystal, swathed as it was in silver and gold. Except . . . he did tell her point-blank he intended to keep her close at hand—whether she liked it or not. And it wasn't because he was in love with her. It was obvious he wasn't.

She never learned how he found out about her identity; Ian hadn't been any more forthcoming than Wyatt, as a matter of fact. Not that she, of anyone, should be throwing stones. Even after Wyatt had helped her remove the blazing hot crystal and then demanded answers, she'd been stubbornly reticent . . .

What's going on, Remy? Haven't you figured out by now that we don't mean you any harm? That we might be able to help you?

I don't have any reason to think that—

We know you're Remington Truth's granddaughter. And you're still here, safe, with us. We haven't turned you over to the Strangers or the zombies. Doesn't that tell you anything?

It tells me that you haven't figured out what to do with me yet.

If it were up to me, I could think of a few things to do with you.

An image of the bare male chest belonging to that very man popped into her mind. Remy opened her eyes. Well, *that* certainly pushed away the hovering memories of Seattle.

She glanced back at the truck, then returned her attention to the fire. She supposed she'd better climb back into the rig and see about getting some sleep. She was beginning to get too warm, sitting here in front of it. Especially the part of her facing the fire.

In particular, her torso *was getting hot.*

Remy looked down automatically and gasped, bolting to her feet. Sure enough, the glow shone through the thin material of her T-shirt.

Not again!

She was already pulling at the tiny silver wires, trying to extricate the crystal. As before, it burned her skin, singeing her fingers as if a tiny fire blazed inside it. Gasping with pain, furious with herself for not changing the way the crystal attached to her, Remy stumbled toward the truck, still trying to pry the jewel free.

The heat had flamed quickly, going from mere warmth to searing pain. She could hardly catch her breath to call out for help, hoping Wyatt wasn't passed out or that Dantès would waken him. The pain was so intense she didn't have the indulgence to be mortified for having to ask for assistance from him.

What would happen if he didn't come? If she didn't get the stone away from her skin? Between stinging tears and gasping breaths, Remy realized she was on the ground, writhing and twisting away from agony that wouldn't leave.

Her awareness sapped, she dimly heard a canine bark and whine, then a shadow loomed over her. It came closer and she smelled whiskey as cool, quick fingers brushed over her skin. She felt the pinch-tug-twists at her belly . . . and at last the pain stopped.

Remy collapsed flat onto her back, the balmy night air brushing over her bare skin, tears trickling down over her temples into her hair. Her eyes were closed; she didn't have the strength—or maybe it was the courage—to look up at Wyatt. For she knew what she'd see: fury, irritation, loathing, greed . . . something like that.

She couldn't even demand he give her the crystal back.

Because surely by now he realized it was something priceless. Surely by now he knew this was why the zombies and the bounty hunters and the Strangers had been searching for Remington Truth for fifty years.

Something thunked onto the ground next to her.

"Son of a bitch."

Then she heard a soft, gritty crunch as he spun away, followed by the creak of the truck door. It didn't slam shut, but it might as well have. Dantès whined once more, then quieted.

Remy bolted into a seated position and looked over. Her crystal, still faintly glowing inside its cocoon of silver, sat on the ground next to her.

Fifty miles away, Texas
Settlement of Glenway

Cat Callaghan slipped from bed and automatically grabbed the fireplace poker she kept leaning against the wall. Weapon in hand, just in case, she padded out of the bedroom to the front window. She hadn't slept, and it was probably just as well. She'd only have nightmares if she did.

In the distance she could hear the mournful, spine-tingling moans: *Ruuu-uuuthhhh ruuuthhhh.*

It wasn't an unusual sound; she'd lived her entire twenty-five years hearing it many nights. Not every night, no. And not always this nearby. But often.

Just like the howling of wolves or crying of wild-cats, the sound portended danger. Everyone stayed in at night, blockaded in homes that were fenced in or raised off the ground.

Now she could see an occasional orange glow—the eyes of the zombies—flickering in the darkness. Until six months ago she'd never seen anything more than that glitter of orange starlight, close to the ground, jolting through the darkness with each labored step of the monsters.

Until six months ago she'd never even seen what they actually looked like—the horrible manifestation of decaying human. The memory flared in her mind before she could stop it: the empty, orange eyes, haunted behind the glow. The sagging, green-gray flesh, the shine of white bone beneath. The putrid smell of death. The sickening feel of skin and bone giving way beneath the thrust of her fireplace poker. A quiet sob caught her by surprise and she pressed her palms hard into her eyes, as if to erase the images. But they were indelible.

Oh, God, Rick.

Cat drew in a deep breath then let it out slowly. Squeezed her eyes closed to hold back the tears. Tightened her grip on the poker. *Rick, I'm so sorry.*

The soft scuff of a bare foot on wood turned her attention from the window.

"Are you all right, honey?"

She couldn't manage a smile. But she kept her voice steady. "Not really, Dad, but I will be. Eventually."

Surely he noticed the poker in her hand, but he said nothing. Instead, he came to stand next to her at the window, wrapping his arm around her shoulders, hugging her close. She closed her eyes and allowed her head to rest against him. Dad was a rock. Thank God she had him.

Thank God he'd taken her away from the memories. It was impossible to walk by every day and see the very place Rick had died, to have to put on a strong face in front of everyone else in their small village. To know that if she'd been a few moments earlier, if she'd been fast enough, brave enough, things might have been different.

Her new home, Glenway, was a nice enough little settlement, and her sister Yvonne and her husband Pete had been welcoming. And when Yvonne's friend Ana and her father had decided to stay in Envy, they'd offered Dad the use of their home. It seemed fitting: a father and daughter had lived here, and now another father and daughter would take their place.

"No one should have to go through what you did," her dad said now. "I'm sorry, Catie. I wish I had been there."

She shook her head against him, closing her eyes against the tears that welled there. "I'm glad you weren't. It was awful, Dad." She swallowed hard, forcing the bile back down to her stomach. "Poor Rick."

Her voice caught and Dad hugged her tight. "He seemed like a good man," he said. "Too young. What a terrible way to have his life cut short."

Cat sniffled, the tears coming faster now. Rick had been a good man. She'd only known him for a month, but they'd had a connection. *Sometimes you just know,* he said to her when she made an offhand joke about it. His eyes had been serious, and her insides fluttered at the expression there. Maybe he'd been right . . . but where did that leave her now?

Dad handed her a handkerchief and she wiped her nose and eyes, drawing away so she didn't dribble on him. "Thanks," she said, wadding up the cloth in her hand.

Ruuuuuuuuthhhhhh . . .

Her father shifted, his attention focusing on the dark world outside. "Do their moans sound different to you? Maybe I'm getting hard of hearing in my old age, but . . ."

Cat's breath caught. She'd been thinking the same thing. "Yes. They do sound different. I noticed it, too, and Yvonne said the same thing. In the last week it's . . . changed. More urgent, it seems. Maybe that's why I couldn't sleep." She forced herself to chuckle, but it came out sounding more like a strangled sob.

"Aw, honey," Dad said, and hugged her. Pressing a kiss on the top of her head, he stroked her hair. "If I could take the memory, the experience, away from you, I would."

Cat pulled away and looked up at him. "You've got your own horrors and memories."

He smiled, but it was sad. "That's why it wouldn't be so difficult to take on yours too. You were fresh and innocent. And now . . ."

"It's part of the world, Dad. I'm not a fragile flower. I'll get over it." In light of everything Dad had been through, watching her boyfriend being attacked by a zombie was only the tip of the iceberg.

"Did you love him?" he asked after a long minute.

Cat drew in a deep breath and closed her eyes. She wondered if he'd been waiting six months to ask her that. "I don't know. I might have. Maybe. Probably."

They stood there for a moment, father and daughter, staring into darkness, listening as the eerie, moaning sounds filled the night.

"I think I'll try and sleep now," Cat said, squeezing her dad around the waist, then pulling away. "Good night."

He turned to follow her out of the room, then she heard him stop. "That's strange."

Cat turned and saw that he was looking toward the doorway that led to George's workroom. A faint orange glow filtered through the crack at the bottom.

He started toward it, and she instinctively grabbed his arm. "Dad," she said.

"It's all right." He gently but firmly pulled away.

Cat followed him, poker in hand. She hadn't been into George's workroom except briefly, on the first day they'd arrived in Glenway. She knew he was a sort of chemist or scientist, and that he'd been growing penicillin for medical purposes, supplying it to a man who was a real doctor, over in Envy. But since she hadn't been in there since, and as far as she knew Dad hadn't either, neither of them could have left a light on.

He reached for the door and she realized she was bracing herself, holding her breath.

But when the door opened at his push, wafting gently into the workroom, all was silent and still. Whatever she'd been expecting didn't come to pass.

Dad, spry and quick for his age, held her back so he could lead the way into the workroom. Cat was right on his heels, poker ready to lash out at the first sign of any movement or danger.

The orange glow was hardly more than that, even now that they were in the room. Dad headed for it and Cat looked over his shoulder to see a small pile of dirt and stones, apparently forgotten on the floor. But some of them were no ordinary rocks.

They seemed to be alive with an orange glow, flaming from deep inside.

CHAPTER 5

Wyatt sat in the dark rig, waiting.

Dantès had recovered from frenzied canine panic over his mistress and her damned burning crystal. He lay next to Wyatt, snoring and then twitching as he chased some imaginary rodent. The dog was bleeding again from the deepest of his wounds, likely from trying to leap from the truck window to get to his distressed mistress.

Whatever the fuck was wrong with the woman? Hadn't she learned her lesson the last time the damned stone tried to fry her? She'd probably have a scar from the burn. Hell, she could already have one from the last time this happened, come to think of it. It wasn't as if he was looking at her damned belly.

Hell no.

Guilt stabbed at him.

His head pounded and he let it clunk audibly back against the wall, closing his eyes. Sleek and pale in the moonlight, that soft, warm skin. Delicate and tender. Probably fried to a crisp now.

Wyatt squeezed his eyes tighter. Not something he wanted to think about. Nope.

They didn't have any burn ointment to put on it. Bummer for her.

It was a long time before he heard the creak of her coming in. The rig jolted as she pulled herself up, and then he heard another creak as the door closed.

Dantès lifted his head, immediately awake, and his tail thumped against the floor, but he didn't get up. Wyatt thought he heard Remy mutter something that sounded suspiciously like "traitor."

He watched her as she made her way carefully in the darkness, obviously assuming he was asleep. Which he wished he were. Or anywhere else but here. Or dead.

Preferably dead.

Desolation washed over him, dull and gray. *Goddammit*. It wasn't supposed to happen this way. He always expected he'd check out early. He knew he'd die young, in his prime. He'd be the one to go. Not his goddamn family.

Not when he put his ass on the line, day after day in Iraq, and then on the fire squad.

Not them. *Him*.

Oh, God, why? Why not me? Why the hell did You do this to me?

"Wyatt?"

He must have made a noise or something, dammit. Now she knew he was awake. Now she was going to want to talk.

"Find somewhere else to put that damned stone," he snapped, then dropped his head back against the wall again.

She didn't respond, but he could hear her picking her way around in the truck. The air stirred as she came closer. He felt Dantès shift and move when she knelt to pet him, then heard the soft sounds of her scratching behind his triangular ears. Wyatt's eyes remained stubbornly closed, and he realized he could smell her too. She was that close. Not the scent of singed or burned flesh—God knew he'd smelled that enough in his life. But the soft, woman essence that clung to a female: unique and yet familiar.

"You gave it back." Her voice was low and husky. And closer than he realized.

He made a sound of disgust, eyes still shut, head still tipped back. "I'm not a damned thief."

"Thank you."

If he hoped that was the end of it, he was wrong. He heard her settle on the floor, Dantès between them, and just as he was about to slip back into his bleak, dark thoughts, she said, "My grandfather gave me the crystal. When he was on his deathbed."

Wyatt's eyes snapped open, but otherwise he didn't move.

"He told me to protect it with my life. That it was the key, and that someday I'd know what to do with it. Unfortunately, he didn't see fit to give me any further information than that. And so I've spent the last almost twenty years doing what he asked. Not knowing why. Not knowing when or how I'd use it. Not knowing *who* wanted it, or when they'd come after me, and what they'd do to me when they found it."

He could see the vague outline of her head, the long swath of ink-black hair obscuring the curve of her neck and shoulder. Somehow, a shaft of moonlight filtered through the grimy truck window, shining on her hair and bouncing down over her arm. He could make out just a hint of jaw and mouth, and the dark shadows hiding her amazing blue eyes.

Raw guilt had him forcing his attention away. "Was your grandfather involved in causing the Change?" he asked.

"He never told me he was, but it seems obvious, doesn't it?" There was no sarcasm in her voice. Just sadness. "He wasn't a happy man. Never a hint of warmth or affection. He was like a shriveled bud of a person, a shell. And when he died . . ."

Dantès groaned between them, clearly bored by all the talk, and Wyatt patted him on the scruff. His hand brushed another hand, smaller and cooler, doing the same thing and he practically jerked his own away.

His mouth was dry and he curled his fingers deep into the warm ruff of fur.

Remy didn't seem to notice; she continued to pet Dantès, and Wyatt felt the rhythm of her movements jolting the dog against his leg. "Grandfather fought it. He clearly didn't want to die. It was an awful time. He didn't want to *die*, but he didn't want to live either. He said a lot of things, and I got the impression he'd done something awful. Something unforgivable. Something he couldn't live with, and something he was terrified of being judged on. It makes sense that he was involved with causing the Change."

"And so he gave you the crystal. Was it a way to make amends?"

The petting stopped. "I'd like to think so."

"Why the hell did he give it to you and not your parents? You must have been young."

"I was fifteen when Grandfather died. Not so young. And my father—I don't know anything about him. He and my mother weren't together for long, and he was gone before I was born. I didn't understand it at the time, but I've come to realize that Grandfather kept my mother and me close and all of us hidden for years. The same thing I've been doing—moving around a lot, staying out of sight, even living in the wilderness at times. He could have been the reason my father wasn't in the picture—maybe he made us move before my mother knew she was pregnant with me. Or maybe he forced us to leave because he didn't want her to get close to him. Or to anyone, and betray his secrets. Anyway, she died when I was eight. And then it was just the two of us."

"So he burdened you with *his* mistake and left you alone and unprotected—and with no guidance at all." Wyatt knew he sounded bitter, but his instinctive dislike of the senior Remington Truth had evolved into something more like disgust. "Nice man. Ruining your life."

Remy gave a short laugh. "Well, the sentiment has crossed my mind."

"You could have thrown the damn thing in the ocean or buried it or gotten rid of it some other way. You didn't have to carry that burden. Especially blindly. That makes you a helluva better person than your grandfather."

This time her laugh carried a note of surprise. "I do believe that's the nicest thing you've ever said to me." Her voice had gone low and husky again.

He flattened his lips. *Nice going, Earp.* Time to change the subject. "How many times has it glowed like that?"

"Tonight was only the second time." Her hackles were back up, her tone crisp. "So something seems to have changed just recently."

Wyatt's mind was working quickly now. Back in Envy, his friend Fence had met up with a woman

named Ana and she knew a lot about the crystals belonging to the Strangers. She had also confirmed what
they suspected: that the Strangers were former mortal
humans who'd conspired with the Atlanteans—yes,
the legendary people living in a sunken city actually did exist; he still couldn't quite wrap his mind
around that—to cause the Change.

"I mean, my crystal glowed once or twice before,
over the years, but very softly and for a short amount
of time. Nothing like this. And not often. So something's changed recently," she said. "That's why I'm
going to Envy. I heard Theo talking about Ana. I
thought she might be able to help."

He nodded in the darkness. "Something happened
about a week ago. When Ana came in contact with
the Jarrid stone—it's a large crystal the Strangers
use, and was stolen from them by our friend Quent—
the stone started to glow and burn. And so did the
crystals Ana had. She seemed to think they recognized each other and activated themselves. Maybe it
activated yours at the same time."

He sensed her interest sharpening, and his thought
was confirmed when she began to scratch Dantès
with new vigor. "I wonder if that's why the zombies
have gotten so . . ."

"Frenzied?" he finished for her. "Yes. In the last
week they seem to have become more desperate. It's
possible they sense the presence of your crystal."

"Yeah. So I feared."

Silence settled between them until Remy spoke
again. "So now you know why I want to go to Envy."

"Except that you were going in the wrong direction before I got here," he informed her.

"Duh. I was doing that on purpose. To try and lose

you. Obviously, it didn't work. Much to my dismay."

"You were going in circles on purpose?"

"Not in circles," she said waspishly. "But *not* in the direction of Envy. I didn't want my destination to be obvious."

He couldn't say anything more to that; she was right. And it had been a clumsy attempt to trick her into admitting she was lost. Which, apparently, she wasn't.

However, she had finally given him some answers. Chalk one up for the good guys. But Wyatt didn't waste any time feeling complacent about that small success. His mind was still working. "Ana told Fence that something called the Mother crystal disappeared from the possession of the Atlanteans around the time of the Change. I don't suppose your grandfather ever referred to the crystal he gave you that way?"

"Not that I remember. I didn't even know he had the stone until he gave it to me. Did Ana say what the Mother crystal was?"

"According to her, it's the key to the Atlanteans' power," he replied, trying to remember exactly how Fence had described it. The man wasn't terribly verbose in his electronic messages, which was how they communicated between Envy and Yellow Mountain. But he guessed he couldn't complain, because the two settlements were more than three days' journey apart—if one wasn't going in circles trying to lose someone—and there was no other way to efficiently send messages.

Theo and Lou Waxnicki, two geeky brothers who'd lived through the Change, had been secretly building an underground communication network that was meant to be the infrastructure for a resistance against the Strangers and, now, the Atlanteans.

They'd hoarded every working electronic device or hardware they could find over the last half century, utilizing what they could to build a sort of cobbled-together Internet and far-reaching network.

"My crystal seems awfully small to be something so powerful. But . . . you just used the word 'key.' The key to the Atlanteans' power. It could be a coincidence that Grandfather described it that way, or it might not be."

"Good point," he replied, reaching over to pet Dantès again. Their hands didn't clash this time because he kept his hand closer to the tail. "But when we get to Envy, you can ask Ana yourself."

He felt a sudden wave of tension, and her hand stopped moving. He supposed he'd be wondering, too, if he could trust Ana and Fence if he were in her position. Twenty years of hiding would make anyone suspicious. Especially if you didn't know who or what you were hiding *from*. Remington Truth was a bastard.

"How did you ever come to name this guy Dantès?" he asked, and realized with an ironic grimace that he was continuing the conversation. Willingly. "It's an unusual name."

"From *The Count of Monte Cristo*," she replied. "It was a book I found—salvaged—once, and I started reading it. I didn't realize I only had part of it, even though it had over eight hundred pages. So I don't know how it ends."

"It's a very long book." Wyatt didn't see any reason to mention he'd spent a god-awful amount of time in Iraq with few entertainment options other than reading . . . and he'd devoured many of the classics, including *Monte Cristo*, *The Three Musketeers*, and *Moby Dick*, as well as a large number of Clive Cussler and Ken Follett novels. The war had done one good thing, helping him acquire a love of reading he'd never had while in school.

"I always wondered whether Dantès and Mércèdes got together in the end," she said, her voice a little wistful.

"It depends whether you read the book or see the movie," he replied.

Her reply was cut off when Dantès shifted and groaned in his sleep. Then his legs moved, obviously chasing another rodent in his dreams. Wyatt stifled a chuckle of affection and removed his hand.

"I don't think he'll be ready to leave tomorrow. He was bleeding again tonight, after he tried to jump through the window and save you."

By the obvious pause, Wyatt suspected Remy was trying to determine whether he was poking at her or not. He didn't care which conclusion she drew.

"What happened to you in the trailer today, Wyatt?"

Oh Christ. If she was looking for a way to poke back at him, she'd found it. He couldn't help it; he shifted his position against the wall, edging away from her and Dantès as a variety of responses ran through his mind.

None of your damn business.

I have no idea what you're talking about.

Nothing—I just got tired of looking through rotting shit.

So he was shocked when the words tumbled from his mouth: "I found something that reminded me of my children."

Sonofabitch.

He let his head tip back against the truck again,

closed his eyes, and waited for the barrage: the interrogation, the pity, the sympathy.

But she didn't say anything. There was stillness;
she'd stopped petting Dantès. He could hear her
breath, steady—maybe a little faster than before. If
she was waiting for him to continue, she was going
to have a long wait.

"They're dead," he said from behind closed eyes,
once again surprising himself. Ah hell. Might as well
get it over with. "My wife too."

Still silence. Maybe she'd fallen asleep. That would
be a gift.

Yet, he couldn't seem to keep his mouth shut. "I
used to read them stories on the nights I was home,
just before they went to bed. I wanted them to learn
to love books."

Silence. A blessed lull. But her question brought
back the bleakness and desolation he fought earlier
today, and now he couldn't help but slip back into
the ugly darkness.

"And you blame yourself. Why?"

Her question surprised him—not only because
he hoped she wasn't listening, but because it was so
unexpected, yet so damn sharp it stabbed. A rush
of nausea overwhelmed him, rising bitterly into his
mouth. Must be the whiskey. Goddammit, he wished
he hadn't finished the bottle. No, he wished he had a
whole 'nother bottle.

Hell. He just wanted to be left the hell alone.

"Go to sleep, Remy."

"Angry, guilt-ridden, closed off, and cold. You've
got a lot in common with my grandfather."

He laughed bitterly. "Not really. Your grandfather
didn't want to die. Me? I wish to hell I could."

CHAPTER 6

When Remy awoke, she found herself alone in the truck. Surprised that she'd slept through Wyatt and Dantès rising and going out to do their business, she was nevertheless glad to have some privacy.

The sunlight seemed dimmer than usual, and a quick peek through the open window told her it was a cloudy day. But the temperature was still warm and humid, and she happily pulled out one of the new, long stretchy tank tops along with an equally new bra and panties to bring with her to the lake. Might as well take advantage of the proximity to wash up while she had it. If they began traveling again tomorrow, she might not have the time or convenience.

She tucked her gun in its place at the back of her pants and finger-combed the tangles from her hair. She was just about to climb out of the truck when she heard Dantès and Wyatt outside, his voice hardly more than a rumble as he spoke to the dog. To her consternation, a little clutch of something caught her in the belly, and she paused to consider its meaning. Something had changed in how she felt about facing Wyatt again, in the daylight.

Sympathetic, of course, now that she knew why the man was so dark and angry. Or, at least, she knew part of the reason.

And, okay, there was a little nervousness, too, knowing she'd have to interact with him after he'd had his hands all over her bare skin. A shiver took her by surprise, fluttering in her stomach. All right, so she was acutely aware of his maleness now that she'd seen him bare-chested and he'd touched her so intimately, but she needed to get a grip.

He's the same rude, arrogant dickhead he's been ever since you put a bullet in the wall above his shoulder.

The sounds of Dantès barking outside broke into her thoughts, and, wanting to appear busy, Remy turned to look in one of the cupboards as Wyatt helped her pooch climb into the truck.

"Were there any other pairs of rubber gloves?" she asked, rummaging through the plastic bin he found the first night. "I want to go back to the trailer and see if there's anything else there, and mine ripped yesterday. They're still usable, but not perfect."

"There might be another pair of gloves in the first aid kit. I'll go with you. We could probably dig in that truck for a week and not find everything."

Huh. He sounded surprisingly amiable.

"Okay, I'll look," she said as he clambered into the cab room next to her. Dantès was there, too, swiping her with his tongue and nearly knocking her over in his pleasure at their reunion. It was a good distraction.

"I'm going to see if I can catch a couple trout in that lake," Wyatt said, standing as tall as he could in the low room. He opened a short, long cupboard that ran along the separator between the driver's seat and the rest of the cab and pulled out a fishing pole. "They were jumping like crazy this morning. How are you at cooking fish?"

"Great, if they're cleaned. But I was going to walk over and wash up—uh—first. Do you mind?"

"Hell no. Knock yourself out."

Well, now, didn't they sound domestic? And not one cross word or cross-eyed look.

Remy turned back to the plastic bin and pulled out a purple cardboard box. "Trojan," she said, reading the label. "What's this for?"

"Nothing," Wyatt said, and snatched the box from her hand before she had a chance to finish examining it. "We don't need that."

Well, okay then. Back to his normal self. She stood. "I'll go swim. Maybe you can find more gloves?"

"I'll look."

The lake was great. Remy felt better after washing up, and even better after she poured herself into a pink and white bra sporting more lace than anything she'd ever owned. It was different because it hooked in the front, and the straps crisscrossed in the back. And it also made her breasts seem a lot bigger than usual, lifting and pushing them together a little. She wasn't lacking in boob size to begin with, but pulling on a new, tight white tank top over this bra made her curves look even more pronounced.

At least, from her perspective it did: looking down. It might not be so obvious from a different angle, and of course she didn't have a mirror. She braided her damp hair in a single over-the-shoulder plait and was just getting ready to hike back to the truck when Dantès loped into the area.

Fair warning that Wyatt was not far behind. Obviously, he was making certain he wouldn't accidentally encounter a naked woman swimming. Heaven forbid.

Remy mentally rolled her eyes, but just as quickly her ire faded. What was wrong with her? She should be thankful he wasn't Seattle. Or even Ian, whose come-on had been nothing more than practicality: *Everyone thinks we're lovers. We might as well make it a fact.*

Not that she had complained. Ian was handsome and had a great body. He definitely knew how to push a woman's pleasure buttons . . . in a mechanical sort of way.

"You decent?" Wyatt shouted from a safe distance.

"Yes," she said, picking up her gun and clothing, then the one towel she had and the small bottles containing soap and hair wash. "I'm going back to the truck. Then I want to go to the trailer and scavenge some more," she told Wyatt when he came around a tree carrying fishing equipment.

His eyes swept over her and his face changed. He opened his mouth to say something and then closed it and pivoted, turning to look out at the lake. He shielded his eyes from the pasty sun filtering through the clouds. "You're going to get sunburned," he said in an odd voice.

Frowning, Remy looked down at herself. In lightweight nylon pants, she was completely covered except for her tanned arms and the U-neck of her tank top . . . although there was a lot more pale breast skin showing than usual. She tugged the neckline up a little as Wyatt added, "Trout aren't jumping right now. I'll wait till later in the day to fish."

"Okay."

He was still looking out over the water, as if trying to count the nonexistent jumpers. "Did you say you wanted to go to the trailer?" he said, turning back toward her. His expression could only be described as irritated.

"That's what I said," she replied, looking at him closely. He was almost babbling. "Whether you're coming or not." She turned and started back the two miles to the truck rig. Dantès came along with her, his tongue hanging out happily.

To her surprise, Wyatt followed. They dropped their things off and, at her suggestion, emptied out their packs to carry back their loot.

"This isn't exactly traveling lightly," he lectured. "Don't forget, once we bring it here, we have to get everything back to Envy."

"I've got plenty of things I can get rid of if I find replacements," she told him, adjusting the gun in the back of her waistband. Aside from that, once Dantès was recovered, he could carry a pack too. He enjoyed helping that way.

They were halfway to the trailer when Remy realized she forgot her water bottle. She wasn't about to ask Wyatt to share his, so she decided to go back and get her own. He made a disgusted sound when she told him, but waved her off without argument.

"Take Dantès," was all he said as he climbed into the trailer.

The round-trip took almost twenty minutes, but it was hot and she was glad she'd gone back for the water. Dantès would appreciate it, too, although Wyatt would have shared his with the dog, at least.

When she got back to the trailer, she called out, "Wyatt? You decent?" and snickered to herself.

No surprise, he didn't respond. She didn't think anything of it until Dantès went stiff and his ears went up. He was looking into the trailer.

Shit.

The dog gave a low growl, edging toward the opening. "What is it, boy?" she asked, walking closer, using a hand motion to halt him. She could see only a little of the inside: dark shadows, a faint light. Wyatt's silhouette standing near the back, frozen, arms half extended as if surrendering.

"Keep him out of here." Wyatt's voice was tight and low.

Remy's adrenaline spiked as she peered into the candlelit interior. She didn't see anything threatening yet, but there were lots of shadows. "Dantès, sit. *Stay.* Guard."

The dog whined then growled, but did as he was commanded, which left Remy the freedom to get closer to the entrance. It was off the ground about five feet, but she'd used a tree stump yesterday after Wyatt left, and it was still in place.

"Jesus Christ, what the hell are you doing?" Still tight and low and now furious, Wyatt's exclamation bounced off the steel walls when she climbed onto the stump and peered into the space. "Get *out* of here!"

She ignored him. Now she could see the raccoon, who'd been obstructed from view because he was short and amid piles of trash. The creature was about a third of the way into the trailer and he was angry. Spitting, drooling, foaming at the mouth. He'd trapped Wyatt, who couldn't get past the beast. The raccoon's eyes gleamed with a red tinge in the flickering candlelight and his black claws were raised and menacing. He looked as if he were ready to attack at any moment, dividing his attention between the two humans.

"He's rabid," Wyatt said from between clenched teeth.

"I can see that. The foam at the mouth and red eyes gave it away."

"If he charges at—"

"*Stay*." She spun to glare at Dantès, speaking in her firmest, most serious voice even though the dog hadn't moved except to give another low growl. Then she directed her attention to Wyatt, reaching behind to the small of her back. "Are you okay? Did he—"

"Christ, Remy, what the hell are you doing? Get out of here before he turns on— What the *hell*?"

But she'd already aimed the gun at the raccoon. *One, two* . . .

"Are you *insane*?" he shouted as much as one could from between gritted teeth.

Three.

She pulled the trigger. The sound of the shot echoed sharply in the metal cavern.

The raccoon dropped.

And Wyatt vaulted out from the back of the trailer, leaping up and out into daylight before she even put the gun back in her waistband.

"What the *hell* did you think you were doing?" His brown eyes blazed as he stood over her, toe-to-toe, fury vibrating from him.

"You said you wanted me to prove my sharpshooting accuracy," she reminded him. "So I—"

"Not like that! Jesus Christ, what if you'd *missed*?"

"I wouldn't have missed, but even if I did, I wouldn't've come close to you. Totally wrong angle, Wyatt. You were off to the right and—"

"*Christ*, Remy. If you missed, the bullet would have ricocheted around inside that damn trailer and God knows who would've been shot. You *or* me." He looked as if he wanted to strangle her.

"Did you have a better plan?" she retorted, realizing that, well, yeah, he had a point. But it didn't matter because after all she hadn't missed. The animal had been a really close target. Dantès whined and gave a little yip, clearly disconcerted. She gave him the silent release signal and he hurried over, butting his nose against her thigh.

"*Yes*, goddammit, I had a better plan. I was just about to throw a blanket over it when you and Dantès arrived and fucked everything up. The last thing we needed was for him to get into a fight with a rabid raccoon."

"I know that, Wyatt. I'm sorry I shot the damn raccoon, okay? Maybe it wasn't the best plan, but it worked. I was at very close range, he wasn't moving, it would have been impossible for me to miss—"

"There is no such thing as 'impossible to miss,'" he said from between his teeth.

"And I didn't know if you'd been bitten, or if he'd scratched you. And for all I knew, he could have scented Dantès and charged out after him, or me. I acted quickly—"

"Without thinking—"

"—and I bet that part of your pissed-off-ness is because, yes, I am a woman and I happen to be a damn good shot—probably better than you—and *yes*, this is the second time I saved your ass in two days, and *yes*, I am cool under pressure, and *yes*, I probably scared the shit out of—"

His hands closed over her arms, yanking her up

and off the ground. The next thing she knew, her chest slammed into him and his mouth covered hers.

Remy's eyes went wide, her breath catching as his lips fit to her parted ones. Then the shock faded, replaced by heat and pleasure barreling through her and she kissed him back. As the kiss deepened, their tongues twined, sleek and easy, their mouths molding together. She closed her eyes and sank into the delicious taste of him as he devoured her in return. His lips were sensual and erotic, and she realized her hands had settled on his warm, solid shoulders. One of them found a lock of silky hair, then slid up into more thick waves as she felt her toes touch the ground again, his hands releasing her shoulders.

He ended the kiss abruptly, stepping back and looking down at her. She was panting, her legs felt like noodles, and for a moment she wasn't certain she remembered her own name. *Oh my God.*

"I had to shut you up somehow," he said, stepping back farther. His expression was inscrutable, his eyes dark and glittering. He didn't seem to be out of breath at all, damn him with his full, sensual lips glistening with *her kiss.* "Now. I'm going to get that raccoon out of there—hopefully he hasn't bled all over the pile of clothes I found—and I'm going to dispose of it so Dantès or any other animal won't be infected." Without another word, he turned and stalked back to the trailer, pausing to pet Dantès on the way.

Outraged, confused, and still stunned from the pleasurable assault, she opened her mouth to shout at him . . . then closed it. Her fingers were trembling, for God's sake. Her lips pulsed, and other areas of her body throbbed. That had been one hell of a kiss.

And it hadn't affected him at all?

Remy glared after Wyatt. No way. There was no way he felt nothing. Not after that.

At least . . . God, she hoped not. That would be mortifying.

She walked toward the trailer, her breath steady, her lips settling back to normal, just as Wyatt came out. He was carrying a bundle, presumably the raccoon, and he barely gave her a glance as he walked past.

"Should be safe in there now," he said.

"Should be?" she asked, lifting an eyebrow as Dantès ran over to sniff at the bundle. "How do we know there isn't a nest of them in there?"

"I think we would know by now," he said very, very patiently. "And they don't have nests. They have dens. And they're nocturnal—"

She flounced past him, irritated beyond belief and trying very hard not to give him the satisfaction of showing it.

"Remy," he called, just as she began to climb into the trailer. He stood several yards away, ready to disappear into the woods to bury the body. "You might want to, uh—" He tugged at his shirt.

She looked down and saw that her tank top had somehow gotten pulled down and out of place, and pretty much half of one pink-and-lace-covered breast was exposed.

Dickhead.

Apparently, he'd succeeded in shutting her up. Although, he felt more than a twinge of guilt about how he'd gone about doing it. Christ, the woman was the survivor of a horrific sexual assault. What the hell had he been thinking, manhandling her like that?

That was it. He hadn't been thinking. This dark, desolate world had finally gotten to him. He'd never laid a rough hand on a woman in his life—unless he was trying to save hers.

Yet, surprisingly, she hadn't seemed traumatized, and he wasn't certain whether he should be relieved or terrified that Remy actually responded to the kiss. He decided to settle on relieved that he hadn't damaged her even more—though the last thing he needed was her wanting something more from him.

He had no business even thinking about that.

Thus, he was glad to work in silence as they dug through more old and rotting packages in the trailer. Maybe he was distracted, but he didn't have much good luck today. The only thing he found worth keeping was a leather belt and a shrink-wrapped iPod. *Why the hell hadn't anyone shipped a case of wine or liquor? This olive oil isn't going to do us much good, old as it is.*

"Veronica Mars?" Remy said, breaking the silence.

"Who's that?" Wyatt looked over and saw her holding a DVD package. He shrugged. "Never heard of her. Are you ready to wrap it up? I want to do some fishing." After two days cooped up in one place with a crazy, gun-toting female, he needed some quiet solitude. Some *sober* quiet solitude; yesterday didn't count.

"Sure. I'm ready to go back," she said, and began to gather up her things.

The trip back to their camp was uneventful except for the discovery of wild scallions and some raspberries, and once back at the rig, Wyatt didn't delay in taking off again.

Less than two hours later he and Dantès once more

returned to the truck rig, to find Remy crouched by
a small fire in the clearing. She was still wearing that
damned white tank top that fit like a second skin and
showed a ridiculous amount of cleavage. Thanks to
this afternoon's incident, Wyatt now knew she wore
a lacy pink bra that belonged in a Victoria's Secret
catalog—not in a gritty, dangerous postapocalyptic
world. He knew from firsthand experience that the
women here generally wore simple white sports bras
out of necessity and practicality.

Dantès rushed over to greet his mistress, who
looked up at his approach. Her eyes lit with pleasure and she lifted her chin as her pet swiped it with
loving kisses. She had a long neck that looked pale
and delicate next to the loose black braid. Too bad
he wanted to wrap his hands around it more often
than not.

And that, he told himself, was a good thought to
focus on. *Not* what had happened this afternoon.

"I have two fish, more potatoes and asparagus,
plus some wild tomatoes I found," he said, laying the
offerings on the cloth-covered stump she indicated.
Her makeshift kitchen. He noted with interest that
she had the basics—a skillet and a few metal uten-
sils—as well as some things he hadn't expected: salt,
dried garlic, oil of some sort, green onions, and . . .
flour? For frying the fish?

This could be the best meal he'd had in a while.

And so he set about trying to ruin it.

"About this saving my ass twice," he said, sitting
down across from her. He picked up a tomato and
began to slice it with his knife. "What the hell are
you talking about?"

She looked up at him from dredging the fish in

flour, lifting an eyebrow. Her eyes were such a brilliant blue they startled him every time she fixed them on him. "Who thought of the torch? Who gave it to you? I do believe that was me. And without the torch . . ."

"Right. I remember you screeching my name the whole time, distracting the hell out of me so I couldn't think clearly. If I hadn't been distracted—"

"Right," she said. "That's just about as bad an excuse as the one you gave me today."

Wyatt suddenly had an unpleasant feeling in the pit of his stomach. He knew better than to ask what she meant so he kept slicing tomatoes.

But of course she was going to tell him anyway. "Your so-called excuse for kissing me."

He picked up another tomato, his hand very steady, and said, "I'm not Ian Marck. I'm here to get you safely to Envy. That's all." He kept his voice perfectly casual, with just a hint of disdain. *But there's a box of Trojans in the damn truck, Earp.*

She bristled, as he expected she would. So predictable! "I don't see how what I did with Ian has any bearing on your conduct this afternoon."

She sounded like the principal at his middle school, prim and outraged at the same time. And she had neatly confirmed what he suspected: she and Ian Marck had been lovers. He wasn't certain why he wanted to know, but now he did.

"That was a sorry excuse," she continued in that prim, princessy voice. "I hope your curiosity was assuaged."

"It certainly was," he said, his voice emotionless. "And you can be assured it won't happen again."

If they had been in a real kitchen, she probably

would have thrown a frying pan at him—or a knife. Instead, her face went blank with shock and then rosy with fury and she pressed her full, pink lips together so hard they became little more than a white line.

Then they softened enough for her to mutter something that sounded like "Dickhead."

Yes, indeed. That, he could be, when he felt there was cause for it. Cathy hadn't ever used that word in particular, but there had been times she probably wanted to. But at least with her, he'd always made it up to her later. The stab of grief laced with guilt left him breathless, and he forced his thoughts away from the funny, bright-eyed woman he'd loved deeply.

The important thing now was that he'd reset the boundaries, reinstated the barrier between him and Remy. He began to cut the tough ends off the asparagus, idly tossing a piece to Dantès just to see whether he'd eat it. He didn't.

By the time the meal was ready, it was twilight and Wyatt's mouth was watering. It smelled unbelievably good for such a rudimentary setting. He wondered at the last minute if she was angry enough to feed his portion to Dantès, but Remy didn't. She merely handed him a laden plate and settled back into her spot to eat.

"This is really good," he said after the first bite of flaky trout. Nothing like fresh-caught fish over the fire, and she'd done a great job. "Thanks."

Remy shrugged. "You caught 'em and cleaned them."

He took another bite. "We can leave tomorrow. Dantès seems ready to go."

This time she nodded. "I agree."

"It'll take about two more days to get there," he

said, spearing a potato. These wild ones were smaller and sweeter than the large brown ones he'd grown up on. Cooked directly in the coals, their skins were crispy and the insides creamy.

"I know."

He swallowed, took a drink of water, then manned up. "Look, Remy, I'm sorry about today. I was a little . . . uh . . . rough when I grabbed you, and after what happened—"

She looked up at him, her brilliant blue eyes calm and steady. "You were being a jerk, but you don't need to worry that you upset me. It was a kiss, not an attack. Seattle . . . uh—" Her voice cracked, but she forged on, swallowing visibly. Her eyes went hard. "There was no kissing . . . then." The words sat there, cold and stark.

Christ. Now he really felt like shit. "Hell, Remy, I—"

He stopped as Dantès sprang to his feet. They both turned and Wyatt saw Remy reach behind her for her gun. He tensed, peering into the darkening forest, listening.

The dog's ears were up but his mouth was closed. He was neither panting nor growling; just at attention. Watching and waiting.

Wyatt was about to duck into the truck to get his gun when the shape of a man emerged from the trees. Dantès gave a short bark of recognition and ran over to him.

The intruder looked around, patted the dog on the head and said, "I thought I smelled your cooking, Remy."

Jesus. Wasn't Ian Marck supposed to be dead?

CHAPTER 7

Remy bolted to her feet the moment Marck came into view. "Holy crap, Ian, what are you doing here?"

He gave her a cool, crooked smile. "I told you. I smelled your cooking." His attention went to Wyatt, who'd taken his time rising to his feet. "Who's this?"

"Ian Marck," Wyatt said, ignoring the question as he examined the lanky dark blond man. "I've heard so much about you."

"Then you have the advantage over me." Ian's blue eyes were the cold ones of a man who'd seen and committed great violence—and didn't care.

"I intend to keep it that way." Wyatt gave him a cool smile of his own, then sank back into his place and continued eating. He'd never actually met Marck before, but he'd seen him once back in Envy, albeit from a distance and in a dimly lit bar. His friend Elliott had pointed him out as the son of the man who'd abducted his girlfriend Jade.

Wyatt hadn't been there, but he knew all the details of how Ian and his father Raul had tracked down Jade in order to bring her back to the Stranger who'd kept her captive for three years—all for the bounty, of course.

But when Elliott and Theo showed up to free her, Ian had secretly helped them in exchange for Elliott's assistance in treating an ill young woman named Allie. Then, weeks later, Ian inexplicably showed up at the bar in Envy and gave them a message meant to help them find Remington Truth. How he knew Wyatt and Elliott and their friends were searching for the old man, they didn't know. Why he wanted to help them was even more of a mystery, especially since no one at the time was aware that the original Remington Truth was dead.

Ian's clue had eventually led them to Remy, but not directly due to his information—which left Wyatt and the others wondering if Marck had been sending them on a false trail or not.

In other words: Wyatt didn't trust the bastard one whit.

The man looked about his age—pushing forty— with short dark blond hair and high cheekbones. He had a look about the forehead and eyes that reminded Wyatt of a Russian guy he'd gone to college with. From the pallor of his skin, the hollows in his cheeks, and the fact that he was unshaven, it was obvious he'd been ill—or injured.

"You look like hell," Remy said, handing him what was left of her plate.

"Nearly dying will do that to you," Marck said, and fairly dove into the food. "Thanks."

"How did you survive?"

Wyatt settled back, making himself appear relaxed as he observed the two conversing. He noticed Remy hadn't greeted her presumed-dead lover with an embrace, or even great warmth, and wondered if that was due to his presence or for some other reason. Had she known Marck was still alive? How? Her body language was a combination of surprise and tension, but not fear or apprehension. Nor great joy. Hell, he hoped that if he suddenly showed up in front of Cathy after being presumed dead, she'd be a lot happier to see him.

Despite Remy's lukewarm reaction to his appearance, Marck settled in as if he'd been with them on this journey all along.

And Dantès . . . he was the most interesting of all. He greeted Marck briefly when he first came on the scene, but now settled down in a pile of dog between Remy and Marck. He lay down but didn't sleep, watching and listening just as Wyatt did.

"I got lucky is how I survived," Marck said, finishing the last bite of fish. "I don't know. I don't remember— much of it was a blur. I just managed to take care of myself enough until I healed." His look became intense as he focused it on her. "What happened?"

Even in the fading light, Wyatt saw Remy's hands curl into themselves and he gritted his teeth. If the bastard who was traveling with her had been on his guard, paying attention, *protecting* her, she wouldn't have the terrifying memories of her abduction by Seattle.

"What you'd expect," she replied in a tone that discouraged further questions.

Marck's expression tightened and his jaw moved, but he said nothing more. He turned his attention to Wyatt. "You got a name?"

He told him, partly because he didn't want Remy volunteering her old nickname for him: Dick. As in Head. Crazy woman. One thing about her: he always knew what she was thinking. "I'm a friend of El-liott's." He gave Marck a meaningful look. *I know exactly who you are.*

Recognition flashed in the man's eyes, followed by something that might have been grief. "The doctor." His expression eased slightly and he nodded. "I did him a favor."

"The way I heard it, he did you one back," Wyatt replied evenly.

"We're square."

"What are you talking about?" Remy asked, her attention ping-ponging between them.

"It's complicated," Marck replied. "What I'm really here for is to tell you the Strangers are out for blood."

"And that's news?" Wyatt said dryly.

"They're looking for you, Remy, and they're des-perate. I can't believe I found you first."

Wyatt couldn't believe it either. In fact, he suspected it was less of a wild coincidence and more of . . . some-thing else. Marck didn't strike him as relying on hap-penstance as opposed to executing his own plans.

"Haven't you noticed the zombies being even more crazy than usual? Something's happened. Something happened and now they're looking for you," Ian was saying. "They have an idea of where you are—or at least, they know you exist."

Wyatt noticed Remy's hand jerk toward her navel, to the crystal, before she caught it and stilled. So Marck had noticed it too: the increased frenzy of the zombies. But did he know about the crystal?

They'd slept together. Of course he knew about the crystal.

"How do you know they're looking for me?" Remy asked.

"They're taking dark-haired people now. Not blondes anymore. They leave the blondes behind." Marck's words were flat and tense, and Wyatt understood the implication. The zombies had spent fifty years looking for an old man—Remington Truth—with white hair. The monsters couldn't recognize pictures, but they understood hair color and so would capture anyone blond. The dark-haired ones, they'd maul and feast upon.

"They're taking brunettes now? How? How do they know about me?" Remy asked, and for the first time he could remember, Wyatt heard a note of fear in her voice. "Did you tell them?"

"No, I didn't fucking tell them. Remy, I didn't spend three months traveling around with you, keeping you close, so I could tell anyone who you were."

"Then why did you?"

That was precisely what Wyatt wanted to know. Ian Marck wasn't the kind of guy to do anything unless it benefited him. So why had he spent so much time with Remy, and why was he here now?

He didn't like it.

Marck looked at Remy but didn't respond to her question. Some message that Wyatt wasn't privy to passed between them—a message between lovers.

Well, three was a crowd. He got up and excused himself.

He'd leave them alone, but he sure as hell wasn't *leaving*.

Remy watched as Wyatt stalked toward the truck rig, clearly glad to be away from them. However, his choice to go there instead of anywhere else wasn't lost on her: he was staking his claim—to the shelter at least.

Most definitely not to her.

The tension in the air was thicker than dried pea soup, and Remy wasn't certain she understood all of the layers. There was definitely an alpha dog thing going on between the two of the males, but that was no surprise. They were both intelligent, dangerous men who didn't know each other—and clearly didn't trust each other.

"Who's the guy?" Ian asked, not even waiting till Wyatt was out of earshot. Surely he heard. Surely he was meant to hear.

"A guide who's traveling with me." Remy kept her answer simple, and for the sake of privacy, edged closer to Ian. It was almost dark, and the fire was the only source of light.

"That it?" he asked, spearing her with hard blue eyes. His were icy cold, so different from her blue-violet ones.

"Are you asking if we're sleeping together?" she replied. "It wouldn't matter to you even if we were."

"I know you're not sleeping together—it's obvious. I want to know if you're here willingly. With him."

Remy looked at him, trying in vain to read his expression and intent. "Do you mean, more willingly than I was when I was with you?" she retorted. "As I recall, you gave me the choice of handcuffs or . . . well, sleeping with you."

Ian's face grew dark, appearing almost frightening in the orange-red glow of the fire. "I never forced you. I never would have, and, by God, I hope you know that. You were a willing partner—"

"In our sexual relationship, yes. I was willing. I was

lonely and . . . well, you're a good lover," she told him, and was startled when his awful expression shattered into bleakness and grief . . . then returned to the cold mask it usually was. The change was so quick, she nearly missed it. "But I would have left you for many other reasons if you hadn't forced me to stay."

"It was for your protection. If I knew who you were, then it was possible someone else would too."

"Like Seattle?"

Once again his face altered. "I'm sorry," he said in a voice she hardly recognized. Soft and broken. "So sorry." He reached for her hand and closed his fingers around it. Probably the only time he'd ever touched her with authentic gentleness and affection. "I can only imagine how bad it was."

Remy's throat was tight and she could only shake her head, battling back the dark images. She wasn't going to talk about it. With the help of her friend Selena, who also had terrible grief of her own to live through, she'd managed to lock away those memories, or at least control them. She couldn't allow them out or they'd consume her.

Ian seemed to understand and he squeezed her hand again, then released it. Never too much intimacy for him, she thought wryly—glad to refocus her thoughts. "Nice boots," she said. "Did you have to kill the man to get them?"

His eyes snapped to hers, and she saw surprise and even a rare flash of humor. "No. He was already dead when I got there. So that's why you weren't surprised to see me."

"I was surprised to see you, but not surprised that you were alive. What are you doing here, really, Ian? I know it's not for me."

He looked away, back at the fire, staring into the hypnotic flames. "It is for you."

She watched him for a minute, considering. No. That wasn't right at all. He didn't love her. He might mean to protect her, but there was another reason for him doing so, for coming here. She wasn't naive. "I asked you once why you always looked so angry when you kiss me. And you said, 'Because I'd rather be kissing someone else.' But did you mean you'd rather be kissing *anyone* else but me, or *someone* else—someone in particular?"

His face didn't move, but his fingers did. Almost like a spasm. "Someone else. In particular."

Remy nodded to herself. That explained a lot. But it also opened up more questions. "The girl Elliott helped to save?"

"He couldn't. She died." His mouth flattened, his lips twisting, turning them ugly. "That was my sister, Allie."

"I'm sorry. I know Elliott has a gift for healing. He . . . helped me after . . . Seattle." She swallowed and forced herself to continue. "If he couldn't save her, then no one could."

"He was her only hope."

"I'm really sorry," Remy said again. She moved close enough to put her arm around his shoulders. To her surprise, some of the tension eased from him. "I'm sure he did everything he could."

Ian nodded, his head moving against hers. "He did. He nearly died too."

"But Allie wasn't the woman you'd rather be kissing."

The tension returned to his body. "No."

"Where is she?"

"I don't know."

Of course, Ian was going to share their quarters for the night. Remy saw no reason for him not to, especially with incensed zombies and furious leopards roaming about and him still not completely recovered.

She could tell he still had many questions—where she was going, why Wyatt was with her—but she wasn't certain whether or how to answer them, so she announced she was ready to turn in for the night.

The sounds of *ruuuthhh ruuu-uuuuthhhhh* filtered eerily through the darkness as Ian kicked over the fire and turned to follow Remy and Dantès up into the truck.

It was practical and safe to ask Ian to stay, but Remy hadn't considered how awkward it would be, sharing a small space with two attractive—if not irritating—men, plus her wolf-sized dog. Especially since one had been her lover, and the other was most definitely *not* going to be her lover.

When she came back into the sleeping area, she saw that not only was Wyatt awake and sitting up, reading a book he'd scavenged . . . but he was barechested. His gun rested on one jeans-clad thigh and he looked up as she came in.

His attention went from her to the man climbing in behind her, and she actually felt the impact as the two of them made eye contact.

There must be some sort of underlying male communication going on here, she thought as Wyatt gave Ian a brief nod and stood abruptly.

As he made his way past her, though, he stopped in that close quarters. She would have moved out of the way, but there wasn't enough room, and before she could do so, Wyatt slid an arm around her shoulders. Her breath caught in surprise as he pulled her up against a warm, solid, broad male chest. It was a shock to feel his skin against hers, and her hand got trapped between herself and the rough dark hair covering the solid muscles of his chest. Remy was so stunned, she hardly registered it when Wyatt muttered into her ear: "Did you tell him where we're going?"

She managed a squeaky sort of negative sound, and he must have gotten the message, for he said, "Don't." Then, just as smoothly, he brushed a kiss over the sensitive skin of her neck, released her and continued on his way through and out of the truck. Ian turned and followed him.

What the hell was that?

Remy sank onto the floor, glad to have the space to herself for a moment. She needed it.

Wyatt brushed past Marck and out into the cooling night air. It felt like heaven on his suddenly burning skin. He probably hadn't needed to pull her quite so close. And the quick kiss . . . well, that was for Marck's benefit. Keep the prick off-guard.

He only had to wait a moment before the other man joined him. Their mutual desire to talk privately had been unspoken but understood when their eyes met in the truck.

Dantès whined briefly at the open window, but Wyatt made a dismissive hand gesture and turned away. The dog needed to stay with his mistress for a variety of reasons, including whether only one of them made it back into the truck.

Ruuu-uuuuthhhhh . . . ruuuuthhhh. The zombies were close; if they scented the humans, they'd be here within minutes. But they were downwind, and there were things that needed to be said away from Remy's ears. And Wyatt wanted the other man to speak first. He didn't have to wait long.

"Is she doing all right?"

More than mildly surprised at this topic, Wyatt replied, "She hides it well. Elliott healed her. And another friend, Selena, has a gift for . . . helping. But she dreams." He found himself inexplicably irritated that Marck's first question was about Remy's well-being. But perhaps that was guilt in the other man's eyes, mixed with desperation and anger. Oh, the anger was so deeply embedded it could never be extracted. Wyatt recognized it because he'd seen it in his own eyes.

"Do you know what happened? How long?"

"We found her chained beneath Seattle's truck. And that was after she'd been assaulted over several days." Wyatt forced the words out, trying to forget the battered Remy he'd pulled from under the truck. Even then, in the midst of her horror and pain, she hadn't been glad to see him. *You*, she'd said. *Dick*.

That was before she knew his name, but still. The sentiment was clear.

Marck's shocked and sickened expression mirrored his own feelings. Wyatt felt an unexpected twinge of connection with him, so he elaborated, "She fought back as well as she could. Pulled a gun on him. Nailed him with a rock. Cut him with a rusty piece of metal. That only made him angrier. He was getting ready to drive off with her chained beneath when we got there."

"Fucking tell me the bastard's not dead," Marck said, his jaw visibly tight.

"Oh, he's dead. Dantès tore his throat out."

"Lucky motherfucking bastard. I'd have killed him myself. Taken a week to do it. Or longer."

Wyatt felt another unexpected nudge of solidarity with Ian Marck and gave him a nod of agreement. "Dantès was a little too neat and quick for my taste," he admitted.

Marck gave him a humorless smile. "At least we agree on something."

Wyatt didn't respond. This wasn't football. He didn't need to be friendly to the opposing team.

"You're a friend of Elliott's, which also makes you a friend of Quent Fielding," Marck said, surprising Wyatt once again. His eyes were sharp even in the darkness, and they focused on him steadily. "Were you in the Sedona cave with him?"

Wyatt couldn't have been more taken off-guard if Marck had dropped on one knee and asked to marry him. How the hell did he know about that? But no sooner had he registered the question than his mind began to work, and he surmised some of the answers. "You knew that Quent was Parris Fielding's son," he said, referring to a member of the Strangers' Triumvirate.

There were three men who had been known as the triad of power: Prescott, the Stranger who'd held Jade captive for years; Parris Fielding, who was Quent's father and one of the masterminds behind the Change; and the third was the original Remington Truth. All three of them were now dead, but according to Quent, the ruling power had been passed on to others, including a man named Liam Hegelson.

Marck nodded. "Parris Fielding was filled with glee and jubilation when he learned his secret experiment had worked. That his son had lived through the Change—or, as they call it, the Evolution—and hadn't aged at all. He even brought Quent into the fold at Mecca, introducing him as his heir apparent—and then his son betrayed him and stole the Jarrid stone."

"You are remarkably well-informed."

"I've worked hard to be in that position," Marck replied coolly.

"I'll bet you have. How wide is the trail of blood you've left behind?"

Marck's jaw shifted. "My real question relates to you. Elliott was with Quent in the caves, and I expect you were too. Which makes you about fifty years older than me."

"That's one hell of an assumption," Wyatt replied.

"It's not an assumption. It's a fact."

"What does it matter to you?"

"I like to know who I'm dealing with."

Wyatt smiled, allowing every bit of unpleasantness he felt to show in the curl of his lips. "And why would I do anything to give you an advantage?" He tilted his head to listen. "The zombies are coming closer. I'm finished with this. Stay or go, your choice." He turned on his heel and walked unhurriedly to the truck.

"What's your gift, Wyatt? What power did you gain in the caves?"

Marck's question followed him, snagging Wyatt in his smooth climb up into the truck. But he recovered immediately and kept going, yet with more force and jerkiness in his movements than before.

Holy shit. How could Ian Marck know about that? How each of the men who'd been trapped in the caves for fifty years had acquired a special super-human ability?

It was inexplicable but true. Elliott had discovered the unnatural ability to heal with his hands. Quent could read an object's history merely by touching it. Fence and Simon, the other two men who'd been trapped with them, also had superhuman abilities.

All of them, with the exception of Wyatt, had noticed a special alteration in their bodies. He wasn't certain whether he simply hadn't discovered his yet or whether he didn't have one. He didn't really give a shit, figured it would be just one more thing to have to deal with in this new horror of a world. He'd seen Quent and Elliott, and especially Fence, try to learn how to handle these changes and their powerful abilities, and it hadn't been pretty. It had been downright dangerous and frightening in many ways.

It wasn't bad enough that they had been thrust into this world—losing everything they'd loved—but to deal with extranormal abilities? That just made things worse.

Still unpleasantly surprised by Marck's question, and irritated by the interrogation overall, Wyatt stumbled into the dim interior of the truck. There was a small light in the back. Remy was up, reading or doing something. Good God, she'd probably have questions and demand answers and generally work hard to piss him off. If she asked him why he kissed her—

He almost turned around to go back out, but decided he would give neither her nor Marck the satisfaction. He'd faced down gun- and bomb-toting terrorists in the Middle East, days and nights without rest, and blazing fires that went on for days. He sure as hell could handle a woman.

And damned if his eyes didn't go right to her as he came into the back. She was watching him and the entrance behind him expectantly. No longer wearing that skintight tank top, she'd changed into something more modest—a loose dark shirt. But there was enough light to see the elegant curve of her neck and shoulder, precisely the place he'd buried his face only a few minutes ago. Her soft dark hair was tousled and free of its braid, falling in shadowy waves against her fair skin. And those damn blue eyes.

Guilt, guilt, guilt. He thrust it away, turning it into anger and impatience.

"What the hell did you expect?" he drawled. "Blood? Broken bones?"

Her expression remained cool. "I heard the zombies."

"They're coming closer," said Marck, his voice coming from the front of the truck. "Might make sense to keep watch tonight. They're on a tear. I'll take the first watch. Sit in the front seat here."

Wyatt grunted his assent, then crawled back into the darkest corner he could find. "I'll spell you. Wake me at two."

"I'll take the next shift," Remy said firmly. But no one responded, and Wyatt knew Marck wouldn't be waking her up.

He settled in and closed off his mind. Sometime during college, he'd picked up the valuable habit of forcing himself to go to sleep instantly, regardless of what else was going on around him and in his head. Most of the time, it worked.

It must have worked tonight, too, despite the whirlwind of thoughts that plagued him, for Wyatt suddenly came awake, feeling movement. *Earthquake?*

His first thought was instantly banished as he noticed the rhythm. The truck was rocking from side to
side. But he was already on his feet, banging his head
on the ceiling as he scrambled over a slower-moving
Remy on his way to the front. The cries and groans of
the zombies were loud, and even from inside he could
smell the stench.

"Why didn't you wake me?" Wyatt demanded,
shoving into the front of the truck next to Marck.
The violent rocking jolted him into the other man,
but he stayed on his feet. He heard Remy shouting
something behind him but ignored her. Dantès was
barking frantically, leaping around, trying to get out.
"Quiet, Dantès!" he commanded. "Sit."

"Goddammit, I was trying to keep them from
tearing the door off," Marck snapped. "What the
hell took you so long to get here?"

Wyatt bit back a retort as he looked out. Zombies
everywhere. Christ. Thirty of them, maybe more.
He didn't think he'd ever seen so many in one place.
They could easily tip the truck over if they all figured
out how to work together. Or got mad enough.

Remy pushed her way between them. "Oh my
God," she whispered as another violent jolt sent her
falling into Marck. "They found me."

Wyatt couldn't help but glance at their new companion. He showed up tonight and all of a sudden
a whole band of frenzied gangas appeared. Coincidence?

His jaw tightened as the truck tipped sharply, then
slammed back upright. He'd deal with Marck later.
Right now they had to get out of this mess.

"Get me a torch," he shouted. "At least we can try
and hold some of them—" The truck jolted again,

cutting him off, but by the time he'd righted himself, Remy was there with a rolled up piece of cloth that was trying to burn on one end. A pair of *jeans*? Christ, wasn't there anything else? Denim burned like shit.

Marck was doing something under the steering well of the truck, and Wyatt realized he was trying to see if there was a way to get it started. "Not gonna work," he shouted, brandishing the torch out the glassless window. "Gas tank's bone dry."

There was a curse and then Marck's face reappeared. "Trying to see if I can get some wires to spark," he said, then disappeared back under.

Wyatt shook his head, wondering what the hell sparking wires would do to help. The only way he knew of to kill a zombie was to smash his brains. Not a pleasant task, nor an efficient one.

Remy shrieked when the truck jolted violently, and this time it nearly went over.

Sonofabitch. Wyatt lunged back to the window and hung out of it, waving the soft, sagging torch at the monsters. It did little to deter them; they merely moved to Marck's side of the truck and began to push at it.

The group was surprisingly coordinated; zombies didn't usually comprehend teamwork. Especially when there was a potential meal involved. Wyatt shoved that thought away. According to Marck's information, he and Remy would be safe—if one could call being abducted by zombies safe—while Ian Marck would be the one in danger. And Dantès.

The poor dog was whining and shoving his head against Wyatt's arm, and then Remy, and then back again. He was just as frightened as the rest of them.

The truck was rocking harder. It was going to go over any time now, and there didn't seem to be anything—

"Remy. You have that bottle of alcohol? Grab it. And the alcohol pads in the first aid kit. And the empty whiskey bottle." Damn. He knew he should have saved some of the Jameson's. "And whatever books and paper you can find."

She gave a little cry as the truck tipped again, sending her to the floor, hard, but she leapt up and dashed back into the darkness, taking Dantès with her. Marck emerged from beneath the steering well just as the glass on the driver's side window shattered. A thick zombie hand, gray and putrid with rotting flesh, reached in blindly, just missing Ian's arm.

"Hurry!" Wyatt shouted, smashing at the hands of zombies as they tried to pull themselves up, using the empty window ledge. He still waved the torch, but it wasn't burning very well at all.

Remy was back, shoving the small bottle of alcohol into his hands. He'd grabbed a piece of something soft from the floor and now he shoved it into the bottle, leaving a little tail hanging out. One small fucking bomb, and maybe a second one if he got lucky. A few burning books. That was the most he could hope for.

The truck rocked again, and he realized the zombies were now pushing from both sides—which was actually a blessing. They weren't coordinating, they were fighting against each other. Good. If they could just hold them off till dawn, when the zombies would leave . . .

He lit the tail dangling from the small bottle and waited for the cloth to burn down as low as he could . . . He didn't want to wait too long, but—

"Duck!" he shouted, and flipped it out the window just as it exploded. Glass shattered against the metal of the truck door and a few shards even flew inside. *Fuck.* That was too damn close.

The small bottle bomb had frightened the zombies enough that they backed away, but the reprieve didn't last long.

"Got any other ideas?" Still holding the smoldering denim torch, Wyatt called to Marck, who was doing pretty much the same thing he was on the opposite side of the cab: keeping the door closed and using whatever was at hand to fight them away.

"I'm thinking!" Marck shouted back, beating at a zombie head with something he'd found on the bottom of the truck. "Isn't there any other way out of this thing?"

"No," Wyatt responded over the roar. "No back door. No rear entrance." He crumpled up the page of a book Remy tossed on the seat behind him, then lit the ball. When it flared into flames, he tossed it out the window, then followed with a second one out Marck's window. The burning missiles had effective but short-lived effects on the zombies: they caused them to spread out, and one or two might catch his clothes on fire, but once they staggered away, screaming gutturally, the others swarmed back to the truck.

He threw the last book—damn, it was the Jack Reacher thriller he'd just salvaged—and then something was thrust into his hand. A metal pan. Excellent. Still holding the makeshift torch, he swung out the window and caught one of the monsters in the head with the pan. The skull crunched and he fell away, only to be replaced by another one, trying to claw his way in.

"Remy," he shouted over the loud cries of the zombies, "open as many alcohol pads as you can and stuff 'em inside the whiskey bottle. And get me a soft piece of cloth."

One more. They had one more bomb, maybe, and then he was fresh out of ideas.

In the midst of the chaotically rocking truck and the increasingly frenzied cries of the zombies, someone yanked on Wyatt's arm. He spun from the window to see Remy doubled over, hand at her waist.

A faint orange glow burned through and behind her cupped hands, illuminating her shirt.

Christ. Not again.

He dropped the waning torch on the seat. The cab jolted hard and he crashed into her as he stumbled to her side, but by the time he got there, amazingly, she had the crystal in her hands. He didn't waste time commenting how she'd removed it or congratulating her for having done so; he simply took it when she shoved it at him. The stone was hot, no doubt about it, and glowing like a fire, but he held onto it. He couldn't take the time to look at it closely, but he saw that it was no longer enclosed in its cocoon of metal wiring. She must have taken his advice.

Remy looked up at him, her eyes wide and a little crazy, and said, "Let's show it to them. Maybe it'll stop them."

Wyatt shook his head. "No, it's what they've come for. It'll just make 'em crazier." He handed her back the stone. The glow had eased slightly, but it was still hot.

"But didn't Theo and Selena say the crystals embedded in their brains are orange? Maybe there's a connection," she argued as Marck shouted from the front, "I can't hold them off! Do you have another bomb?"

"Here," Remy said, swooping down to the floor, rising, then jamming the whiskey bottle into Wyatt's gut. "I put in as many alcohol pads as I could. But if it doesn't work . . . what are we going to do?"

Their eyes met and for a moment everything around him stopped. Wyatt's chest felt tight. He caught himself just before he reached for her, his hand falling back to his side.

I won't let anything happen to you. He thought the words, told her with his eyes. Then he turned away, his heart pounding furiously, his insides in turmoil. What *were* they going to do?

He hustled to the front, snatching up the torch, which had gone out. Only a few sparks were left clinging to the denim, and the truck was rocking violently again.

"How long till dawn?" he shouted to Marck, trying to light the damn bomb as he was being jolted from side to side. "Remy, I need fire!"

"Too long," Marck shouted back. "Two hours."

Remy was there, her arm jerking sharply. Then a flare illuminated the darkness and he snatched it from her as the cab rose up on two side wheels, sending everything falling. Remy grabbed him as they tumbled to one side and he lost his grip on the bottle and the small light as they all crashed to the ground.

The truck hung there, suspended, for a long, long time, but once he recovered from the surprise, Marck moved fast, and Wyatt right with him. They bolted up, climbing over to the uppermost side of the truck, and the propulsion of their weight and movement brought it slamming back to the ground, still upright.

The force jarred everyone, and Dantès was freaking out in the back, whining and barking and scrabbling at the floor.

"That was fucking close," Marck said.

"I've got to show it to them," Remy said, grabbing at Wyatt's arm as he scrabbled for the whiskey bottle.

"Where's that damn bomb?" Ian shouted from the front.

"No fucking way," Wyatt snarled at her. "Don't show it to them. We don't know what it'll do." He found the bottle and grabbed it triumphantly, saying, "Where's the light?"

She had it for him seconds later, her drawn, frightened face illuminated by the golden light. Grabbing her arm, he yanked her close to his face. "Don't show it to them. Don't show it to anyone. It's all we've got, Remy." He took the light and turned away.

He didn't have an answer. He couldn't promise her anything.

He just had to find a way out of here.

Wyatt lit the bomb, looking out at the swarm of zombies. Even if this bastard worked—which would be a miracle—it wouldn't do anything more than the others. Hold 'em off for a minute and then they'd be back.

At the right time, he flipped the bomb just out the window and it exploded as it fell into the soup of zombies. Glass shattered and a brief surge of flames roared. The zombies cried out, their *ruuuuuthhhh-hhs* rumbling into high surprised groans, and staggered back.

"That's it," he told Marck. "That's all we got. They're gonna push us over. What's the plan? Think we can fight our way through them when they do?"

"Gonna have to," Ian said, his face as grim as Wyatt felt.

The reprieve from the bomb ended, and the zombies recovered sooner than he hoped. And he was flat out of ideas.

Remy brushed past, bumping against him as she pushed her way into the front of the truck. He caught sight of a soft glow just before she reached the window, but it was too late.

She was already showing them the crystal. Holding it firmly, the illumination dancing over her face like a candle flame, she lifted it well out of reach of the suddenly undulating, desperate crowd of zombies. Her face was a study in concentration and hope, along with despair.

"What the *hell*," Marck whispered, staring at her. "Where did you—"

"Remy, no!" Wyatt went to drag her away from the window, but the zombies had already seen the gem, held high above them. Stunned, he released her.

The crystal the monsters sought was alive, glowing orange. And when they saw it burning above them, the zombies had gone silent.

CHAPTER 8

Remy held the crystal aloft, relief and apprehension rushing through her. The night was silent, the zombies were still. Wyatt stood behind her, tension and fury and wonder emanating from him. And Ian . . . he must be feeling the same.

Then, as if by some silent signal, it all changed.

The zombies surged back into motion, crying and shoving each other in renewed desperation. They were more frenzied than before, if that was possible, and now she could see the fury and need in their orange eyes. The truck rocked again, more violently now, for all of the monsters had crowded to the side where the crystal was.

"Son of a bitch," Wyatt said from between his teeth, his voice in her ear as he pulled her away from the window. He fairly shoved her into the rear of the truck.

Remy's short-lived relief evaporated and now she could do nothing but stare down at the glowing crystal. She held it by one of its metal pieces, which kept it from burning her fingers too badly.

"I'll just give it to them," she said, suddenly very

tired. "They can have it, Wyatt. It's not worth our lives, whatever it is."

"No," he said, looming over her in the darkness. It was just the two of them back there; Ian was effectively blocked into the front by Wyatt's solid figure. Remy could see him trying to fight off the grasping hands behind Wyatt. "We'll find a way. You can't give it up. Not now." He took her shoulders. "Ian didn't know?" He could hardly believe it.

She shook her head. "No."

The truck shuddered violently and rose again. It crashed to the ground moments later, but the message was clear.

"But it's not worth dying for." Remy tried to push past him, but he grabbed her arm. "We don't even know what it is."

"It's definitely something. They know it. Look at them!"

"If I throw it at them, maybe they'll chase it and we can escape," she said, pushing against his solid chest as the truck lurched again.

"Getting a little rough up here!" Ian shouted. "What the hell are you doing?"

"How far do you think you could throw it?" Remy asked, looking up at Wyatt.

"Not far en— Wait." He stilled, and she could see his mind working. "If we had a decoy . . ."

She caught on immediately. "Yes! But how? We could light a stick and throw that . . . ?"

"No, that wouldn't work," he said impatiently. "But maybe this would." He shoved past her as the truck tipped again, and fumbled in the precious plastic box.

"What are those?" she asked, looking at the slender greenish sticks he brought out.

But he ignored her, speaking rapidly. "We need something plastic or glass. Clear, and find my orange shir— No, *wait*. Find that small medicine bottle in the first aid kit. The golden glass one. Yes, that'll be perfect. Then we won't need my—just empty it out, pour out whatever's in it. Quick, Remy."

Wyatt moved to the front of the truck. "Going to try something," he said to Ian as Remy scrabbled around, trying to find the bottle that met his description. "You know how to make a slingshot?"

There was a loud screeching noise as one of the mirrors was torn off the truck.

"The fucking door's gonna be next," said Ian, tearing a piece of cloth off his shirt. "I can do a sling. Don't have any rubber."

It took her forever, but at last Remy found the small glass bottle. Its label said merthiolate and it had some bright red liquid in it. She dumped it out into a wad of blankets, smelling the pungent scent of the medicine.

The zombies surged and Remy felt the door rattling as they pulled on it, then shoved at the truck. It was like being on a boat at rough sea, rocking and dipping constantly.

Wyatt had taken the slender green things and snapped one in half. "Damn," he muttered. He took a second one and broke it too.

"What are you trying to do?" Remy asked.

"These are glow-stick flares," he said shortly. "They're supposed to glow when you break them. They're not working. They must've gotten wet or are too old."

There were only three more left.

"Got your sling," Ian said. "What's the plan?"

"There may not be any plan," Wyatt snapped, picking up a third flare. He looked at it, closed his eyes as he jolted from another lunge at the truck, and then broke it. This time there was a faint greenish light, but it went out immediately.

Remy's palms were damp and she was aware of the heavy, hot crystal in her pocket. She'd wrapped it in thick cloth to keep it from burning her, but she feared she was going to have to bring it back out again. She wasn't about to sacrifice their lives for the sake of a stone. It just wasn't worth it.

Another stick snapped, and this time the glow stayed. *Yesss.* Satisfaction and determination shone in Wyatt's face as he held out his hand. "Give me the bottle."

She handed it to him and he did something she couldn't see, taking part of the flare and shoving it inside the bottle. "Whoa," she whispered when she saw the effect.

Inside the bottle, the flare burned with a reddish-orange glow. It could . . . maybe . . . pass for the crystal. If anyone was dumb enough to be fooled, the zombies were.

"Remy, are you ready?" Wyatt asked. "Marck, the sling. I have to get on the roof. Otherwise it won't go far enough."

"You can't do that," she said, grabbing his arm. "They'll knock you off."

"Stand on the seat," Ian suggested. "Put your head and shoulders out the window. We'll leverage you."

Wyatt gave a short nod. Then he turned to Remy. "Pull out the crystal," he said. "You have to show it to them again. They sense it somehow—"

He was cut off as the truck was lifted high again.

Remy held her breath, her heart in her throat as Wyatt and Ian lunged to the side to weight it back down.

"I understand," she said when the truck stopped rocking. "Ready?"

She pulled out the crystal and Wyatt climbed out the window. She and Ian each grabbed a leg and she pressed the hot crystal into Wyatt's palm. He wasn't expecting her to give it to him, but he took it, holding it high. As the zombies fell silent again, he replaced it with the glowing bottle in his hand and showed the fake crystal only briefly as he slipped the real crystal back into her hand. The zombies were getting restless again, and from below, she watched as he fitted the bottle into the cloth sling Ian had made.

Holding onto one muscular thigh—and trying not to think about the fact that she was—Remy felt Wyatt's body move as he swung it around once, twice, and then the snap as he whipped it, sending it flying.

The orange glowing object arced through the air, over the watching heads of the zombies, and deep into the woods.

The monsters screamed and stumbled over each other as they turned to lumber after it.

Remy didn't have more than a moment of relief before she was being manhandled from the truck and onto the ground. "Run," Wyatt breathed in her ear. "Northeast. Take Dantès."

She hesitated, but he gave her a fierce look and a little shove. "Go! I'm right behind you, but I'm going to try and hold them off a little longer."

Dantès was there, butting her with his nose urgently. He, at least, was ready.

"But—"

"Go, Remy. You've got to take that crystal to Envy.

We can't let the Strangers get it. Whatever you do, get to Envy."

Remy gave Wyatt one last look as Ian jumped out of the truck. At least there were two of them.

Then she turned and ran.

Dantès kept pace with her, bounding over cropped-up pieces of concrete and dodging bushes and rusted out mailboxes. The moans from the zombies faded as she ran as fast and as hard as she could, going uphill whenever there was a choice to do so.

But even as she ran, Remy wondered how Wyatt would find her again. And Ian.

She paused once, out of breath, the stitch in her side making further movement unbearable. Leaning against an old signpost, gasping for air, she listened for the sounds of her companions crashing through the wilderness behind her. But the only noise she heard besides her own breathing was Dantès, who was panting next to her, and the low hoot of an owl.

Bending, she patted her dog, looking and feeling around as well as she could for the blood seeping from his wounds. Nothing; just the heaving of his rib cage from the first run he'd had in two days. She smiled in spite of the moment. Dantès was never happier than when he was running or chasing something.

Remy knew she should start moving again, but she waited for a little longer, straining to listen for Wyatt or Ian. As she did, she looked around for possible shelter. Through the trees and skeletons of buildings, she could see the faint lightening of the sky in the east. Dawn wasn't far off, and the zombies would seek shelter before the sun came up.

She was standing in a wooded area threaded with ivy and other vines. Low growing bushes dotted the space and a long, one-story structure stood nearby, across an expanse of what might have been a concrete parking lot. There was little glass in its windows on which the moonlight shone. Not a good place to hide from zombies, but as it was nearing dawn, she might be able to stay here for a while. Give Dantès a chance to rest too.

And wait for Wyatt to catch up.

If he did.

Remy started toward the building. In the faulty light, she could see some metal lettering still clinging to the outside: ACKS ELEM SCH L.

The nearest door was rusted closed, so instead of wasting time trying to open it, she knocked the remaining fragments of glass from the nearest window and hoisted Dantès up. It was a low window, and using the leverage of his paws on the edge, she was able to get him inside with little trouble. They were used to working together like this. Once he was inside, she gave him the command to stay.

She paused, listening once more. Then, just as she was about to follow her pet inside, she saw the glint of moonlight on a familiar metal shape. A chill zipped down her spine and she gave Dantès the "quiet" command as she vaulted through the window. Once inside and safely in the dark room, she looked back out at the gleaming steel.

A Humvee.

The shape and size was unmistakable, and even the brief glance told her the vehicle wasn't an old, rusted out truck. It looked as new and intact as the one she and Ian had driven around in.

Ian.

An uncomfortable feeling turned in the pit of her stomach, and she bit her lip. She couldn't be more than five or six miles from the camp she'd shared with Wyatt—and where she'd found Ian's old boots. Could the truck belong to Ian?

Or did it belong to someone else, who might be lurking about . . . or sleeping in this very building? Remy reached automatically to the back of her jeans for her gun. *It wasn't there.* As her belly dropped with a sickening thud, she realized she hadn't been wearing it when Wyatt dragged her out of the truck. *No. Oh, no.*

No weapon. No pack. Nothing. She had nothing.

Nervous and unsettled, she glanced at Dantès. He seemed only calm and curious, watching her for a command, but clearly ready to explore their surroundings. His ease relaxed her a little and she released him so he could sniff around the area while she considered the situation.

There was the possibility that the Humvee was abandoned. It happened more often than one might expect. That sparked a flare of excitement in her. She could get to Envy more safely and quickly if, miraculously, she could steal the truck. Even if its owner was sleeping in the building, she'd have the chance to drive it off. That would more than make up for not having her gun.

Because of the way the bounty hunters and Strangers used the Humvees, many of the vehicles had no keys, or if they had them, the keys were left inside. Instead, there was a hidden compartment with a switch that started the truck so that any of them could utilize a vehicle as needed. This came in handy, she'd learned when traveling with the bounty hunters, in the case of quick getaways or if otherwise attacked. They didn't want to be sharing or losing the keys to their escape.

All of which meant that if she could get to the truck unseen, she could steal it.

Now Remy had a different reason to listen and wait. But she'd been here for at least ten minutes and had heard no other human sounds. Seen no other movement—not even from Wyatt, who said he'd be right behind her.

A prickle of unease slipped over her shoulders. What if he and Ian hadn't made it away from the zombies? She slid her hand over the pocket of her jeans to feel the crystal—the lure that surely had drawn the mob of zombies to them, and would call them to come for her again as soon as the sun set tomorrow.

Her heart stopped when she realized *her pocket was empty.*

The crystal was gone.

CHAPTER 9

Remy frantically searched all her pockets, but the crystal was gone.

Her heart thudding, nausea roiling up, threatening to choke her, she sagged against the wall. It was impossible for the crystal to have fallen from her pocket while she was running. The pocket was too deep.

Which meant someone had taken it.

Wyatt.

It had to be him; he must have done it when he pulled her out of the truck, practically shoving her off into the woods. Ian hadn't been close enough, and he didn't even know she had the crystal until she showed it to the zombies. Had he?

Remy closed her eyes. She'd trusted Wyatt. Why had she trusted him? How could she have been so stupid? Fury mingled with the sick feeling deep in her belly.

Dantès butted his head against her hand as if to ask what was wrong. She wanted to tell him he'd been taken in by a thief and a liar, that the man he'd cheated on her with wasn't worthy of his affection.

She'd actually begun to soften toward him, especially after learning about his wife and children. And—hell, admit it—after that kiss. No wonder he told her it wasn't going to happen again. He probably planned this all along. After all, he was the one who told her to find somewhere else to put the crystal.

And she'd listened to him. She'd made a necklace-like belt so she could still wear the stone beneath her shirt, around her waist, while providing for easy removal if it began to burn again.

But he gave it back to you.

Twice.

Remy shook her head. It didn't make any sense. Why would he give it back if he really wanted to keep it? Even with her gun, she knew she'd be no match for him if he wanted to steal the crystal.

But he hasn't shown up yet. If he was really following you, he'd be here by now.

She wanted to bang her head against the wall. She wanted to cry. For twenty years she'd protected that crystal, given up her life for it—and now it was gone. Now what? Should she go back and try to find him or keep going on to Envy? But should she go to Envy if his friends were there?

At least the zombies will be after him now, not me.

That was small comfort.

She opened her eyes. The best option was the Humvee. She drew in a deep breath and, after warring with herself, commanded Dantès to sit and stay quietly. Then she climbed back out the window, still silent and wary. If she could get the vehicle, maybe she'd be able to backtrack and find Wyatt. The landmark of the tall signpost would help her find the old truck rig again, and it was beginning to get light in the east.

A cyclone of thoughts and possibilities—not to mention fantasies of inflicting torture and pain on Wyatt—flooded her mind as she made her way toward the Humvee. Staying in shadow, taking her time, Remy nevertheless moved quickly, and soon she was right at the vehicle. It was hidden by a large scrub of bushes in the shadow of the building. She'd only seen it by chance because of the way the moonlight hit the metal.

She listened. Waited. Breathed.

She heard nothing. Crouching low, she ran up to the truck and rose slowly on her toes to look inside the windows. It was dark, and hard to see for certain, but she didn't spy any shape that looked human.

Once she was sure no one was about, she carefully tried the door. It was unlocked.

Heart beating nearly in her throat, she eased it open, aware that an interior light might come on but that she had to take the chance. When the white light cut into the darkness in what felt like a silent explosion, she hardly winced. After another quick look around, she climbed inside and closed the door silently. Blessedly, the light went out.

Hard to discern details in the dark, but she saw that the front seats were empty. On the floor in the rear, however was a duffel bag. It could contain some goodies—including a hint as to whether this was Ian's truck or not—but now was not the time to dig through it. There could even be a *gun*! Once she got away from here . . .

Remy bent down to look under the steering wheel well, where the secret compartment with the ignition switch had been located on Ian's truck.

All at once the light went on and she felt a waft of chill air over her back.

"Well. What do we have here?"

She froze. The woman's voice skittered over her skin like a thousand spiders. She knew that voice. Very well.

Pulling out from her awkward position, Remy found herself facing a woman who was holding the gun she coveted. Her white-blond hair was even more silvery than usual thanks to the moonlight, and the harsh shadows highlighted her attractive but hard features. Her thin lips were curled into an unfriendly smile, red with color even in the dead of night. She was tall, slender, and wiry with muscle.

"Hello, Lacey," Remy said, so tense she felt ill.

"This must be my lucky day, Goldwyn," Lacey said, speaking to the man who stood behind her. "Remington Truth. In the flesh. Actually climbing into my truck. As if she *wanted* to go with me. How much better can it get?"

At her words, Remy's heart plummeted and her knees turned wobbly. *Oh God. She knows my real name?*

Lacey was nearly as powerful and ruthless as Ian. Not only was she a bounty hunter, but she'd been crystalled by the Strangers as a reward for her loyalty and hard work, which made her immortal and that much more difficult to kill. Her small blue crystal, embedded in the soft skin just below her collarbone, was displayed by a special hole cut into her leather corset. Laced tightly, the corset hugged the bounty hunter's slender, boyish figure, making her small breasts appear larger. Her arms were long and slender, corded with muscle and decorated with leather wristbands. But the blue crystal, smaller than Remy's missing gem, showed proudly through its special opening, glowing in the night.

Remy had encountered Lacey when she first met up with Ian, and several other times after that. The woman hated her on sight, partly because she was with Ian—who was the best at what he did, and whom Lacey wanted to partner with—and partly because Lacey wanted to be Ian's partner in *every* way.

"I'll shoot the signal flare," Goldwyn said, also holding a gun. Remy had only met him once, briefly, but she remembered him well. He was an albino with watery red eyes, and his chest was as wide as the Humvee's door, although he wasn't crystalled. Nevertheless, getting away from either of them was going to be pretty damn impossible.

"The fla— *No,* I don't want you—" But Lacey was too late; Goldwyn had raised his gun and shot it into the air.

A brief arc of light curved above the trees as Lacey turned on her partner. "Not yet! You cocked it all up now," she said, gritting her teeth. "Damn." She turned to Remy, her features brittle. "Well, we'll have a little time before he gets here." Her smile became even more unpleasant and Remy's insides curdled. "We have some catching up to do, don't we, my dear? Step out of the truck, nice and slow now. Where's that dog of yours?" she asked, looking around sharply.

Remy clamped her mouth shut. She definitely wasn't going to call Dantès now. The bitch would probably shoot him on sight. *Damn.* Now her best hope was that Dantès would find Wyatt—no, wait. Wyatt had double-crossed her.

He wasn't going to be coming after her if he'd taken the crystal, was he? She was very confused. And very alone.

Remy felt a cold shock, as if a bucket of water had

just been dumped over her head. What were they going to do with her, now that they knew they had Remington Truth? Bluffing was her only option, so she said, "Remington Truth? What are you talking about?"

Lacey backhanded her with her gun hand, and Remy saw stars. Black waves of nausea engulfed her and the pain sent her spiraling into the dark memories of her ordeal with Seattle. Her cheek hurt and her head pounded, but she fought out of the black vortex and forced her eyes open. She made herself look at the ground through her flashing, watery vision, focusing on the shapes and the reality of where she was . . . and the fury she felt toward this woman.

"Don't waste my time pretending. I know who you are," Lacey said. "And you're going to make me rich and powerful. I won't be hoboing it around all the time anymore, once I get you back to the Strangers at Mecca. I'll be a cocking *hero*."

"I can't imagine how that's going to happen," Remy said, keeping her voice strong with conviction. For now her only option seemed to be to confuse and delay.

Lacey's eyes narrowed, and for a moment Remy thought she was going to hit her again. But Goldwyn put a hand on Lacey's arm and said, "Won't help us if she's dead or messed up. Wait till he gets here."

"I'll mess her up all right," Lacey promised. "Then we'll see if he—" She clamped her lips shut and glared at Remy.

Her insides were a mess, her cheek and jaw throbbed, and now Remy had more questions: who was "he" and what had Lacey been about to say? Possible answers trammeled through her mind— none of them pleasant. She felt as if she'd been placed in the middle of a nightmare and had no idea what was going on.

"How long should we wait?" Goldwyn asked. "He didn't respond to the signal flare. Maybe he's out of range."

"Another ten minutes. Then we book. In the meantime, bind her." Lacey gestured with her gun, and Goldwyn grabbed Remy's arms, forcing her hands behind her back.

She felt him digging in his pocket, then the strong, slender plastic the bounty hunters favored for handcuffs were twisted around her wrists. It was painful and tight, cutting into her skin. When Goldwyn finished, he smoothed his hand up and down over the curve of her rear, slowly and intimately.

"Very nice," he breathed into her ear before stepping away.

Remy swallowed hard and kept her mind blank as black terror edged there. This was not going to be like Seattle. She couldn't live through that again.

No. She struggled, fought back the fear and the memories with every bit of mental strength she had. If she let them in, she'd be done. She wasn't going to think about anything but how to escape. Not the future. Not about who was coming. Not about Wyatt. Just now. And here. How.

Lacey gave her a shove and Remy bounced against the Humvee, her face smashing into the metal edge of the door, then away. Pain burst over her lip and she tasted blood as she spun helplessly. She caught herself before she fell to the ground, tumbling instead onto the front seat of the Humvee, barely missing the steering wheel. She landed facedown, her injured cheek and cut lip crushed into the seat. *Bitch.*

The minute Lacey put her gun away, Remy was going to whistle for Dantès. It was her only chance. Once she got put in the truck and driven off, she was done.

Lacey and Goldwyn conferred in low voices and Remy tried to keep an eye on them, waiting for them to let their guard down. But Lacey still held the gun, and the pain in Remy's head made it hard to focus. She had to fight to keep from succumbing to the hovering darkness of oblivion.

Then her captors stopped talking and Remy heard the sound of someone approaching. It took great effort, but she dragged herself up and out of the truck, wobbly on her feet, just in time to see Ian Marck walk into the moonlight.

CHAPTER 10

Remy's first reaction was relief, which immediately changed to uncertainty when her captors greeted Ian readily. She leaned against the truck, the only thing keeping her upright. Blood dripped from her lip and her head felt two sizes too big.

"You found her," Ian said as he approached with long, easy strides. When he barely glanced over, Remy's heart sank into her nauseated belly. The fact that he didn't sound surprised made her feel even worse.

"You didn't respond to the signal," Lacey told him.

"I saw no need. As you can see, I was close enough to get here quickly." Now Ian turned to look at her. "Damn. What the fuck happened to her?"

"She was mouthy," Lacey said. "Pissed me off."

Remy didn't have the energy to speak, but she was certain he read the sentiment in her murderous glare. Ian shook his head and turned back to Lacey. "She doesn't have the crystal."

"How the hell do you know that?"

Remy wondered the same thing.

"She didn't tell you?" Ian said, moving to stand

next to her. "I was with her for a while, then we had to scatter when the zombies attacked. I thought I lost her." He gave Remy a tight, cold smile, and it was all she could do not to spit in his face. But she wasn't stupid enough to let her emotions get the best of her. She had to remain calm and cool and think about her next steps.

"She didn't say nothing," Goldwyn replied. "You were with her?"

"Didn't I say that?" Ian replied, his tones unpleasant as he raked over Remy with his eyes. "Watch her," he ordered the albino, gesturing to Remy. Then he turned to Lacey and took her arm, leading her far enough away that their conversation was inaudible.

Still hoping for any opportunity to escape, Remy eyed the two of them. Lacey bristled as she faced Ian, speaking intensely. But as Remy watched, Ian's body language changed: he relaxed, eased closer to the silvery blond woman in the sort of sexy slouch a man did when he was interested in a female, bringing his hips a little closer, head tilting to the side as he looked down at her.

Remy had asked Ian about Lacey once, when they were together. One of the reasons Seattle hated Ian enough to kill him was because he wanted Lacey, and he believed she and Ian were lovers. But when Remy asked Ian about Lacey, he responded negatively, with great disgust. *Fuck, no*, were his exact words.

Apparently, his opinion had changed.

Lacey relaxed visibly and Remy heard the low, husky rumble of her laugh as she fairly melted into Ian. They shifted so that Ian's back was toward the Humvee, blocking Lacey from view, and Remy saw him bend to kiss her. It was not a brief one.

"Jealous?" said a deep voice in her ear. Goldwyn's presence engulfed her, causing her stomach to pitch unpleasantly. "I can take your mind off that."

Before she could move away, he slid his arms around her from behind, pulling her back against him so her bound hands were against his crotch. Remy gagged as he pressed his erection firmly into her hands as his fingers moved around to caress her cheek, then slide down from her shoulder over her breast.

She shuddered, closing her eyes as she tried not to vomit, tried to stave off the ugly, dark memories that swarmed her as she struggled to ignore the feel of his hands on her. *Breathe.* She slammed her heel down onto his foot then squeezed the soft part of him pressing into her from behind.

Goldwyn cried out in rage, and the next thing she knew, she was spinning toward the ground.

Someone caught her before she landed on her battered face, yanking her upright with an uncomfortable jerk of her bound wrists. Remy looked up and saw Ian through her angry tears. He wasn't looking at her, but at Goldwyn. "No," he said, his voice deathly cold.

"But you—"

"That's right. *I.* Not you." Ian smiled down at her with a hard, cruel mouth, then propelled her sharply toward the Humvee. He wasn't rough enough to make her fall again, but she bumped against the wall.

"Ian," Lacey said, her voice questioning, and flavored with the slightest whine.

His mouth tightened, then softened as he turned to her, sliding one finger up her arm suggestively. Then, just as smoothly, he asked, "Where's the dog?"

She shook her head mutely. She wasn't sure she could even whistle for Dantès, with her mouth cut as it was. But she sure as hell wasn't going to tell Ian anything.

Betrayed by two men in less than an hour. What the hell.

"Remy," Ian said, taking her by the arms and yanking her toward him. "Where the hell is your dog?" He was so close she could feel his breath on her cheek, his eyes boring into hers. "I'm sure you don't want anything to happen to him."

Something about his tone cut through her pain and anger and she met his eyes. A little ping of hope flitted through her when she saw the intensity in his gaze, then it faded. She knew better. "I don't know," she managed to say through a swollen, bloody lip. "He took off."

Ian gave a short nod, then shoved her away. Not enough to make her fall again, but enough that she stumbled. Lacey was watching them with a suspicious, furious expression, and when her eyes settled on Remy, they were filled with hatred. Then, to Remy's horror, Ian whistled and shouted, "Dantès! Come."

She started to shriek "No!" when Lacey jammed the gun into her throat as Dantès bounded out into the clearing, leaping through the school window as if he'd been waiting for the chance.

Ian looked at Lacey. "Keep that on her. You— don't say a word," he ordered Remy as he walked over to stop Dantès from rushing up to his mistress.

Remy held her breath, feeling the pressure of the gun barrel on her skin. If it was pushing into her, it wasn't aiming at Dantès. She had that at least. She tried to relax, because if her dog knew she was in distress, he'd attack even without her command. And then the gun would go off. Ian knelt and greeted her pet, who kept looking around him at her. Remy closed her eyes briefly, praying, trying to dissolve any tension Dantès might sense.

"Remy. Tell him it's okay," Ian called from where he crouched by the dog.

"It's okay, Dantès," Remy called in as steady a voice as she could muster. *Let him be okay. Let him go. Please.* The wave of despair and fear that rushed through her was so strong, she felt a great band of pressure constricting her chest. Darkness flickered at the edge of her vision despite the rising sun, and for a moment her knees felt as if they were going to give out.

Then Ian made a sharp gesture, and after one hesitant glance at Remy, Dantès dashed off into the woods.

"Let's get her out of here," Ian said as he returned. "Now, before the mutt comes back." When Lacey opened her mouth to protest, he snapped, "The dog's a loose wire. You want to take the chance he might tear out your throat like he did to Seattle?"

"Seattle's dead?" Lacey sounded gleeful. "Rocks."

As she alternated between relief that Dantès was being spared and despair that she was being taken away so she couldn't be tracked, Remy was shoved into the back of the Humvee with rough hands. She landed on her face again, but at least the seat was softer than the ground. To her dismay, Goldwyn climbed in the back with her and Ian went behind the wheel, with Lacey joining him in front.

The truck took off with a lurch, and Remy bounced along, half on the floor, half on the seat, as they barreled over the rough terrain. Exhaustion, pain, and fear eventually had its way, and she at last succumbed to the darkness edging her vision.

When Remy became aware again, it was to a bright, jolting world filled with throbbing pain and a constant rumble beneath her ear. Her mouth was dry and when she tried to swallow, she realized her swollen, bloody lip had stuck to the leather seat. Her back hurt, her arms strained behind her ached, and her head pounded.

She blinked gritty eyes, and as the sound of voices penetrated her discomfort, she tried to listen to the conversation. It went in and out, but she caught some of it over the sound of Goldwyn's snoring and the vehicle's motor.

". . . stop for a while." That was Ian, who was driving.

"But it's just past dawn," Lacey argued. ". . . get to Mecca . . ."

". . . find out where she hid the crystal . . ." Ian again. So he thought she'd hidden the crystal. But how did he know?

"She'll tell me," Lacey said, the anticipation in her voice. "I have . . . getting information."

Ian laughed. "I'd love to see you in action."

Remy closed her eyes as a dart of renewed fear shot through her. What she wouldn't give for a drink of water. A knife. A gun.

Even Wyatt.

She squeezed her eyes tighter as tears stung them. She'd been alone before. Alone and hopeless. She'd figure out a way to escape, or die trying.

But the crystal was out of her hands now, so she didn't have to protect it. She didn't have to stay alive.

That realization was, in a bleak way, a relief.

Now if there was a chance she could convince them that she had nothing they wanted . . .

No. She could be terrified later. Now, she had to think. And in regrouping and assessing her situation, she realized the softness beneath one of her knees was the duffel bag she'd noticed earlier, when she searched the inside of the Humvee. Maybe there was something useful inside.

It took some uncomfortable contortions, but Remy was able to squirm down to the floor and find the zipper on the duffel, her face buried in the space between the back of Lacey's seat and the rear. When she found the metal tab, it took forever to get at the right angle to catch it in her teeth—and the bouncing, jouncing, jolting of the ride didn't make it any easier. But she bit firmly onto it and then tried to work the zipper open. She caught her lower lip in the metal as the truck jounced and caused the zip to surge open, but in the grand scheme of things, it was a minor discomfort.

But she'd barely begun to open the duffel when the truck stopped abruptly. She jolted forward, slamming against the back of Lacey's seat. She stifled a moan of pain and tensed as the doors opened and Ian and Lacey got out of the truck.

When the door next to her opened, she prepared herself for an onslaught of renewed violence, but it was Ian, not Lacey, who pulled her out.

"Fuck. You're a mess aren't you?" Ian looked at her with those cold blue eyes. He steadied her on her feet, holding onto her arm as if afraid she would bolt.

"I don't want her to get infected or sick. Liam won't be pleased if she dies before we get the information he wants. We've come too far to fuck things up."

"Who's Liam?" Remy managed to ask, although the question came out more like a growl.

Lacey started to retort angrily, but Ian stopped her with a raised hand. "Liam Hegelson," he told Remy. "He'll be delighted to welcome you to Mecca. He's been looking for Remington Truth—and the crystal—for a long time."

"I don't have the crystal."

"I know," he replied. "But you're going to tell me where it is." The soft menace in his voice was an unsettling promise, and Remy's heart thudded heavy and hard in her chest.

The four of them went inside a small brick building that was relatively clean and unlittered. Obviously, it was a regular stop-over place with which the bounty hunters were familiar. The inside was dim and sparsely furnished with a sofa, chairs, and a table.

To Remy's surprise, Ian arranged for warm water—heated over a small solar-powered device—to wash the blood and dirt from her injured face. He also ordered Goldwyn to snip away the plastic cords around her wrists, and Remy fairly cried with relief when she was able to move her arms again.

"There are three of us and one of her," Ian snapped when Lacey protested. "You don't think you can handle that?"

"Whatever. But let me find out where the crystal is." Her colorless eyes danced with anticipation.

"Be my guest," Ian said, gesturing to a chair. "I don't like to get messy. But what's the hurry? I've got other things on my mind." The look he gave Lacey was so slow and heavy, even Remy felt it.

The bounty hunter relaxed, nearly oozing against him. Then she looked at Goldwyn. "You stay here. Watch her. We'll be back. Later." She gave Remy a cold, cruel smile as she slipped her wiry, muscular arm through Ian's. "That'll give you time to rest. You're gonna need it."

"Take the stones to Envy?" Cat said, looking at her father. She put down her cup of tea. "Why?"

Everyone knew about Envy—the largest settlement of people since the Change. It had sprung up in the months after the massive catastrophe that destroyed twenty-first century America—and, presumably, the rest of the world. Practically a city, although from what Cat knew, it was nowhere near the size or extent of pre-Change cities like New York or Los Angeles, or even Denver. It sounded like a foreign land to her.

The place had been called Envy for so long many people had forgotten it actually began on the site of Las Vegas, originally being named New Vegas, or N.V.

Regardless, Cat had no desire to go to a big, busy, crowded place like that. Even though she heard there were actual restaurants there, where you were served food at a table like in the old days, and it offered a variety of tradesmen making clothing and even a few places to barter for or buy rebuilt appliances, she didn't want to go. She liked it in Glenway. She was comfortable in the small peninsular town, protected from the zombies by a deep trench on two sides and the ocean on two more. She felt safe here. Safe, and able to heal.

But Dad seemed excited about the trip. It was almost as if he were looking for an excuse to go—after all, why would they need to make a three-day journey to deliver some stones? Even if they had glowed in the dark?

"You don't have to go with me, Catie," he said, stirring honey into his tea. "In fact, it might be better if you didn't. Yvonne can always use your help with Tanya, and don't think I haven't noticed Benjamin Mandova spending a lot of time talking with you." He smiled, the corners of his eyes crinkling deeply. "Maybe he'd get up the nerve to do something else if your papa wasn't around glowering at him."

"If you think I'm letting you go by yourself, you're nuts," Cat said flatly. "But I don't understand why you think it's so important."

He shrugged. "Call it instinct. I've been around long enough that I've learned to listen to it. Stones don't just glow. And the fact that the zombies have become more erratic lately, and they have glowing orange eyes that look a lot like those stones . . . I think George needs to know."

Cat got up, mug in hand, and went over to the sink. She pumped water into the basin with rough movements and was just turning back to Dad when the front door opened.

"Grandpa!" A whirlwind of energy burst into the room, hurling herself into his arms. She had springy dark hair and happy brown eyes.

Yvonne—Tanya's mother and Cat's sister—followed her daughter. She looked fondly at her father and daughter, who were smooching, hugging, and tickling each other. "Good morning. Sorry for the interruption, but since you've moved here, Tanya seems to think your house is just an extension of ours. Usually I can keep her contained until after nine, but this morning she got away from me."

"We're always glad to see you!" Cat said with real warmth. Moving here was the best decision she and Dad had made. Which was why she felt such an inkling of mistrust about this proposed trip to Envy. She was afraid it would change everything again.

"What's going on?" Yvonne looked from Cat to their father, obviously sensing the underlying disagreement.

"Last night when the zombies were out, we noticed a glow coming from George's laboratory," Dad said. "It was orange, and when we investigated—we were careful! Sheesh," he interjected when Yvonne drew in a sharp breath of alarm. "Anyway, we found the glow coming from some stones. Like crystals."

"Dad thinks we should take them all the way to Envy for George to look at," Cat said, not trying to hide her dislike of the idea.

Yvonne pursed her lips. "Tanny, honey, can you run home and make sure I turned off the . . . uh . . . water. In the sink? And while you're there, why don't you get your new doll to show Grandpa?"

Cat didn't say anything until Tanya was gone, but she watched her sister with calculating eyes. Once the door closed behind the little girl, she said, "What's going on?"

Yvonne shrugged. "Tanya likes to talk. I didn't want her to be spreading this around, but . . . Dad. I think you're right. You should take them to Envy." She hesitated, smoothing her hand over the battered kitchen table as if to sweep away a bit of crumbs. "You know Ana and I were very good friends. Although we were close, she was a little secretive about some things. About her background. So I don't really know what the situation was, but . . . one time, by accident, I saw her bare torso. Like, the side of her belly and rib cage. And she had crystals embedded in it."

"Crystals?" Dad sat straight up, his dark eyes sharp. "Like the Strangers?"

"No, no. She definitely wasn't a Stranger—these were different. And they were in the wrong place on her body; not up by the collarbone." Yvonne shook her head, pinching her lip between two fingers. "I always sensed she was different, that there was something she wasn't telling me. Not in a bad way, Cat. I'd trust Ana with my life. It was like she was . . . hiding from someone. Or something."

"I still don't see why that has anything to do with the glowing crystals we found," Cat said stubbornly.

"I'm not sure either, but if they were found in George's workroom, and his daughter has crystals in her skin . . . I doubt it's a coincidence." Dad drummed his fingers on the table.

"But . . . what if George and Ana are . . ." Cat allowed her voice to trail off as she struggled for the right words. ". . . not to be trusted? I mean . . . crystals? When I think of crystals, I think of the Strangers. And I can't say it makes me very comfortable knowing your friend Ana wears crystals." She glanced at Yvonne, who frowned back at her.

Dad sighed and settled back in his chair, then ran a hand through his thinning gray hair. He looked from one daughter to the other, then sighed again. "All right. Girls"—he still always called them girls, even though they were both in their twenties—"there's something I need to tell you."

Oh shit. Cat didn't like the sound of that, nor his arrested expression.

"What?" Yvonne demanded, her face and voice as tense as Cat felt. "I *knew* there was something going on with you, Dad. I knew it."

Cat resisted the urge to roll her eyes. *She'd* been the one living with Dad for the last six years—since Yvonne got married. As if her sister had any clue what was going on with their dad.

But apparently she herself didn't either.

"You have to keep it a secret. It's imperative. My life—and that of others—depends on it. Can you do that?"

Her heart pounding, Cat nodded. "Of course, Dad. I'd never do anything to endanger you." She exchanged glances with Yvonne and saw the same apprehension and confusion in her sister's face.

"I'm . . . uh . . . involved in a group," he said, obviously choosing his words carefully. "A secret group that's trying to . . . well, hell, how do I explain this? A group that's banded together to build up a resistance to the Strangers. We're in the process of building a rudimentary communication network using computers."

"Computers?" Cat breathed. "Like the old Internet?" A tingle of excitement blipped through her.

Dad nodded. "It's real spotty, but one of the locations is now here in Glenway. Thanks to me." He held up a hand when his daughters would have peppered him with questions. "I can't give you more details right now. I *can't*," he added sharply. "The fewer people who know, the safer we all are. But I can tell you this much: Ana and George can be trusted. I know this for a fact. They're part of the group. And so that," he said, spearing Cat with his eyes, "is why I have to bring those crystals to Envy. They mean something. I don't know what, but I think someone there can help. They need to know about them. Things are happening."

Cat became aware of her heart pounding in her chest and a queasy feeling roiling her belly. A secret group. A resistance.

All at once little things began to fall into place in her mind: hushed voices, her father leaving their house at odd times. The cloth-wrapped packages he occasionally brought home. He'd always claimed it was part of his job as a medic, which made sense. But now those details took on new meaning.

He'd always tried to help people when they needed help, using whatever medical training he'd been able to get over the years from other people and from books; there was no formal place to learn medical practice like in the days of *Grey's Anatomy* or *ER*. But she'd never thought of her father as a person who bucked the system, who caused ripples. She thought of him as a peacemaker, a healer.

He'd always been just Dad: comforting, supportive, and strong. Funny. Stern. A terrible cook.

"Wow," she breathed, looking at him with new eyes.

"So," he said, looking back at her, "I'm going to Envy. If you want to come, I'd like it. And they're having a big celebration sometime this week—I'm not sure which day, but it would give us a little bit of a cover for going. Survivors Day, it's called."

"Remembering and celebrating all the people who

survived the Change," Yvonne added helpfully. As if Cat couldn't have figured that out for herself.

Dad winked. "It might be fun, you know. I've always wanted to go. But, Catie, if you feel more comfortable staying here with Yvonne, I completely understand. I'll find someone else who wants to travel with me. I won't go alone. Brady Luck looks like he's old enough to have been a survivor." His eyes still glinted with humor.

Cat was shaking her head hardly before she realized her decision. "No, Dad, I'll go with you. I'd like to find out more about this resistance group."

His smile wavered, then turned affectionate. "Ah, yes. I was afraid you'd say that."

Wyatt looked down at the orange crystal.

It was about the circumference of a nickel, roughly spherical in shape and rough around the edges. Certainly not something that had been polished and prepared for a jewelry setting.

Could it really be the Mother crystal? The source of power for the Atlanteans? Something this small and irregular?

Regardless, it affected the zombies. It seemed to call them. And it was important to the Strangers. Therefore he had to do whatever it took to keep it safe and out of their hands.

He shifted, looking down from his perch high in a massive tree with widespread limbs. The zombies were long gone, having disappeared once dawn began to color the sky. But Wyatt had taken no chances, so late last night he climbed high onto a sturdy branch, tying himself in place so he could sleep safely.

It also gave him a good vantage point, this high off the ground.

Now he rose, standing on the branch. The trees were close and the leaves thick, but he could see pretty well in a circumference of two miles. Nothing. No sign of movement. No sign of Remy.

A twinge of conscience pricked at him and he pushed it away. He'd done the right thing.

Instead of dwelling on that, he climbed down and landed on the ground. It was daylight and he had time to go back to the truck rig. There were several things they'd left during their unexpected flight. After retrieving them, he meant to catch a wild horse and be on his way.

But just as he turned to start back along the overgrown road, he heard a bark.

A very familiar bark.

CHAPTER 11

Remy was relieved and surprised when Ian insisted that Goldwyn give her something to eat and keep her arms unbound. She was tied by her ankle to the table leg, however, and her captor made certain to keep his weapon in full view.

Ian pulled Goldwyn aside and got in his face, hopefully telling him, in his low, sharp tones, not to touch her. Then he and Lacey left without another glance.

Despite the soreness and pain of her injured face, Remy managed to eat the beef jerky and hunk of bread she was given and gulped down three glasses of water. Her captor sneered every time she asked for a refill, but whatever Ian threatened him with must have been serious, for Goldwyn capitulated.

Nothing like feeling as if she were the calf being fattened up for later. A little shiver ran over her shoulders when she remembered Lacey's cold, promising smile. As she refueled, she looked around the small room, hoping to find some inspiration for escape. But she saw nothing optimistic. The space was windowless except for one high, small opening she'd never be able to get to. Goldwyn sat between her and the only door, eating his own meal. Her leg shackled to the table gave her only a small radius of movement.

By the time she finished eating, Remy hadn't come up with any possibility for escape. The aches and pounding of her head had eased with the water and food, but she was exhausted and still in significant pain.

With nothing else to do but wait, she pillowed her head on the table, injured side up, and closed her eyes. She didn't expect to fall asleep, but realized she must have dozed off when something jolted her awake.

A hand closed over her mouth, something metallic and cold pressed into her neck.

"Don't make a sound."

She was terrified and startled and at first she didn't realize who was holding a gun against her neck. But when he bent to slice away the plastic cord binding her to the table leg, Remy realized it was Ian.

"Let's go," he said, his voice low and taut. He yanked her up off the chair, half dragging her against him as he hurried to the door.

She caught a glimpse of Goldwyn in a pale heap on the floor as they passed him. There was no way of knowing whether he was dead, but she didn't see any blood.

Not that she cared either way.

And, she guessed, if he were dead, there'd be no reason to hurry or be silent.

With the gun pressed into her ribs, Ian hustled her outside and into the Humvee. He was none too gentle as he shoved her into the truck from the passenger side, then used the gun to gesture her all the way over behind the steering wheel.

"Drive. Now," he ordered, the firearm still aimed at her as he looked back toward the building.

Remy's hands shook but she found the small compartment under the steering wheel well and, still stunned and confused, managed to push the ignition button. The truck leaped forward when she pressed the accelerator and she gripped the wheel tightly as it careened over the rough, uneven terrain.

"Double-crossing your friends," she said once she had the vehicle under control. "Nice."

Ian lowered his weapon and buckled himself in. "I wouldn't call them friends." He lifted his hips to tuck the gun into his jeans. Apparently he didn't consider her a threat any longer.

Or maybe he never had.

"That's true. Lacey definitely thinks of you as more than a friend," Remy said, swerving to avoid a sheet of rusted metal. "And vice versa."

"Fuck," he said, his voice filled with loathing.

Remy couldn't hold back a humorless chuckle. "Exactly."

"And here I thought you might show a little gratitude. She had plans for you."

Remy couldn't hold back a shudder. She didn't want to imagine what Lacey would have done to her. "And what about you?" she retorted. Even now, after the confusing events of the last few hours, she didn't know whether to thank him or despise him.

"I have plans for you too," he said. "Just not the same ones."

Her throat went dry. There was a note of promise, a little bit of rough desire in his voice . . . or maybe not. It was hard to tell with Ian. And she'd just witnessed the man seducing that skanky woman, which, apparently, was not top on his list of pleasant things.

Or so he wanted her to believe.

Remy wanted to shake her head to clear it. She was so damned confused. "Whose side are you on, anyway?" she demanded.

He swore as the truck slammed into a massive hole, then lurched forward without slowing its speed. "Mine."

She chanced a look at him. "Well, finally. A bit of truth from you."

"I've never lied to you."

Remy snorted. "I find that hard to believe." A thought struck her and she slammed on the brakes, causing Ian to jolt violently.

"What the hell!"

"I want to go back and find Dantès. I'm not leaving him in the wilderness by himself. He won't have gone far from where I was, even if you sent him off."

Ian didn't look happy, but to her surprise he capitulated without further argument. "Only because it's on the way. Head northwest. If he isn't there, we're leaving."

"And then where are we going?"

His lips tightened as he pressed them together. "Just fucking drive."

Remy was unsettled, but at least he seemed willing to allow her to retrieve Dantès. And with Dantès in the truck, if she was lucky enough to find him again, she'd have a modicum of protection.

She'd already decided she had to get to Envy, with or without Ian, with or without the Humvee. Wyatt had the crystal, and surely that's where he was headed.

You've got to take that crystal to Envy. We can't let the Strangers get it. Whatever you do, get to Envy.

That what he'd said to her, in those last moments before he shoved her off into the wild jungle.

Those last moments . . . when he was slipping the stone from her pocket, the bastard. She grimaced and felt a twinge from her sore lip.

Then it occurred to her. He could be sending her to Envy while he took the crystal and went in a totally different direction, to a totally different place. For what? To do what? She'd never locate him.

She couldn't tighten her busted lips so she gritted her teeth. She had no choice. She'd find a way to give Ian the slip and she'd get to Envy. At least Elliott was there. Maybe he, at least, would help.

It took more than an hour of slow, bouncing driving, but at last they came to the overgrown clearing with the old school building. Remy leaped from the Humvee, calling Dantès before her feet hit the ground. She heard a joyous bark in the distance and her heart leapt as she called him again.

Moments later the dog burst from the dark forest and barreled up to her so crazily he nearly knocked her over. Crouching next to him, she buried her face in his fur and allowed him to kiss her chin. *Thank God*.

"Thanks," she said, looking up at Ian with watery eyes.

He was watching impassively, but he also had the gun back in his hand. Now he gestured with it. "The dog goes in the back, or he doesn't go."

Remy froze and rose to her feet. "What do you mean?"

"He goes in the back of the truck, behind the screen, or he stays here. I can't have any loose cannons. Let's go."

Her mind numb with questions, feeling a skitter of nerves, Remy walked over to the truck with her pet. Ian opened the back and ushered Dantès in, then closed the door. So much for the added protection from her dog.

She was about to climb into the driver's seat when Ian took her by the wrist. "Remy," he said, backing her up against the door of the truck.

Her throat closed up and her heart stopped. But he merely took her gently by the chin, turning her face to the side so he could look at her injuries.

"Who did this?"

"Your friends," Remy replied tightly. "Who did you think?"

"I assumed. But there was the slight possibility you hurt yourself running from the zombies." His jaw was tight, shifting as he looked down at her. With a light touch, he traced the side of her face that was swollen and tender. "You could use some ice."

"I'll be all right." She started to ease away, but he tightened his fingers around her wrist.

"I got there as soon as I could," he said. For a moment she thought he was going to kiss her, but then he abruptly released her. He tilted his head as if listening, then whipped around to look behind him. After watching the jungle, he turned back. "Let's get out of here."

A little shaken, still uncertain about him and his role in this mess, Remy climbed back into the truck and started it up. "Where are we going?"

"We're going to Envy."

Remy navigated the Humvee for many more hours than she wanted to. It was rough going—both mentally and physically. She still ached from her injuries, and the constant jouncing and jolting only made things worse.

"Time to stop," she said at last. It was just easing into twilight and one of the headlights on the Humvee was catty-wonker, offering little help in the way of illumination, while the other was hardly more than a glow.

"Another mile farther and we can stop," Ian said. "There's a place to hide the truck."

She followed his directions, which led them to a tall, slender, brick building. Even in the dim light she could see the masonry crumbling and covered with ivy. There were no windows, but there was an entrance large enough to drive the Humvee into. She decided the structure must have once been a fire station.

Inside, it had a high ceiling and one large space into which the fire trucks had presumably been parked. Ian had her drive the truck deep into the building and to the side, where shadows would help conceal it.

"There's a creek nearby," he told her. "If we're quick, we'll have time before the zombies come out."

"To do what?"

He grimaced. "Lacey. My skin is still crawling. I want to wash up . . . and you could do the same for your injuries."

"Or, in other words, you won't leave me here alone while you go." She eyed him coolly. "Well, I can't blame you for wanting to get rid of the remnants of that skank. I couldn't believe you went with her."

"I had no choice. She was going to carve you up—or worse—if I didn't distract her somehow."

Remy raised an eyebrow, then winced as pain twinged. She certainly wanted to believe him, but could she? "You could have pulled a gun on them instead of screwing her," she suggested blandly.

His eyes were cool. "If only it were that easy."

"Hmm. So how many times did you feel the need to wash after you touched me?"

Now his mouth relaxed into a smirk. "You know the answer to that."

And well she did, for previously when traveling together they'd slept close every night whether they had sex or not. He certainly hadn't rushed off to a nearby creek at the first opportunity. He'd made it clear the proximity was partly to keep her from running away, and she believed him.

At the time, she accepted his decree with the practicality of knowing he wouldn't hurt her, and that being with him would actually help protect her—from the other bounty hunters as well as zombies and any other dangers that might approach. Aside from that, she'd been waiting to catch him off-guard and take the opportunity to run.

Now, after going with him to the creek, she had to admit he was right: it felt good to wash away the last bit of grime and blood. And the cool water soothed her swollen, throbbing face. But Ian had insisted she leave Dantès behind, and that made her uncomfortable.

She was treading water, aware of the softly fading light, listening for the telltale *ruuuuuuthhhh,* when he swam over to her. Her heart began to pound when she recognized the look in his eyes.

"My, how quickly you've moved on. Lacey would be devastated," she said when he took her arm and drew her toward him in the water.

"Damn, Remy, did you have to remind me? Nothing like a downer to ruin the mood." His expression indicated he wasn't joking.

One of her hands was on his broad, sleek shoulder, and their feet brushed as she frog-kicked to stay afloat. He brought her closer and they kissed, his mouth warm and soft over her chilled lips.

Remy allowed herself to ease into the kiss, pushing away the flicker of memory from the unexpected, knee-weakening kiss Wyatt had given her out of anger. But it wouldn't go, that flare of memory. And so she kissed Ian harder, trying to drum up more interest.

He made a soft sound into her lips and curved his arm around her waist, pulling her up against him. She was still wearing her shirt and panties, but it hardly mattered: the fabric plastered against her like a second skin, and he was bare from the waist up. His body, strong and warm, pressed into her curves. And from the growing hardness between his legs, it was clear he'd managed to get beyond any distracting thoughts of Lacey.

But it wasn't quite so easy for Remy to dismiss her distractions—and the dark memories lingering at the edge of her mind—and she pulled away. For a moment she thought Ian wasn't going to release her, but after peering into her eyes in the dim light, he did.

"You okay?" he asked.

"I'm sorry," she said lightly, knowing what he was really asking. "I'm not interested in being your consolation prize for subjecting yourself to Lacey, although I am grateful you chose to do so." She paddled backward easily, feeling his eyes on her.

"I wasn't asking for a quid pro quo," he replied.

She could make out his irritated frown. "You're just damn hard for a guy to resist."

"Not for some," she muttered before she could stop herself, thinking of Wyatt. Fortunately, her feet touched the bottom then, and she turned and waded out of the water.

Ian didn't say anything, but he followed her back to shore. They gathered up their things in silence and he led the way to the old firehouse. Dantès was ecstatic to see his mistress again, and she and Ian fell into their old routine: he built a fire, using an old sink to contain it, while she scrounged through his supplies—or whoever the packs in the Humvee belonged to—for sustenance.

As they dined on beer, smoked fish, dried apples, and some soft, flat bread, she felt Ian's attention coming back to her in between him listening to sounds of the darkening night.

"I still can't figure out," she said, as much out of curiosity as to divert his attention from her, "whether you double-crossed Lacey and Goldwyn or whether you double-crossed me. You showing up when you did, and then me finding Lacey so close by . . . I can't imagine that was all an accident."

"Not many things in this world are an accident. But believe me when I say I have no allegiance whatsoever to Lacey or Goldwyn." He took a drink from a bottle of beer, holding her with his eyes as he set it down. "I want that crystal, Remy."

She had a momentary pang of surprise. "But you know I don't have it."

Now his face changed. "What do you mean you don't have it?" For the first time, she saw real anger in his expression.

"You heard me tell them I don't have it. You said you *knew* I didn't have it."

"What do you mean *you don't have it*?" His voice was flat and hard, and a flare of nervousness rushed through her. "I saw you with it when the zombies attacked."

"I . . . don't know where it is. I lost it. It came out of my pocket. Probably when I was running away from the zombies." Remy wasn't certain why she didn't tell him that Wyatt had stolen it. Well of course she knew why she didn't tell him: she didn't want to have to compete with Ian to get it back. Or to mete out her revenge on him for taking it.

"You *lost* the Mother crystal?" His voice was deathly low and his eyes . . . they were hard and glittery and furious.

"I didn't think you knew about it," she said. "You never said anything before."

"I *didn't* know, dammit. I suspected you knew where it was, but I didn't know you had it until you brought the fucking thing out and showed it to the zombies. If I had known you were carrying it around all the time, back then, I . . ." He turned away, his jaw clenching visibly.

"You what? Would have taken it from me before? You would have left me to Seattle?" She was getting angry now, and damn it, her eyes were growing wet with furious tears.

"No, Remy. Have I ever hurt you? Haven't I protected you, and even saved your ass more than once?"

"But it was all because of the crystal. That's why you took care of me: you figured I'd lead you to it at some point. Or you'd take it from me. If you'd known I had it, things would have been a lot different."

"How do I know you aren't lying to me? There's no way you protected that thing for years and suddenly lost it in one night."

She lifted her chin, crossing her arms, speared him with her glare. "Feel free to search me. It's not as if you haven't seen everything before."

"I'm going to have to," he said, standing suddenly. "I can't take that chance."

"Fine." She stood, too, and whipped off her damp shirt, then yanked down her jeans. "Here you go. Have at it. Want me to take off my bra and panties too?"

Ian glared at her for a minute, then snatched up her jeans and felt through them quickly. He did the same with her shirt then tossed them back at her. "You could have hidden it somewhere before Lacey found you."

"I could have," she replied. "Somewhere in the wilderness, where the zombies could easily find it. As you saw, they're attracted to it. That would make a *lot* of sense, seeing as how I spent the last twenty years trying to keep it safe." She made no effort to hide the derision in her voice.

He swore, his hand coming up to rub his temples. Ian's whole body seemed to sag, his devastation obvious. If she weren't so furious and disappointed in him, she might have felt sympathetic.

"Look," he said at last, looking up her. His eyes were terrible: cold and bleak. "I've spent eight years risking *everything* for that crystal. I need to have it. I have to find it."

"You and everyone else, it seems. Besides, I don't even know what it is," she said. "I don't know for sure that it's the Mother crystal."

"Well it's fucking something," he snapped. "Something important. Your grandfather gave it to you, didn't he?"

She nodded, swallowing around the lump in her throat. "Yes."

"What did he tell you about it?"

Remy shook her head. "Nothing. He just told me to protect it."

Ian turned away. "Damn," he said. His voice was quiet. Broken.

She watched him for a minute, alternately wanting to smash him in the head with something hard and pull him into an embrace. He was a dangerous, violent man . . . but there was something at his core that didn't fit with that persona.

What was his weakness? His soft core?

"What do you need it for?" she asked finally. "What does it do? If it even is the Mother crystal."

He sat down heavily, his expression drawn and dark. His hands hung loosely over his crossed legs. "I need it because the Elite want it."

"The Elite? You mean the Strangers," she added to herself. "So you want it in order to keep it from them—to use whatever power it has. Or you want to *give* it to them. In exchange for something, perhaps? Money? A crystal of your own, so you can live immortally?" A thought struck her, way out of the blue, and she tilted her head, looking at him closely. "Unless it has to do with *her*."

It was hardly noticeable, but she was watching for it. His fingers spasmed, then relaxed.

"Who is she?" Remy asked. "What's her name?"

Ian looked up, his eyes boring into hers. She caught her breath at the odd light in his gaze; she couldn't tell if it was loathing or despair. "Liana. Her name is Liana."

She opened her mouth to ask more, but he stood abruptly. "That's it." He held up a hand to ward her off, then looked down at her. His expression was not pleasant. "It occurs to me that your companion Wyatt might somehow have acquired the crystal—with or without your knowledge. If that's the case, you'll help me get it from him."

"Or?" she retorted, her pulse spiking.

"I have no allegiance to anyone. I'll do whatever I have to do to get it. You can count on it."

CHAPTER 12

The last time Remy was in Envy, she'd thrown a snake at Wyatt. Literally.

With that tense moment long past, she couldn't hold back a smirk as she and Ian approached the walls of the city. It had been sort of funny.

Wyatt had been chasing her and Dantès through a deserted, dirty underground hallway and when she finally came to a set of stairs that offered escape, they'd encountered a snake. It wasn't a big snake—not like the ones that lived in the old sewer tunnels—but it was much bigger than those little garden snakes.

It was the element of surprise working in her favor when, after she climbed several steps ahead of Wyatt, she turned and flung the reptile into his face. Probably not what he was expecting.

That was more than six months ago, and it was how she made her escape from the people who wanted to keep her in Envy—Elliott, Wyatt, Quent, and the others. She hadn't seen any of them again until Wyatt found her under Seattle's truck.

Now Remy looked at her current companion as he

climbed out of the Humvee. "Have to leave the truck here, and hidden," Ian said.

It was true. If they approached the gates in a vehicle, they would be presumed Strangers or bounty hunters. She helped him pull the steel door of an old garage closed behind the truck and then they swung up their packs.

"I think," she said as they started toward the city, Dantès padding along at her side, "it would have been faster, as well as more comfortable, riding a horse."

Ian glanced at her. "Duly noted."

She rolled her eyes and looked away. The sooner she ditched him, the better.

Since Ian learned she didn't have the crystal any longer, he'd been quiet and distant—more so than usual. He'd also kept a very close watch on her. They hadn't talked other than necessary for the last day and a half of travel, but to ensure she didn't run off in the night, he made sure they slept close together. Body heat notwithstanding, it actually allowed her to rest more deeply—knowing he was listening for danger (zombies, wild animals, Lacey) too.

Despite being enclosed in his arms, she had a nightmare about Seattle that first night, likely because of her capture by Lacey and Goldwyn. It was the first one she'd had in months. But Remy was able to pull herself out of it and fight back to consciousness using some of the techniques Selena had taught her. If she'd wakened Ian, he gave no indication . . . but his arms had remained close around her.

The walls of Envy loomed above as they approached. The enclosure was twenty feet tall and built of remnants from a long-gone twenty-first century civilization: billboards, pieces of cars, airplane hangar walls, large piles of rubble, massive segments of buildings or vehicles. The purpose of the barrier, or so Remy had been told while she was in the infirmary under Elliott Drake's care, was not to keep people out or in, but to offer protection from the zombies and other predators.

Thus, although there was a watch at the entrance, the large gates—made from two massive garage doors—were kept open from sunrise to sunset. Entering and exiting Envy wasn't like being given access to a medieval castle. No one was denied, no one was retained.

But she suspected that didn't mean there was a lack of communication about who was entering or exiting.

She, Dantès, and Ian walked past the guard on duty as he waved and smiled at them. A few yards farther inside they found themselves in the wide, bustling streetfront previously known as the Las Vegas Strip. Tall buildings, structures unfamiliar to her, rose on either side. If it weren't for the expanse of the street, she might have felt boxed-in. A Statue of Liberty stood at the base of the street as if to welcome newcomers, just as the original statue had done in Manhattan more than two hundred years ago.

There were two intact buildings on either side of the wide street, and neatly kept flowers, trees, shrubbery, and even streetlights paraded between them. Except for the lack of motorized vehicles, the area looked almost identical to the pictures Remy had seen of pre-Change civilization. Beyond the two flanking buildings were the remnants of other, smaller structures: some maintained and others in utter disrepair. And at the top or north end of the street, rose the tall, metal skeletons of buildings that didn't survive the Change. Beyond them and in the perimeter of the main thoroughfare were more ruins, the rest of the wall, and, to the north and beyond: the Pacific Ocean.

It was months ago she'd been here last, but Envy felt different this time. There was an air of excitement or expectancy in the people moving about.

"Wonder what's going on," she said, looking up at Ian, who shrugged.

"Looks like some sort of celebration," he replied in a tone that indicated his disinterest.

"Well, look who the fucking zombies dragged in."

Remy and Ian turned at the same time. The woman standing there was lean and athletic, with short, blue-black hair that flung about in choppy waves around her jaw. She was beautiful, with her almond-shaped eyes and rich, mahogany skin, but she also had a no-nonsense air about her and fairly bristled with sass.

"Ian Marck," the woman continued. "I'd say you were a sight for my sore damn eyes, but that'd be a fucking lie."

"Well, well, Zoë," Ian said, the hint of a sneer in his voice. "You're looking well. I see that captivity suits you, locked up behind these walls. Remind me to ask Quent how he does it."

"He acts like a fucking human instead of a murderous asshole, that's how," Zoë replied. "Maybe you ought to take lessons." But her sharp eyes had transferred to Remy and then Dantès. "I remember this big-ass guy," she said, crouching to pet him. "He hung out here for a while with Wyatt. I'll have to introduce him to Fang. There aren't any other dogs big enough to play with him without getting their asses kicked," she said, standing up to look at Remy again. "That is, assuming you're gonna fucking stay this time."

Remy nodded, feeling Zoë's attention linger on her face. The bruises had faded, but they were still a little yellowish, and the nasty cut by her eyebrow was still red and swollen. She wanted to ask about Wyatt—although surely he wouldn't be here yet. But from the time she'd spent at Yellow Mountain, she knew he had some way of being in contact with the people here. She needed to find out where he was. She had to get that damned crystal back, and she'd murder Wyatt in the process if she had to. She'd *trusted* him, dammit.

But she had to do it without Ian knowing.

"Yes. I . . ." She looked around, again noticing all the activity. "What's going on here?"

"This shit?" Zoë looked utterly disgusted. "Hella big-ass party, more noise and food and people than should ever be in one fucking place, you ask me. Survivors Day is what they call it. Been wasting an ass-load of time getting ready for it. Fricking pig roast, ice creams, something called—what the hell, rhino ears or—"

"Elephant ears, luv," said a clipped voice. "They're called elephant ears. And they're delicious."

Remy looked up at the handsome blond man who'd appeared from nowhere. His hand settled proprietarily on Zoë's shoulder and he was looking at Ian with unadulterated dislike. "Ian Marck. To what do we owe the pleasure?"

The words were polite enough. Even his accent—which sounded like the people in all those Harry Potter DVDs—made it sound pleasing and almost formal. But the expression on his face and the inflection in his tone belied anything related to sincerity.

"Just passing through," Ian replied. "Don't get in my way, Fielding, I won't get in yours."

"It's Quent. I don't use my father's name."

"There you go—we have something in common. I don't use mine either." Without another word, or even a glance at Remy, Ian walked off.

"Remington Truth," said Quent, thankfully pitching his voice low. "The last I heard, you were with Theo and Wyatt in Yellow Mountain. Then you took off."

"You traveling with that asshole?" Zoë demanded, glaring after Ian. "Because if you are, we've got some serious talking ahead of us. Asshole didn't decorate your face like that, did he?" Her lips were flat with disgust as she looked pointedly at Remy's face.

Glad to be extricated from Ian's presence—although she was by no means confident it would be permanent—Remy replied, "No, he didn't. And we met up because we happened to be traveling in the same direction. Two is safer than one, even with Dantès along."

"Where's Wyatt?" Quent asked. "He went after you, didn't he? He find you?"

Probably better not let on she was ready to kill the man. Play it cool, lure them in . . . "Yes. We got separated during a zombie attack. I was hoping he'd be coming here."

"I haven't heard from him recently."

"I . . . was hoping to speak with the woman named Ana." Remy looked from Quent to Zoë. "I understand you know her?"

"Zoë! There you are!"

"*Shit.*" Zoë's face went pale under her dusky skin.

Remy turned to see two women coming toward them, purpose in their steps. One of them looked familiar—she had amazing red-gold curls that shined like a flame in the bright sun. Remy remembered her: she'd been with Wyatt and his friends when they found her in Redlo. Her name was Sage. Her companion had darker, auburn hair and clear green eyes. "Flo's been waiting for you for an hour!" she said.

"Oh, fuck, I'm so outta here." Zoë would have bolted away but Quent had her by the arm and hauled her back. "Let go of me, genius." The sass was gone, replaced by desperation. "I'll make it worth your while. *Really* worth it." Her voice and eyes had gone smoky—but still with a hint of panic—and she fairly melted into him. "Please?"

Quent merely chuckled, keeping a firm hold on her arm. "It's not going to kill you to get a little primped up for tonight," he said. "You're already glowing," he added, the corners of his eyes crinkling as he patted her belly, "but if you let Flo have her way, you'll be even more stunning than usual. And *then* you can make it worth my while."

"I am *not* letting that dominatrix put any of that face paint shit on me," Zoë said. "And she's not making me wear anything with a skirt."

"But Zoë," said Sage, giving Remy a curious glance. "Your grandmother is being celebrated tonight. You should honor her and what she did by putting on something special."

"I promise, it will be painless," said the other woman. "Flo is a genius!"

"She's a bloody damned sadist," muttered Zoë, still trying to weasel out of Quent's grip.

Chuckling, the second woman turned to Remy. "Hello. I'm Jade. Elliott's wife. You look familiar . . ."

"Hi . . . yes, I'm Remy. Elliott . . . um . . . helped me a few months ago. When my leg got all cut up. Zoë brought me here to him."

"She's the one who threw an assload of snake at Wyatt," Zoë put in. "I don't know which pissed him off more—when she shot at him or threw the damn snake in his face." Her panic receded as her eyes gleamed with relish. "Wish I'd been there to see that."

Remy felt her cheeks warm. "Yes, I guess I did piss him off a little." *Guess we're even now.*

"Well, that's not hard to do, frankly, Remy," Jade said with a smile. "Wyatt's . . . well, he's not an easy—"

"He's got an ass-crap-sized boulder on his shoulder big as that fucking building there," Zoë said.

"He's a wonderful man," Sage put in. "A very *good* one. He's just got some . . . stuff. To deal with. Like we all do," she added, spearing Zoë with her eyes. "All of us."

"Right," Zoë replied with great insincerity. "Anyway, Remy just arrived here, and I was going to show her around, get her settled—"

"That's wonderful," Sage interrupted with a sunny smile. Her voice was soft and sweet, but firm. "She can join us in getting freshened up for the party tonight. Would you come with us?" she asked, looking at Remy. Her aqua-blue eyes were guileless, and concern lingered there too. She probably wondered about the bruises as well.

Looking from Zoë to Quent to Jade, Remy had the

sense that Sage would get her way even if she tried to refuse. She had no reason to do so. These people were not only friends with Ana and Wyatt—and would be the first ones to know when and if he arrived— but she loved the idea of freshening up. Ever since the zombie attack, she'd been wearing the same loose shirt she'd planned to sleep in and jeans. It was too bad she'd been forced to leave her new clothes behind at the truck rig, but at least she was still wearing the new pink and white bra. "Yes, thank you."

"Traitor!" Zoë hissed at Remy. "I saved your ass from Ian and his father, and this is how you fucking repay me?"

Sage and Jade laughed, and Remy shrugged. "Sorry. It's been a few days since I showered." She smiled.

"I'll see to . . . Dantès, is that his name?" Quent offered. Clearly, he was willing to do whatever it took to get Zoë sent off and taken care of. "If you're comfortable with that." He glanced up at her.

Remy nodded. She crouched and hugged Dantès, saying, "Friend. Go with Quent." She made the hand gestures and her dog immediately transferred his attention to the blond man. Remy turned back to Sage. "So who is this sadist named Flo and what is she going to do to me?"

"Torture," moaned Zoë. "A shitwad of *torture*."

It wasn't torture at all.

In fact, although her agreement to go with Sage and Jade had been more practical than anything else, Remy found herself completely enjoying Flo and her ministrations.

The so-called sadist was a soft, fluffy woman of about fifty, with hair the color of moonbeams except for a wide pink streak. This breach of color went from the front of her part around to the nape of her neck, where it was twisted and pinned up into a puffy coiffure that looked like clouds coming out of her.

Zoë took one look at Flo and covered her own head. "I don't care what Quent says, you are not doing anything to my fucking hair!" Blue-black wisps stuck out from between her fingers.

"I'm not going to touch your hair," Flo said mildly. "Don't want to try anything that might hurt the baby, you know. Skin and hair absorb things, you know."

"Seriously?" Zoë's eyes popped wide. "You mean the kid means I'm safe from all that shit you're putting on *them*?" She cupped her stomach, her face a study in sudden bliss.

Baby? Ah. Now some of the comments she'd heard between Elliott and Wyatt back in Yellow Mountain made sense. Zoë was pregnant. Remy looked at her and frowned. She couldn't be too far along—the woman looked slender and fit except for the slightest rounding of her belly.

A baby. *Wonder what that would be like.*

She'd not given it much thought before. How could she? With the life she had, moving around, running and hiding all the time, it was an impossibility.

Remy didn't know if she'd *want* to have a baby, even if she could. Even if she found someone to have one with. It was a dangerous world. A bleak one, at times. Would she want to bring a child into a place like this?

A little shiver surprised her. Thank God Ian had always been very careful when they had sex. The last thing she would have needed was to be pregnant with his baby.

God. Or Seattle's. Remy felt weak. She stopped that horrifying thought abruptly, pausing only to give thanks it hadn't come to pass.

Flo was smiling. "I have something in mind for you, Zoë. *Not* a dress. But who is this?" She turned to Remy.

"A friend of Wyatt's and Theo's," Sage said in her smooth, modulated voice. "Her name is Remy and she's just arrived. Jade and I brought her along so she could freshen up."

"Yeah," Zoë said. "Feel free to torture the shit out of her with all the crap you were going to do to me and leave me the hell alone."

Remy looked around the spacious, well-lit room, which had a collection of mismatched mirrors lining one wall and a row of cupboards on another. A variety of chairs and tables littered the area, pieces of clothing hung everywhere on hooks and hangers, and beyond, she could see a bathroom with a large tub and shower. There was also a curious item that looked like a large metal helmet on a stand. She'd seen one in the *Legally Blonde* DVD. It went over one's head, for a purpose she wasn't altogether certain about.

"Just a little lip gloss, some nail polish—and definitely something other than those ratty pants," Flo said to Zoë.

"No damned way am I wearing any ass-crap dress," she warned. "Those assholes in Mecca had me all suited up in a skintight dress and shoes that just about fucking killed me. And I told Quent he was going to have to remember that, 'cause there is *no* way it's ever going to happen again."

Mecca? Remy looked at Zoë. What had she been doing at the island headquarters of the Strangers? She opened her mouth to ask, but then the short, fluffy whirlwind that was Flo descended upon her.

"I've never seen anyone with eyes as amazing as yours, dearie," the older woman said, taking her by the chin so she could get a better look. "Like Elizabeth Taylor's, but a touch bluer. And your lashes! So long and dark, you don't even need mascara. A little eyeliner would be good . . . and what are we going to do with your hair . . . some fancy updo would be good."

"Yeah, try the pink on *her*," Zoë suggested. "She's one brave-ass chick. She's the one who threw the snake at Wyatt."

"And lived to tell about it?" Flo looked at Remy consideringly. And then hummed in a way that made her nervous. "Interesting."

"Now who's the traitor?" Remy said, suddenly worried that Flo might actually turn her hair pink.

Jade laughed. "Looks like Zoë might have met her match here, hey, Flo?"

"No, no pink for this young lady," the older woman muttered, as if she hadn't heard any of their conversation. Her fingers—adorned with too many rings to count—tapped her chin. "And something *red* to wear. That'll give them—no, no, wait. *White*. You're going to wear white, dearie. With your eyes and your hair, and you've got the perfect dusky-peachy-rose skin to offset the white . . . Oh, this is going to be fun!"

Remy was relieved that Flo didn't make a big deal about her bruises and cut, although obviously she noticed them as she continued her rapturous commentary. Nevertheless, she looked at Sage and Jade. "Are you sure about this?"

"No," hissed Zoë urgently. "Don't let her touch you! Escape while you still have time!"

Sage giggled and flapped a hand at her friend. "I'm going to get in the shower. Flo has *the* best showers here," she added, looking at Remy. "That's because she's—wink, wink—*friends* with Ana's dad, George. And he can figure out pretty much anything."

At the same time, Jade rolled her eyes at Zoë and said, "Don't worry, Remy. You just have to let Flo do her thing. She's what they used to call a cosmetologist, and she's got quite a collection of old *Vogue* and *Elle* magazines, most of them courtesy of Theo and his travels. She experiments with making all her own cosmetics right here—lipstick, mascara, hair dye, everything. And when she gets her hands on a new person, she can go a little crazy." Jade gave her a sidelong look. "I promise, she'll make you look so hot even Wyatt won't be able to keep his eyes off you. Or—better yet—his hands."

Remy's face went warm and she shook her head. "I could care less what Wyatt thinks." But her heart gave a little bump at the mental image of his strong, tanned hands on her bare skin. Then she reminded herself she was *pissed* at the man for *taking her crystal.*

"Holy fucking crap, don't tell me you're banging *Ian*?" Zoë demanded.

"Um . . ." Remy's cheeks threatened to get even warmer, but she managed to stave off the blush. "No. Hell no."

"It's not that it wouldn't be a hella good jump in the sack," Zoë continued. "I even considered it once.

But I don't trust that man anymore than a hair ball."
She prowled the room like a caged tiger, but Remy
noticed she made no effort to escape the so-called
torture even when she came near the door.

Minutes later Remy was ushered into a shower
stall next to the one Sage was using. Both had real
running water that ran not warm but *hot*. The redhead was right—it was heaven.

If she'd wanted privacy, Remy was bound to be disappointed, but at least there was a curtain hiding her
from view. Still, the conversations bounced around
with an occasional outburst from Zoë. Sage passed
Remy a bar of pale pink soap over the top of the di-
vider. It smelled unbelievably good and looked like it
had tiny pieces of flowers and leaves in it.

"I don't think I've ever smelled so good in my
life," Remy confessed as she stepped out, wrapped
in a towel. "Or felt so relaxed and clean. Hot running water is such a luxury. We didn't even have it in
Yellow Mountain; it got warm, but that's it."

"Oh, that's right! You were in Yellow Mountain
with Theo and Selena," Sage said. Her blue eyes
danced and her freckled, peachy skin was flushed
from the shower. "You have to tell us all about
Selena. We haven't met her yet, and—"

"And Sage wants to make sure she's good enough
for her old flame Theo," Jade put in. She had curlers
in her hair and was sitting in a chair with her head
tilted back. Flo was painting something bright and
pink around her eyebrows. As Remy watched curi-
ously, Flo dabbed a white cloth over the pink gunk
and then *ripped* it away.

Jade didn't even flinch, but Zoë shrieked. "Holy
mother assload of *crap*! I told you! She's a freaking,

ass-kicking *sadist*! You are *not* doing that to me, Flo. Over my cold, dead, zombie-meat body!"

"Ugh," Sage said. Her hair was in a towel, with only one bright coppery strand falling loose over her shoulder, and she was flipping through a rack of dresses. "Spare me that image, please. My stomach's a little weak lately." Her smile could only be described as sweetly sly.

"Oh yes I am doing it to you," Flo said. "Your brows are out of control, Zoë dear. They're practically spiders. A well-arched brow makes all the difference," she said, turning to lecture Remy. "It's the foundation of elegance."

"She read that in a magazine," whispered Jade.

"Where did you get all of these gorgeous clothes?" Remy asked Flo, looking at rows and racks of dresses. She'd never seen anything like most of them—the glittery fabric, the fur, the feathers, the impracticality of it all.

The older woman smiled, showing a juicy dimple on one cheek. "My mother was one of the survivors of the Change, and she worked here as a showgirl when this city was Las Vegas. The glitz, the glitter, the glam, she used to say. The way she explained it, she raided as many of the wardrobes as she could—I have no idea why, when people were trying to survive. I guess it was her way of holding on. Maybe she thought they would be important for history's sake. Anyway, she saved a lot of these things. I've made some. And remade others. Collected even more from scavengers. It's sort of an obsession." She grinned wider.

"Obsession's a freaking understatement," Zoë muttered.

"So tell us about Selena," Sage said. She turned, holding a bright blue dress with a flowing skirt. "How's this, Flo?"

"You always wear those long, loose skirts," Jade said, lifting her head a little to look. "Why don't you try something different? Something short? Let Simon get a look at your legs for once."

Sage smiled slyly, which gave her innocent face a layer of something naughty. "Simon gets plenty of chance to look at my legs, trust me. And I like this style. It's the color I'm wondering about. Flo?"

"I approve," replied the older woman. "But Jade's right—you could try something a little shorter. What do you think about this, Zoë?" She held up a small piece of black material that sparkled. "It'll be great with your skin tone."

"What the hell is that?" Zoë approached cautiously, but with curiosity in her face. "Don't tell me it's a frigging *skirt*."

"No, it's a tube top. It goes around here." Flo demonstrated on her own torso. "You could wear it with that white jacket and black skir— Oh, all right— *pants*," she added with a sigh. "Although a long skirt would look better."

A knock on the door interrupted whatever argument Zoë might have been about to make. "You all decent?" a female voice called.

"Come in," Flo called. "The more the merrier!"

One look at her face told Remy the motherly woman meant it. She was in her element with a roomful of females who needed her.

At the invitation, two more women came in. One was very tall—probably at least six feet—with long, streaky blond-brown hair and a rich caramel-golden tan. She had such a beautiful smile it took Remy a moment to notice that she walked with a pronounced limp. "Hey, all. This looks like fun. *Whoa.* Is Zoë holding a *skirt*?"

"Over my dead-ass body. It's called a tube top. Which *you* wouldn't be able to wear because you've got an *assload* more boob than I do."

"I don't know, Zoë. That baby's giving you a lot more curve than you had before," teased the tall woman. "Even Fence noticed."

"Aw, fuck that. When *doesn't* Fence notice a woman?"

"When he's looking at Ana," Sage said, unraveling the towel from her hair.

"Damn straight," agreed Zoë.

"Welcome to the zoo, Ana," Jade said with a grin. "And welcome to you, whoever you are. I hope you came ready for Flo to take you under her wing." This last was said to the second young woman, who was looking around the room with the same sort of trepidation that was on Zoë's face.

"This is Cat," said Ana. "She and her father arrived from Glenway just in time for Survivors Day. Her sister is my friend Yvonne." There were quick introductions of the rest of the women, including Remy to Ana.

This was good. Now she knew who Ana was. Hopefully, she'd be able to find time to talk with her sometime tonight and see what she knew—if anything—about the crystal.

"Cat doesn't have anything to wear," Ana explained.

"I didn't realize this Survivors Day thing was such a big deal," interjected the newcomer. She had dark brown hair that curled in tousled waves around her face and jaw. Her eyes were the color of coffee beans and she had a smattering of youthful freckles across her nose. Even so, she looked as if she were in her twenties.

"It is a big deal," Sage said. "There's an official Thanksgiving celebration in memory and gratitude for the people who managed to live a year after the Change; sort of like the one Americans used to celebrate in November. That happens in June and has been celebrated ever since the first year after the devastation. But a while back, Vaughn—Mayor Rogan, I mean—thought it would make sense to honor the people who actually survived the Change. Some of them are still alive. They did so much to rebuild our world by planning and saving all sorts of things. Without them, we wouldn't have a lot of the things we have today—things like black pepper and strawberries. Information about solar panels. And a whole lot of other basic things."

"Besides that, it's a great reason to have a big party," Jade said with a laugh. "And the only thing we're missing, I think, is a bottle of wine."

"Well, funny you should mention that," said Ana, setting a bottle on the table. It was filled with pale yellow liquid. "Yvonne's husband Pete sent a few bottles of the mead he makes. And trust me when I tell you—it's wonderful."

"I'll get some glasses," said Flo, bustling over to one of her cabinets. "Zoë, you're next. Take Jade's place, please."

"Okay, Remy, now back to Selena. Give us the dirt," Jade said, shoving Zoë into the chair she'd just vacated.

"Selena is a very special person," Remy said, hiding a grin at Zoë's terrified expression. "She's got a special gift for helping people—as they're dying, but also when they have something . . . terrible . . . happen. And she does this thing with the zombies that . . . helps them." She glanced at Zoë and decided not to go into detail.

From Wyatt and Theo, she knew that Zoë had a much different approach to handling the zombies than Selena did. "There's something peaceful about her. She really helped me, uh, get through a difficult time. *But*," she added, "Selena's not a pushover. She and Theo are really happy together. He helps her stay strong with her gift—which can be really difficult. And he's completely nuts about her."

"I'm so glad," Sage said, sincerity in her voice and demeanor. "He's a very special guy. A good friend. He used to bring me books all the time when he was out—"

"Holy mother of the world, where did you get *this*?" Zoë's exclamation had everyone turning to look. She was miraculously out of the chair and holding up Remy's new bra. "This is beyond hella *awesome*."

Remy grinned. "I scavenged it. We found an old truck trailer and there was a lot of stuff in it. I found a bunch of other things—panties and tank tops. But I had to leave them behind in the zombie attack. And there was this one pair of panties . . . at least, I think they were panties. It was black, and nothing but a triangle in front, and a string—er—up the back. You know what I mean?"

"A thong," Flo said, handing Remy a glass of the mead.

"It has a fucking *string*?" Zoë repeated, taking her own glass—which was only about a third full. "Up the *back*? You're supposed to have a string up your ass-crack? How in the hell can that be comfortable?"

They all laughed, and for the first time she could remember, Remy realized she was having a good time with other women. *This must be what it's like to have sisters. Or best friends.*

How had she missed this much of life?

CHAPTER 13

Wyatt had completely forgotten about Survivors Day.

Just what I do not *need.*

Hoping to avoid people, he'd come into Envy through the back way, using the secret tunnel Theo and Lou Waxnicki had designed half a century earlier when the protective wall was being built around the city. The old, cracked Wendy's sign marked the entrance from the exterior, and the route included passage through an old railroad car and a massive metal culvert. It came out on the far west side of the enclosed part of the settlement, an area that was abandoned by all but rats, stray cats, and more than a few ugly snakes.

Hidden beneath and inside the barrier built of rubble, the throughway was known only to a limited number of people. As Lou Waxnicki had told Wyatt and his friends: *You always have to have a back door, whether you're writing code or building a fortress.*

You never knew when you were going to need a way out . . . or a way in.

Now, back in the inhabited part of the city, Wyatt

stalked grimly through the structure that had once been the Vegas resort New York–New York. The building was the place where most of the residents of Envy lived, using the hotel rooms as small living spaces. Of course few of them were outfitted with kitchens, so meals were generally taken at one of the two community restaurants run by the City of Envy and staffed by the residents of the settlement. Everyone took a turn on KP, or somehow supported the co-op by growing or raising food, or contributing other resources like keeping the appliances working, the solar panels in shape, and the water flowing. There were a few small, private kitchens, he'd learned, but most people liked and preferred the community setting. It was like *Cheers* on steroids.

Every single day.

Unfortunately for Wyatt, this meant if he wanted to eat, he'd have to brave the frivolity and celebration below. And he had been traveling rapidly and efficiently for two days, hardly stopping to eat or sleep, so he was hungry and tired.

Once he'd assured himself Remy was safe—although whether being with Ian Marck could really be considered safe was a good question—he stopped following them. The tender scene he'd witnessed between Remy and Ian, when Ian eased her up against the Humvee and reached up to stroke her cheek, was an early indication. But just to be sure, he tracked them a little farther, easy to do while in the trees and following the very slow progress of the vehicle. It was the passionate kiss in the creek that had convinced Wyatt he didn't need to keep watch any longer, and at that point he took himself off to find a horse.

Unfortunately, it took longer than he anticipated

and he wasted nearly a day trying to find a wild herd and then lure one of the animals to him. Normally he didn't have a hard time at all—animals were generally pretty easy around him. But for some reason none of the horses would approach, even when he offered a nice brown apple.

He should have just gone on foot from the beginning, but he didn't.

Finally reaching his floor, he unlocked the door to his room and eyed the bed. Damn, it looked inviting.

But he was nothing if not disciplined. He wanted to eat, true, but he also wanted to find out if Remy had made it to Envy, or whether she and Ian had gone somewhere else. He hoped like hell she'd listened to him and come here.

But then again . . . this was Remy. That woman had a mind of her own, and most of the time what went through it was completely incomprehensible to him.

He was going to have to venture down into the chaos. And so he dumped his stuff on the floor, stripped, and headed for the shower.

A short time later Wyatt stalked out of his room and headed for the stairs. After twenty flights, his damp hair still dripping over the back of his neck, he hit the ground floor and was immediately assaulted by delicious smells.

Maybe this wouldn't be so bad after all.

The gathering was happening outside beneath blue and red neon lights—remnants of the blazing Vegas strip still hanging on, carefully conserved, fifty years later. Braziers and lanterns also lit the area in preparation for the descent of the sun. Another hour at the most and it would sink behind the city wall, and after that darkness would fall quickly.

Two pigs were roasting, three huge metal cans of clams and crawfish parked amid golden coals. Unhusked ears of corn were piled in massive tubs, still steaming. Wyatt swore he saw a vat of potato salad, which seemed so *not* postapocalyptic. And . . . *pies*. There were rows of pies on a table. He could only guess the flavors, but he figured apple and cherry were good bets. But he wasn't picky. Not about pie.

The sultry voice of a woman singing something blue wove through the constant rumble of conversation and laughter, helped by a good old-fashioned mic and some amps. He thought he recognized Jade's voice, and a glance toward the large brazier onstage next to her confirmed it. She'd been singing in the pub the first night he and Elliott and the others had come to Envy.

Wyatt walked along the fringe of the celebration, toward the dark and quiet. The party went on behind him and off to the side. When he turned, standing in the shadows, far from everyone, he saw the energy, the lights, the silhouettes and shadowed forms of people. He scented cooking food, grills, and, subtly, the salt of the ocean.

If he closed his eyes and didn't think for a minute, he could open them again and almost believe he was back . . . Back under the stars for the blues fest or the county fair or the church carnival . . . Back home. The smells, the sounds, the lights, the energy. All were the same.

But when he looked again, beyond the glow and the people and the stage, he saw the skyline of a ravaged city outlined by a lowering sun. Skeleton buildings, jagged structures, devoid of light and activity.

Kind of how he felt, pretty much all the time. Empty. Destroyed. Angry.

"Wyatt. You're back."

He turned to see Simon Japp, who'd been one of the survivors from the Sedona caves. Although Simon hadn't been in the original group on that caving trip that included Elliott and Quent, along with himself, and led by their guides Lenny and Fence, he'd been caught in this strange time lapse with the rest of them.

"Yep," Wyatt replied. He glanced around; they were outliers, standing at the far edge of the gathering. "Where's Sage?" The two were nearly inseparable—at least when she wasn't working in the secret, subterranean computer lab that Theo and Lou Waxnicki had built, and when Simon wasn't doing his part to keep the peace in the city. Sage was a lovely woman in appearance as well as deed, and Wyatt had come to like her quiet, peaceful personality. She was one of the few people he'd actually talked to about his past. She listened.

"Ah, she's all busy helping with the food or something. Vaughn wanted me out here, watching for any security issues. You know how it goes when you get a bunch of people partying. Beer flowing and all. Everything all right with you?"

Wyatt opened his mouth to respond with a short, no-nonsense affirmation, then stopped. Of all of them who'd been in the caves, Simon was the one he knew the least. He was also the quietest, most sober of the bunch. Kept to himself for the most part. And from what Wyatt knew about his background, Simon had been in a very bad place before the Change. Ironic, then, that he was the face of law enforcement—such as it was—here in Envy.

"You ever come to Vegas . . . before?" Wyatt asked, surprising himself by saying just about precisely what was on his mind.

"All the damned time." Simon's tone held the flavor of a Chicano accent along with an underlying bitterness. "Too damn often. Too much . . . shit . . . happened here. You?"

"I came here on my honeymoon."

"Jesus, Wyatt."

"Yeah. What a cock-up." But the anger that normally edged his voice was missing. "How the hell did you . . ." He stopped, shaking his head. He couldn't even put into words what he wanted to say. His eyes burned and he squeezed them closed. What the hell was wrong with him?

Somehow Simon seemed to understand. "I was the only one of us who saw—who could see—*this* . . . as an opportunity. An awful, horrific one . . . but it was the chance to create a new life in the wake of devastation. A resurrection."

Wyatt shook his head, still staring at the disrupted skyline, the jagged, empty, gutted buildings. "A resurrection." His breath was a little ragged. His throat hurt. "Like a damn phoenix. Destroyed, then rising from the ashes, pristine and reborn. Christ, I'd just as soon have stayed in the damned ashes. I don't understand *why*—" He bit off the words sharply, curled his fingers into an angry fist. "I just want to live again. Goddammit, I just want to *live*. And at the same time, I just want it to end. I want to be fucking *done* with it." The guilt. The anger. The pain.

Simon nodded next to him, and for a moment they were silent. Then he spoke, softly. "When it all happened—just before the cave started collapsing around me, just before all hell broke loose—I was praying. On my knees. Couldn't remember the last time I'd really prayed. I was praying for my life to end . . . or for some miracle to happen."

"Well, hell, Simon, you got your damned miracle."

The other man looked at him, grief in his expression. "In a matter of speaking. Fact is, we can't change—nor are we responsible for—what happened. It's done. It's over. It's gone. But there's a reason for all of us making it through, you know. Elliott, me, Quent, Fence. Even Theo. You have to find yours. You know our being here has already made things different."

"Hm." Wyatt slipped his hand into his pocket. Felt the warm, solid weight there. Sifted it through his fingers, then let it slip back into the depths. He shook his head. "No. No thanks. I'll take the ashes."

Simon looked at him, his perfect, chiseled features limned by the dancing light of a nearby torch. "That's what I used to think." His mouth twisted in a wry, sad sort of smile. He clapped him on the back, his hand lingering long enough to let Wyatt know he truly cared.

Wyatt might have responded, but before he could, something barreled into his leg. He looked down to find himself accosted by an ecstatic bundle of fur complete with delighted whines and frantic tongue. "Dantès!" He crouched to greet the dog.

She's here.

"You seen Ian Marck anywhere?" he asked Simon as he stood back up, his hand still settled on Dantès's head. Wyatt looked around. Where Dantès was, she was never far away. But there were too many people and the light was too faulty.

"Yeah. The bastard's here. How'd you know?" Simon didn't trouble to hide an inflection of surprise.

Wyatt shrugged. "Just had a suspicion. What's he up to?"

"Nothing, so far. *Chavala*'s just sitting in the corner alone. Watching. Having a beer. Fence and I are keeping an eye on him."

Alone. Wyatt considered the implications. "I'm hungry," he said, realizing that he still hadn't done anything about his empty stomach. "That pork smells amazing."

Simon, not much of a talker himself, seemed willing to let the conversation drop. "There's cherry pie too. But I've got to make one more patrol around before I can eat. And Sage said something about dancing later." He didn't sound all that enthusiastic about the idea. "Later."

"Thanks, Simon," Wyatt said as his friend disappeared into the crowd.

He turned back toward the revelry. Back to the world. Back to his life.

It was about thirty minutes into the celebration before Remy realized she was having a good time. She was relaxed. She laughed. She sipped a glass of white wine studded with slices of orange and lemon and strawberries. She managed to navigate in the silver high-heeled shoes Flo had fairly shoved on her feet. A collection of wide silver bangles clanked at her wrist. And she couldn't help the tingles of appreciation when an attractive man seemed to notice her. Particularly Vaughn Rogan, the mayor of Envy.

Of course, the long white dress helped. The bodice was tight, fitting her curves through the hip and then falling in a loose, flowing skirt that brushed the tops of her toes. The neckline was cut in such a wide, low vee in the front and rear that Flo had stitched a delicate silver chain from shoulder to shoulder across the back of Remy's shoulders, connecting the wide straps to it so they didn't slip down. A short length of silver chain hung perpendicular, with a pendant on the end that bumped gently against her bare back whenever she moved. And because her hair had been pinned up at the back of her head, leaving her neck and shoulders bare, she felt every change in the tropical breeze filtering over her skin.

When Remy protested about the fuss, Flo merely brushed her off, saying, "Humor me, dearie. This is what I *do*. And how often do you get to dress to the nines like this?"

"It's no use fighting it," Jade told her with a smile, as she submitted to a new shade of lipstick. "Flo will have her way."

So, dressed to the nines—whatever that meant— Remy hung out at the festival with her new girlfriends until the mayor happened by and they were introduced.

"Remington Truth," he murmured in a low voice, his gray-green eyes settling on her. They sparked with interest that told her he knew precisely who she was. "Welcome to Envy."

"Thank you." Remy glanced at Sage, who quirked her brow and nodded. *Yes, you can trust him*, seemed to be the indication. "This is a nice celebration, Mayor Rogan. I don't think I've ever been to such a large event, with so many people. And it's so well-organized."

"Call me Vaughn," he said. "Please." His attention seemed to wander off for a moment, to where a cluster of men and women stood talking. An elegant, sable-haired woman with lush curves was laughing with one of the men. Vaughn refocused on Remy. "I hope you're enjoying it, despite the crowd."

"Oh yes. It's very enjoyable," she said sincerely. "And the food is excellent. I always wondered what cotton candy would taste like. It's not at all what I expected."

"Did you try a corn dog?" Vaughn grinned. "They're my particular favorite, and we only get to have them very rarely."

"Good reason to plan a party then, hmm?" she replied, aware that this could be considered flirting. "So that's why you came up with the idea for another holiday. Very sneaky."

He chuckled. "Ah, you've discovered my ulterior motive. Don't tell anyone, all right? And I hope if you need anything while you're here, you'll let me know. I mean that sincerely. I understand from Sage that you're going to be staying in her place while you're in Envy?"

"That's right. Apparently, her room's been vacant for a while." Ever since Sage and Simon had gotten together, according to Jade. Remy smiled to herself. While she was being buffed and fluffed, as Flo called it, she seemed to have gotten the entire history of half the people of Envy—or at least of Wyatt's friends.

She knew, for example, that the curvy, dark-haired woman who kept drawing Vaughn Rogan's attention was Marley Huvane, and that she and Quent had some sort of history. And that Jade and Elliott had been an item ever since Elliott heard her singing in the pub shortly after arriving in Envy. They'd gotten married only a month ago. And she learned that Fence and Ana had some sort of connection to the sea. And that everyone was relieved Theo had met and fallen in love with Selena, since he'd originally had a thing for Sage . . . and when she fell for Simon, that had made things a little bit awkward.

But there was something else about this group of men and women. Something that wove them together, that made them a cohesive group. Something between them that went beyond mere friendship.

Remy felt as if she were missing something. Not that she was being excluded—no, they'd all been more than nice—but that there was something else she merely hadn't yet discovered or comprehended.

And she got the sense Vaughn Rogan felt the same way.

So, feeling that kinship, she smiled at him, appreciating his rugged good looks in the same way any warm-blooded female would. He reminded her of that old famous soccer player—Becker, Beckton, something like that. But a little rougher around the edges. Like he could go a few rounds with something more dangerous than a black and white ball.

"Ah. Jade's singing one of my favorite songs," Vaughn said, turning toward the stage. He smiled with affection rather than lust as he looked over at the songstress. "She usually manages to fit in at least one set because she knows I like it. One of the perks of being friends with the band."

By now the sun had sunk below the walls and most

of the illumination came from flames dancing in braziers and torches set into the ground. Light from the moon and stars filtered stubbornly from behind clouds in the night sky. The air was still warm and muggy, but there was an edge to the breeze that indicated it would cool off soon. Smoke from the barbecues mingled with the scent of summer flowers and something baking.

Remy listened to Jade singing about an island in the sun, and for a moment she was heavily aware of the fact that, despite being surrounded by people, she wasn't with anyone. The realization of loneliness shocked her with a sudden intensity.

But why? She'd been alone for so long . . . why did she now feel so *lonely*?

As the song ended and a rumble of applause broke out, a nudge at her hip startled her. Remy looked down and gently pushed Dantès's nose away from her white skirt. It wasn't her dress, and she didn't want to be responsible for dog slobber on it. "Hey, bud," she crooned. "Where have you been?" She hadn't seen him since Quent took him off so Flo could have their way with her and the others.

Dantès butted her once more in the leg. Then, instead of waiting for more attention, he slipped off into the people. A prickle of awareness skittered down her spine, and she scanned the shadowy crowd.

Her eyes locked with Wyatt's.

Ignoring the little jump of her heart, Remy focused instead on the well of fury inside her. "Excuse me," she said to Vaughn. Without waiting for his response, she started off, pushing her way assertively through the crowds. She figured Wyatt would be slinking off as quickly as he could in order to avoid her.

But to her surprise, he seemed to have the opposite intent. Threading his way through the crowd, he kept his attention focused on Remy as he made his way toward her. He was wearing a white shirt that picked up the light like a magnet, making his dark hair and golden skin look even richer in color. When they finally met up near a group of people, she jabbed a finger at his chest. "What the *hell* do you—"

"Christ, Remy, be quiet," he muttered before she could get the words out. "Shouting is not a good way to stay under the radar. And who the hell hit you?"

She reached up automatically to touch her bruises, amazed that he could even see the injuries in the low light and covered with makeup. "I ran into a duo of bounty hunters," she replied, then, irritated that he'd redirected her demand for the crystal, began in a more strident voice, "Where the hell—"

"Sonofabitch." He cut her off again, this time curling his strong fingers around the wrist of her hand, which was still pointing at him. "Looks like they did a number on you," he said as he slipped something small and solid into her palm. Closing her fingers around it, he looked down at her. His expression was as it always was: exasperated and unapproachable.

Remy's mouth snapped closed as she realized she was holding her crystal. Her ire evaporated, leaving her confused and speechless. He'd stolen it and then given it back to her? What the hell? When she started to barrage him with questions, of course he interrupted.

"And clearly, you don't have anywhere safe to put the damn thing," Wyatt said, his eyes scoring over her. "No pockets or even—Jesus—a place loose enough to slip it into without it showing. Christ, could you be wearing anything tighter?" The disdain had her hackles rising.

Before she could gather her wits beneath this verbal assault, he spun and stalked off. To add insult to injury, he took Dantès with him, bending over to scratch the dog behind the ears as they walked away.

Remy stared after him, curling her fingers tightly around the crystal. She couldn't believe he'd given it back to her so quickly and easily. She didn't even have to ask for it. She shook her head, wondering what the hell she'd missed.

"What was that all about?" Jade's amused voice startled Remy, and she turned.

"He's a jerk," she replied, still eyeing those broad shoulders in crisp white cotton as they edged their way through the crowd. Then she did a double take. "I thought you were up there onstage."

"I just finished the set and was heading over to get some water when I thought I saw you talking to Wyatt," Jade replied. "I didn't realize he was back in Envy. So . . . what happened just now?"

Remy shook her head. "He returned something of mine he had, demanded to know who hit me, and made an obnoxious comment about my dress." She tightened her fingers around the crystal even more. "Then he stalked off."

"Really." Jade sounded utterly fascinated. "Wyatt didn't like your dress? Well, Vaughn and every other man in the vicinity seem to think you look wixy hot. You're attracting a lot of attention."

"I am?"

Jade laughed. "You don't get out much, do you, Remy? So what exactly did Wyatt say about your dress? Ugly color? Too long? What?"

"He just made a comment about it being too tight." Remy's gaze snapped back to Jade as comprehension dawned. "*Oh.*" A warm little flutter in her belly surprised her.

The other woman was nodding and smiling. "Yeah."

Remy couldn't help but turn to look in the direction he'd gone. To her surprise, not only was he within sight, but he was looking in their direction. When their eyes met, he didn't even try to hide his irritation.

She looked away, biting her lip, and realized Jade was still there. Watching her with that knowing amusement.

"Wyatt would be a tough one to crack," said Jade. "He's going to fight it every step of the way, no matter how badly he wants it. That man has more anger and guilt weighing him down than anyone I've ever met. He's at war with himself—about everything. But I have a feeling he'd be well worth the trouble. I mean—those *shoulders.* And all that thick, dark hair. I can only imagine what he looks like under that shirt."

Remy shook her head, mortified that this woman she hardly knew was . . . sort of . . . giving her advice about a man she could hardly have a conversation with without getting into an argument. He made her feel prickly and uncomfortable. "I don't think I'm interested in cracking that nut."

"Right." Still with that grin, Jade turned just as Elliott came up behind her. It was as if she recognized his presence before she even saw him. "Hi, honey. How's the expectant mom doing?"

"She's going to pop that baby out sometime in the

next three to four hours. Which means I'm going to miss your next set, and maybe the one after it."

"That's okay," Jade said, her hand settling easily on his chest. "I'll give you a private performance later on."

Remy's cheeks flushed warm and her mind was reeling. Such easy affection and joking between the two of them made her feel a combination of envy and discomfort. She turned away, blundering off into the crowd, unsteady on her high heels. Wyatt was right: she didn't have anywhere to put the crystal and she needed to get it somewhere safe.

Not three steps later she found herself face to face with Ian Marck.

"Well, well, well . . ." he said, looking her over. "That is some outfit, Remy." Appreciation showed in his face, and he reached out to touch her bare arm with a finger, trailing it gently all the way to her wrist. "You look . . . unbelievable. Even more difficult to resist than usual."

She eased her other hand—the one holding the crystal—just behind her back. "Almost makes you want to forget about Liana, huh?" she said tartly.

His eyes narrowed and the warmth drained away. "Sorry, Remy, but there's not anyone who could do that. Even you."

"Then why do you keep trying?" she returned.

His smile turned hard. "I'm not a monk."

"Either you love her or you don't—"

"Love?" Ian sneered. "I never said anything about love. And I didn't tell you about Liana so you could use her as a prod. I told you because you deserved to know at least that much. So consider this fair warning: don't bring it up again."

"Don't worry, I won't. I don't have any intention of having the opportunity. Excuse me," she said.

But Ian edged into her path and slid an arm loosely around her waist. "Not so fast, Remy. I need the crystal. I saw you with Wyatt. I suspect he has it, or knows where it is. You need to get it from him or I'll get it myself." The threat was clear.

"And why the hell would I do that?" She looked at him in disbelief, pulling out of his embrace. But he'd planned well, for even as she moved away, Remy realized they were near the shadow of a tall building just set away from the crowd. Private and out of eyesight. Still, he didn't frighten her. He just pissed her off.

"Why? Because you owe me for keeping your secret from the Elites—and the bounty hunters—for so long. Because you don't even know what to do with it, or what it's worth. Because you know I'm not going to let anyone stand in my way. You're off limits, Remy, but just barely. And that can change—" He stopped abruptly, looking behind her. "Speak of the devil."

But Remy had already sensed Wyatt behind her, and she turned toward him. She couldn't read his expression: it was even more ambiguous than usual.

"I hope I'm not interrupting anything," he said. His voice was ultra smooth and casual. He didn't spare even a glance for Remy; his attention was completely focused on Ian.

"As a matter of fact, you are." Ian's reply was just as pleasant. "We were having a private conversation."

"Were you." Wyatt's smile showed a gleam of straight, white teeth, but not a hint of humor. His dark hair, in need of a cut, brushed the collar of his pristine shirt and he was clean-shaven.

"You two boys chat," Remy said, easing away. "I'll see you later. *Much* later," she added darkly, pushing her way back into the edge of the party. Heart pounding, she clutched the crystal and navigated boldly through the crowd—easier said than done on her spindly heels amid a throng of half-drunk revelers on rough, grassy ground. Her only intent was to get far away from Ian and Wyatt and to find somewhere safe to put the stone.

But she hadn't even reached the door to the New York–New York building when Wyatt reappeared, directly in her path. *How the hell did he do that?*

"I told you to put that somewhere safe," he said, swooping down on her. He took her arm firmly and directed her into an alcove near the building. "Or were you going to hand it over to Ian Marck at the earliest opportunity?"

"Did you *see* me give it to him?" she retorted, pulling from his grip. "Don't be an idiot." Suddenly chilly and off balance, she rubbed her arm briskly.

He snatched her fisted hand and raised it. "You still have it."

"He wants it, though," Remy told him. "Badly."

Wyatt's fingers tightened around her wrist. "How badly? Did he threaten you?"

"Not me."

"Smart guy. I hope like hell he isn't responsible for those decorations on your face," he added, his eyes glittering darkly.

"No. It was a bounty hunter named Lacey. Ian extricated me from the situation, or I'd look a hell of a lot worse," she told him.

As if realizing he had hold of her like a lifeline, Wyatt released her arm. "I wouldn't recommend putting that stone in your room. There's no security there. So what are you going to do with it?"

"Is this your way of trying to steal it back from me?"

He made a disgusted noise and stepped back. "I just gave it back to you thirty minutes ago, and now I'm going to weasel it away from you again? That makes sense."

Remy deflated, surprisingly relieved to release the anger she'd harbored. "I know. I'm just confused that you did. Why bother to take it if you were going to give it back?" She looked up at him, trying to read the answer in his face.

But he was half shadowed, and his expression blank as usual as he looked at her closely. Even so, when their eyes met, her heart gave a hard little thump. "You really don't have a clue why, do you?" he asked.

She shook her head. "No. But thank you. I mean that sincerely. This makes three times you've given it back."

"Maybe now you'll begin to trust me—us. We're no fans of the Strangers. And I think that puts us on the same side."

"I think I do . . . trust you." She was looking at him, but he pivoted away, scanning the crowd behind them. For a moment she was struck by the beauty of his profile, highlighted by a hint of moonlight—the strong nose, the thick, wavy hair, the set jaw. Something inside her hitched, welling up hot and powerful. *Those shoulders. All that dark hair.*

That kiss.

He'd be worth it.

She swallowed and looked away, then down at the

crystal in her palm as she tried to ignore the crazy fluttering in her belly. The gem was still enclosed in part of its setting, left over from when she wore it around her waist. "Where am I going to put this? I don't even have a necklace . . . wait." She reached up and around behind her neck, following the slender silver chain that connected her two straps until she reached the dangling part finished by a pendant.

Wyatt turned from his examination of the crowd, clearly attracted by her awkward movements. "What are you doing?" he asked. But his voice was mild, less abrupt than usual. Almost affectionate.

"I could replace the pendant with this," she told him. "No one would notice, especially in the dark. For now, anyway."

"Unless it starts to glow again," he reminded her. Nevertheless, he took her shoulders and positioned her so her back was to him. "Which, unfortunately, it did several times while I had it," he said, his fingers deftly working on the chain. "But it's as good a chance to take as any. For now."

"I'm so glad you approve," she said, keeping her voice dry.

But even so, she closed her eyes. It took effort to keep her breathing steady. His hands brushed her bare back, light and warm, as he removed the pendant Flo had attached. She felt the weight lift away, then the light tickle as the empty chain fell against her skin, swaying like a pendulum. She waited, a very detailed fantasy of Wyatt pressing his lips to the back of her shoulder roaring into her mind. The very thought sent delicious, expectant prickles over her.

"Remy."

"Yes?" She heard the husky timbre of her voice, the breathlessness in the single syllable.

"Are you going to give me the crystal?"

Oh. Her eyes bolted open as she handed the crystal to him over her shoulder, relieved he couldn't see her face.

Was it her imagination, or did it take a lot longer for him to twist the links to attach the stone than it had to remove the other one? Were his hands slower, taking their time, brushing against her spine and scapula more often than necessary? Did they linger, settling on her shoulder, brushing a stray wisp of hair away? She could almost see the strong, tanned fingers skimming over her paler skin . . .

"There," he said after what seemed like forever. Breathless, Remy felt the weight of the stone suddenly fall, bumping her spine at the level of her shoulder blades. It was heavier than the one he'd removed.

Wyatt's fingers lifted away and, bracing herself, she turned to face him. "Thank you," she said.

His hands, still poised as if caught in mid-touch, fell to his sides. He stepped back, returning his face to the shadows. All she could see was a hint of dark eyes, but she felt them fastened on her. "It's only a temporary solution," he said. "If you want—if you trust us—I know a safe place you can put it. Then you won't have to carry it all the time."

With a surprise, she realized it would be almost a relief not to have to wear it, or have it with her, *all the time*. To not have to worry about it constantly. "I'll think about . . ." All at once comprehension dawned and she looked up at him, startled. "You took the crystal so the zombies would chase you . . . not me. On the way to Envy."

He'd turned slightly, watching the crowd again, but she could tell he was still attentive to her. "Bravo, Remy."

"You took on my burden, you risked yourself—"

"It's what I do," he said, his lips in a flat line. "I told you."

"Thank you. Again."

It must have been the tone in her voice that drew him to look at her fully, surprise and a little bit of caution in his face. And as he did so, as their eyes met, she took matters into her own hands and stepped into him.

Her heels made her taller. Easier to settle her hands onto the tops of his solid shoulders, to lift her face and find his mouth.

Wyatt stilled, tall and warm against her. His lips were still firm with irritation, but Remy didn't let that daunt her as she fitted her mouth to his. It was a brief kiss—a gentle, tentative, almost-nibble, and it sent heat swarming through her as sensitive lips brushed sensitive lips.

Even through the rush of pleasure, she recognized that he remained frozen. She felt the tension in the warm muscles beneath her hands, felt the way his body remained immobile, and knew she'd made a mistake.

"Well," she managed to say, keeping her voice light as she stepped back. "I guess—"

He followed her, his mouth settling down over hers again. This time hungry and insistent. A large, warm palm planted itself between her shoulder blades, pulling her up to him as the other cupped the back of her head.

Remy closed her eyes, sinking back into a kiss

that was even better than the first. Long rolling waves of heat trundled through her as the passion deepened and she felt the imprint of his body against hers: solid, firm muscle and heat bleeding through her dress, brushing her bare skin. His mouth was no longer firm and annoyed but full and sensual, devouring hers as she melted into him. His fingers curled up into her hair, his other hand slid down over the curve of her bottom then settled at the base of her spine. He smelled fresh and masculine, but there was a tinge of smokiness clinging to his clothes and the subtle flavor of beer on his tongue.

When he pulled away, it was abrupt and sharp. All at once the heat and sensuality was gone and Remy found herself looking up at him, dragging herself from the lull of passion.

"What the hell are you doing?" he demanded.

CHAPTER 14

Wyatt wasn't certain whether he was asking Remy or himself. *What the hell are you doing?*

No, definitely himself. *Stupid* fucking *idiot*.

Remy was looking up at him, her eyes wide with shock and, probably, hurt. Christ.

"You do this often?" he asked, trying and failing to keep the roughness from his voice. His knees were about ready to give out and it had taken every bit of conscience to pull himself out of that dangerous vortex of desire. He could hardly catch his breath, found it hard to focus his emotions where they should be: on disgust. Instead, his body hummed with desire and *more*. More, more, more.

No, he told himself flatly. *You can't.*

"What . . . what are you talking about?" Remy recovered quickly, he noted with relief. That flash of spirit was back in her eyes—at least as far as he could tell in the iffy light.

What? Why not? He struggled desperately for a reason. Any reason that wasn't the truth. "I'm not interested in walking in Ian Marck's footsteps. But you

can try for Vaughn Rogan . . . he might be desperate
enough not to ca—"

She shoved him. Hard enough to catch him in the
lungs and cut off the rest of his sentence, but not hard
enough to make him stumble. "You're damn lucky I
don't have my gun with me. God, Wyatt, it's like every
time I begin to like you, to think you actually have a
human side, you have to act like a real bastard."

Like him? Holy shit, he'd fucked things up more
than he realized.

Wyatt shook his head, which was, thankfully, beginning to clear. "Were you or were you not sleeping
with Ian Marck for the last two days? And were you
or were you not flirting your ass off with Vaughn
Rogan ten minutes ago? And now you're coming on
to me because . . . why? Because I'm standing here?
Because I'm convenient?"

He didn't know why he was even explaining himself, or giving her the chance to do the same. He didn't
generally bother. If someone screwed with him, that
was it. He was done. He didn't have the time or the
stomach for excuses and platitudes.

"The only sleeping I've done with Ian—or with
anyone since . . . since . . ." Her voice broke, sending
a sharp stab of guilt through him, but she soldiered
on before he could say anything. ". . . since I came to
Yellow Mountain, is the simple sharing of body heat.
Which, I might mention, you couldn't even bring
yourself to do when we were in the truck."

Wyatt snorted. "You expect me to believe that?"

Then all at once understanding lit her face. She
straightened and glared up at him. "And how the hell
do you know I was with Ian two days ago? Were you
spying on me?"

Fuck. Didn't think that one through. Just went to show how scrambled his brains were. A mistake like that could have cost him his life over in Iraq. And it was just as dangerous now.

"Only to make sure you were safe," he said, dredging up a haughty tone. "So it's hard for me to believe you're not jumping from one sack to another. You two seemed very cozy when you were swimming in the creek." Damn. Too much detail again. He was getting sloppy.

"Who said anything about jumping in the sack with you, Wyatt? I just kissed you, for pity's sake."

"Right. Thanks for the clarification." Oh, the sarcasm just rolled right off his tongue.

"I was just checking on things," she said. The tone of her voice was different now.

He knew better, but the words jumped out before he could stop them. "Checking on what things?"

"I was doing a little comparison. Between kisses."

Oh Christ. Hell, she was the last person he would have expected to play games, to taunt and tease and flirt like this.

Cathy didn't play games. She was as straightforward as they came, honest to a fault. Sunny-dispositioned most of the time . . . *Cathy. That's right, think of her. You can't forget her yet. Too soon.*

Grief welled inside him. Grief and guilt and anger. He channeled it into control. "I hope it works out for you," he managed to say. "The comparison." He turned to get the hell away from Remy.

"Um . . . Wyatt."

Damn. He needed to keep walking. He wanted to, but he couldn't. It was the tone of her voice: husky and yet peremptory at the same time. It was like a massive magnet, pulling him back, turning him to face her even as he knew he needed to get the hell out of there.

"What?" he said from between clenched teeth. Trying not to look at Remy, her lips, still full and soft and glistening from the kiss. Ignoring the silvery slide of moonlight over her long bare neck and creamy shoulders. And he was definitely not looking down at the deep shadowy vee between her breasts—the ones that had just been smashed up against him. He tried and found it damn near impossible to swallow when he thought about that long curvy body plastered against his.

Remy hesitated, then looked toward the party. "It sounds like the ceremony is starting," she said, obviously revising whatever she'd planned to say. "Are you going to go watch?"

No, he wasn't going to go watch. He was going to find himself a nice dark corner with a big-ass beer; the biggest fucking beer he could find—maybe a whole keg—and be alone. Blessedly alone. And then later he might see if Kellie from the Irish pub was around. She didn't talk too much, she sure as hell didn't argue, and she didn't want anything but a good time.

Best of all: being with her didn't make his knees weak.

"I'd better go with you," he heard himself saying. "In case Marck tries to get that crystal from you again tonight."

Dammit. He knew he should have stayed in his room.

Remy juggled a glass of Pete's mead in one hand and a napkin-wrapped piece of cherry pie in the other as she and Wyatt made their way toward the stage. Dantès had been put inside in a safe place with a couple of teenage boys who were playing cards, Wyatt told her. He'd thought it best to keep the dog safe from the discarded chicken bones and other garbage generated by the party that could make him ill. And apparently the teens were much more interested in cards than survivors.

The crowd was too thick for them to get very close to the stage, but Wyatt pulled her through the throngs so they found a place to stand off to the side but near enough to see and hear. She wasn't certain what to expect, but she thought it was an interesting and appropriate idea to honor the survivors who'd helped rebuild the city.

"Have you been to this before?" she asked her companion—the man who was at war with himself, and, it seemed, everyone around him. Including her.

Still, he was here with her, and although she wasn't certain how she felt about it, his reasoning was sound. She wasn't fond of the idea of running into Ian again tonight. What little trust and affection she'd felt for her former lover had disintegrated. She might not be in physical danger from Ian, but he was still ruthless and determined. And since she now had the crystal again . . .

In answer to her question, Wyatt shook his head. He had a bottle of beer in his hand and leaned against a tree. His white linen shirt shone like a beacon against the dark trunk, the rest of him muted in shadow. "Nope. I only arrived in Envy a little less than a year ago." Despite his relaxed stance, his voice sounded tight.

"If Lou were here, he'd be honored, too, wouldn't he?" Remy asked, trying to keep the conversation light.

"I'd expect so. Too bad he's still in Yellow Mountain. I would have liked to have seen him up there."

She would have responded, but Vaughn Rogan was speaking into the microphone, introducing himself and explaining the idea behind Survivors Day.

As Vaughn called up one of the survivors onto the stage, a cool breeze stirred the air and an unexpected shiver took Remy by surprise.

"It's no wonder you're cold, wearing that," he said. "I don't suppose you have a sweater."

"I'm fine," she replied, sipping her wine, holding back another tremor. It got chilly rather quickly, here by the ocean. She was surprised when Wyatt left the tree and actually moved in closer behind her. He stopped short of actually touching her, but warmth emanated from him anyway.

"I don't have a jacket, and I'm sure as hell not taking off my shirt," he said.

Thank God, she thought. She wasn't sure which would be worse: wearing his warm, masculine-scented shirt or having that muscular bare chest in close proximity. A little shiver caught her by surprise.

"If you took your hair down, it might help. But it looks nice up."

Remy's eyes widened. An actual compliment? Really? She reached up to touch it automatically and felt parts of it sagging. A flicker of heat licked her inside. That was from Wyatt. From the kiss. From his hands, all over her, shoving up into her hair, loosening the pins, sliding down over her spine . . .

From the stage, Vaughn was speaking again. It took Remy a moment to drag her thoughts from the man behind her and focus on the ceremony.

"Our next honoree is Mangala Kapoor. Unfortunately, she's no longer with us, but her granddaughter Zoë is."

Remy grinned as Zoë stomped up onstage, reluctance evident in every bone of her body. She could see Quent standing near the front, his tawny head highlighted from the lights onstage.

"Who got ahold of Zoë?" Wyatt murmured. His voice was low and rough near her ear, raising little prickles over her skin. "That must've been a battle. And holy shit, I can't imagine what the other woman looks like." There was amusement in his voice.

"Flo's just fine. I think Zoë got the worst of it, so to speak." Remy managed to respond coherently despite the warm tickling sensation near her ear.

"If that's the worst, that's pretty damn good. She looks different, but very ho—nice."

She had only met Zoë twice, but Remy agreed: the other woman had never looked better. Her choppy hair had been tamed into a sleek sophisticated look that curled up at the ends and was tucked behind her ears. Two tiny jewels sparkled in its darkness. She was wearing the black tube top along with white slacks and white shoes. Flo had been on a white streak today, apparently. Even though she was five months pregnant, Zoë's belly was hardly more rounded than Remy's, and even with that curve, she looked long and crisp and sleek. At the same time, she appeared spectacularly uncomfortable as Vaughn ushered her to stand next to him.

"Mangala Kapoor was a mechanical engineer. She was instrumental in not only maintaining and developing some of the mechanics that kept water running and electricity on hand in one of the small outlying settlements, but she also made a point of collecting seeds and, through years of trial and error, propagated a variety of non-native plants and spices. If it weren't for Zoë's grandmother, we wouldn't have access to food like cinnamon or peanuts and almonds any longer."

The applause was loud and boisterous, and Zoë made her escape from the stage as quickly as she could. Remy could see her complaining as she stepped off, and she could imagine she was griping about why she had to go up there and stand in front of everyone for a total of two minutes, dressed like this, and so on. At least she wasn't wearing the skirt Flo had threatened her with.

When she got to the ground, Quent snatched her up in a big bear hug that had Remy smiling wistfully. Apparently, even bad-tempered people had someone to love them. Of course, that meant the bad-tempered person had to actually *allow* themselves to be loved.

She watched as they wandered arm in arm away from the stage and toward her and Wyatt. When they came close enough to see them, Remy saw the surprise in Quent's face. Whether it was because they were together or simply because of Wyatt's unexpected presence, she didn't know.

"Fucking glad *that's* over," Zoë grumbled, bending over, her arm jerking vigorously. She suddenly became about three inches shorter and Remy chuckled when she straightened up, holding the white heels. "All that crapload of hassle—*hours* of getting fussed on—for two measly minutes. I am *never* doing that again."

"Oh, yes you are, luv. Especially when our children are old enough to understand what their great-grandmother did for humanity. Just think . . . without

her, we'd never be able to have peanut butter. Or cinnamon buns."

"Bite me," was Zoë's reply.

Remy heard Wyatt snort behind her and murmur
something to Quent. The other man laughed and the
two spoke in low voices, leaving Remy to marvel at
Wyatt's altered mood. He seemed to be in unusually
good humor.

But as Vaughn read off a few more names, Remy
felt Wyatt beginning to get restless behind her. She
was just about to see if Zoë wanted to get another
glass of mead when the mayor spoke into the microphone.

"We have one last honoree tonight. An unexpected
pleasure, for he's a newcomer to Envy and traveled
here just to join us today, for the first time, on Survivors Day. Recently arrived from Glenway with his
daughter, Cat, he previously lived in Tyrell Valley—a
hundred fifty miles east of here and too great of a
distance to even know about our celebration. Tonight
I'd like to introduce you to a survivor who was only
eight when the world was Changed. Living in the remains of the city of Denver, Colorado, David Callaghan survived by . . ."

Remy felt Wyatt snap to attention behind her. He
made an audible sound, a shocked, choked noise of
unadulterated disbelief. He pushed past her, suddenly
walking toward the stage.

"Bloody buggering hell," Quent whispered behind
her.

"What the hell is up his ass?" Zoë demanded as
she and Remy turned to look at him.

"David Callaghan . . . that's Wyatt's *son's* name."

CHAPTER 15

Wyatt felt as if a bucket of cold water had been dumped on him, and then as if he were shoved into a burning building. Icy cold then flaming heat. The chill of disbelief. The rage of hope.

Everyone and everything fell away as he slogged through a heavy, murky world, as if he were wading through an ocean of gray Jell-O. He couldn't get there fast enough, but he felt as if he wasn't moving either.

He got to the front just as David Callaghan took the stage, standing next to Vaughn. Wyatt didn't hear anything they said, nothing about the reason for the honor, nothing at all. His ears were filled with a roaring sound. Everything around him was dark except for the light shining on the man onstage.

He stared up at the man there, next to Vaughn. Was it possible? Could it be *possible*? He realized he was shaking.

There were—had been—a million David Callaghans in the world. Hundreds or even thousands of them near Denver in 2010. And probably dozens or more of them had been eight in June of that year.

He wanted to jump up there, to look this man in the eye, to see if it was him . . . but the longer he waited, the longer he could hold onto the hope.

That forgotten feeling of *hope*. Of light.

So he watched, waited, prayed. Tried to get a good look at the man's face from his position on the ground. Tried to imagine what the boy of eight would look like now at nearly sixty. Tried to keep himself from seeing resemblance where there might be none.

Applause broke out just as Wyatt felt someone move in behind him. A rush of awareness penetrated his murky world and when Remy touched him, he tensed, but didn't pull away. He didn't even wonder what she was doing there. He just . . . let her, allowing himself to appreciate it.

Then as the applause died down, as David Callaghan waved then began to walk offstage, a new sound filled the air.

Distant at first, then growing louder. A *tdt-tdt-tdt-tdt* that came from overhead. Wyatt recognized it immediately, but he knew he was one of the few who would. The sense of alarm was so strong, it washed away the shock and hope and murkiness about the man named David Callaghan.

This couldn't be good.

Silence fell over Envy . . . a sudden, arrested reaction as everyone looked toward the sky. Beneath the moon-stoked clouds, the large vessel came into view like a monstrous bird. Wyatt heard the collective gasp, the intake of breath, as the helicopter centered over the city.

A white beam of light shot down in the middle of the crowd, and people stumbled back from the illumination as if afraid it would burn them.

The air whipped up now, sending the canvas walls of tents flapping and dust whirling. Yet, aside from that, everything was eerily still. *Tdt-tdt-tdt-tdt* . . .

A disembodied voice boomed from above, carrying over the thrumming beat of the rotors. *"Remington Truth."*

Somehow, over the noise, Wyatt heard the gasp at his shoulder. He reached back blindly and angled an arm around her, shoving her behind him, holding her there as he looked up, shielding his eyes from the beam of light and the clouds of dust. His mind raced even as the voice continued.

"Turn Remington Truth over to us and Envy will be spared."

Wyatt tightened his arm around Remy, holding her immobile. He could feel her shock and trembling, the jerking breaths she was trying to control. *Don't make a sound. Don't move.*

He felt her shifting, tensing against his back, and he grabbed her arm, trying to keep her quiet without drawing attention to them. Surely she wasn't crazy enough to announce herself, to give herself away . . .

"You have forty-eight hours to produce Remington Truth," declared the clear, booming voice. "This will be your only warning. Our conduits will arrive tomorrow for the acquisition of Remington Truth. And *this* is only a precursor to what will happen if you do not comply."

The beam of light was suddenly extinguished as the helo rose . . . and then something streaked from the mechanical bird in a glowing red arc, flaming to the ground.

"Run!" cried Wyatt, shoving Remy to safety as he shouted again to anyone who would listen. *"Run!"*

Now there was noise: people shouting, screaming, moving . . . and then the soft, dull pop of an explosion. He looked to make sure Remy was gone, that she'd listened to him for once. And as he spun back there was a sudden flare of light, the billowing red-gold of hungry fire.

Wyatt hesitated only a moment, turning to see that Remy was still running. Then he ran toward the flames.

Pushing through people, he propelled them past him as he charged toward what had become a rolling ball of flames. Someone shouted his name but he didn't stop.

Whether by accident or design, the bomb or whatever it was had landed on the roof of one of the tents. It took only a moment for it to surge into a blaze, and by the time Wyatt got there, the canvas was a ball of fire.

"Water! Buckets! Anything you can find!" he shouted to the crowd at large, directing them away as he looked at the roaring fire. The familiar smell of smoke filled the air, stinging his eyes. The roof sagged, pulling down its supports, and as Wyatt watched, it collapsed into a mountain of flames.

Coughing, still shouting, Wyatt looked for some source of water. If the fire wasn't extinguished, it would set the building next to it ablaze. Fuck. It already had.

"Water!" he cried again, knowing Envy could only have rudimentary firefighting tools at most. A bucket brigade. Maybe some sort of hose . . .

He bumped into Quent, who'd somehow appeared, and Jade, and a sea of other familiar faces as someone shoved a container of water at him. Vaughn.

Fence. Ana. Others he knew from the pub. The night
became a blur of activity and grim intent. Shadows
of more people. Pots and pails of water. A few puny
hoses. The sizzle of wet on flame. The roar of fire.
The crack and pop of new fuel for the blaze. The
crash of something collapsing.

"Holy hell! Look at that!"

A column of flame tore into the sky, sending ash
and chunks of burning timber tumbling to the ground.
Damn. Must've hit one of the grease-laden barbecue
pits. The golden-orange glow threw eerie shadows
and discoloration over the people battling the fire, the
desperate warriors gathering up anything that could
be used to subdue the flames. Blankets and pieces of
canvas beating on small pools of fire. Pots of water.

Wyatt remained in the thick of it, giving orders,
shouting from a smoke-etched throat, dry eyes stinging and watering at the same time. Yet he was in his
element: he knew this. It was his world.

Then he heard it. Somehow, above all the roaring,
shouting, crackling, his ears tuned in and he heard it:
". . . in there! She's in there!"

The terrified, desperate cries shot straight to his
consciousness. A phrase he'd heard countless times
before. "Someone help! Someone save her!"

Wyatt spun and ran toward the sound—acting
on instinct more than anything. He was hardly able
to see through the billowing smoke caught up like a
black tornado. It was a small building away from the
collapsed tent. Some ash or flaming piece of rubble
must have popped over and set it on fire. The roof
was blazing, yellow flames licked up the wall. Black
smoke, outlined by the very blaze from which it
came, roiled from the sagging door.

"She's in there! Patty! She's in there!" An older woman stood with black streaks on her face, wringing her hands, tears making shiny paths through the soot. Her hair was thin and gray and her face stretched in a shiny mask of shock and terror. She reached an ineffectual hand toward the fiery building that was hardly bigger than a garage.

"Who is it?" Wyatt demanded, already dumping a bucket of water over him. Soaking his clothing and hair in an effort to keep from going up in flames himself. Because he knew he was going inside. "How old? How big?"

"My dog. My Patty!"

He snatched another pail and poured it over himself again, hardly noticing the frigid water. "Kind of dog? Where?"

The woman stammered out information—enough that he knew he was looking for a mid-sized brown dog . . . but she was so terrified and upset he could hardly get details.

Wyatt started toward the smoking black door, the cascade of water already drying from the immense heat. A strong hand yanked him back and he nearly stumbled into Fence.

"You aren't fixing to go in there," Fence said. "Over my motherfucking dead body."

"Gotta try," Wyatt said, shaking off the large hand.

"You're bloody crocked." Quent was there, panting. His face was black and his hair stuck up in tufts. "Nothing in there's still alive. If you go in, you aren't coming back out."

"Gotta try," Wyatt said again. And he started toward the black doorway.

"It's a damned *dog*!" someone shouted. "You're risking your life for a *dog*!"

And that was precisely why he kept going. Because if it were Dantès . . .

Calm stole over him. Clamping a mass of sodden shirt over his nose and mouth, offering up a prayer, Wyatt charged inside.

The minute he breached the wall of ugly smoke, he felt the searing heat. It pressed in on him, heavy and suffocating, instantly turning his cold wet clothes steamy.

Pitch-dark. He took two steps and stumbled over something. As he crashed to the floor, he knew he'd found Patty.

And as a flaming wall collapsed, tumbling over him in a rage of flames, he figured this was it. He wasn't coming out.

Carrying a sloshing pail, Remy pushed her way through the crowd just in time to see Wyatt dash into a flaming building.

"Wyatt!" she screamed, flinging her supply of water wildly onto a patch of flame as she ran. Someone yanked her back and she found herself face-to-face with Quent. "Did he just go *in* there?" she panted.

He didn't need to reply; his face was set with fear, streaked with ash. He merely shook his head, pursing his lips as if in an effort to stave off some other emotion. "*Bloody sodding fool.*" It was a whisper, but Remy heard it nevertheless. "Went after a dog trapped inside."

She stared. There was no way any living creature

was still alive in that building. There was no way anyone could survive stepping even a foot inside.

Did you really want to end it that badly, Wyatt?

Then Quent's words registered. *A dog.*

Oh, God, now she understood. If it were Dantès . . .

And she knew Wyatt. He'd at least have to try, the damned idiot.

"Keep working!" shouted someone.

The order spurred her into action—there was nothing else she could do other than stand there and wait. And pray. And try to put the rest of the damned fire out.

And try not to be terrified that it was because of her that this fire had even started in the first place. They'd found her. The Strangers knew who she was.

And now the only person she really trusted had run himself into a flaming building. It would be a miracle—beyond a miracle—if he ever came back out.

Numbly, Remy turned to fill her bucket from the ineffectual hose. Just as she spun back, taking three short steps to hand it off to someone, there was a loud crash followed by a rolling wave of heat.

"Motherfucker," someone breathed.

Her heart in her throat, already knowing what she was going to see, Remy looked over. The building into which Wyatt had dashed was now nothing more than a vee-shaped, collapsed pile of rubble.

She dropped the bucket, running automatically toward the renewed blaze, into where she'd last seen him. *Wyatt. No, please, no!* But something—some*one*—hooked her arm, yanking her away so hard her head snapped and the crystal whipped sharply on its chain, slamming against her back.

She looked up into Ian's face. His cold expression sent a bolt of fear through her. She tried to pull away, stomping down hard on him with her bare foot, and wished she was still wearing her silver shoes. The spiky heel would have done some damage. "Let me go, Ian."

"Not a chance," he said, edging her away from the activity. "You heard what they said. Turn you in or Envy's toast." In the eerie light of the leaping flames, his smile was frightening.

She opened her mouth to shout, but it was lost in the roar of the fire battle.

Wyatt closed his eyes. The unbearable heat from the flames seeped into him . . . through fabric onto skin and then muscle and bone, finally settling deep in his organs. He felt it with every pump of his heart, every pulse of blood in his veins. Eating into his liver and lungs. Searing into his very marrow.

The weight of the ceiling or whatever it was that crashed onto him pinned Wyatt in place. He couldn't move even as the fire dug into flesh and bone. He could see the blaze dancing along his arm, felt it nibbling on his hair and searing into his nostrils, eyelids, and ears.

Finally.

He closed his eyes and the world behind his lids was just the same: bright, blazing light, heat, shadows. As he slid into a final sleep, pieces of his life filtered through his mind in a gentle lullaby.

Cathy at the altar, sparkling in white, glowing with love . . . the dark black heat of a Middle East night, a heavy weapon resting on his shoulder . . . The weight of his fire gear, hose in hand, boots clumping on his feet . . .

Loki as a pup, with his mischievous eyes and too-big ears . . . holding Abby in his arms for the first time, her soft, fuzzy head hardly bigger than his palm . . . watching David toddle his first steps before falling into a soft blue sofa . . . snatching Abby out of a fast-rushing stream . . . holding hands with Cath by the fire . . . flipping burgers on the backyard grill . . .

The grateful, sad smile of a Haitian woman when he opened her repaired door . . . angry tears in his wife's eyes . . . bright pink flowers on Mom's grave . . . Dantès's intelligent, amber eyes and upright ears . . . his first glimpse of Envy . . . Remy and her shotgun, blasting at the rabid coon . . . Dantès and Remy asleep on the floor . . . Brilliant blue-violet eyes and full pink lips and comfort . . .

And then . . . nothing.

He was floating. Darkness came and went and then there was a brilliant white light.

Wyatt.

Someone was calling his name.

A heavy weight was lifted from his chest. He could move. He could breathe. He did.

Someone shouted. Someone touched him.

He gave a great shudder and felt the exhaustion and ache rushing through his body. It was like waking from a dead sleep after the longest, hardest day of his life. Worse than the first day of basic training. Worse than the end of a week in Haiti after the hurricane. His muscles protested. His lungs hurt. His eyes wanted to stay closed but he forced them open.

The light was strong and bright, bringing tears to his eyes. He had to look away, reaching up to shield his face. Something tickled his skin like the flutter of fingers or something delicate falling on his cheeks and he opened his eyes again, still blinded by the light.

"Holy Mother of God, he *is* alive!"

Who? Wyatt pulled himself upright, even as something—some*one*—pushed him back down.

"Easy now, Earp," said a familiar voice.

Wyatt knocked Elliott's hands away and sat up. *What the hell?*

"My God," someone said in a hushed voice.

"What the hell is going on?" Wyatt managed to say aloud this time. He squeezed his eyes closed, still seeing the dancing flames bright behind his lids, and then opened them again. It was daylight.

He happened to be looking down, and the first thing he saw was his hands. *Jesus Christ.* They were shiny, coal-black. The skin was peeling, curling up in large pieces.

Beyond his hands . . . below . . . was his torso, his legs. What was left of his clothing was charred beyond recognition and his skin was the same . . . soot black. Ashy. Flaking and peeling away.

He looked up, still squinting in the sunlight, and found Elliott. Wyatt licked his lips—God, he was *dry*—and tasted . . . burned skin. Charcoal. Grit. Salt.

Elliott was looking at him with an expression he'd never seen before. A combination of horror and wonder and question. "Wyatt. Are you . . . how do you feel? *Do* you feel, um . . . anything?"

Wyatt shook his head, shifted, and felt the groan of his muscles, an achy sort of heat trundle through his body. And he noticed more black skin flaking away. He drew in an experimental breath, feeling his lungs expand, and drew in deeply, more and more and more. He felt as if he could inhale forever . . . Cool, fresh oxygen surged through his body like a lake breeze. Energy and life tingled through him. He felt it rush to the very ends of his capillaries, to every neuron in every nerve ending . . . to the well of every hair follicle through to the tip of its hair . . .

"Yeah," he replied carefully. An odd prickly comprehension was sliding over him, like a shade being dragged away and allowing the sun to shine through. This was . . . wrong. He'd seen burned bodies. They didn't look like this.

Then he looked back at Elliott, understanding. Yes. His friend had healed him. Saved him from death.

"You should be . . . dead," Elliott said. He was crouching next to Wyatt, and they both watched as he reached out and gingerly brushed a fingertip over Wyatt's forearm. Black skin fluttered away . . . and beneath it was . . .

"*Holy crap.*"

Beneath it was clean, smooth, unmarred skin. Sleek. Muscular. Sprinkled with dark hair. *Unblemished.*

"You healed me," Wyatt said, looking at his friend. He shifted and felt the ache rush through him, knew it would be a day or two before the lingering discomfort finally dissipated. But, hell. He was alive.

For the first time, that thought wasn't a disappointment.

But Elliott was shaking his head, wonderment and understanding in his eyes. "No. I didn't do anything."

Wyatt frowned and felt the tightness of his face. He reached up to massage his brows and more dark flakes fluttered down. His jaw, his cheeks, his mouth . . . they were tight and hard and shiny . . . and they shed.

"What happened?" he asked, and experimentally got to his feet. Simon was there, and so was Fence. They were both looking at him as if they'd never seen him before.

"Take it easy Wyatt," Elliott said again—but he made no move to stop him. Instead, he positioned himself as if to catch his friend should his legs give way while watching in awe.

Wyatt stood there, on his own two legs, in the middle of smoking rubble. Charred wood and other debris littered the area. Early morning sun blasted down, bright and new. The smell of smoke was everywhere.

"What happened?" he asked again.

"I think," Elliott said, a ghost of a smile touching his lips, "you've discovered your special ability."

"Yeah?" Wyatt replied, letting that sink in as he looked down at himself. More burned skin had fallen away, and bigger patches of fresh, undamaged skin were showing.

"You came out of that fire covered in ashes, your skin just peeling away," Simon said, kicking away a smoldering piece of wood. "And now look at you."

"Holy shit," Fence said. "You're a motherfucking phoenix." He looked down. "And, bro . . . you need a new pair of pants."

CHAPTER 16

Once someone brought him a new set of clothing, Wyatt found he was perfectly capable of participating in the recovery work Simon, Fence, and other residents of Envy had been doing, even as he continued to "shed" the last bit of his old skin. He joined in the work immediately, knowing how important it was to locate any survivors as soon as possible. His body was achy and his eyes gritty, but those were minor discomforts. Other than that and the fact that his mind was a little muddled, the rest of him seemed to function just as well—or even better—than before. He actually felt quite . . . *new*.

"Can't decide whether you're a phoenix or a freaking snake," Fence said as his buddy brushed away more burned skin from behind his knees. It seemed to cling more stubbornly there than elsewhere. "Either way, it's fixin' to be a helluva mess every time you do . . . whatever you do."

"I could use a shower or a swim, that's for damned sure," Wyatt replied. "But there's time for that later. Most of it's gone."

"Yeah. And, you know how the Hulk is when he

changes, he busts out of all his clothes, so he always wears his pants way too big? Well, man, you better find some fireproof shorts for yourself, bro. Or you're gonna be making a stir with the ladies, showing your junk around like that." Fence rumbled a chuckle, showing his brilliant white teeth.

They were clearing the remnants of debris from the two tents and the one building that had gone up in smoke. Wyatt wasn't surprised to learn that he could pick up and move smoldering pieces of wood with his bare hands. He felt the heat but it didn't burn.

"Any casualties?" he asked Simon as they tossed the burned-out remains onto a pile that would later be burned to the ground.

"Other than you?" His smile was wry. "Only the poor dog you tried to save. Some burns and other injuries, but that's it. As far as we know, anyway. But we're still looking to make sure."

Wyatt heaved a large piece of door onto the pile. "Me?"

"Yeah, mo-fo. When that roof came down on your head, we knew that was all she wrote. The damn fat lady had sung," Fence said, swiping an arm over his soot-streaked face. But his eyes danced with humor as only his could during such an unpleasant topic. "No one could get to you either, brother—you were buried in flames. Not till we got the fire out and it cooled off this morning enough for us to dig your ass out."

Hell. Wyatt tossed an unidentifiable piece of furniture onto the pile. "Thanks for pulling me out." He wondered what would have happened if they hadn't dug him out. Would he have died? Or had it been only the heavy ceiling that kept him from being able to walk out under his own steam? Because it sure as hell wasn't the fire that did it. Neither the fire, nor the smoke—either of which should have finished him off.

It didn't really matter: he was alive. And he wasn't sure he wanted to go through it again to find out how or what happened.

"Elliott's up to his balls in work in the infirmary, but he came out to find you first thing," Simon told him. He didn't need to add that the doctor would have done whatever he could to save him, and knowing what a double-edged blessing that skill was, Wyatt was relieved Elliott hadn't had to try. "And once this is cleaned up and the injured are taken care of, Vaughn wants all of us—"

"You know, *us* us," Fence added meaningfully. "We bad-ass dudes. And our bad-ass women, too, of course." He looked around as if to make sure no one had heard him tacking on that last bit. Heaven forbid if Zoë thought she was an afterthought.

"He wants all of us to meet and strategize about what to do next," Simon continued. "We've only got forty hours to figure out what to do."

Wyatt stopped what he was doing. In the craziness of his reawakening and the blur of urgent work that needed to be done searching for survivors, he'd forgotten about all of that. The memory of all that happened before the explosion and fire came rushing back in a cold, shocking wave.

David. A surge of hope and optimism fluttered inside. As soon as they were finished here, he'd locate the man and find out if the miraculous had happened. If—

He froze. The Strangers. The helicopter. How could he have forgotten *that*?

Remy.

"Where's Remy?" he asked sharply.

No one immediately answered, and he said it again as an unpleasant feeling curdled in his belly. "Where the hell is Remy?"

"I don't know for sure," Fence said. "But I'm betting she's with Ana and the others. She and Jade have been helping Elliott in the infirmary, and I think Sage and Zoë were fixing to do some other cleanup inside."

Fence's words were easy, and they should have put Wyatt at ease . . . but, hell, he knew better. And his gut told him it might not be that simple. He glared around at the mess that had changed an area of celebration into a place of fear and pain. Tendrils of smoke still curled up from one pile of rubble, and soot and ash danced in the breeze. People were talking quietly as they worked, and much had already been accomplished. The damaged area was a relatively small space and cleanup was under control.

"I'm going to look for her," Wyatt told Simon. Their eyes met and the other man gave him a sober look of understanding.

"No one knows who she is, man," Simon told him in a low voice. "That she's Remington Truth. Just us. And Vaughn."

"And Ian Marck," Wyatt snapped. And wondered if he could really trust Vaughn Rogan—especially when his city was at stake.

"*Pinche,*" Simon muttered. "You go. I'll take a look around too."

Wyatt's long legs took him off quickly and efficiently. He went to the infirmary first, where he found Elliott well in control of the ill and injured.

And just about ready to deliver a brand new baby as well. That might have been a spark of optimism after a night of darkness, but since no one there had seen Remy or Dantès, Wyatt found little reason to smile.

His next stop was inside the pub, where he'd left Dantès in the care of a couple of teenage boys last night. Neither of them were there, but one of their moms was and she told Wyatt that Dantès was safely with her son.

But that meant Dantès *wasn't* with Remy.

"Zoë," Wyatt snapped when he saw her rushing off somewhere. She was still wearing the clothes from last night, and her white slacks were streaked black with soot, and were gray everywhere else. She was wearing hiking boots and her face was haggard.

"Holy fucking shit." She nearly dropped the tray of food she was carrying. Her eyes bugged out. "Are you alive or a damned ghost? There's no damned way—"

"I'm alive," he said shortly. "Long story. Have you seen Remy?"

She stared at him, blinked, and then refocused. "No. Not since last night, right after you went up to the stage." Her face went grim. "Now that I think of it . . . I haven't seen her at all."

Wyatt tried to quell the icy feeling creeping over him, but he couldn't. Remy wasn't the type of person to hide away when there was work to be done, people to be helped. The Remy he knew would have been out in the middle of everything, giving orders and telling everyone what they were doing wrong—even if they were right.

Which meant something had happened to keep her from being there.

"What about Ian Marck?" he demanded.

Zoë shook her head.

The cold sharp claws of fear gripped him tightly now. Not good. This was not good.

He had to get Dantès. If Remy was still in Envy, Dantès would find her.

Remy paced the room. It was a well-appointed, comfortable space; she should be able to relax, calm herself and think clearly. But her stomach was in knots, tightening and loosening in turn.

I shouldn't be here.

But Vaughn had convinced her it was the best, the only, option, for now. Until they figured out what to do.

Forty-eight hours. It had been ten o'clock last night when the helicopter appeared and it was eight o'clock now. That meant the timeline was down to thirty-eight hours. Hardly more than a day and a half.

She swallowed, pacing faster. *I could just turn myself over to them. They wouldn't do anything to me if I hide the crystal. They'd need me to get it back. To tell them where it was.*

Of course, there was always torture. She shuddered. She didn't think she'd do well with torture.

Maybe there was a way she could bargain her way out of the situation. Maybe it wouldn't be so bad for them to have the crystal. After all, she'd had it for twenty years and it didn't seem to do anything.

But she knew in her heart that wasn't the case. They wanted and needed the stone for something important enough to be searching for it for half a century. One woman—or even a whole city—standing between the crystal and the Strangers wouldn't matter to them.

But she had some time to think. And maybe Vaughn would have a solution.

No one knew she was here, in his private suite—and Remy wished she weren't. She should be down on the ground, in the remains of the party, helping to clean up. Helping . . . whoever needed help. Whoever might be buried in the rubble.

Her throat closed up. She wasn't going to think about Wyatt.

Instead, she made herself focus on inane things, like her surroundings. Not only was the mayor's suite much larger than the room she was staying in, but it had a small kitchen area, a living room, two bathrooms and a bedroom, plus the office. Spacious. Clean and bright. High off the ground. Very unlike any living area she'd known.

She caught a glimpse of herself in the mirror as she stalked past it. Good grief. What a mess! Dirty face, soot-streaked and exhausted. Eyes bloodshot and puffy. Hair falling in a terrible tangled mass. Her white dress was more gray and brown than white and sported a bloodstain on one side, not to mention dirt along the hem, thanks to Ian.

She couldn't hold back the twitch of a humorless smile. He was probably still nursing the clout she'd given him on the head with an empty beer bottle. Served him right for trying to manhandle her off somewhere . . . wherever.

Even now she wasn't certain whether it had been good fortune that she'd encountered Vaughn shortly after, still in the midst of the chaos. But he seemed to have been looking for her, and he seemed to know what to do right away. "Hide yourself," he muttered, pulling her away from the craziness. "Keep safe until we figure out what to do."

Remy looked at herself again. A shower wouldn't be a bad idea. She had nothing better to do, and who knew how long it would be before Vaughn returned?

But time was ticking . . .

It was beneath the rhythmic pounding of the water that she let herself go. The warm cascade—nearly as hot as Flo's—was like a catalyst for the release of her emotions. She let the tears come, her sobs deep and harsh. Confusion. Stress. Fear. Loneliness.

Grief.

Wyatt.

How could she feel such a sense of loss for a man she hardly knew? That she wasn't even sure she liked? The image of the roof caving in over him replayed in her mind over and over . . . and there was no happy ending.

No one could survive that. She knew it.

What she didn't know was why it affected her so deeply.

Maybe it was because he was the only one who knew about the crystal, who understood what she'd been through. She'd lost the only person she could talk to.

Or because of the stoic, matter-of-fact way he'd said, *That's what I do. I risk my ass. For people.* And the way he'd always just seemed to turn up when she needed something, whether she wanted him to or not.

And now the world was less such a man. An arrogant, angry man with a good heart. A man battling himself and everyone around him. Her eyes stung.

The memory of him sitting in the semi-truck trailer, staring down at the children's books . . . the empty, dark pits of his eyes, filled with hell and grief. *Are you at peace now, Wyatt? Are you with them?*

The tears came with a ferocity she hadn't expected.

Remy didn't know how long she was in the shower, sobbing, soaking, trying to numb herself from the horror of her reality: that the Strangers had found her, that she was a hostage for an entire city, that the one man she trusted and cared about was dead . . . but it wasn't until someone knocked on the bathroom door that she became aware of her surroundings once more.

"Yes?" she called, grabbing a towel and turning off the water, which had gone cool. Her fingers were so wrinkled she wondered if they'd ever smooth out again.

"Remy, are you all right?" It was Vaughn. He didn't open the door; he didn't even try—and he could have, for she'd not thought to lock it. He just called through the barrier.

"I'm fine. Be out in a minute." She rushed. Maybe he had some news. Or a solution.

Maybe she shouldn't rush, because the news might not be what she wanted to hear.

He had large, soft, fluffy towels. A little threadbare in places—they must be old—but still, more luxurious than she'd ever experienced. She wrapped one around her hair and used the other to dry herself, considered wearing it out into the living room. There was no way she was going to put that filthy dress and those underthings back on. They lay in a pile on the floor just outside the bathroom door. The crystal was still attached to its silver chain, hidden by the folds of cloth. As soon as Vaughn left again, she would retrieve the gem.

When she saw the large robe hanging on the back of the door, she got herself into that and padded out of the bathroom, hair still dripping.

"I thought you might want some clean clothes," Vaughn said as she appeared. His rugged face appeared drawn and exhausted and his eyes were sober and worried. Dirt and soot streaked his face, and she saw that his clothing was hardly in any better condition than hers had been. He gestured to a pile on the table.

"Thanks," she said. Numbly, she walked over and picked them up, wadding the bulk of soft yellow cotton in her hands. "What's going on down there?" she asked, wanting to know and yet not wanting to know.

"Mostly cleanup." He avoided her eyes, turning to the small counter in the kitchen. She heard the soft clink of glass on glass, then the sound of liquid splashing. "Everyone is talking about Remington Truth."

Her throat tightened. "Vaughn, I'm not going to stay here and let the Strangers come back and—"

He turned, holding a short glass of amber liquid. His expression was cool and determined. "We'll figure it out. You can't leave here. Not yet. If anyone finds out you're here—that you're Remington Truth . . ." He shook his head firmly. "Remy, I don't know what the sentiment is. They don't even know who—or what—Remington Truth is. People are still shocked and frightened over what happened last night. They'd never seen a helicopter before, and this threat from the Strangers . . . well, it has everyone in an uproar. They've never been so overt before. I have to let everyone calm down first, clean up, take care of any injured or casualties, and then we'll figure it out."

Casualties. She pushed the ugly thought away. "What about Dantès?" she asked. "Is he all right? Can he come up here with me?"

Vaughn shook his head. "It's not a good idea. He might bark or something. No one can know you're here. He's fine, by the way. He's with Rod Macedon's boy for now."

She opened her mouth to argue when someone knocked on the door. Remy looked at Vaughn, who rose. "Yes?" he called.

"Vaughn, are you in there? It's Marley."

Remy might have found the mayor's reaction amusing if the circumstances were different. He went rigid, then his eyes shot from her to the door to the bed and back again. Guilt and chagrin were written all over him and she could almost hear his mental curse.

"I'll just go in here," she said, giving him an easy out as she ducked into the back bedroom. But even though she was out of sight, Remy left the door cracked so she could hear.

Vaughn let Marley in. "What are you doing here?" he asked. Remy shook her head. He didn't sound very welcoming, which was precisely the opposite of what she'd seen in his eyes. Men. She shook her head.

"I just came to see . . . to see if you were all right." Marley's voice was softer, but it carried back to the bedroom.

"There's a lot going on," Vaughn said. His tones were cool. "I have a lot to deal with, Marley. Everyone's very upset. The clock is ticking. So what do you want?"

"You left pretty quickly after they uncovered Wyatt."

The stab of pain was so sharp, Remy had to hold back a gasp. She closed her eyes, leaning against the wall as tears gathered again. *No. Not now. Think about it later.*

It took a moment for her to collect herself, and by then Marley had moved farther into the suite. Now Remy could see her through the crack of the door.

This was the first good look she'd had of the woman. Even disheveled from working all night, Marley exuded an air of elegance. She was, as Flo might have said, "put together." Very beautiful, with shiny dark hair streaked attractively with blond, falling in perfect waves around her face and shoulders. Long red fingernails, except for the first one on her left hand.

As Marley turned, Remy saw something that made her turn cold. A faint bluish glow coming from beneath her clothing . . . just below the collarbone. *Exactly where the Strangers wore their crystals.* As she watched, the glow seemed to grow brighter, shining through the clinging dark blue blouse.

She couldn't breathe for a moment. Marley was a Stranger? What did this mean? Vaughn must know she was one. *Oh God . . .* was he going to turn her over to Marley? Or had Marley somehow come here, looking for her? Did she know?

We will send our conduits.

Her heart pounded and her palms went damp. She looked around for something to use as a weapon as she strained to hear their conversation, which remained stilted and short.

". . . have a lot of decisions to make," Vaughn was

saying. He sounded almost pompous. "But the most important one is taking care of the people of Envy. My people. You of anyone should know that." Then something changed, and he moved suddenly, blocking Remy's view. "What is it?" His voice was urgent. "Marley?"

She couldn't hear anymore. There was a flurry of movement and Marley made a noise that sounded like pain or surprise. She couldn't see anything but Vaughn's solid figure, but she heard something that sounded like "crystal."

Her breath caught and ice shot into her belly. *Oh no.* The crystal—*her* crystal—was still on the floor, caught up in the pile of clothing she'd left right outside the bathroom door. Was it recognizing Marley? Was that why the blue crystal embedded in her body had started to glow brighter? Would the other woman see the orange glow from beneath the clothing? Would she know it was there?

Did she dare go out to try and retrieve it—

"Who's back there?" Marley's voice rang out sharply. Remy froze as Marley's face appeared from behind Vaughn. She was looking toward the bedroom.

Remy automatically ducked away from the opening. The last thing she needed was for a Stranger to see her.

"You don't want to go back there," Vaughn said. He moved to block her, cutting off Remy's view again.

"Oh. I see." Marley's voice was like ice. "I didn't realize I was interrupting." Whatever had been bothering her was obviously no longer a problem. "Ah," she said, her tones brittle now. "And here are her clothes. I most *definitely* see."

Vaughn said something else, but Remy couldn't hear anything other than the tone: brief and hard.

Then she heard the opening and closing of a door. Not a slam, but a very deliberate *click*.

Followed by a soft, heartfelt curse.

Confused and shaken, Remy realized one thing: she didn't want Vaughn to know she'd witnessed any of that. She had a lot of thinking to do. Who was her enemy? Who could she trust? It was better to play ignorant until she figured it out.

She lay down on the bed, curled up and facing away from the door, and forced herself to lay still and even out her breathing. Easier said than done with her heart pounding like it was. But it must have worked, for when Vaughn pushed the door open a few minutes later and said her name in a low voice, her lack of response seemed to assure him she was asleep.

Remy heard the door close behind him and opened her eyes.

What the hell did all of that mean? And what was she going to do now?

She looked at the clock. *Less than thirty-seven hours.*

"My first loyalty is to the people of Envy," Vaughn Rogan said. His eyes were steely and determined as they swept the room. "I know some of you might not agree with me, but that's where I stand. I'll do whatever it takes to keep them safe."

"Of course the first priority is to keep Envy safe," Jade said mildly. "You don't need to convince us of that."

"We've got thirty-five hours," Simon said. "What do we have to work with?"

They were gathered in the mayor's ground-floor office, the people in the inner circle—or, as Fence had jokingly termed the group, the bad-ass guys. And their bad-ass women. Jade and Elliott, Quent and Zoë, Sage, Simon, Fence, Ana, and Wyatt. The air in the room was as brittle as ice.

"What's the general sentiment of the people?" Sage asked. "What's everyone hearing out there?"

"The most common reaction I've experienced is confusion mixed with fear. People have never heard of Remington Truth. They don't know who or what it is so they don't know how to react or what to do. Remember, it was only because of Jade and the fact that she was imprisoned by Prescott that we realized Truth was a person's name," Elliott said. "So they don't know what to do or how to do it, and they're scared."

"So there doesn't seem to be a big push to find Remington Truth and turn her over to the Strangers?" Ana asked. "They're not tearing the city apart, looking for Truth?"

"I wouldn't say that," Elliott said. "At least, not yet. From what I heard, there's a lot of talk among them. It's only a matter of time until someone lets it slip, or someone figures out who or what Truth is. After all, we have a whole group of survivors here right now. It's an unusual name, and someone might remember that Remington Truth was the director of the American NSA back when the Change happened and put two and two together."

"We know Ian Marck is here, and there must be someone else who already knows about Remy—

otherwise, how would the Strangers even know she existed, let alone that she was here?" Sage added.

"That brings me to my main concern," Wyatt drawled. Keeping his voice slow and low was the only way he could keep from shouting. "Where the hell is she? Has anyone seen Remy since last night?"

Grim-faced, each of them shook their heads.

"So it could be a fucking moot point," Wyatt pressed, his voice dangerously calm. "If we don't find her, someone else can. Or already has done so. So why the *hell* are we sitting here *talking about it*?"

"She's not with Ian Marck," Simon said. "Or if she is, he hasn't interacted with her since last night. I have Brad Talley keeping an eye on him just in case."

Wyatt managed to control a sneer. Instead, he gritted his teeth and tried to keep from charging out of his seat and taking matters into his own hands. *Thirty-five hours. Less than a day and a half.*

The only reason he was here was because he'd hoped that with the group gathered, he'd have an efficient way to learn whether someone had heard anything from Remy. In about two minutes he was getting the hell out of here to do some reconnaissance on his own. With or without the others.

"The other worrisome thing," Quent said, "is that the Strangers made their threat and instituted a deadline . . . but they gave no way for us to communicate back with them—yet. Their so-called conduits haven't arrived, or haven't made themselves known. If we were going to turn Remington Truth over to them—presuming we intended to—we have no way of knowing how or where to do so. Which implies to me," he continued, speaking louder as Wyatt opened his mouth, "that they have some way of monitoring the city."

"What the fuck do they want her for anyway?" Zoë asked. "Seems like an assload of work to be looking for her for fifty damned years. Must be something important."

Wyatt glanced at Ana. He hadn't told anyone about Remy's crystal, and as far as he knew, no one else was aware of it besides himself, Remy, and Ian Marck.

Ana didn't seem to notice Wyatt's attention, but, as he hoped, she spoke up. "I heard things, living in Atlantis. Bits and pieces. The original Remington Truth disappeared during the Change. And at the same time, something called the Mother crystal also went missing." She shrugged. "It's logical to assume the original Remington Truth had something to do with it, but no one knows for sure or how."

"What exactly is the Mother crystal?" asked Sage. "Maybe if we knew that, we might . . . I don't know . . . have a better bargaining chip when dealing with the Strangers? Is it related to the Jarrid crystal—the one Quent and Zoë stole from Liam Hegelson?"

"All of the crystals are related," Ana said. "At least, the living ones are. There are energy crystals, which are different from living crystals. But the way I understand it, all the living crystals are connected somehow. And some of the connections are stronger than others, and between different types."

"Marley would probably know something," Quent said, suddenly looking around. "Where is she, anyway? She should be here."

Vaughn shifted in his seat and ran a hand through his hair. "I didn't tell her about the meeting. I wasn't certain she should be included. She is, after all, crystalled."

"Against her bloody *will*," Quent reminded him flatly. "If you recall. I don't think she's particularly sympathetic to the Strangers."

Vaughn nodded, his jaw visibly tight. Wyatt found himself feeling unwillingly sympathetic at the misery in the other man's face. Something was definitely up there. "I do recall. I didn't want to make an assumption that everyone here would be in agreement that she should be trusted. And included, however. After all," he looked at Wyatt, "Remy's safety is at stake. As well as that of the entire city. We have to find a way to get out of this situation with both intact. And the clock is ticking."

A prickle went down Wyatt's spine and he went cold. *Vaughn knows. He knows where Remy is.*

But what did that mean? *My first loyalty is to the people of Envy.*

Wyatt heard that loud and clear. The question was whether the mayor's priority included offering up one life to protect and save many if it came down to that.

There was a knock on the door and the room went silent. The place wasn't a secret location, like the underground computer lab built by Sage and the Waxnicki brothers, but this was a private sanctum in Vaughn's public office. Not many people knew it existed, let alone how to find the entrance.

Vaughn himself rose and went to the door, easing it open a crack. He spoke quietly to the person on the other side, then opened it fully. "Please join us," he said. "I expect you'll have something to add to the conversation."

The mayor stepped away from the door, casting a warning glance around the room. His expression indicated prudence in the topic of conversation.

"Hi, Dad," Ana said when her father walked in accompanied by another man. "Does everyone know my father, George? He's the one who grows Elliott's penicillin," she added with a smile. "And keeps Flo's showers running superhot."

"And this is David Callaghan," George said, gesturing to his companion as he introduced him to the room at large. "He's just showed me a most curious . . ."

Wyatt's head was filled with a loud buzzing sound. He started to get up but his knees wouldn't hold his weight. His chest tightened so he couldn't breathe, and he felt Quent reach over and close his fingers over his arm.

Then the man named David noticed him. Their eyes met and the newcomer's face went slack with shock and then turned white as a sheet.

He gripped the nearest chair and stared at Wyatt. "Dad?" he whispered. "No, no," he added, shaking his head. "I'm sorry. That's . . ." But even as his voice trailed off, he couldn't seem to look away. "You look . . . just like . . ."

"Your father." Wyatt found his voice and a blaze of joy surged through him. "Wyatt Callaghan. Married to Catherine, father of Abby and David. Resident of Lockwood, Colorado. Fire chief and burgermaker extraordinaire." Now he managed to stand. "David, it's me. Your dad."

CHAPTER 17

"*David. I am your father,*" said a very deep, breathy, bass voice.

Of course, that was Fence, bringing levity to the situation as usual. Wyatt barely heard him, however, for the roaring, rushing sound that filled his ears obscured everything but his son, David, saying again, "Dad? But . . . how is this possible?" His expression was a combination of joy, disbelief, and confusion.

Wyatt wanted to explain, but he found he didn't want to waste his energy doing such a mundane thing while he could be drinking in the sight of his son. Examining every detail of the man he'd become. Noticing the gray in his thick, dark hair, the wrinkles radiating from the corners of his eyes. The smooth, slight sag to his skin. Whiskers. No more freckles. And he was much taller than he'd been fifty-some years ago.

And so he was grateful for Sage, in her calm, organized way, who explained to David how his father came to be sitting here, fifty-one years later and unchanged. Mostly.

When Sage finished, Wyatt said, "I have so many

questions for you . . . but first, I have to know—"
His throat closed up then, suddenly, and it burned
when he tried to swallow. Tears stung his eyes and he
blinked furiously.

David's expression was still shocked, but now a
veil of sadness slipped over it. He shook his head.
"Abby and Mom . . . they didn't make it. They survived the storms, the earthquakes—I'm sure you've
heard about it all. They were some of the many who
died suddenly days later, for no apparent reason. It
was quick and painless," he added quickly, with a
matter-of-fact air. "They didn't suffer. It wasn't until
two weeks later that we figured out why some people
survived and others didn't." He'd probably said these
words countless times. Made the explanation simply
and smoothly, as if he were teaching a history class
talking about the Holocaust or the Civil War, or re-
counting a family story about walking five miles to
school in a snowstorm.

But Wyatt saw grief still there, and he clenched his
fingers tightly into his palms. Rage and black fury
roared through him, tempered by a surge of nausea.
He wanted to scream and shout and hit something
. . . some*one*.

Yes, it might have been quick and painless. But
David was left alone. An eight-year-old boy. *Alone.*
In the middle of inconceivable destruction and devastation. *The end of the fucking world.* Losing his
mother. His sister. Wondering where his goddamn
father was. Wondering and wishing and waiting and
hoping *every single fucking day.* For fifty years.

Tears burned his eyes and Wyatt had to squeeze
them closed to keep from sobbing. How could he
have failed them so? How could he have been absent

during the most terrifying, desperate time of his family's lives . . . especially when he'd been a savior for so many others?

Someone touched him—a gentle hand on his shoulder. Wyatt looked up, blinking, and realized he'd retreated into the darkness of despair once again—even in the face of what should have been happiness. But David was there, rubbing his shoulder, his face sober and his eyes hopeful. And glad. There was joy in his expression. Joy and sorrow.

Wyatt didn't think any longer, he just pulled his son—his *son!*—into an embrace. And he let the tears leak from his eyes, felt David's trickle against his cheek, and they held each other for a long time.

When they pulled apart, clearly both filled with infinite questions and things to say, Wyatt realized the room was empty. The others had left them alone, and he was grateful for it.

"I can't believe it," he said, looking at his fifty-nine-year-old son, unable to keep from staring at him.

"You?" David said, and chuckled with happiness. Wyatt saw Cathy there in that moment, and he felt the pang of grief . . . but it wasn't as deep or sharp as it had been. "Here I am, old and wrinkled and worn out . . . and my father shows up and he looks half my age." His laugh rang out in jubilation. "If only I could look that good at . . . how old are you now? Ninety-eight? It's like a Benjamin Button thing."

Wyatt laughed too. The first time he'd really laughed, really felt pure happiness in a year. "I don't think it'll happen that way for you, Davey." Then he sobered, took his son by the shoulders and looked him in the eye. "I'm sorry, David. I'm so sorry." Grief welled up in him again, mingling with the beautiful happiness, making him feel as if he were in that murky Jell-O again . . . but at the same time, looking at a ray of sunshine he knew he could eventually reach. "Can you ever forgive me?"

David was shaking his head, his old eyes filling with tears. "*No*, Dad—"

"I should never have left you and your mother and Abby. I shouldn't have gone to Sedona. I should have stayed home." Wyatt's throat burned, his voice was dry and rough and he could barely force the words out.

"No, Dad, *no*. You can't do that to yourself." David was earnest and intent. And he spoke like an adult. A *man*. Good God, his son was a *man*. "No one could have known. No one could have prevented what happened. And even if you hadn't gone to Sedona . . . what would you have been doing anyway? Yes, you'd have been out there, pulling people out of the rubble, putting out fires, helping them . . . and you would have died three days later anyway."

Wyatt shook his head hard, trying to clear it. Trying to make sense of everything. Every unfucking-believable thing that was happening right now. "What do you mean? Who knows if I would have died? I might have been one of the few who survive—"

David shook his head. "No. Dad. Trust me." He covered Wyatt's strong, tanned hands with his own, older, veiny, age-spotted ones. Surreal. "The people who survived . . . they all had something in common. We figured it out. All of us who lived, who didn't suddenly expire, had had a tetanus shot two days earlier."

Wyatt stared at him, waiting for the information to filter through and into his brain. "You're telling me that the people who survived did so because they'd had a tetanus shot?"

"Two days earlier," David confirmed. "It's true. Trust me," he added with a wry, sad grin. "When you're eight years old, you remember shots. They're almost as bad as—well, no, forget it. In the grand scheme of things, they aren't that bad. But as it happened, my friend Johnny Raybourn—do you remember him?—we'd had shots on the same day. I remember, because we were complaining about it at school. He survived too. We found each other at the school, where people went after things . . . got crazy. And from there we got to talking to people and realized that everyone who was still alive had just had the shot." He shrugged. "I can't explain it any more than I can explain you being here . . . but, Dad, it's a miracle. And I'm sure as hell not going to question it."

"I know." Wyatt closed his eyes. Tried to push away the images of his young, bewildered, grief-stricken and frightened son.

"It was *fifty-one* years ago," David said, as if reading his mind. "It was beyond terrifying. It was . . . unbelievable darkness and fear and devastation. But it was a long time ago, Dad. I've accepted it and built a life—a good life—with that in my past. And now . . . the most miraculous thing has happened. Something I could never have imagined. You're here." His eyes filled with tears again, but they were joyful tears. "And I can't wait for you to meet your granddaughter."

Granddaughter. Wyatt's heart nearly stopped. "I have a granddaughter." He tried out the words, listened to them as they seemed to float in the air between them, and let them sink in. "I have a *grand-daughter*." He felt his lips stretch in a smile of won-derment.

"You actually have two of them," David said with a grin. "And a *great*-granddaughter. But only Cat is here."

"Cat?" Wyatt said, looking at him.

David nodded. "Catherine Michelle. After Mom. Of course."

Tears gathered in his eyes and he blinked hard, harder. "I can't wait to meet her." Something warm inside him flowered, expanding warmly and sweetly through his body. After a year of cold and emptiness, of battling back any possibility of *feeling* again, he was alive again.

He'd been reborn. Twice in one day.

"You'll meet her as soon as possible," David prom-ised. Then his expression became sober once again. "But it seems that right now, there's a sort of crisis happening We're on a countdown."

"Yes," Wyatt said. Some of his joy melted away as he remembered the far more urgent problem of Remy and her whereabouts. He was going to find Vaughn and make him tell him where she was. "Right now we've got a nasty situation."

"I'm here to help. And I should probably tell you," David said as they both stood, "that I've known Lou and Theo Waxnicki for years. And I've been a part of their . . . network . . . for the last three of them."

Wyatt felt a rush of surprise tinged with pride. "You're part of the Resistance?"

He nodded. "That's why I'm here. I've never ac-tually met Sage, but I've been in touch with her via the network for years. She can vouch for me. And I mainly know the Waxnickis through the same interface, although I met Theo in person a few times when he first came to set up the network access point near where Cat and I lived."

"How did you get here, now?"

"I found something in Glenway that I thought George should see, and I brought it here. Now that I'm here, I want to help—with whatever you're going to do regarding this threat about Remington Truth. That," he added, looking at Wyatt steadily, "is what George and I assumed this big meeting with Mayor Rogan was about."

Wyatt nodded slowly. "Yes. I want to tell you more, but I have to get the agreement of the others to do so."

"Absolutely. I understand completely." His smile was one of chagrin. "I made the mistake of mentioning to Cat—and Yvonne, my other daughter—that I was sort of involved in a resistance group, trying to explain to them why it was urgent that I get to Envy. And now Cat wants to join . . ." He shook his head. "She'd jump in feet first if she could." Then he looked up at Wyatt and a proud smile curved his face. "She takes after her grandfather."

Thirty-three hours.
  Tomorrow night at ten.
  Remington Truth.
Everywhere she went, Cat heard people whispering about it. Or arguing, with desperation and panic rising in their taut bellows. They gathered in groups and every pair of eyes turned to watch whenever anyone new walked by.

She wandered, feeling lost and impotent. She wanted to be doing *something*, but she knew no one but Dad and Ana, and they were nowhere to be found. She suspected they were meeting with the others in the resistance group . . . but she hadn't been invited.

Remington Truth. What did that mean? Was it *the* Remington Truth . . . like some sort of book or document? A canon or writ or something? Or was it an object? A statue?

Could it be a person? Remington Truth. A little tingle, a little *pop* in her thoughts told her that made the most sense. But that would be like finding a needle in a haystack. *And if I were Remington Truth, I'd be keeping way out of everyone's way.*

"Come on, Jason. We're leaving. We're getting out of this city!" The high-pitched, strident voice of a woman filtered through the constant level of noise to Cat's ears.

She turned to look and saw the woman rushing along with a large pack over her back and another slung over a shoulder, crosswise over her chest. She held the hand of a small boy whose legs pumped to keep up with her determined strides, and an older child followed.

There were others too. Groups scuttling nervously out of the building, carrying their belongings.

"I'm going to demand a meeting," cried another voice. This one was a woman as well, and her pronouncement was greeted with shouts of agreement and urging. "Rogan's got to answer to us! He's got to tell us what he's going to do!"

"We can't wait for the mayor and the city council," someone said. "They'll argue about it for hours. We have to act!"

"Start a search for Remington Truth. Someone's got to know what it is. I'm going to *demand* that Rogan step up to this!"

The voices were growing louder and more strident, and Cat edged away as the rowdy group, propelled by fear and ignorance, surged by.

This could get ugly.

She shook her head, wishing she could do something. Wishing she knew some way to help.

Wishing Dad would *let* her.

As she turned to go back outside—at least she could help there, although much of the cleanup was done—she noticed the huge dog.

He seemed lost and distraught, and although he was frighteningly large, she couldn't bear to see an animal in distress. Since he was inside the building and didn't appear to have any concern with or from the people walking by, she suspected he belonged to someone living in the place. Hopefully he was just separated from his master.

"Hey buddy," she said, crouching next to the auburn, brown and black wolflike animal. Even when on her knees, she found her face at eye level with him, so she didn't approach too quickly. Carefully and slowly she held out a hand for him to smell. "Are you lost? What's wrong?"

He had intelligent amber eyes that seemed to understand exactly what she was saying. His ears perked up into sharp triangles and he allowed her to pet him, then butted at her with a whine.

"What is it?" she asked. "Who are you looking for? Do you want me to help you find your daddy? Or your mama?" He went to attention at that and bumped her harder . . . then turned and started off.

Although she didn't have a dog of her own, Cat understood. *Follow me.*

"Okay then," she said. "I'll bite."

She followed him as he trotted rapidly down a long corridor that ended at a door. "Ah, so that's it," she said when he scratched at the door.

She opened it and followed the dog inside. They were in a . . . what was it called? . . . a staircase that went up and up and up . . . a stairwell. The dog bounded up the steps, then paused on the landing to look down at her.

He gave a short, peremptory yip as if to say "Come on!"

Cat shrugged and followed him up, and when she reached the next floor, she understood why. He was waiting for her to open the door to the hallway. The expression on his face was one of *Duh!*

Laughing at the dog's attitude—plus the fact that he was so damn smart—she opened the door to the corridor. He took off, his nose to the ground, sniffing as he went along. Cat waited to see what he'd do next, and was mildly surprised when he went to the end of the hall and turned around to come dashing back. He pushed past her into the stairwell and bounded up the next flight.

She followed, opened the door to the corridor, and watched while he did the same thing. Obviously, he was searching for someone.

"Okay, I'll play," she said, ruffling his fur. And so they went on and on, up each floor in turn.

The dog became more efficient as they went on . . . he merely walked a few feet past the door, sniffed around, then came back and bolted up to the next level. Cat couldn't help but wonder how many more stairwells he was going to lead her to once they got to the top of this one, but she found the process so fascinating and intriguing she stayed with him.

"Look buddy," she finally said, almost an hour later, "this is the last floor. If he's not here, I don't know where he's going to be."

But unlike the others, this top door didn't open. It was locked. It was also a different type of door: a nicer one, but without the small rectangular window that allowed a view into the corridor. It was new, and the fittings were shiny, and there was a peephole . . . but for the person on the other side. "Damn," she said, jiggling the knob again. "Looks like you're out of luck, pup."

The dog did *not* like that. He whined and bumped the door. Then he gave a sharp, high-pitched yip. Then sniffed at the bottom of the door again and barked another time.

"Hush, buddy," Cat said, wondering if she should get out of there. Whatever place this was, it seemed forbidden . . . as if she shouldn't be here. But the dog was insistent and he barked again, louder and more urgently.

When Cat heard someone on the other side of the door, she got nervous and edged away. Was she going to get in trouble for trespassing? The dog was barking louder and more excitedly, and she stepped back, trying coax him away with her. "Come on, buddy," she crooned in a soft voice. "Let's go. You're disturbing people."

But he would have none of it, and she heard the clinking of a lock on the other side of the door. She bit her lip and stood in front of the door. Maybe this *was* his master's—or mistress's—place.

The door swung open.

"Dantès!" The dark-haired woman crouched and the dog charged into her arms, nearly knocking her over in the process. In the midst of a good face-washing, she looked up and they immediately recognized each other. "Cat! What are you doing here?"

"Hi Remy," she replied. Then her brain stopped. Remy. *Remington?* No. That was absurd. "Is this your dog? He was distraught, looking for you."

"Thank you for bringing him to me. Do you . . . uh, do you want to come in?" She stepped back from the door.

Cat could see past her into a spacious, well-lit room. "Wow. Is this where you live?" She stepped in. That little *pop* she'd felt earlier . . . it was back. Her heart pounded and curiosity sizzled through her.

"No. I'm . . ." Remy looked uncomfortable and wasted. "I'm glad you're here. I'm glad you brought Dantès. I was thinking about leaving . . ."

She looked at the other woman, noticing her amazing blue eyes. And all the inky-black hair she had, which, unlike her own, seemed to stay under control. Instead of curling up all over the place like Cat's, it hung in long, sleek waves that shone almost blue-black. She was tall for a woman, but not overly so, and older than her—but she wasn't sure how much. Maybe ten years? But it was her demeanor that she found compelling: not intimidating so much as in control, self-assured. Even yesterday, when they were at Flo's place, Cat had noticed Remy's confidence and strength. But today she looked exhausted and stressed-out, with dark circles under her eyes and a cut by her eyebrow, but she still exuded determination.

"Dantès? That's his name?" Cat said, petting the dog. When she stood, she realized that Remy was looking at her, as if assessing her.

"Do you believe in signs?" Remy asked, closing the door behind them. "Sort of like a cosmic nudge, in the right direction?"

Cat stood and faced her. "Maybe," she said, remembering that funny little *pop*. Something was going to happen. "My dad does. I know that."

Remy looked around the room, and Cat's gaze followed hers. She'd never seen a place so open and new and bright, so much like the pictures of the world her father had known, before the Change. It reminded her of the houses rich people lived in on the DVDs she watched with Dad.

She realized Remy was looking at her again, in that measuring sort of way, as she spoke. "I was just sitting here a while ago, wondering how I was going to figure out whom to trust . . . wondering if I should leave here and take matters into my own hands . . . and here you are. And you brought Dantès—that's sort of the clincher. I'm choosing to think of it as cosmic guidance. My friend Selena would approve, I think." Remy gave her a crooked smile, then tipped her head, still looking closely at Cat. "Do you know who I am?"

Cat blinked, unsure whether she should verbalize her suspicions. This had to be Remington Truth— apparently someone the Strangers felt strongly enough about that they wanted her back. *Back* . . . was she a hostage here in Envy? Was that why she was tucked away up here? But she hadn't been acting like a hostage yesterday.

Or did the Strangers want her . . . for other reasons? As a prisoner.

Yet, Cat didn't feel uncomfortable or apprehensive. It was as if she'd walked into a riddle—or a story—and hadn't quite figured out where she was or what she was doing yet . . . but that her instinct was guiding her. A cosmic nudge, if you will. "You're . . . Remy." She shrugged. "Friends with Zoë and Sage and all of them."

"My name is Remington Truth."

Well. That was easy. "I . . ." Cat said, then decided to be honest. "I just now figured that out."

Remy didn't move. She just looked at Cat, still assessing, as if waiting for something.

Then Cat realized . . . the other woman was waiting for her to react. To shout an alarm, to do something. "I can understand why you've been hiding," was all she could think of to say. "Unless . . . unless you're a prisoner here."

"I'm not a prisoner . . . and I don't like to think of it as hiding," Remy replied. Her stance relaxed a little. "Vaughn—Mayor Rogan—thought it was best if I was out of sight, especially since there's the chance that more than one person would be willing to turn me over to the Strangers if they knew who I was." Again that hesitant, pregnant pause. Waiting.

"*I'm* not going to turn you over, if that's what you're worried about," Cat said. *As if.* "My dad—" *Better not say anything about his work.* "Well, I'm not a fan of the Strangers. I don't trust them, and neither does my dad. And to be honest, yeah, you're right. There are people below—I've heard them talking—who are pretty much ready to get pitchforks and find you and turn you over. Why do the Strangers want you anyway?"

"It's a long story," Remy replied. "Which I will tell you . . . if you'll help me."

Cat felt a spike of adrenaline and determination. Just the opportunity she'd been waiting for. Anything to mess with the Strangers and keep them from getting what they wanted. "Yes. I'll help you."

A small smile curved Remy's lips. "Thanks." She seemed about to say something else, but cut herself off. "Let's get out of here."

"What is this place anyway?" Cat asked as Remy gathered up a bundle of things.

"It's the mayor's private apartments. I think I'd better leave before he gets back. He might try to talk me into staying."

"What can I do to help?" asked Cat, following her new friend and Dantès out the door.

"Well, first, you can be my lookout," Remy said, gesturing for her to go ahead of her. "There are only a few people who know who I am, and I don't want them to see me. Not because I don't trust them, but just until I figure out what to do."

Cat stopped halfway down the flight of steps and turned to look up at Remy. "You're not thinking about turning yourself over to the Strangers, are you?"

"Not unless it's my only choice," she replied. "But if it's an option between all of Envy getting blown up or me going with them . . . the choice is easy." There was strain around her mouth despite the certainty of her words.

Cat shook her head. "No. We'll find another way." A determined energy filled her. This was something she could do. Something worthwhile. A way to change things, make them different . . . make up for not getting there in time to save Rick. A life for a life.

A chill of understanding caught her by surprise. Was this what she'd been waiting for? Something to do, to set things right?

Cat decided at that moment there was no way she was letting Remington Truth offer herself up as a sacrifice. Anyone who was even *talking* about doing so had to be worth helping.

"So," Remy said. She started down the steps, forcing Cat to continue on as well. "I need you to keep an eye out for anyone who'd recognize me."

"I guess that would include everyone who was in with Flo yesterday? Ana and Zoë and the rest? And I think I met Simon and Elliott too . . . do they know you?"

"Right," Remy said. "Yes, they do know me. And there are a few other people who might recognize me. One is named Ian Marck. I definitely don't want to run into him. I have to find a place to hide out in the meantime."

"You could stay in the room I have," Cat offered. "It's just me and my dad, and he's busy right now." She wanted to tell Remy about the Resistance, and that Dad was involved . . . but it wasn't her information to tell. She didn't want to put her father at risk.

They'd gone down several flights of steps, with Remy describing the man named Ian Marck as well as she could. "And then there's the mayor. You know who he is, right? From onstage last night?"

"How could I miss him? He is wixy *hot*," Cat said with a grin. "A little old for me, but definitely worth noticing—in a different way than that creepy albino guy who was checking me out. Anyway," she said, feeling a little foolish. This wasn't the time to be drooling over men. Good thing she didn't mention the über-hot dark-haired guy who'd come up to stand right next to her last night when her dad was up onstage. *He* was someone she'd been hoping to run into again, now that the chaos was over. "What's the matter?" she said when she realized Remy had gone stock-still, five steps above her. Even Dantès recognized his mistress's concern, for he gave a short little yip.

"Did you say 'albino'?"

"Yes. It's not that I have anything against them," she added hastily. "I mean, I don't care if they have—"

"Never mind that," Remy said, urgency and fear in her expression. "You saw him here? In Envy? Was he with anyone? Was he alone? What did he look like?"

"Yes, he was still here this morning. I saw him when we were cleaning up the rubble. He was with a woman. She was kind of skanky looking with white-blond hair in little—I don't know what you want to call them—*things,* like short ponytails all over her head. *Crap.* You know them? This is bad, isn't it?"

"I should go back," Remy said, spinning on the stairs. "If they're here, I need to tell Vaughn. And get somewhere where they can't find me. They're the ones—they have to be the ones—who told the Strangers where I am. And that I have—" She stopped abruptly.

"You can stay in my room," Cat offered, wondering what she'd been about to say. She had . . . what? "It's just me and my dad, and he's . . . busy right now. No one would think to look for you there. Plus . . . how would you get back into the mayor's place? The door was locked, wasn't it?"

Remy bit her lip. "Damn. True. Okay. *Wait.*" She

stopped, held her hands out in front of her as if telling herself to pause. "I'm not going to go running off and hiding from them. I've been running for twenty years. It's time I took control of things."

Cat smiled, that spike of adrenaline back. "I like the way you think. I'll do whatever I can to help, Remy."

The other woman gave her a brief smile. "Well, you say that now . . . but this could be dangerous. And you don't even know me." Her blue eyes fastened on Cat, serious and intent.

"I need something to do," Cat told her. "Something to do with my life. I've been feeling lost and empty for a while." To her embarrassment, her voice cracked. "So what's the plan?"

"We find the albino and the woman. And we get some answers."

CHAPTER 18

Thirty-two hours

It was, Remy reflected, better to have that awful deadline to focus her mind on, to keep herself sharp. For, despite all of the other problems she faced, her thoughts kept wanting to slide back to Wyatt . . . and the fact that she'd never see him again. And that she wanted him here, to help her. To give his flat, terse, no-nonsense advice.

Her eyes stung and she squeezed them shut tightly. No. Not now.

For some reason, Cat reminded her of Wyatt. Maybe it was her no-nonsense manner. Or the way she interacted with Dantès. Or maybe it was just simple transference—her confidant in Wyatt was gone, and Cat happened to be the next possible candidate.

Either way, she knew she'd have to deal with her feelings for Wyatt eventually . . . but right now she kept telling herself there was a more urgent matter at hand. People's lives were in danger and she was the catalyst for it all. She had to be the one to find the solution, because she was the only one who knew the whole story. And she was the only one who could make the decision for her own future—one that was now entwined with that of an entire city's.

Step by step. Little by little. Take your time, figure it out. You have time. *You have time.*

Remy waited with Dantès in Cat's room while their hastily assembled plan was put into action. It would likely work, but she would have been much more comfortable being the one walking up to Lacey and sticking a gun into her side than allowing Cat to do it.

But it had been Cat's idea—simple and ballsy— and Remy couldn't take the chance of being seen while she was looking for the bounty hunter. And Cat, who'd never met Lacey, could literally walk up to her without the woman knowing she was a threat . . . it was just a matter of finding the right moment, when the bounty hunter was alone, and letting her feel the gun Cat held beneath her sweater.

So once again Remy knew she could do nothing but sit and wait and see if the plan succeeded.

The firearm was one good thing—a stroke of luck, really. She'd acquired it from Vaughn's apartment. After he left, she'd been busy, searching for anything she could find that might help her decide whose side he was really on. She found the handgun—a Glock, just like one she'd had when she was with Ian—and some ammunition in a hidden space in the back of one of his dresser drawers. Likely he hadn't anticipated her being in his bedroom, but when Marley arrived unexpectedly, that was where she'd gone. And that was how she had the chance to be nosy.

And now she sat, petting Dantès, letting her mind run over those events and the last few days . . . avoiding only the knowledge that she'd never be kissed again the way Wyatt had kissed her. Who else, she thought with the faintest, saddest of smiles, would kiss so arrogantly and sensually at the same time? Who else would be kissing the hell out of her at the same time as he was fighting himself from doing so?

She wished she'd had more of a chance to talk to him. To understand what went on in that mind of his. To ask for his advice. To be embraced and touched . . . and feel safe. Even if it was only for a moment. Even if it was only an illusion.

Wyatt. I hope you're at peace now.

When the knock came, Remy stilled, her heart pounding. She made a firm gesture to Dantès not to make a sound. *This is it. Or, at least, it's something.*

She went silently to the door to look through the peephole.

Lacey's furious face, awkward and bulbous through the tiny spherical window, glared up at her. And behind Lacey stood Cat, a grin on her own countenance.

With a gust of relief, Remy opened the door and Cat fairly shoved Lacey into the room.

As soon as the bounty hunter saw Remy, she bared her teeth in fury. Despite the gun, she would have lunged toward her as Cat turned to close the door but for Dantès, who growled.

That was all he needed to do to stop Lacey in her tracks.

"Dantès, guard," Remy said, gesturing to their guest. She smiled humorlessly at her former abductor. "He won't attack unless I give him the command. Or unless you make a move to hurt me. So I suggest you take a seat and make yourself comfortable."

Lacey had no choice but to comply, and gave Remy

a look of loathing before sitting in the chair at which Cat pointed. But as she sat, an odd expression crossed Lacey's face, and she clapped a hand to her chest as Remy heard—or felt—the faintest sizzling *pop*.

"What the *fuck*," Lacey exclaimed, frantically looking around the room. "What's—oh hell *no*," she breathed, curling her fingers tighter into the shirt she wore. Remy realized the bounty hunter was gripping herself at exactly the location of her crystal, which was hidden by a black leather vest that did not have its usual peephole.

"You *do* have it," she said, looking at Remy. Her expression was a combination of greed and fear. "After all these years, all the searching—"

She cut herself off with a groan as Remy asked, "What are you talking about?"

"The Mother crystal," Lacey panted. "It's here. It's right here. And it's . . ." She was still clutching her shirt, but her face had gone gray and pale as Remy watched, thinking the bounty hunter either an amazing actress or in great agony.

Cat was watching, too, with confusion and surprise, but still held the gun. And now the faint smattering of freckles stood out more sharply in her face. "I'll keep her covered, Remy, if you want to take a look and help her." She moved close enough that the gun barrel was pointed right at Lacey's head.

Remy nodded. Her new partner was too smart to take any chances. By now Lacey was collapsed in her chair, trying to breathe. Her face was slick with sweat and she continued to grip the stiff vest that obscured her crystal.

"Get . . . it . . . away . . ." she breathed, clutching at her leather top. "Take it away."

Remy had moved forward with the intention of loosening the vest to find out what was happening. Maybe Lacey's immortality-giving crystal was burning like hers had. But at the woman's agonized words, she stopped. Did Lacey mean her own crystal? That she should take it out of her skin?

Or . . . she looked over at the small bundle of clothing she'd taken from Vaughn's room, in which her crystal was wrapped. It was on the table right behind Lacey, a mere yard away.

"It's here," Lacey gasped, her eyes wide with pain. "Take it . . . *away*."

Feeling Cat's curious eyes on her, Remy walked over and retrieved the small orange crystal. It had come to life and was burning and warm, but not with the same ferocity as before.

She walked around to Lacey, who was still panting, and had unlaced her vest and pulled it away enough so the crystal embedded in the soft skin below her collarbone was exposed. Normally, the small round gem would have been lit with a soft ice-blue glow—just as when Remy had seen it a few days ago. But now it was gray and cloudy, like a moonstone.

"What . . . have . . . you . . . *done*," Lacey whispered, looking down at it. Fury and loathing blazed in her eyes when she lifted her face, and Remy knew if she had the energy, the woman would be out of the chair and coming for her—Dantès or no. "You've killed me."

"I've done nothing," Remy replied. "Tell me about this. Tell me about this crystal. I don't know what it does or where it came from. Is it really the Mother crystal?"

"You . . . don't . . . know?" Lacey managed an

unpleasant laugh, even in the midst of her pain. True character, blazing through. "Joke's on me," she added bitterly. "I didn't . . . know either."

"Know what?" Remy pressed. Was the woman really dying? Or was she just in pain—as if it were a sort of kryptonite or asthenia that made her weak while in her presence? She experimented by stepping back and away from Lacey, putting distance between the bounty hunter and the crystal. "Does this make a difference? If it's farther away?"

"It's too late," the other woman said from between gritted teeth. Sweat trickled down her face. "It's dead. My stone's . . . dead. And I will be . . . soon."

"Then tell me what you know," Remy said again. "And I'll get Elliott here. He'll help you."

Lacey's smile was bitter. "No one . . . can help . . . me . . . now. Once the stone . . . dies . . ."

Remy knew her only chance to get more information was to drag it from the woman. Dying or no, she wasn't going to give it up without a fight. "So you've been chasing me—and this crystal—for years, and now that you've located it . . . what? Its proximity kills you? That's kind of a kick in the teeth, isn't it?"

The bounty hunter's lips were a flat white line. Her face was as pale as Goldwyn's, matching her hair. The sweat of agony collected at her temples and dribbled down her cheeks, gathered at the bony hollow of her throat, glistened everywhere on her skin. Her eyes were two dark orbs, sunken in hollowing sockets, the circles beneath them were darkening even as Remy watched.

"Never . . . knew . . . that," the woman replied. "Never . . . was told. Don't know . . . if . . . *they* even know . . ." Her lips twisted in an evil sneer. "Hope

. . . they . . . don't. Hope . . . they find . . . you. Take
. . . the . . . stone. And all . . . fucking . . . *die*."

This impassioned speech seemed to cost too much
effort, and she sagged lower in her chair, her head
falling against the back. Her corded neck bulged
with blue veins, her pulse throbbing visibly in her
throat.

"Did they send you here to get me? After they
made the threat last night?"

Lacey opened her eyes, fixing them on Remy. "*I*
. . . knew you were here. Guessed . . . followed . . .
Ian. *I* . . . told . . . Hegel . . . son. Not Ian." Her
lips stretched in a tight, pleased smile. "I wanted . . .
reward. Ian . . ." She shook her head, closed her eyes.

"You knew I was here, and so Liam Hegelson—
yes, I know the name," Remy said when she saw the
flare of surprise as Lacey's eyes shot open, "sent you
to follow up on their threat. To take me to them,
after they promised to destroy Envy. What will they
do when I don't go? When I don't appear? What do
they plan to do to Envy?"

But Lacey had closed her eyes. Her labored breathing rasped in a silence broken only by Dantès vigorously scratching his side.

"Lacey." Remy prodded the woman with her voice.
"What are they going to do?"

"Destroy . . . Envy," she replied. And showed a
malicious hint of teeth.

"Yeah, I got that. But how? More bombs? A fire?
An invasion?"

Lacey didn't respond. She just watched her through
black, blank eyes, malice exuding from her even as
the life drained away.

"Okay, let's try this: why do they want the Mother

crystal? What does it do?" Remy brandished the stone, holding it up for Lacey to see.

"Very . . . powerful. Too . . . dangerous . . . for anyone." Her bloodless lips twisted in a parody of a smile. "Didn't know . . . how . . . dangerous. Want to have . . . control."

"What did it do to you?" Remy asked. "The crystal. What happened?"

Lacey shifted her head weakly in a negative movement. She was going. Remy could almost see the life draining from her.

"Is there a way to destroy the crystal? What if I get rid of it . . . then the Strangers won't be able to get it."

Somehow, the dying woman was able to force a rough, wheezing laugh. "Yeah . . . do it . . . destroy the crystal. That . . ." She moved her lips up at the corners. ". . . would . . . serve . . . right. All . . . die . . . then. All connected to . . . crystal . . . would . . ." Her voice trailed off and she closed her eyes. For a minute Remy thought she was gone.

But then she heaved back into motion with a deep, shuddering breath. One of her fingers twitched as if to emphasize something she'd said.

I'm losing her. Damn. Then a thought struck her. "Who's Liana?"

To Remy's surprise, Lacey opened her eyes and fixed them on her. A blaze of consciousness shone through the dullness for a moment. "How . . ." She shuddered a breath and lifted a trembling hand as if to ward off some threat. ". . . do . . . you . . . know . . . about . . . Li . . . ahh . . . na . . . ?"

And then her eyes went blank. Her hand fell. And she was gone.

Wyatt was pacing Vaughn's office because he sure as hell couldn't sit. He ached everywhere from holding his muscles tense, from doing *nothing*. His head pounded. His belly gnawed. *Where the hell are you, Remy?*

At the moment, he didn't even know where their so-called fearless leader was either. During his reunion with David, the group scattered to temporarily handle other pressing matters, and afterward Wyatt had gone to look for Vaughn, in vain. And now the mayor had yet to arrive at the appointed time for the meeting's continuation.

Thirty-one hours. Closing in on less than a day.

The door opened and everyone looked up.

"New development," said Quent as he came through the door and Wyatt gritted his teeth. Where the hell was Vaughn? Quent slid onto a seat next to Zoë. "Sorry I'm late. But one of our questions has, unfortunately, been answered."

Fuck that. The only question Wyatt wanted answered was for Vaughn Rogan to tell him *where the hell Remy was.* The longer the mayor kept her whereabouts hidden—and even the knowledge that he had it—the less Wyatt was inclined to trust him. He'd always liked the man, respected his leadership, and even enjoyed chatting with him over a cold one. But as Vaughn had already clearly said: his priority was the mass of Envyites as a whole.

Wyatt's, on the other hand, surprisingly enough, had become the personal safety of one woman.

And therein could lie an ugly conflict, especially if the rest of the group sided with the mayor. Or even if they didn't.

Vaughn could be keeping her imprisoned somewhere as a last ditch bargaining chip if every other option failed—not that anyone had presented any other fucking options. They were all just sitting here, waiting, trying to clean up, trying to *guess* at what to do.

They needed reconnaissance. They needed *action*. He wanted to punch someone. He wanted to shout and get out of this room and tear the damn place apart until they found her . . . and yet, he knew that any searching or tracking had to be done very carefully.

Because if the general public became aware of the fact that Remy, a young, beautiful woman, was Remington Truth, *everyone* would be looking for her.

"What's the new development?" Elliott asked. "And where's Vaughn? He was supposed to be back here by now. Are things getting crazy out there?"

"The new development is that we have the answer to one pressing question: how to communicate our response to the Strangers," Quent replied. "They sent a team of bounty hunters—a bloody fright of a woman and her albino partner. Walked right up to Fred Newbergh at the gate and bloody announced they wanted to see the mayor." He ran a hand through his hair and looked at Fence. "Remember when Seattle put that damned bullet in Theo? That blond wench who was with him?"

"She visits me regularly—in my damned nightmares," Fence said. "Lacey. That was her name. Couldn't be a worse choice for a name, if ya'll ask me."

"Spoken by the guy who goes by Fence," muttered Ana. "What happened? Did they see Vaughn?"

"Don't know. Last I heard they were looking for

him." Quent turned his attention to Wyatt. "Simon's—"

Before he could finish, the door opened and Vaughn strode in. *'Bout damn time.* Wyatt narrowed his gaze on him, taking no care to hide his precise feelings about the situation. If the others hadn't been present, he'd have the damn man—mayor or no mayor—by the throat until Vaughn told him where Remy was. He might anyway.

"How is it out there?" asked Sage. She flickered a glance at Wyatt as if to ease his mood. He gritted his teeth and looked away.

"Getting unpleasant," Vaughn replied. "There's a group of about two dozen being whipped up into a frenzy by Susan Proudy, about finding Remington Truth. She's trying to get them on board to start searching every damn room and home in the whole city until they find it. Yes," he added, his mouth in a wry grimace, "they are searching for *it*—not her. Or even him. Got people leaving too. Packing up their things and taking their families and going."

Vaughn looked exhausted. If Wyatt wasn't so fed up with the situation, he might have felt a little sympathy for the man. But not much. Hell, he'd seen guys who'd had it much worse: digging through piles of hurricane rubble to find corpses that had once been family in Haiti. Walking through a Baghdad market after a suicide bomb had decimated it.

Coming out of a damned cave and finding the entire world different. Everything you ever loved, *gone.*

His mouth tightened and he drew in a deep breath. *Calm.*

"But even that's not our biggest problem right now." Vaughn looked right at Wyatt. "She's gone."

It took a minute for the words to sink in. "What do you mean . . . she's 'gone'?"

"You know where Remy is?" Jade interjected. She sounded just as pissed as Wyatt felt. "What the *hell*?"

Vaughn drew himself up and scanned the group with cool, no-nonsense eyes. "I made the decision to protect her and keep her out of the way until we decided how to proceed. To be perfectly clear—Remy was in my custody with her full agreement."

Wyatt was aware of a rising fury bubbling inside him. What the hell gave Rogan the right to do such a thing? And to lie about it, to people who knew her?

"It was safer for Remy," the mayor said, fixing him with a cold gaze, obviously reading his mind. "Safer if no one knew where she was, or *who* she was. There would be no chance encounter, no accidental recognition—"

"But what you're saying now is that she's *fucking gone*." He couldn't sit any longer, and now he was eye-to-eye with Vaughn. His vision went dark, edged with red fury. "And there are people out there—a mob—just waiting for the chance to—"

The knock on the door was probably the only thing that kept him from taking a swing at the man—either literally or figuratively. And Wyatt didn't figure he cared which way it would have gone. His muscles trembled with the effort of holding back.

Rogan turned with dignity—but not without measuring Wyatt back with a dark look of his own—just as Ian Marck stumbled through the door. Behind him was Simon, clearly the force behind the propulsion.

In retrospect, Wyatt realized it was probably a damn good thing things happened the way they did. Being able to grab Marck by the scruff of the shirt and whip *him* up against the wall instead of the mayor was doubtless a better choice in the long run.

"Get your fucking hands off me," Marck spat, recovering quickly from the surprise assault. He grabbed Wyatt's arm with strong fingers.

"Not until you tell me where Remy is," Wyatt said from between clenched teeth.

"If I knew, I wouldn't tell you. But since I don't, I don't even have *that* satisfaction."

Marck tried to head-butt him in the face, but Wyatt dodged the blow and jammed the other man harder against the wall. It was all he could do not to plow a fist into his face or gut, and then let the rest fly . . . but, unfortunately, he believed Ian. With great reluctance, stiff with fury, Wyatt loosened his grip on Ian's shirt and let his feet rest back on the floor.

"Last time I saw Remy, she smashed me on the head with a fucking beer bottle," Marck said, twisting sharply away from Wyatt's grip. His movement revealed a lump the size of a golf ball on his head, and a bright red scar shining amid matted blond hair.

"Well, that's a hell of a souvenir." Wyatt nearly smiled. *Nice going, sweetheart.* "When did that happen?"

"Last night. Right after all hell broke loose. What the hell am I doing here?" Marck glared at Simon, who'd been watching the proceedings with his arms crossed over his chest—blocking the door.

"When did you see her last?" Wyatt demanded, looking at Vaughn.

"About three hours ago," he replied. "And now she's gone."

Damn. Wyatt turned back to the bounty hunter.

"The two bounty hunters who just arrived in Envy. Do you know them?"

Marck shrugged, insolence oozing from him. Had to give the guy credit for balls. He was up to his chin in a mess, and he still copped an attitude.

"An albino man and a bleached-blond woman in black leather," Quent said, his tones flat and impatient. "Know who they are?"

"Lacey's here? Sonofabitch." Ian Marck's sneer turned disgusted and a little discomfited. "Thanks for the warning. I'll be going now."

"I don't think so," Vaughn said. Simon hadn't moved anyway, so Marck's retreat was foiled regardless. "Not until you give us some more information. We're working on a damn timeline here."

"Yeah," Marck said with a humorless smile. "I know. Thirty hours until everything goes up in smoke. Me included."

"You've had a big-ass death wish for years," Zoë said. "Should be no big deal for you now. Unless you want to help us."

Marck's response was a dry chuckle, clearly indicating his position.

There was a knock on the door and everyone swiveled to look. "Seriously?" Fence said. "Who the hell is it now?"

Being closest, Simon poked his head out the door and had a brief conversation with whoever was there. When he pulled his head back in, he looked at David. "Your daughter is looking for you. Apparently, she has a problem."

David frowned and exchanged glances with Wyatt. "What sort of problem?"

"Apparently, there is a dead body in your room."

CHAPTER 19

"A dead body? In our room? Are you okay?" Her father's reaction was pretty much what Cat had expected.

"I'm fine," she told him. But "fine" was such an inaccurate word to describe how she was feeling after the events of the last few hours. Jumpy, fired up, confused, and determined were probably better.

Dad had asked the question just as he came out of the room where he'd been in some clandestine meeting, probably having to do with the resistance group he'd told her about. It had taken her forever to find someone who knew where he was, and it was only because she'd mentioned Ana and George that she was able to track him down anyway.

But to Cat's surprise, Dad didn't come from the room alone. Her breath caught when she recognized the man accompanying him. *The hot guy from last night, by the stage.* Her cheeks warmed and her heart stuttered. *Lucky me.*

"Cat, this is Wyatt," Dad said. He had a funny expression on his face. "He's . . . uh . . ."

"I'm going to help take care of the body, but

quickly. Remy's still missing," Wyatt said. "We can explain everything else later. What happened?" he asked Cat, turning his full attention on her.

Intense. That was the only word to describe him. Up close and talking to this guy, she realized there was a lot more to him than mere hotness. He seemed barely restrained, like he was ready to explode into action at any moment. His eyes were dark and a little too hard; they kind of glittered, with some emotion she couldn't identify. He was older than her, probably at least ten years, and looked as if he'd *lived*. Not in a debauched sort of way, but in a *real* life-sucks sort of way. Like Dad.

Cat realized with a start that Wyatt and her father were both looking at her. They had identical expressions on their faces: expectant, impatient, and concerned.

"Yeah, right. Well, this blond lady just kind of showed up at the room," she explained, telling the story she and Remy had agreed upon. As close to the truth as possible without giving away anything important.

Not that she really knew much, even now. Just the little she'd gleaned from the conversation between Remy and the woman. And she'd seen the small crystal apparently known as the Mother crystal—which Remy told her was causing all of these problems, and apparently could be the cause of Envy's destruction.

"I guess she was looking for help, because she was knocking on doors. I must've been the only one around because she knocked on ours and I opened it. She was sick," Cat said as they started to walk out of the offices of the mayor and city council. "I could tell that almost right away. She came in and sat down . . .

got all short of breath and clammy and weak . . . and then she died." She spread her hands. "I didn't know what to do, so I came to find you, Dad."

"That's unfortunate for the woman and her family, of course, but I don't think it's an insurmountable problem," Dad said. He seemed irritated with the simplicity of the story, tense in an unusual way. "I thought something . . . else . . . might have happened." He and Wyatt exchanged glances.

"Well, I figured since she had a crystal," Cat added deliberately, "it might not be as simple as that." She was rewarded when Dad and Wyatt both paused in their steps.

"What kind of crystal?" Dad demanded as Wyatt said, "She was blond? Not dark-haired?"

"Blond," Cat replied. "Her hair was almost white. And she's a Stranger. Or at least, she's got a crystal right where they usually have them."

"Was she wearing a leather vest?"

"Well, yeah. She was. Is." How did Wyatt know that?

He gave no indication, instead saying something sharp and violent under his breath. Almost as if they read each other's minds, Dad and Wyatt picked up speed and nearly left her behind.

Hurrying to keep up, Cat admired Wyatt's powerful stride and broad shoulders, the confident, arrogant way he moved. He had great arms, all muscular and tanned. Then, noticing his dark, intense expression, she couldn't help wonder if he might not be a little too much man. Even for her.

"And she's dead? You're certain of it?" Wyatt's expression made her even more unsettled as he looked down at her.

"She's not breathing and there's no pulse. I'm guessing she's dead," Cat snarked back as they reached the stairwell. As if she couldn't tell a dead person when she saw one.

Wyatt's lips twitched a little, then he said a little more mildly, "Strangers don't usually die . . . unless their crystal is removed." Then he opened the door and gestured her through.

"You can see for yourself," Cat replied. "Her crystal is still embedded just below her collarbone. I've never seen one up close, but how many people have crystals embedded in their skin?"

She started up the steps ahead of them. She figured it couldn't hurt for Wyatt to have the chance to check out her ass, which, she'd been told, was quite a piece of art.

When they got to the room, Cat took her time opening the door as a way to warn Remy they were returning. The plan was for her to stay hidden in the closet while Dad removed the body, and she was supposed to duck inside when she heard the sounds at the door.

Everything went as planned: Cat opened the door to reveal the dead bounty hunter still slumped in her chair. Remy was nowhere in sight. Dad and Wyatt slipped in quickly, closing the door behind them.

"It's her, all right," Wyatt said, bending to move the leather vest away and examine the crystal.

Then all at once there was an eruption from behind the closet door. Barking, whining . . . and then the door flew open and Dantès burst out.

"What the hell?" Dad said, and at the same time, Wyatt exclaimed, "Dantès? What are you doing here?" As he crouched to greet the ecstatic dog, who

clearly knew him, he looked up at Cat. His eyes
flashed. "What is this dog doing here?"

Utterly confused and discombobulated, Cat tried
to respond with something that made sense. "Um . . .
I just found him." That was the truth . . . sort of.

"Wyatt?"

The disbelieving whisper somehow filtered over all
the other noise.

"You're . . . alive." Remy stood at the entrance
to the closet, staring at the scene in front of her. "I
thought you were *dead*. I thought you . . . burned."

One moment Wyatt was crouched, petting Dantès
. . . and the next moment he was there, taking Remy
by the arms, pulling her up close. He looked down at
her as if he'd seen a ghost. "Where the hell have you
been?" he demanded . . . but the tone was not peremptory. It was relieved and thick, filled with emotion.

"You're supposed to be dead, you jerk," Remy
said, shoving at Wyatt's chest. He didn't release her
arms. "You have no idea what I've gone through in
the last—" She threw herself into his embrace, fairly
melting into that powerful torso.

And as Cat watched, openmouthed, Wyatt's arms
curved around her and he drew Remy up against
his chest, filtering his fingers through the hair at her
neck. She was sniffling and shaking, clutching at his
shirt as if drowning.

Wyatt's expression changed. Softened. Cat saw the
way his arms tightened, pulling Remy closer. Noticed
the way he brushed his cheek against the top of her
head . . . and even as he loosened his hold, releasing
her, he dragged his hand over her head, buried his
nose in her hair for the briefest of moments. Taking a
good sniff before setting her away from him.

Well. There goes my chance for the hot guy.

"I'm definitely not dead," he said in the most bland understatement of all time. Once again he gazed at Remy, this time as if he'd just found an entire cache of that rare thing called duct tape.

"I can see that," Remy responded, swiping the back of her hand under her eyes. "You are such a jerk." But she was smiling behind the words, and Cat understood she was missing a whole lot of subtext between them. She actually felt hot and light-headed, seeing how Wyatt looked down at Remy. If someone ever looked at her that way, she didn't think her knees would hold up.

"Ahem." Dad's bemused but pointed interruption drew their attention. "I think there's more of a story here about this bounty hunter than what Cat told us," he said, his eyes settling on his daughter purposefully.

"Well, yes," Cat admitted, glancing at Remy.

Then the most extraordinary thing happened. Wyatt, whose attention had been completely focused on Remy, looked at Dad, then at Cat, and all at once he changed. He stilled and the expression that crossed his face was fleeting, but raw and uncomfortable. Then his features settled into something else. Harshness—stony and cold.

He moved away from Remy and returned to Lacey's side, examining her. "Well? How did she end up here? Knowing you," he jerked his head toward Remy without looking up, "it was no accident."

"Of course not," she replied. Her voice was just as brisk as his and her expression revealed nothing of her feelings. A subtle chill had descended on the room, filling the space between Remy and Wyatt, leaving Cat bewildered. Her attention bounced from one to the other as her new friend explained what happened.

To Cat's mild surprise, Remy told the entire story of how they'd come to meet up and how Lacey came to be in this room.

"You pulled a gun on a bounty hunter?" Dad turned toward her.

She wasn't sure if he was pleased or shocked, but she grinned anyway. "Maybe now you'll let me join your secret group," she said.

"Fat chance," her father replied. "Someone in the family has to stay safe and sane."

He and Wyatt exchanged glances and grim smiles. Once again Cat was struck by the fact that they not only wore the same expression, but they bore a resemblance to each other. *Someone in the family.* A prickle slid down her spine. Her grandfather's name had been Wyatt. Was that just a coincidence?

"So Lacey came into the room, and almost immediately after, she began to show the symptoms of her illness?" Wyatt asked. His voice was businesslike, clearly directed at Remy . . . but he was looking at the dead woman again.

"It was the presence of the crystal," she explained. "At least, that was what Lacey said—and I believe her. It was sitting on the table there, hidden in a pile of clothes. I actually felt a little zing in the air, and Lacey must have, too, because she reacted immediately. I don't think she realized what happened right away, but it didn't take long before she was in pain, grabbing at her crystal."

"It's opaque gray now," Wyatt said, lifting the vest. "Not blue, like they normally are."

"It wasn't before. I can't say when it changed, but when she and Goldwyn had me, I—"

"Had you?" he interrupted, glancing over. "Oh. The bruising. On your face." His mouth tightened but he continued his examination of the body.

"The crystal was definitely blue then," Remy continued, her tone matching his. "Four, five days ago." Then she drew in her breath sharply. "Oh my God. Marley. Someone needs to find Marley Huvane."

Remy couldn't help gawking at the room lined with banks of important-looking machines that hummed and whirred in a constant rumble. Theo and Lou Waxnickis' secret subterranean computer lab was windowless, brightly lit, and also furnished with desks, chairs, and a collection of mismatched sofas. A blue and yellow license plate with WIXY 98 and California stamped on it hung on the wall. A *Lord of the Rings* poster was the only other decor.

"This looks like something from a movie," she said to Wyatt as Sage stood from the chair at which she'd been furiously typing on a keyboard.

Finding and entering the laboratory had made her feel like she was in one of those James Bond DVDs too. In order to get here, they went to the abandoned, decrepit-looking part of the hotel building and located a particular elevator. Wyatt pushed the up and down buttons in a certain pattern and moments later the elevator doors opened. Then they descended a short distance and he punched in a code using the floor numbers. The rear door opened to reveal a stairway that led down into the actual room.

Remy looked around the room and realized she knew everyone here. Elliott and Jade, Quent and Zoë, Simon and Sage, Fence and Ana and George, plus Wyatt, David, Cat, and herself. *What a group.*

Again she thought, there was something very special about the cohesiveness of these people. Something that went beyond simple camaraderie.

And then with a start she realized: these are my friends. *These are people I trust. And they're going to help me.*

I'm not going to be doing this alone.

She looked at Wyatt for the hundredth time, drinking in the sight of him. How could he still be alive? She'd *seen* him go into that flaming building. She'd seen the roof collapse on top of him. But here he was, and he didn't appear to have a scratch or a burn anywhere on his smooth, golden skin.

"Shouldn't Vaughn be here?" she murmured to him.

She couldn't read Wyatt's expression as he replied, "He's a little tied up right now. Besides, he wasn't invited."

"Hey everyone—I've got Theo and Lou connected," Sage said. "They'll be joining us on that monitor there." She pointed to a large flat screen that looked like a television. As she did so, the faces of the two computer geeks appeared.

"Can you hear us?" Theo said.

"Yes," Sage confirmed.

Just then Selena appeared in the screen behind the Waxnickis, and Remy thought it was very cool when her friend actually waved to her.

She waved back, feeling a little odd to be greeting a picture of someone. But then she realized this was just as if they were in the room with them, even though the Waxnickis and Selena were more than fifty miles away in Yellow Mountain.

"We are gathered here today—" Fence intoned in a deep voice, then snickered as Ana elbowed him in the gut.

"All right, Wyatt," Elliott said. "The floor is yours. Tell us what you've got."

"Remy has the Mother crystal," Wyatt announced. "Which is what the Strangers have been searching for since her grandfather procured it fifty years ago and, presumably, is why they want her turned over to them in the next—" He looked at one of the computer monitors. "—twenty-eight hours. We've got hardly more than a day."

Despite his sobering words, the reaction from the others couldn't have been more surprised, particularly Ana's.

"You have the Mother crystal? Seriously?" Her voice was reverent, hardly above a whisper. "Here? Could we see it?"

Remy glanced at Wyatt, who said, "I'm not sure it's safe for Ana to get too close to it. Right now, it's in the other room, wrapped in asbestos. The crystal has already destroyed Lacey merely by being in the same room. It seems to have killed her crystal, and she died shortly after."

"And something happened to Marley," Remy added, "this morning, when she came into—into close range. She seemed fine when she left, but . . ." She worried her lip, looking around. "Has anyone seen her? I hope she's okay." She'd already raised the concern to Wyatt, who said he'd send someone to find her, but there'd been no word yet.

"I saw her just a while ago," Jade said. "She seemed all right. A little distracted, but healthy. She was talking to a family who was leaving the city." Remy's concern for Marley relaxed as Jade's elegant features tightened. "People are going in droves."

"Like I said," Wyatt glanced at Remy, "the mayor's tied up, trying to keep his city under control."

"And Marley knows you have the Mother crystal?" Quent interrupted.

Remy shook her head. "She didn't actually see it. I don't think she knows. But Lacey did. She realized almost right away what happened."

"What did happen?"

Remy explained about the little sizzling pop and how Lacey's life simply drained away.

"The Mother crystal won't hurt me," Ana said. "I'm not immortal. My crystals only help me breathe underwater; they aren't my source of life. Can we see it?" Her eyes gleamed with interest.

Remy felt a little tremor of unease, for Ana seemed voraciously, almost greedily, interested in the crystal. But Wyatt curled his fingers around her hand and gave a little squeeze as their eyes met. A leap of heat sizzled along her arm. This was the first time he'd touched her since that awkward moment in Cat's room . . . which still had her upset and confused.

He'd been genuinely happy and relieved to see her then. The emotionless facade slipped from his face, clearly showing his feelings when he moved across the room to embrace her. His strong, solid arms curved around her, so welcome and secure. But then the warmth was gone. Just as so many times before—the same pattern.

It was as if he could only allow himself a brief

moment of joy or release, then he had to tuck anything good or happy away. Bury it deep inside and cover it up with guilt and anger.

She shook her head, wondering if there was ever a chance for happiness or joy to take root and make its way out of the darkness to grow permanently.

And how trite, these mental metaphors of hers.

"All right, Remy?" Wyatt was looking at her.

She realized with a start he'd been waiting for her permission to show them the crystal. *Well that's new.* He was asking for her opinion? She nodded, and he disappeared into the next room.

This gave her the opportunity to lean toward Elliott and whisper, "I thought . . . didn't Wyatt get caught in the fire? He doesn't look burned. But I saw him go in there."

He looked at her, his expression one of sympathy and compassion. But before he could respond, Jade interjected, "You mean he didn't tell you what happened?"

"No."

Jade rolled her eyes and made a *tsking* sound. "Men."

"I think he might have a few other things on his mind," Elliott replied dryly. "Like the fact that we're basically under a death watch."

"Which is exactly why he should be telling her things. *Everything,*" Jade added loudly and pointedly enough for Wyatt to hear as he walked back in. "Our days might be numbered." She glared at him.

Wyatt didn't seem to notice; or if he did, he ignored Jade. Upon reflection, Remy figured it was probably the latter—he was very good at ignoring things. Without a word, he unrolled a dark piece of clothlike substance and set the small orange crystal on the table where everyone could see it.

Remy realized she was holding her breath, waiting to see if something happened: another sizzle or pop or a flare-up or a flash of light . . . but the crystal merely sat there, glowing softly, as if a small orange flame burned deep inside.

"So this is what they've been looking for," Quent said. "All these years."

"Don't fucking touch it," Zoë snapped, yanking away his outstretched hand.

He looked at her, and Wyatt saw him roll his eyes before returning his hand to his lap. "Remy's had it in her possession for years, haven't you? And it hasn't caused her any harm."

Zoë snorted. "Maybe not, but you have this other damned thing, genius. That sucking vortex that drags you into a black hole whenever you touch something new? Remember that sweet little gift?"

He looked at her and his expression changed from one of annoyance to affection. "And look who I have to always pull me out of the—what did you call it?— sucking vortex, Zoë, luv."

She *hmphed* and folded her arms over her chest as Remy wondered what Zoë was referring to.

"It's much smaller than I imagined," Ana said, her voice still filled with wonder. "When I heard the legends and the stories about the powerful Mother crystal, I assumed it had to be bigger—like the Jarrid crystal. So much power in such a small stone."

"What's the Jarrid crystal?" asked Remy.

"We have a piece of it here," Quent told her. "Zoë and I stole it from the Strangers' stronghold of Mecca. According to Ana, and to what I learned while we were there, it's the conduit the original Cult of Atlantis members used to communicate with the Atlanteans."

Remy raised her brows. "Cult of Atlantis?"

A loud *ahem* from behind jolted their attention to the flat screen. "Maybe if you all moved, we could see this stone too?" Lou Waxnicki said. "Hold it up to the camera, someone, so we can get a look."

Sage hesitated a fraction of a moment, then picked up the crystal and brought it toward the small black object mounted on one of the monitors.

"The Cult of Atlantis," Simon explained as she did that, "was an elite group of ungodly wealthy and powerful people who lived before the Change. They each paid a very large sum of money to be part of the secret group—Quent's father was one of the founding members—and eventually they were the people who caused the Change. We suspect that your grandfather was one of them. I don't know if you were aware that he was the director of the United States National Security Administration during that time, which made him very powerful and very well-connected. As well, he would have had access to confidential and dangerous data that could have contributed to creating the destructive events."

Remy shook her head, her throat tight and dry. "I don't remember ever hearing him mention the Cult of Atlantis, or even Atlantis. But I did know about the NSA."

"Yes, it was your grandfather's old identification card from the NSA that eventually led us to find you," Sage put in.

"But why would a group of people *cause* the Change? What was the benefit? How could they live with themselves after being part of such destruction?" Something plunged in her stomach, sharp and low. "My grandfather . . . you said he was one of them. He was one of the ones who planned and caused the Change." An ugly nausea bubbled inside her. She'd always suspected he'd done something awful . . . but this was inconceivable. "That's why he lived such a life of remorse afterward. And why he didn't want to die."

Wyatt nodded, his face grave. "It's likely. Or else he had the knowledge of what was going to happen, but wasn't able to stop it. Or didn't try. We'll never know."

"But we might," Quent said, eyeing the crystal Sage had returned to the table. "I—"

"No fucking *way* are you touching that thing," Zoë exclaimed. "I'll smash the damned thing myself before I let you place one pinky nail on it." Her dark, almond-shaped eyes snapped with ferocity . . . and fear.

"You can't destroy it," Ana said. "I mean, it's possible . . . but it's the Mother crystal, the source of life for the Atlanteans and the Strangers. If it's destroyed, they'll all die."

There was a shocked, taut silence. Then Wyatt said, "Are you certain? If the crystal is destroyed, they all die? Do you mean we have here the power to destroy all of the Strangers and the Atlanteans—at one time?" His voice was low and careful, filled with tension.

"Lacey told me the same thing," Remy said. "If the crystal dies, everyone dies."

They stared at the small orange crystal.

CHAPTER 20

Twenty-four hours

They'd left the crystal safely in the computer room with Sage, George, David, and Cat—and Dantès—while everyone else scattered to see to other business and get any updates on the situation in the city at large. Meanwhile, the Waxnickis were working remotely to see if they could hack into the Strangers' communications system, which was just as secure as their own and, fortunately, less complicated. If they could learn what the Strangers had planned for retaliation, it would be easier to circumvent if necessary.

Wyatt was taking Remy to find something to eat when they ran into Simon, Elliott, and Jade.

"They've blocked the gates. The evacuees can't get through." Simon's features were tight and his eyes weary.

"How?" Elliott asked, sliding a comforting arm around Jade as he exchanged glances with Wyatt.

"Four Humvees. Sitting out there about a thousand feet beyond the gates. *Chavalas* opened fire on a family—with *children*—as they came out, carrying their belongings."

"They fired at children?" Rage punched through him and Wyatt curled his fingers tightly. "Tell me no one was hurt."

"Thank God, no," Simon replied. "But the threat is clear, and so they've stopped the stream of people leaving. Now people have to stay. And now the situation is even worse." He passed a hand over his face and glanced at Elliott. "Tell him."

"Someone has revealed that Remington Truth is a woman, and given a basic description of her. That means the likes of Susan Proudy and her gang are getting even more riled up. Louder, more violent."

"Who would have done that?" Wyatt said, feeling Remy tense next to him. *"Ian Marck."* That rage bubbled up sharply again.

"Ian wouldn't do that."

Why the hell was Remy always defending the bastard?

"Marck's still in custody," Simon said with a thin smile. "Vaughn's got him under house arrest. He hasn't had communication with anyone."

"How the hell did they find out, then? Besides us, the only other person who knew was Lacey and her—"

He stopped and looked down at Remy just as she said, "Goldwyn. Her partner."

"Had to be him."

"And he knows what I look like," she said, furtively glancing around, even though it was dark out here. "He could draw a good picture, or tell someone how." She edged closer to Wyatt, and he resisted the urge to slip an arm around her.

Instead, he scanned the area. They were standing outside in front of a worn-out New York–New

York. The area was lit by streetlamps, but it was still shadowy from the night. A smattering of people were moving about, talking in groups or rushing from place to place. Inside, more people were in the pub or the common areas. An albino wouldn't be hard to find even in the dim light. He could take care of him in about thirty seconds . . .

His gaze panned back and clashed with Simon's. The very same deathly look was in his dark eyes, but he gave Wyatt a subtle shake of the head. *Not the way, brother.*

Fuck that, Wyatt flashed back.

"It's too late," Elliott spoke up. He may or may not have read the unspoken dialogue between his friends. "Goldwyn's probably safely out there with his friends in the Humvees. Waiting for the countdown, twenty-four hours from now."

"Vaughn wants to meet in his office at midnight," Simon said. "Go over all the options. The city council is meeting now and he'll have their recommendation by then."

"That's nice," Wyatt sneered. "I'm sure we'll be kissing their collective ass and going along with whatever they decide is the best move."

Elliott's mouth twitched. "Vaughn's playing the game. He has to. This might be the last bastion of civilization, but it's still a democracy. Er . . . to some extent," he added when he saw Wyatt's expression.

"Let's go," Wyatt said abruptly, looking down at Remy. "We'll be back at midnight," he added to the others as he drew her away.

Remy found herself walking quickly to keep up with Wyatt's long, purposeful strides. She supposed it was best to be moving, for it was less likely someone would catch sight of her beneath a streetlight or the flashes of neon.

She wasn't really worried about being easily recognized. After all, it wasn't as if Goldwyn had a photograph of her that he would be showing around. Nevertheless, as Wyatt went into the community kitchen to scrounge up some food, she stayed off in a corner, pretending to be examining an old painting on the wall. She couldn't remember the last time she'd eaten, and when he handed her a sandwich, she realized she was ravenous. They ate and drank quickly, still lingering in the corner, Remy with her back to the room at large, then he said, "Come on."

A few minutes and several flights of stairs later, Wyatt opened the door to his room (or so she assumed; true to form, he hadn't actually given her any explanation as to where they were going) and she stepped inside. Closing the door, he flipped a switch and the soft glow from a series of wall sconces and lamps filled the space.

The room was simple, sparse and neat. Moonlight shone through the open curtains and large windows on one wall. A row of books lined the windowsill; too far away for her to see the titles. The bed was made, its sheets and coverlet tight and sharply creased, the pillows positioned at right angles, their cases smooth and wrinkle-free. A few items sat on one dresser and in a small square pile on the floor. She could see a hint of the bathroom through an ajar door, smell the faint, pleasant scent of man clinging to the space, and noticed a small rectangular object on the table next to the bed.

"Your stuff's over there," Wyatt said, jerking his head toward a bundle on the dresser.

"My stuff?"

"Your things from the truck."

"Really?" She was over to the bureau in a flash. Her pack—which she'd had to leave behind during the craziness of the zombie attack and her slim chance to slip away—was there, and filled with her stuff. "How did—you must have gone back the next morning," she said, answering her own question before she could even ask it.

It was all there: her new tank tops, the bras and panties, the cute blue sundress, and the other treasures she'd found. "Oh, thank you for going back to get my things, Wyatt. You have no idea—*thank you*." Then, a little embarrassed by the naked emotion in her tones, she glanced over to see his reaction.

She caught him by surprise; she must have, for he whipped his attention away from her. But not before she saw the look in his glittering eyes. Heat, raw and dark.

Her belly dropped, her mouth went dry, and she faltered, her attention skittering away as if she'd seen something she shouldn't have. Something so private and personal that she had to pretend it didn't exist. Her insides were a tangle, fluttering and hot and confused, and she didn't know what to say, how to react—of course she couldn't react. His now stony expression, bordering on angry, discouraged any sort of response. His stiff posture, his fists, tight at his sides, his flat, cool eyes.

"No problem," he said, turning away to dig through what appeared to be his own pack.

And then, as she tried to find a way out of the awkward moment, Remy noticed the other item on the dresser. A thick, heavy, hard-covered book. Com-

pletely intact. "*The Count of Monte Cristo*," she
said, picking it up. Her heart thumped, hard.

"I thought you might want to finish it," he said,
still busy with his back to her. His voice sounded
strange. "Since you never did."

Something shimmered through her, warm and
tingly, swelling inside her like a warm flower blos-
soming large. "Thank you." Her reply, she realized,
was hardly more than a whisper. "This is your copy?"
She glanced toward the makeshift bookshelf.

He stilled for a moment, then went over to draw
the curtains closed, hiding the books on the sill. "I
. . . uh . . . came across an old library on the way back
here and scavenged around to see if I could find it."

"You just came across an old library?" Remy's
heart was thumping harder now, and that warm rush
continued to bloom through her insides. "Just by accident? Really." *And just happened to find a copy of
this book?* She turned to face him. His expression
had eased into chagrin and impatience layered with
chill.

A man at war with himself.

"It was only a little out of the way," he said. De-
fensively.

Remy put the book down. Before she realized it,
she'd walked across the room toward him. Stark
panic flared in his eyes when he realized she'd positioned herself so he was trapped in the corner by the
curtain pull, or he'd have to actually walk past her—
possibly brush against her—to move away.

"You could have just told me how it ended," she
said, looking up at him. *Whoa.* He was so close,
so solid, so dark and forbidding . . . and yet at the
same time, he looked like little more than a trapped

animal. Her chest swelled and she found it hard to breathe. "Instead of taking the chance of being found by the zombies. While carrying my crystal." She let her voice drop low, let the huskiness slide into it.

"What the hell are you doing, Remy?" His voice was sharp and hard, and she saw the defenses shoot up like a shield. His lips went taut and he actually held up a hand, as if to ward her off.

"Thanking you."

"Great, you've thanked me. Now could you—"

But she'd taken his upheld hand and raised it so she could see better in the light. His skin was warm, his wrist solid and strong. But something else had her attention. "What's all this black stuff?" she said, looking at the delicate skin on the underside of his wrist. There was black in the creases there, which wasn't so unusual in itself . . . but a patch of it was flaking off . . . almost like a burn. "Is this from the fire? You *did* get burned, didn't you?"

Wyatt snatched his arm away and pushed past her. He strode across the room, and when he turned, he was grinding his thumb and forefinger into his eyes and the bridge of his nose. "I'll tell you about it. But first, I'm going to shower. Get the rest of it off."

Remy blinked. "Get the rest of what—"

But he was already stalking toward the front door, throwing the bolt lock into place with a loud clank, clicking the chain lock into its slot. "Do not open the door to anyone," he said, his eyes boring into her. "Anyone. I don't care who they are."

"What if Elliott or Que—"

"*No one*, Remy," he said, already on his way to the other room. He paused on the threshold to the bathroom. "If someone comes to the door, you let me know."

"Right. I'm going to walk in on you in the shower?" she said, just to see what his reaction would be.

"*Knock,*" he said, then slammed the door shut.

Remy stared after him, shaking her head as she heard the spray of water start in the shower. And then she couldn't help but picture what was happening on the other side of that door: Wyatt peeling off his shirt, sliding out of those long jeans and whatever he wore beneath. She felt hot and breathless, unable to keep her imagination from running rampant. With a chest like his, arms and shoulders as sleek and muscular as they were, legs so long and lean . . . she knew the rest of him had to be worth going breathless and fluttery over.

But . . . jeez . . . Wyatt. He was an angry jerk of a man who couldn't seem to let himself feel.

A man at war with himself.

Jade was right; there was no better way to describe him.

Despite that, Remy still found herself wanting to be with him. Attracted to him, yes—who the hell wouldn't be?—but despite his prickly nature, his moods, and that underlying rage, she was drawn to him. She trusted him. Cared about him. Sometimes even liked him.

Am I crazy?

Her attention went back to the book. To the pile of her things on the dresser. To the fact that he'd stolen her crystal and kept it in order to protect her from the zombies. And that, while carrying it, he'd taken a detour to an old library . . . and then that moment in Cat's room, when he'd realized she was there. An instant of naked emotion.

That burst of heat swelled inside her once more, making her a little light-headed. He did care. He didn't want to, but he did. In some way, some small way, he cared about her.

But was it worth it to try and find out how much? Especially . . .

The rush of cold fear swept away her soft, bubbly, warm feelings. Reality returned, gouging out the heat and leaving her empty and cold in the pit of her stomach.

Less than a day. What am I going to do?

The options were pretty limited. And although she'd tried not to think about it too much, Remy knew what she would have to do. After all, there was no way to keep the city safe from an attack by the Strangers—especially since they seemed to have helicopters, and who knew what other weapons. How did one protect people from dropped bombs and mechanical vehicles in this day and age?

And now that there was no way to evacuate the city . . .

Her insides twisted, sharp and hard. There wasn't much choice. There wasn't any choice, really. She'd have to go to them. Find out what they wanted . . . even though she pretty much knew.

At least she could leave the crystal here . . . maybe as a bargaining chip. That might keep her alive.

But she sure as hell didn't want the crystal getting into the hands of the Strangers. One life wasn't worth the havoc they'd be sure to wreak once they had the Mother crystal.

A sharp knock on the door startled her out of her thoughts, and Remy froze, her breath catching. She glanced at the bathroom, heard the sounds of spraying water, then back at the door. Someone knocked again, harder and more loudly.

Heart thumping, she tiptoed over and looked through the peephole. David and Cat stood there and she reached for the chain lock, then hesitated.

No one.

What put Wyatt in control of her life? Why did she have to listen to him? This was Cat and David . . . they'd already helped her. Both of them. She trusted them—just as much as she trusted Wyatt.

But her hand fell away and Remy stepped back from the door, not altogether certain why she didn't open it. Was it because she trusted Wyatt's judgment over her own? Or because she knew that any interruption would disrupt their time together?

Moments later she heard David and Cat move away, their voices low as they went off down the hall. And only then did she go to the bathroom door and knock.

The water stopped immediately, and before she could consider whether she should peek in, the door cracked open. She expected warmth and steam to come rolling out, but there was only Wyatt.

"What happened?" He poked his face around, his hair dripping in crazy dark wings, his eyes sharp and alert. She could see only a glimpse of tanned neck and a sliver of water-dappled shoulder before she jerked her attention away.

"David and Cat just came to the door and knocked. I didn't answer," she added before he could respond. "They went away."

"Good. Be out in a sec." He shut the door.

Oh God, I hope he doesn't come out in a towel. Or maybe I do. Remy bit her lip, looking at the closed bathroom door. She felt flushed and warm again.

If he did, she didn't know where she'd look. Or what she'd do.

In an effort to distract herself, she walked around the room, looking at his things. The neat pile of clothing on the other dresser. His pack on the floor, with a variety of other things she recognized from the semi-truck: the first aid kit, duct tape, the box with Trojan on it, a pair of boots. Then she wandered over to the table next to the bed. Earlier, she'd noticed the small rectangular item, a hand-sized, sleek electronic device. A cord ran from it down behind the table, and when she picked it up, the surface lit to show a picture. Remy's breath caught and she went still, something sharp and sad twisting inside her.

The picture was of a woman and two children, all smiling and beautiful. Heartbreaking in their beauty.

This is why.

She nodded to herself, still looking at the picture, seeing the bright, laughing eyes of the red-haired girl whose face was an explosion of freckles, the mischievous grin on the towheaded boy's face—he looked like a devilish one—and, the wide, white smile of the woman, whose blond-brown hair curled in a riot around her face, held back at the top by a sparkly barrette. She had a sweet, happy face that wouldn't be called striking so much as pretty or perky. Intelligence and warmth shone in her eyes, even in this picture.

She must have been looking at someone she loved. And who loved her in return.

The bathroom door opened and Remy put the device down with a clatter. Turning, guilt written all over her face, she faced Wyatt.

His eyes went from her to the table and back

again, but he said nothing as he walked over to one of the dressers and yanked open a drawer. He was, as she'd feared, wearing nothing but a towel. Rivulets of water ran down over his arms and neck, dripping from too-long hair plastered to his skin, and she couldn't help but admire his long, lean back and the slide of muscle there as he dug through the drawer.

But the tension was different now. Her awareness of him was tempered by sorrow and sympathy, and the reality of what he'd lost. A feeling of inadequacy. And discomfort at being caught snooping.

He disappeared into the bathroom again, then came out moments later wearing a T-shirt that clung to his damp skin and a pair of loose, drawstring shorts. He'd shaved, but his face was still tight and drawn.

"Now that you've assuaged your curiosity," he said, his voice cool and remote. "I suppose I owe you a little more of an explanation."

"You don't owe me anything," she replied automatically, forcing herself to use the same emotionless tone.

His mouth quirked without humor. "Another bad movie line. Yet, there are some things you should know . . . about me, and the others. Before we meet downstairs. In"—he glanced at his watch—"forty-five minutes."

"Fine."

"Have a seat," he said, and sat down in a chair as far away from her as possible.

She sat on the edge of the bed and leveled a stare at him.

"Quent, Elliott, and I went on a hiking and caving trip in the mountains of Sedona, Arizona. Fence and another guy named Lenny were our guides. While we were in there, all hell broke loose—there were earthquakes, storms, all kinds of events. Something happened and we were knocked unconscious. When we woke up, we found Simon there, too, and we all came out of the cave." He focused his gaze on her, steady and intent. "It was fifty years later."

Remy blinked and tried to assimilate his words. "Fifty or fifteen?" she said, knowing what she'd heard, but knowing it was impossible. Yet, his expression was one of calm certainty.

"Fifty. A half a century."

"So you're telling me . . . you . . . what . . . ?" She worked to grasp the concept, to wrap her mind around his words. She shook her head. Crazy. "How?"

"We don't know. Time-traveled, maybe. Frozen in time, maybe. We don't know. All we know is, one minute it was June of 2010, and then when we woke up or came to, it was 2060. And the world . . . was . . ." His voice cracked.

Gone.

She looked at him for a long moment, and he met her eyes unflinchingly. Truth shone there. "Really?" she said finally in a low voice.

He nodded. "Really."

"So . . . you're . . . really old." Remy wasn't certain why *that* was the first thing that came out of her mouth. She wasn't certain if she really believed him. But . . . hell, if there were zombies, and immortal beings, and crystals that could kill merely by their presence . . . she supposed time travel wasn't completely out of the realm of possibility.

Before he could respond to her silly, thoughtless

statement, she spoke again. "I can't imagine how terrible that must have been. For you." Her attention slipped over to the bedside table and its device with the photo, then back again. "I'm sorry, Wyatt."

He nodded, and she saw his throat work as he forced himself to swallow. "I . . . kissed my wife and children goodbye one day and got on a plane. The next thing I knew, it was fifty years later . . . and they were gone. *Everything* was gone. Every fucking thing."

Remy felt sick. "Wyatt." Her eyes stung and a horrible, empty ache swept over her. How could anyone handle that? How could anyone be normal, sane . . . happy . . . after that? "My God. I'm so sorry."

"If I hadn't gotten on that plane . . . if I hadn't left them . . ."

He didn't seem to be talking to her any longer . . . the words tumbled out quietly, taut with grief and guilt and desolation. She didn't remember getting up, getting out of her chair. But the next thing she knew, she was sliding her arms around his shoulders, sliding onto his lap, pulling him into her. Close to her.

She felt a tremor ripple over his wide shoulders, the stiffness in his arms and neck, the ragged breaths. His hair pressed wet against her cheek, dripping and seeping into the front of her shirt, sleek and cold under her hands. But his body melted against her, warm and solid, and for a moment . . . just a moment . . . she closed her eyes. Breathed in, smelled him, felt that little fluttering warmth in her belly. *Ah, Wyatt.*

He moved, gently taking her arms from around him, extricating himself. "I . . . Remy, there's more. And I can't . . . think . . . when you're—when—like this." He kept his face averted as he slipped away, standing to walk across the room.

She watched him, settling into the chair he'd vacated, waiting. Patient, horrified and devastated.

"It's been a year," he said, his voice stronger now. "Since we came out of that cave. One of the guys— Lenny—died shortly after. But the rest of us, the five of us . . . we've changed." He glanced at her now, sort of sidewise, as if to gauge her reaction. "We can do . . . things. Each of us has an ability we didn't have before. Elliott isn't just a doctor anymore, but now he can heal with the touch of his hands—but there's a sort of backlash when he does it. And he can sort of see what's going on inside someone. Quent can touch something and see its past, read its history—but he gets sucked into a trancelike, coma sort of state. That's why Zoë won't let him touch the Mother crystal. She's afraid it's too powerful and he won't come back out of it."

Remy was aware that her jaw had fallen open, and she closed it.

"Simon . . . well . . ." Wyatt gave a strained chuckle, "I wouldn't believe it if I hadn't seen it myself, but he can turn himself invisible. That's how we got past Dantès, that first time we met—when you set him to guard us. Simon turned invisible and sneaked past him."

She wanted to shake her head, to tell him he was crazy . . . but Wyatt? He might be a jerk, he might be arrogant and commandeering and cold . . . but he wasn't crazy.

"Let me guess," Remy said, somehow finding her voice. The pieces—as improbable as they were—had fallen into place. "You can walk through a fire and not burn up?"

His eyes glinted briefly with appreciation. "Basically. I do burn . . . but then it . . . peels away. Or at least, that's what happened last night. I didn't know it would happen. That's the first time . . . and I don't really know if it would happen again. I'm not particularly eager to find out."

Remy looked at him, and he stared back for what seemed like a long time. "You realize how crazy this all sounds," she finally said.

"No shit." He ran a hand through his hair. "There's one more thing." When she didn't respond, he continued. "David . . . well, he's my son."

His son. "Wow." She tilted her head, thought about that. More pieces fell into place as she remembered the moment in Cat's room when Wyatt realized she was there. That moment when he gathered her up to him as if he'd never let her go . . . and then the shields, falling back into place once again. She tried to smile. Now it all made sense. "So that makes Cat . . . your granddaughter?"

His expression reflected the same wonder and confusion she was feeling. "Yes." There was even the ghost of a smile—the slightest bit of happy—playing about his lips.

Remy laughed softly, shaking her head. "Well, she's going to be a little disappointed to know you're her grandfather."

He frowned. "What? Why?"

"I saw the way she was checking you out. She thinks you're hot." Somehow, teasing him a little felt . . . right. It eased the tension, just enough.

"Christ," he muttered.

Silence fell only for a moment, then a sharp rap at

the door had them both looking up. Wyatt made a sharp gesture to Remy, sending her toward the bathroom, but she frowned and shook her head.

He glared as the knock came again, but went to the door and looked through the peephole. His shoulders relaxed and, with a rueful smile at Remy, he unbolted and unchained the door and opened it.

"Well, Grandfather," said Cat as she breezed in. "How wonderful to meet you."

CHAPTER 21

Nineteen hours

Wyatt and Remy were a half hour late to the midnight meeting with Vaughn and the others. The tardiness was due to the unexpected arrival of David and Cat and the sort of family reunion that occurred between grandfather and granddaughter.

But when he and Remy walked into the mayor's private office, Fence looked at Wyatt knowingly and winked. "Duu-uude."

Wyatt gave him a fuck-you glare and went to stand across the room where he could watch or pace, and yet be out of the line of sight. He was also, purposely, near the door.

"Nice of you to join us," Vaughn said. He seemed to make no effort for civility in his tones. Wyatt couldn't really blame him, but he wasn't in the mood to be benevolent. "I trust there were no problems that delayed you?" added the mayor. "Remy hasn't been identified?"

"No problems," said the woman in question, looking around as she selected a chair. She'd been ecstatic about changing into some of the clothing he'd rescued for her, and while Wyatt, David, and Cat were talking, Remy showered and changed into her new clothes. Problem was, she'd pulled on a sleek blue tank top that made it hard to look anywhere but there. And then there was the question that popped into his mind . . . was she wearing the thong, or the lacy black panties?

Hell.

This was, Wyatt reminded himself, viciously re-routing his thoughts, the first time she had been in this room, meeting with the mayor and his friends. She seemed at ease, surprisingly so, and smiled when Sage reached over to squeeze her arm. The two women exchanged brief words, and then Remy looked over at Jade and nodded. The other woman patted her on the shoulder, concern lining her face.

Wyatt leaned against the wall and folded his arms over his chest. "Well?"

"The city council has decided it's in the best interest of the city to turn Remington Truth over to the Strangers," Vaughn announced.

"The city council can go fuck itself." Wyatt would have swept Remy up and been through the door if Simon hadn't moved. Strong fingers closed over his forearm and the other man placed himself in Wyatt's path.

"Wait."

It was the calmness and fierce understanding in Simon's exotic eyes that had Wyatt easing back into his place. He allowed himself a brief glance at Remy, careful not to linger too long—just enough to see that she wasn't horrified or upset. Sage still held her hand, their fingers clasped together.

"The council feels," Vaughn continued as if there

hadn't been an interruption, as if he hadn't just delivered a damned death sentence, "that there is no
way to protect Envy or otherwise divert an attack by
the Strangers. If they come in by helicopter, dropping
explosives, we have no recourse. They have motorized vehicles as well—we have no idea what other
sorts of weapons they have. We're sitting ducks, and
they've ensured that the evacuation process has been
halted. The buildings are old, and although well-
maintained, it's clear that warlike activity can and
will destroy them and cause innumerable casualties."
He looked around at them all. Dark circles swelled
under his sunken eyes and the grooves in his face had
grown more pronounced. "There's simply no way to
protect the people of Envy. And I am in agreement
with them."

He looked over, his steady, calm gaze clashing
with Wyatt's. It took his last iota of control to remain
quiet and still, allowing his eyes to deliver the message of *Fuck you, sonofabitch. I'll show you agreement.*

Vaughn looked away, transferring his attention to
Remy. "Let me be clear: I am in agreement that there
is no way to protect the city. But understand that I
am not, for one minute, suggesting that we turn you
over to the Strangers."

"Which means," Elliott said, breaking the snapping tension, "we have to find another option."

"What other option? There is no other option."
Remy stood abruptly, dragging her hand out of
Sage's grip. "There's no way to protect the city, no
way to get out of it, no place to be safe. That leaves
one choice: give them what they want."

"But it's not really you they want, is it?" Quent

pointed out, his voice clipped and formal, rising over the instant reactions of the others. The voices quieted. "They want the Mother crystal."

"We can't give them the Mother crystal," Ana exclaimed just as Remy said, "I've spent the last twenty years protecting that stone. My grandfather, for whatever reason, risked his life—and mine—to get and keep it. I'm sure as hell not going to just give it to them. Then what would stop them from attacking Envy anyway?"

"What would stop them from attacking us if we gave them *you*?" Wyatt snarled, pushing past Simon to glare at her. "Not a goddamn thing. They'll do what they want. They have the might, the weapons, the technology. So there's no sense in risking—"

"There are the tunnels," Jade pointed out, pitching her voice loud enough to hear over the others. "They don't know about the tunnels under the city. We can evacuate or at least hide down there—like bomb shelters. Even though there are wixy-big-ass snakes." She shuddered and glanced at Elliott.

"Already in progress," Vaughn said, looking at her. His smile was faint and humorless. "We've already begun to evacuate through them, but we have to do it carefully and slowly. If the Strangers find that entrance, they'll blockade it as well. So we're being very careful. And we don't know what information is being passed to them by Goldwyn or anyone else."

Wyatt felt some of his tension ease. At least someone was thinking. "The ocean?" he asked, looking at Fence and Ana.

For once the big man's expression was tight and sober. "Ain't no chance there. Ana and I were there checking things out. The motherfucking Atlanteans have their crazy shield up again—anyone tries to get past it in the water'll fry their asses."

"Which means," Ana said, "they've got to be in communication with the Strangers and are supporting them. The shield just appeared this morning. The timing isn't a coincidence."

"So we put some people safely below the ground, others in the sturdiest structures possible," Wyatt said, his mind clicking along. Hell, he hadn't been in a war in Iraq for nothing. "We have to have some defensive weapons of our own—Molotov cocktails at the very least. And others. We can hold them off—"

"*Listen.*"

Remy's voice cut into the discussion, and, surprisingly, everyone quieted and looked at her. She stood in front of Vaughn's desk, the center of attention, turning to look around the room. Hands on her hips, her glossy black hair pulled into a long, loose braid that fell over one shoulder, her startling cobalt eyes bright and steady, she spoke. "I'm the one they want. The only way to keep them from attacking Envy is to surrender myself to them. And I've decided that's what I'm going to do."

The room surged into a cacophony of negation, but Remy held up her hand and continued to speak. "I'm not finished. First of all, it's my choice. Second, there is *no way* I am going to stay hidden here, cloistered away, while the city is attacked—even if you believe there are some safe hiding places. Someone's going to get hurt or killed, and I don't want that on my conscience. You," she said, whirling to spear Wyatt with fierce eyes, "of all people should understand *that*."

He closed his mouth, pressing his lips into a hard

line. But that didn't keep him from glaring back at her. *Always knew she was fucking crazy.*

"And besides that," Remy continued, "we don't know why they want me—maybe they just want to talk—"

"Jesus Christ," Wyatt exploded. "Of course they don't just want to 'talk'—"

"They probably just want to know where the Mother crystal is." Remy raised her voice to be heard over his, lashing out at him. "And killing me or even hurting me won't get them what they want."

"Unless they just want to torture the information out of you," he shouted back. "Then it might hurt a *little fucking bit*!"

All at once he realized the room had gone silent, that he and Remy were nearly chest-to-chest in the middle of everyone, both heaving with anger, and everyone was looking everywhere but at them.

He stepped back, desperately channeling calm, spinning away even as his hands trembled with anger. And fear.

"The bottom line," Remy said, her voice low and subdued, her cheeks flushed red, her eyes averted from Wyatt, "is that it's my choice. And whether the rest of you support it or not, agree with it or not, it's what I'm going to do."

Wyatt opened his mouth, desperately searching for something to say, but Sage stood. She quelled him with a look, then turned to Remy, putting her arm around her. "Then it's our job to make it as safe for you as possible, you brave woman. You'll go with guards, with an escort. In full view. You can parlay, and we'll have your back."

Remy nodded, and Wyatt saw her lips move in a

tremulous smile. So she wasn't as foolishly fearless as she seemed. "Great plan. Thank you." She turned to Vaughn. "You can tell Goldwyn to bring the message."

The mayor nodded gravely. "Unless some other option presents itself between now and tomorrow night. Which it's my sincere hope it will," he added, rubbing her on the shoulder. "Remy, I'm sorry to tell you this, too, but the mob group led by Mary Proudy is getting louder and stronger. It's imperative that you remain anonymous and safe. My apartments are the most secure—"

"She'll stay with me," Wyatt said, easing away from the wall. His movements were deliberately casual, but the look he gave Vaughn was not. The room stilled, quieted, and he didn't understand why.

"Is that all right with you, Remy?" asked Vaughn, purposely placing himself so Wyatt couldn't see her face, his back presented to him.

"Yes."

"Let's get the hell out of here," Wyatt said. Done. He was done with this, done with all of this. And his hands were shaking.

For safety reasons, a large group accompanied Remy and Wyatt back to his room. But none of them lingered; in fact, they seemed eager to be off—with the exception of Fence, who stepped into the room and wandered around, looking about as if to ensure its security hadn't been breached. Or maybe he was just being nosy. He bounced his palm on the tightly made bed and glanced at Wyatt.

"Haven't lost your touch," said the massive man

with a feckless grin. "You could flip a quarter on this mo-fo."

Suddenly nervous, Remy hesitated as she stepped over the threshold . . . then pushed on. This could be her last night sleeping easy—at least as easy as she could, knowing what was on the horizon for tomorrow—for a while. She wouldn't feel safer with anyone other than Wyatt. There wasn't anywhere else she wanted to be other than here.

She was safe here.

"Holy shit, dude. Where the hell'd you get this? A whole motherfucking box of *Trojans*?" Fence had a huge smile on his face as he swept down to pick it up from the pile on the floor. "Dang! *Un*opened? What the hell—"

"Get the fuck out of here," Wyatt said, shoving the man toward the door. "Take the damn things with you."

"Hell, bro, I think you're fixin' to need 'em more than me," laughed Fence, throwing the box back at Wyatt as he spun out into the hall. "Do you some—"

"Christ, Fence, shut the hell up—"

"Might want to actually *open* the—"

The door slammed shut, obliterating whatever Fence was saying. But Remy heard his giddy, high-pitched laugh even through the door, fading as he walked off.

At least someone was having a good time.

Wyatt turned from the door. If she didn't know better, she'd think he looked almost flustered. He snatched up the purple box from the floor and slammed it into one of the dresser drawers. "*Don't ask.*"

Okay, then.

"I'm going to sleep on the floor in front of the door," he said, grabbing a pillow off the bed. "In case anyone tries to come in."

"We could get Dantès. He'd be a good guard," she suggested.

"He's down in the computer lab, safe. And guarding the crystal. I think I can handle this," he said, his voice wry.

"Right." Remy looked around, suddenly, acutely, uncomfortable. She hadn't thought about putting him out of his bed. She hadn't really thought about this at all. "Vaughn's got an extra bedroom—"

"You want to sleep with Vaughn tonight?" he snapped back. "Is that it?"

"Uh—"

"I can arrange it if that's what you want."

"Maybe this wasn't such a good idea," she ventured.

"Maybe you'd feel safer in the mayor's private suite," he shot back.

They stared at each other from across the room. Remy was aware that her heart was racing, that her insides were all out of sorts. Shaking her head, she turned away. Listlessly, she picked up the remaining pillow and hugged it to her chest.

"No," she managed to say, closing her eyes as she buried her face in the cotton. Of course it smelled like him. "Strangely enough, I feel safest with you."

Wyatt gave a muffled curse and she heard a dull, hard thump. "You don't have to do this," he said. His voice was still hard. Cold as ice. "We can find another way."

"There is no other way," she replied wearily. "I've thought about it and thought about it. I suppose I always knew this day would come—the day I'd have to make a decision about the crystal, the day of truth, I guess. The day it all came clear. Maybe I've been preparing for it for the last twenty years. But at least it'll be over."

She looked up, still hugging the pillow, just able to see above its snowy white case. He was across the room, remote and distant, figuratively as well as literally. *This was a mistake.*

She didn't know what she'd been thinking. That maybe her last safe night might be . . . pleasant? Comforting?

"Don't look at me . . . like that," he said. She could see his jaw moving, the shadows beneath his cheekbones shifting, but his eyes were hidden.

Remy turned away, lifting her head proudly. Definitely a mistake. But what had she expected? She was aware of the stiffness of her movements as she returned the pillow to its place on the bed, walked to the bathroom, closed the door, splashed cold—very cold—water on her face, wiped away what could have been a few tears if she actually let them come.

Remington Truth. *I'm Remington Truth. I can get through this.*

If I can get through what Seattle did to me, I can get through this.

When she opened the door, he was standing there. Tall, dark, tense. Present.

"Remy."

She looked up at him, everything inside her cascading into a messy heap, and she walked into his arms. They came around her, slowly and with control. Her face pressed against his throat. He was warm and damp, his skin smelling of comfort and familiarity.

His heart thumped beneath her, matching her own racing one.

He moved his cheek and jaw, caressing the top of her head. She was aware of the subtlest of tremors in the arms that held her. Her eyelashes caught against his skin as she closed her eyes, and drawing in a deep breath, she pressed a kiss on the madly pumping vein at the side of his throat. Her tongue slipped out just for a moment, tasting salt and heat and man, and he shuddered a little. His arms tightened, then eased.

Remy was prepared for him to push her away, but instead one hand moved, sliding up beneath her braid, as the other pulled off its tie. His fingers, warm at the nape of her neck, combed into her hair, loosening the plait, spreading its three parts into one wavy fall. He rubbed it between the pads of his fingers, pulling gently as if to test its texture, then tenderly massaged her skull as she sagged into him.

She kissed him again, with more boldness this time . . . burrowing into the warmth at the juncture of neck and shoulder, sliding her lips and tongue over smooth, sensitive skin. His breathing changed, his muscles went rigid, and she kept at it, moving to his earlobe, flickering her tongue in the hot, secret place behind it.

The fact that he wanted her was starkly evident; their bodies were pressed together, separated only by clothing and whatever other baggage they each carried. Acutely aware of this, she nuzzled him on the jaw, glad he'd shaved earlier, enjoying the taste of his skin. At last, Wyatt dipped his head to meet her lips, loosening his arms just enough to angle in. During that brief moment, before she sagged into the kiss, she saw his eyes closed, his brows drawn tightly together.

Hot, slick, and deep, the kiss went on like a long, slow ride. Tangled and sensual, easy . . . as if they could go forever. There was care and tenderness in his touch, and Remy felt a well of emotion starting to rise inside. *Oh, yes. This.* This.

His hands moved up along her hips, sliding under her tank top. Warm fingers brushed her bare skin and she shivered, pleasure rushing along beneath his touch. Her bra tightened and released, then his palms covered her bare back, pulling her tight against him, traveling along the curve of her spine and back up to settle below her shoulder blades.

It was then she realized he'd eased himself against the wall, gathering her up to his broad, solid torso. One of her feet slid between his, and she felt the pressure of his thigh between her legs as she melted against him. He buried his face in her neck, that sensitive place beyond her throat, his lips and tongue sleek and warm. She vibrated gently as the bolt of pleasure caught her by surprise, rushing south to her belly and beyond.

After a moment he eased back and looked down. His dark eyes delved into hers. "Remy . . . I'm not sure this is a good idea." His voice was gritty and low, but he didn't release her.

She laid her hand flat on his chest. His heart thudded like crazy, matching her own, and when he remained silent, she said, "Tell me why."

Wyatt shook his head, tipping it back to lean against the wall, and held her, still gathered up against him, one of her legs embraced by his, the other straddling his thigh. His hands still covered her back, warm beneath her tank top. She admired his throat, long and tanned and strong; saw the pulse beating where she'd kissed him. A smattering of hair poked from the collar of his T-shirt, more thick dark hair brushed his neck.

His throat moved as he swallowed, his jaw shifted as he seemed to grope for words. "Tomorrow . . . we don't know what's going to happen. We should be thinking about other things. Finding another way, another option. Planning, preparing, doing *something*. This isn't what you should be doing . . . tonight. Tomorrow could be—"

"This is exactly what I want to be doing tonight, Wyatt. Do you really think I want to go to . . . whatever will be tomorrow—captivity, death—"

"Christ, Remy—" He lifted his head, his arms tightening, feet shifting, moving her.

"—I want to have something good to take with me."

"—there's got to be another way. I—"

"But it's really not about me," she went on doggedly, and he fell silent. "It's you. It's the guilt. The pain. Wyatt, I understand that, oh God, I *really* do—and I don't take it personally. I don't think I'd be ready either, if I went through what you have. I didn't think *I'd* be ready so soon." Memories of Seattle flickered at the corner of her mind, and she closed them off sharply. *No.* Easing out of his embrace, Remy let her hand fall from his chest. "It's all right, Wyatt. I'm truly not upset."

She wasn't. She wanted comfort, she wanted affection, she wanted *him*. But not if he wasn't ready. Not if he couldn't move on, just a little. Pain and anguish took time to work through. She understood that better than most.

And she was used to being solo. And tomorrow

she would be, once again, having to live by her own bravery and wits.

"That's the problem," he said, his voice gritty. "It's too easy. After everything . . . it's too easy. How can it be so easy, to be—to *want* you?" The last part came out in a low, pained accusation. "And at the same time . . . it's so fucking *hard*."

He drew in a deep breath and reached out, touching the ends of her hair. The backs of his fingers brushed against her collarbone as he filtered through the heavy waves. It was all she could do to keep from leaning back into him. "Most of all, Remy . . . I don't want to hurt you," he murmured.

"You won't. You couldn't." *Not after what I've been through.* Those horrific memories hovered, always ready to surge into her consciousness at any opportunity. She battled them back the way Selena had taught her and steadied herself firmly into *here*. With him. "Now, will you please take off your shirt?"

Her command drew a short, surprised huff of laughter from him. But it was gone almost immediately and his eyes remained uncertain. "You're sure?" Concern eclipsed the pain and indecision that had been in his expression.

A little flicker of darkness stopped her from a flippant reply, but Wyatt's sensitivity to that made her even more certain. "Yes. But . . ."

"I'll take it slow." And now she saw a lick of heat and promise in his eyes. It sent a delicious shiver through her belly. "*Very* slow." She smiled back, relief and promise of her own blazing there, and his eyes flared in response. Then he sobered again. "But stop me . . . tell me . . . if you're not okay."

She nodded. "Now can we stop talking? I think I

liked you better when you were grumpy and didn't want to talk."

"I was never grumpy," he said, and slid his hands beneath her tank top again. This time they curved around to the front of her, covering her breasts, pressing gently into the tight points of her nipples. He gave a soft *whuff* of breath and slid his arms around to bring her back to him, covering her mouth with his. She closed her eyes and sank in.

"Your shirt," she murmured when he moved to her neck again, his mouth hot and demanding against her sensitive skin. She gave a shiver as he found that most delicate of places. One hand slid down beneath the waistband of her jeans, pulling her up against his hips . . . and then she was off the ground . . . then the bed appeared beneath her.

He settled her there gently, then yanked off his shirt as he walked over to the dresser and dropped it in a wad on top. Opening a drawer, he fumbled around in it. When he turned back, he wore an odd, almost bashful expression. He was holding something small and flat in his hand, but Remy hardly noticed. She was openly admiring the rest of him: the tight, sleek muscles of his pecs, covered with dark hair that narrowed down over a flat belly, the squared-off edges of broad shoulders, the delicious golden color of his skin, the swell of biceps. The loose shorts rode low on his hips, his arousal ruining their shape but making her heart skip a beat nevertheless; and long, muscular legs extended below, morphing into the elegant feet she remembered from the truck.

She swore she stopped breathing for a minute—he was just so *gorgeous*—and then, biting her lip to keep from gawking openmouthed, she kicked off her shoes and lay back on the bed, watching him. He put the small packet on the table next to them and eased down next to her.

"Did you know when you walked back to camp without your shirt on, I was pretty much drooling?" Remy said, feeling a little self-conscious. "I didn't dare look at you for fear you'd notice."

His lips moved in something like a smile, and even the corners of his eyes crinkled a little. "Did you know I hated that white tank top, for the same reason? But I kind of like this one," he said, helping her out of it, and then her loosened bra as well. He made a soft sound of appreciation that pinged deliciously in her belly and made her throb down low.

She flushed as he looked down at her, his tanned hand moving over her lighter skin, cupping one of her breasts. He was gentle, lifting it, using a thumb to trace over its sensitive point . . . sending a shiver of heat licking through her. She watched his elegant fingers, dark against light, hard against soft . . . There was a moment, a brief flash, when one of those ugly images—brutal hands, rough and invasive—tried to usurp the moment.

"Remy?" he stilled, looking up and into her eyes.

She allowed herself to be caught by his gaze, and her tension eased . . . the dark memory fading. She smiled, reaching up to curve her fingers around his warm neck. "I'm okay." And then she did something she'd been wanting to do for more than a week: smoothed her hand down over his chest.

She loved it: the heat of his skin, the crisp roughness of the hair, the firm muscle beneath . . . the delicate goose bumps that rose on him in the wake of her touch. He gave a little shiver of his own then bent to kiss her: her lips, her chin, her breast. When his hot mouth closed over her tight, ready nipple, she arched up, giving a soft gasp, her fingers curling into his shoulder. His eyes flickered toward her, but his lips and tongue were busy: swirling, sucking, teasing.

Pleasure rolled through her, hot and liquid leaving little throbbing teases in its wake. They settled prone onto the bed, warm skin sliding against warm skin, legs entwined, his mouth doing crazy things to her, his hand finding its way between her legs. The pressure through her jeans was just enough to have her rolling her hips, pushing back, wanting more.

"Let's see," he murmured, sliding her somehow unfastened jeans down from her hips, "which of your new things you're wearing."

If the low, growling sound he made was any indication, the black lace panties had been a good choice. She reached for him, groping for the ties to his loose shorts, but he stopped her, pressing her hand to his warm, flat belly. "Not a good idea," he said, his mouth quirking oddly. "Not yet."

Before she had the chance to protest, he moved again, shifting alongside her, sliding his hand down beneath the black lace. Remy stilled, drawing in a surprised breath when he touched her . . . gently at first, lightly . . . and all the time she felt him watching her. Watching for any sign that she might slip away.

She didn't. He was next to her, she could see and breathe and was free. And there was too much heat and pleasure, too much need pounding gently between her legs. His fingers were deft and delicate but very sure, and his breath became rougher as she vibrated and shivered and sighed. He kissed her, covering her mouth, taking in the low, husky gasp of pleasure as she grew tighter and readier.

Everything dissolved but him: the smell and taste, the unsteady pitch of his breathing, the slow, insistent tease of his hand between her legs. He murmured something soft and throaty in her ear, but she felt only the heat of his words, smelled the delicious scent of this man . . . then she forgot everything but the sharp, spiral of pleasure.

It exploded, trammeling through her in undulating waves of heat and brightness . . . and she smiled in relief and triumph. A moment later, still hot and rolling with pleasure, she opened her eyes to find Wyatt watching her.

"Now," he said, his eyes burning, his face tight, his breath rough.

"Yes," she said, a pang of anticipation shocking her so close on the heels of complete bliss. She reached for his shorts, pulling at the tie; and when it wouldn't loosen, he pushed her hands away with characteristic impatience.

Moments later he was there, long and lean and naked, more beautiful than she'd imagined, sliding alongside her. She could tell, in the back of her pleasure-fogged brain, that he was taking care, still, not to be rough or demanding, not to do anything that would tip her into those dark memories.

But she saw the hunger in his face—pure and good rather than malevolent—and she recognized the price of his restraint . . . and so she set him free. And herself.

CHAPTER 22

One moment Remy was sprawled in a sensual bundle next to Wyatt, her dark blue eyes heavy-lidded with pleasure, an arm thrown up over her head, lifting her breast into a perfect orb . . . and the next, she was all over him.

Her mouth, her hands, were suddenly everywhere, her soft, insanely sexy body pressing against him, rubbing, sliding. She had his cock in her hands before he realized it, and that alone nearly sent him spinning . . . but Wyatt caught himself in time. Just in time. And impossible as it was, he slid from her grasp, twisting away just enough to keep his brain clear.

But he couldn't keep his hands off her, nor from licking and sucking on her glorious breasts and raspberry nipples, his face from burying into her long, sweet-smelling hair. His fingers carried her essence, musky and rich from pleasure, and the scent filled his nostrils as the rest of him raged and wanted. His belly trembled when she kissed along his chest, down, down to where his cock throbbed, ready to explode.

He had to close his eyes, count, think of the furiously cold shower he'd taken today, remind himself he had to be easy, slow, tender . . . but it was damned hard when she was sliding all over him, nipping at his shoulder and making all sorts of sexy noises.

It was when she began to straddle him, sliding her damp, slick, musky self over his thigh and hip that he lost his mind and flipped her over smartly onto her back. The air whooshed from her and her eyes went wide and shocked, and Wyatt froze, cursing himself for stupidity, bracing himself for whatever was to follow.

But instead of fear in her eyes, he saw desire and heat, temptation and welcome, and at that point he let go and dove in. He devoured soft lips, tasted salty skin, slid his tongue long and slowly around a hard, nubbly nipple . . . then drew it into his mouth, dancing his tongue around the tight pink areola, catching his breath when she sighed and trembled with pleasure. His fingers found her sleek, swollen heat, making her twitch with tantalizing little shivers and deep, throaty moans that made him crazy. He made her come again—watched her face go tight, then joyous, and knew she'd won another small battle. The surge of delight and pleasure that gave him made his cock throb sharply with impatience.

Now.

Somehow he remembered the condom on the table, somehow he managed to use his unsteady fingers to tear its packet open and slide it on, praying in the back of his mind that it was still good fifty-some years later. But at that point it would have been too late even if it wasn't.

Her eager hands were in the way, helping him roll the thing on, her fingers unfamiliar and distracting and wonderful, and he finally had to push them away so he could regain control of himself.

She breathed a laugh, said something about him being a dick—or maybe it was something *about* his dick—and then took him by the hips and began to maneuver.

"Easy," he told her, rolling her on top of him, still taking care not to startle her, but giving her control. *Just . . . oh. God.* His mind went blank as she rose over him, breasts swaying just beyond his face, her eyes soft and bedroomy, her hair in tousled, inky waves against her cheeks, the pale skin of her throat . . . and he helped position her, fitting them together.

She slid down, long and slow. A rush of blinding pleasure had him groaning aloud, his eyes, suddenly damp, closing in relief and hope. "Please," he heard himself saying. "Please."

She moved, and he moved, too, working rhythmically beneath her, holding her hips as she leaned over him, taking his mouth with hers. Their kiss was almost vicious, nearly too rough, but hard and arousing, and all the while he kept moving, up and down, up and down, feeling her close around him, her shudders and vibrations as his need built and built . . .

Wyatt tensed, holding his breath—*yes*—and grasped the peak as tears rolled from his eyes . . . *Yes.* White, fiery, incredible pleasure blasted through him and he felt his body release. Pain, pleasure, need, grief . . . pouring from him in a long, rolling, undulating fury.

White. Clean. New.

It was a long while before Wyatt became aware of anything but the draining, soul-threatening gratification that still sizzled through him. Like the last bit of electricity left in a downed wire. The sides of his face were still wet, and he roughly wiped the tears away, mildly chagrined at the display of emotion.

Someone—Remy, because he sure as hell hadn't moved—had turned off the light, and the only illumination was a glow from a triangular gap in the curtains he'd drawn. He guessed it was dawn, or near it. Hard to tell.

He felt the weight of her head on his shoulder, the warmth of her body pressed against his, a piece of her hair tickling him on the cheek. He smelled their mingled scents clinging faintly to the sheets and pillow. Her even breathing suggested she was either sleeping, very relaxed, or an excellent actress.

In the event it was the latter, he remained silent, unwilling to disturb her. He wanted only to bask in the feeling of . . . *new.*

Odd. An odd feeling, but not an unwelcome one. Repletion, satisfaction, pleasure. And . . . *new.*

That word came to mind once more and he frowned over it a little, turning it around in his lust-loosened mind as he smiled in abject happiness.

His body felt languorous and sated. Weak, in a good way. *God, that was amazing.* Beyond amazing. Spiritual.

I need a fucking cigarette—even though he didn't smoke. He started to smile, to close his eyes and sink back into the basking when he remembered. His eyes sprang open and his indulgence evaporated, turning cold.

Last night . . . he'd had sex—no, hell, he'd gone

all the way and made love. To another woman. Who was not his wife.

No comparisons, no guilt, no grief, no anger. No superimposed image of his wife on her face. Just . . . fuck. His heart was thudding hard now and Wyatt felt his calm and joy slip away. *Not good.*

The iciness grew, chilling him from the inside and he closed his eyes, struggling with himself. This wasn't the first time he'd been with someone since coming out of the caves. No—and he wasn't proud of the fact that he'd spread himself around a little. Trying to exorcise the anger and guilt, trying to forget. Trying to find something to keep from going insane. Those nights—or days, or hours . . . they'd been dark and difficult and bitter.

They still were.

But, oh, God . . . not this. He remembered suddenly what he'd said to Remy—his blunt, honest, *It's too damn easy with you.*

But why is it so hard too?

Yeah, that about covered it. His gritty eyes prickled with wetness and he pursed his lips to hold back whatever emotion was causing it.

But he knew what it was. Fear. Cold, frigid fear.

Remy stirred, pulling away, and all at once she was looking at him with those shocking blue eyes, clear and steady. Good actress, he decided ruefully. She'd been awake all along.

"How are you?" she asked.

He could drown in them. The rich blue-almost-violet hue was flecked with black and ringed with more inky color, and the whites of her eyes were pure and bright, even after a busy night. "I'm good," he said. "What about you?"

Her expression turned wary and she flattened her lips. "Good. And . . . a little scared." She looked away suddenly and he felt a tremor through her that had nothing to do with pleasure.

Hell. What was wrong with him? She'd probably lain awake all night, thinking about what was going to happen today . . . while he snored his way past dawn and worried about his flimsy guilt, mentally bellyaching about why he'd shed tears. Dickhead.

"Remy, come here," he said, gathering her to his chest. She felt so good there, dammit . . . and guilt pinged in his belly. "I'm not going to let you do it. We'll tell them you ran away, that you escaped. I'll get you out of here—there are secret tunnels and—"

"Wyatt, stop," she said. "You're making it worse. You know it's not possible. I have some ideas—"

"There is another option," he said flatly, looking at her with determination. "You know there is."

Her eyes shuttered and she bit her lip. It wasn't a coy pose, but she did it often enough that he noticed and found it extremely sexy. Except at this moment. Now, he saw a confused but brave-faced woman, and something inside him moved sharply, deeply. He was breathless.

"We could destroy the crystal," he said, pressing on.

She looked at him with unreadable eyes. "We could."

Wyatt was aware of a hollow, odd feeling in his chest. He didn't know what it meant, but it was unpleasant and frightening. "If we destroyed the crystal, they wouldn't be after you any longer," he said.

"Because they'd all die."

Their eyes met.

"Yes. All of them."

"They destroyed the earth, Remy. They killed millions."

She nodded, her expressive eyes now dull. "I know." She tugged out of his grip, rolling away. "Do you think I haven't thought about it? How easy it would be? How *free* I'd be?"

"They took my life," he said, his voice broken. "Mine and everyone else's. I *hate* them."

Remy's back, bare and fair and sleek, was facing him, but she nodded.

A sharp knock startled them both, and Wyatt surged from the bed as she dashed for the bathroom with a flash of pale flank and bouncing breast. He looked through the peephole and saw David and Cat, then heard the whine of Dantès as he scratched at the door.

Wyatt darted a look at the bed, the mussed sheets, the used condom, and the clothing strewn around the room. Not precisely the information he wanted to announce to his son and granddaughter, for Christ's sake. They knocked again, more insistently, and he called, "Just a sec."

Scooping up Remy's clothes, he shoved them in a drawer then attacked the bed as she poked her head, shoulder, and one breast out of the bathroom. "Give me my pack," she said. "Who is it?"

"David and Cat. They brought Dantès."

Her face lit up, and he tossed over the satchel of her clothing, then yanked on his shorts—accomplishing all of this preparation in less than a minute.

But when he opened the door, he swore there was a knowing glint in David's eyes—a reality that set his teeth on edge and made his insides feel even more unsettled. He took the opportunity to crouch down for a reunion with Dantès, glad to not have to look at his *son's* expression.

At least it wasn't Fence darkening his door this time. The jerkoff would probably be checking the box of Trojans to see how many were gone—and nagging him about the lack of usage. *Just one, brother? What the fuck're you thinking, with a crazy-hot piece like that in your arms?*

Wyatt closed his eyes briefly, thanking God Fence wasn't here, and wishing—

"Remy in the shower?" said David, glancing toward the closed door.

"Yes." Wyatt released Dantès and rose, noticing with discomfort that Cat was studiously *not* looking at him. She seemed very interested in gazing out the window and examining the row of books on the sill. Great. Now his granddaughter thought he was a pig.

Christ. He rubbed the spot between his eyebrows and tried to think about what to say.

"Sorry for being so early," David was saying. "Vaughn wants us to meet at eight, and I thought Remy might want to see Dantès first."

"I don't give a shit what Vaughn wants," Wyatt replied coolly. "Remy is not going to spend the day at his beck and call." But at the same time, the knowledge that they had a mere fourteen hours until the deadline made his veins turn to ice.

"I'm not what?" The bathroom door opened and Remy came out in a waft of steam. Her face was flushed, her lips full and red, and wet hair clung to her neck and throat. She was wearing a short blue dress that made her eyes look more brilliant—if that was even possible. It also showed off more cleavage than Wyatt thought necessary. His knees felt weak.

Any response would have been drowned out by Dantès, who, finally seeing his mistress, barked, whined, and bounded across the room to her. Wyatt swore he saw something damp glinting in her eyes as she knelt to hug the writhing mass of happy dog. She buried her face in his copper and brown fur, and even from his position Wyatt could see her clinging to the dog with every bit of strength she had.

I've got to fix this. She can't go.

Remy stood up a few minutes later and greeted David with more warmth than Wyatt would have been able to expect her to muster, given the circumstances. Cat turned from the window and seemed glad to see her as well, but she still hardly said a word to Wyatt.

"How about putting on a shirt," Remy said, picking up the one he'd tossed on the dresser last night. She gave a meaningful look toward Cat, and then understanding dawned.

Oh, yeah. Awkward to have one's granddaughter checking you out. As he pulled on the shirt, he realized it was probably even more awkward for the granddaughter . . .

"Vaughn has asked for everyone to meet at eight," David said.

"You don't have to—"

"It's fine," Remy said. "He might have news." But the light that had been in her eyes when she hugged Dantès, and the glint of humor when she gave him his shirt, was gone. Although she tried to hide it, he could see the fear and pain in her face. He recognized it from his own reflection, and he wanted nothing more than to get rid of it.

I have to destroy that damned crystal.

On the way to Vaughn's office Remy caught Cat for a moment alone and said, "I need you to help me."

"How?"

"You need to find a way to distract Wyatt—get him out of the way. I've got something I have to do."

Cat looked at her searchingly, and seemed about to say something but stopped. "I'll try. You don't want to tell me why, or what?"

Remy shook her head. "Just get him away. He's stubborn. So make it good. Okay? And . . . you can take Dantès back to the computer lab."

"You're not taking him with . . ." Cat's voice trailed off, as if she didn't want to say the words: *with you to the Strangers*.

"No. They'd just hurt him. He'll be happier here, with Wyatt. But don't say anything to him yet—he'll just argue."

To Remy's surprise, Marley Huvane was in the mayor's office. She, too, looked weary, and less put-together than the other times Remy had seen her. Her thick dark hair was pulled in a loose ponytail and she was talking quietly to Quent and Zoë when Vaughn walked in.

"Marley's here because she has . . . news." The mayor's voice was formal, and he took his seat behind the desk after a brief glance at the newcomer.

"My crystal has changed," Marley said. "It's cracked." She pulled the neckline of her shirt away to reveal the small blue stone, set in her skin just beneath the collarbone.

Remy leaned forward to take a good look. It was the size of a pinkie fingernail or an old pencil eraser— and looked like one too. Smooth and round, it rose like a large translucent beauty mark from the delicate skin surrounding it. "It's not the same as Lacey's," she said. "Hers went gray and opaque. Yours is still blue. But I can see the crack running through the inside of it." *And you're still alive.*

"It doesn't glow anymore," Quent said. He was looking at Marley as if trying to read her mind. "How do you feel?"

She shrugged. "A little tired. But that's most likely related to everything else that's going on. Haven't gotten much sleep the last two nights."

"Ana, do you have any idea what this means?" Vaughn asked. "This alteration of her crystal?" He didn't come right out and ask if it was a death sentence for Marley, but he might as well have.

Ana had leaned forward, and Marley allowed her to touch the small crystal. "Usually when a crystal goes dark—loses its glow—that means it's lost its life. It's dead. Eventually, it goes gray and opaque." Her voice trailed off and she glanced at Fence as he rubbed her back. "I've not seen one cracked like this before."

"Does this mean she's going to die?" Quent demanded. He turned to look at Elliott. "What happened with that woman you tried to save for Ian Marck—the one whose crystal died. What happened then? Is this the same?"

"Her situation was completely different." Elliott, too, had taken a turn to examine the crystal. "Allie—that was her name—her skin presented brittle and black around the stone, and the infection, or whatever it was, grew from there and eventually took over her whole body. From what Ian told me, the crystal had been introduced and it wasn't accepted. Like a transplanted organ might be rejected from a body. And the stone itself was a sick, yellow color. I don't see any resemblance here to what happened then."

Remy was watching Vaughn, and his fingers, curled on the desk, relaxed slightly at this pronouncement. Still, he said nothing.

"How long do you think I have?" Marley asked. She was looking at Ana, and, to Remy's surprise, at her.

"Lacey came in close contact with the crystal," she told Marley. "And the effect was immediate. She . . . expired within five minutes. It's been well over twenty-four hours since you were near the crystal."

Marley nodded, her face grim but accepting. "Well, I guess after living more than eighty years, I should be ready to go at any time."

"We should all be ready to go at any time," Sage said quietly. She patted Marley on the arm, then drew her close in an embrace. "None of us ever know which day will be our last."

"On that happy note . . ." Fence said, looking around. But he, too, was sober.

"Zoë had a thought," Quent said. "If we went out through the Waxnickis' secret tunnel, we could come up behind the Strangers and their Humvees—ambush them while they're distracted from the front. It would at least give us the chance to evacuate."

"The entrance to the secret tunnel by the Wendy's sign is within view of them," Elliott said. "I checked. But using one of the old city sewage tunnels, where Jade's favorite snakes live, we can come out far enough out of sight, like the evacuees are doing. It should work if we can figure out how to ambush them. Nice thinking, Zoë."

"It's worth a try," Vaughn said. But he didn't seem optimistic.

Remy felt for him. When they first met, she found him very attractive with his rugged looks and easy flirtation. But in the last thirty hours, he'd seemed to age before her eyes. She knew he was torn up inside about the decision facing him and the city . . . and that was part of the reason she'd made the choice she had.

They mulled over the prospects of what to use for the ambush and when to do it—when Remy was surrendering herself later tonight under cover of twilight, or during the day, well before the so-called witching hour. She didn't participate, and neither, she noticed, did Wyatt. Instead, he watched the proceedings with his inscrutable expression, casting an occasional glance at her.

Someone knocked and Wyatt, in his customary position, checked and then opened the door to admit Cat. She'd taken Dantès to the computer lab and was only now returning—but with some urgency.

"There's something going on out there," she said, looking at Wyatt and then Vaughn. "I heard someone shouting 'Fire!' And there was a lot of smoke coming from near the kitchen."

"I'll go," Elliott said, and Jade rose to follow him. Fence was in their wake, but Wyatt didn't move.

"It's a *fire*," Cat said, looking at Wyatt. "They might need you. What if someone's trapped?"

He gave a brief nod and glanced at Remy, then the rest of the room. "I'd better go check it out. Be back as soon as I can." He looked at Cat. "You going to show us where?"

"Yeah," she said, and slipped out the door.

The dangerous blaze in the kitchen turned out to be a small fire in a metal wastepaper basket stuck in the corner not too far from the restaurant area. Cat seemed properly embarrassed about raising the alarm, but Wyatt was too distracted to be annoyed.

It was the perfect opportunity.

As soon as he was assured everything was under control and no one needed to be dragged from a fiery room, Wyatt found what he needed and slipped off to the computer lab on his own. Confident that Remy was safely in the custody of the others, he knew he had the time to do what had to be done.

Up, up, up, down. He pushed the buttons and the old elevator doors slid open. The spiral staircase was revealed and down he went.

Dantès greeted him with a whine and a lick, and Wyatt took the time to hug him back, accepting a few good swipes from a canine tongue. The dog, as always, made him feel calm and at home. Loved.

After a moment Wyatt stood. He looked around and confirmed what seemed obvious: no one was here. That would make things so much easier.

He knew where the crystal was kept—in the second room, stored in a file cabinet. One of the drawers held the piece of Jarrid stone that Quent and Zoë had stolen. Another drawer contained the Mother crystal, currently wrapped in asbestos he'd removed from the semi-truck cab's brakes. He had no idea if the asbestos did anything to contain the crystal's heat or otherwise mask it, but he figured it was worth a try in case it started to burn again. Not that it would matter for much longer.

Placing the crystal on the surface of a sturdy table, Wyatt unwrapped it. It sat there, orange and glowing, unassuming in its width and breadth. Hard to believe it held so much power; it was hardly larger than his thumbnail.

He hefted the sledgehammer in his hand, looking down at the object that, if destroyed, would save countless lives—not only the people of Envy, but anyone else who would ever get in the way of the people who sought it.

Remy.

The memory of her face rose in his mind. Strained and frightened, heavy with knowledge. Acceptance.

He gritted his teeth. She wouldn't have agreed to do what he was about to do, for the same reason that she'd decided to give herself up to the Strangers. Which was why he'd made the choice.

She could make hers. He would make his. Someone had to do it.

He lifted the sledgehammer. One blow with its massive steel head and the crystal would shatter, be ground to dust. And it would all be over. Remy could be free. Envy would be safe. The Strangers destroyed.

His family—and all of the world—would be avenged.

Maybe then he could find some peace.

The hammer was heavy above his head. Wyatt closed his eyes, thought of Cath and Abby . . . everyone he'd ever known, and those he knew now. David. Dantès. Remy.

And he brought it down.

No sooner had Cat dragged Wyatt from the meeting place than Remy looked at Simon. "I . . . uh . . . left something up in the room. Personal. Will you go with me to get it?"

"I'll get it," Sage offered. "It's probably better if you stay hidden. Especially with the deadline so close." She couldn't help but look at the clock, and Remy's eyes followed.

Thirteen hours.

Or less, if Remy had her way.

"Oh, you wouldn't be able to find it," Remy said, and gave Sage a look.

The redhead's eyes widened in understanding, and she frowned. Her expression said, *Are you sure?*

"Simon, do you mind?" Remy asked again.

"Of course not." He seemed oblivious to the silent communication between the two women, and stood. Because of Simon's background and the fact that he was the security and authority figure for Envy, Remy knew she'd be well-protected.

Besides. They weren't going far.

As soon as they got out of Vaughn's office, she turned to Simon and said, "Take me to Ian Marck. I need to talk to him."

He paused, looking her over with expressionless brown eyes. "You planned all that, didn't you?"

"I had to. Take me to him, please? Before Wyatt gets back."

He didn't look pleased, but took her arm and led her off through a short warren of hallways. They came to a door and he drew a handgun from his back waistband, then unlocked the door.

Remy went in and found Ian sitting on a sofa in accommodations just as comfortable as her own. He rose when they came in, and she was gratified to notice that Simon replaced the gun in his waistband and took a seat near the door.

"Could we speak alone?" she said, turning to

Simon. His cool eyes went from her to Ian and back, but he didn't argue. He simply stood, opened the door, and disappeared into the hallway.

When the door closed behind him, Remy turned back to Ian.

"To what do I owe this pleasure?" he asked.

"I need you to tell me everything you know about the Mother crystal. Why the Strangers want it, what you know about its power . . . how my grandfather obtained it . . . everything."

His lips shifted into a humorless smile. "And then what?"

"I'll make sure you're released. When I surrender myself to the Strangers."

His ice-blue eyes widened. "You're going to go to them?"

"Yes. And you're going to take me. You're a bounty hunter, right? You track down bounties, right? I'm pretty sure I'm the biggest damn bounty you've ever had the fortune of getting."

"You do know what they'll do when they have you?" he said. Some of the chill eased from his eyes and he looked at her searchingly.

"I have my ideas. None of them are pretty." She swallowed and tried to force the thoughts away. "They want the crystal, and I know where it is. They won't actually kill me until they find out what they want to know . . . and I'm hoping by then I'll either have escaped or I'll be dead . . . my own way. Painlessly." Remy forced her lips into a shaky smile.

"You're unbelievable," he said. He shook his head, still looking at her. "You're a hell of a woman, Remy. It's too damn bad I don't do relationships." His smile went a little crooked. "But you'd sure as hell be the one if I did."

"How kind of you to let me down easy, Ian." She narrowed her eyes. "Now that we've got that out of the way—time's running out. The Mother crystal. Tell me everything."

"I will tell you what I know . . . but understand there's no way of verifying it all. The Mother crystal and what happened with Remington Truth has been the stuff of whispers and hearsay for fifty years. I don't think anyone knows for certain what happened except your grandfather, Preston, and Fielding . . . and they're all dead now, aren't they?"

"Okay, fine—I got the caveats. Tell me what you've heard."

"The Mother crystal. A piece of the ultimate power source for the Atlanteans, and the source of the immortality that lives in the Strangers' crystals. It was a gift from the Atlanteans to the Cult of Atlantis—you know what that is?" When she nodded, he continued, "They gave it to the leaders of the Cult of Atlantis to enable them to cause the Change—and in gratitude for doing so. All the Atlantean crystals—at least the life-giving ones—are connected. So when one comes in proximity with another, depending how strong its power is, they can communicate or transfer energy between them. That's how they caused the Change. They chose places throughout the world to align powerful crystals along natural energy centers, deep in the earth or the ocean. The way I understand it, when the Cult of Atlantis used the Mother crystal's power—in conjunction with some other energy generated beneath the sea by the Atlanteans—all of those areas sort of erupted or exploded in a catastrophic manner."

"Causing earthquakes, tsunamis, and the entire earth to shift on its axes?" Remy had heard enough from Lou and Theo Waxnicki about their theories—which were surprisingly corroborated by Ian's information. They'd been correct.

"Yes. It was like a domino effect that affected weather and climate as well as civilization."

"And you've allied yourself with these people," Remy said, her voice unsteady. "My God. No wonder you're . . . the way you are."

His face went rigid. "You have no idea, darling."

She drew in a deep breath and continued. "Something happened a few weeks ago to make my crystal—the Mother crystal—start to burn."

"It must have been activated somehow, by some other powerful energy stone. Until then it was dormant and that was why they've been looking for it for fifty years. Once it came back to life, or whatever you want to call it, it reignited its energy and burned. And it can be tracked and located."

"Why do the Strangers want it?" Remy knew what Lacey had told her and what Ana had surmised . . . but she wanted to know if Ian had the same understanding.

"It's powerful. And it's dangerous to them at the same time," Ian said. "You never want your enemy to control something that can destroy you." His eyes glittered with loathing. "That's why I need to have it, Remy. Let me have it, come away with me, and I promise you'll never be in danger again."

"You want it so you can destroy the Strangers?"

He bared his teeth. "Oh no . . . it's not that simple.

I want it so they know I have it. I want it because *they* want it. I want it for revenge."

"Lacey died when she came in contact with it."

"So that part *is* true," he said to himself. "Which means they have to have a mortal . . ." His dark smile became harsher. "Perfect."

"But Marley . . . she didn't die. At least not yet. Her crystal is still blue, but it's cracked. And it doesn't glow. Lacey's turned solid gray and she died within minutes."

His eyes narrowed. "That's interesting. Could be proximity. Could be the type of crystal—Lacey's is obviously newer, since Marley has had hers for fifty years and Lacey only a year or two. Might just take longer for some . . ."

"But if the crystal is so dangerous, why do they want to have it? Why do the Strangers want it if it will kill them?"

"Because if someone else has it, they can annihilate all of them at once—you said it yourself. All they have to do is smash it, and *boom*! The energy evaporates from their crystals and they're all dead. Surely you know your history, Remy. The United States had a nuclear bomb and so the—who was it?—the Soviet . . . Union? . . . had to have one too. It was a stalemate."

She was shaking her head. "But if the crystal will kill them, how will they do anything with it? I mean if they obtained it, whoever got near it would die."

"That," he said, his eyes turning cold, "is what they have the zombies for. Their orange eyes? They're from minuscule crystals—grit from the same node the Mother came from. The zombies are immune to the Mother crystal—they're actually probably attached to it. Somehow. Unlike the Strangers who wear the blue crystals."

"Orange and blue, fire and water," Remy murmured. "Opposites. Destructive opposites. Makes sense."

"Right. That's how the zombies found you once the crystal started burning. They were coming a lot faster and crazier in the last few weeks, weren't they? So they'd use the zombies to protect and guard the Mother crystal once they get it. That was how I found you this last time. I followed the zombies." There was no remorse in his eyes.

Remy nodded. It was as she'd suspected. "But again, how would they get it if they can't go near it? The zombies are stone dumb. They'd need . . . Oh." She looked at Ian, who had the balls to meet her gaze steadily. "Bounty hunters. Mortal bounty hunters."

"And there you have it," he replied.

CHAPTER 23

Striding along the hall toward the main area of New York–New York, Wyatt looked neither right nor left.

"Yo, Wyatt."

Curling his fingers into a tight fist, he stopped at the sound of Simon's voice, but didn't turn. He didn't want to talk to anyone right now.

He needed to be alone . . . or with someone who wasn't Simon.

"What's up?" he said, making little effort to hide his reluctance as Simon approached.

"You okay?" his friend asked—which was clearly not what he'd meant to say.

"What's up?" he repeated.

Simon got the message and moved on. "After you left . . . Remy asked me to take her to see Ian Marck. I thought you should know . . . she's leaving with him."

Wyatt felt his face drain of color. "What?"

"She wanted to speak to him alone, but unbeknownst to them I . . . uh . . . stuck around. I heard the entire conversation—"

"What do you mean, she's 'leaving with him'?"

"The gist of the conversation is she offered to be his bounty. He's taking her to the Strangers to collect. I heard enough to know that she was going to make another excuse and come back to get him in an hour and they were going to leave. It took me a while to find you . . . Where were you?"

Wyatt squeezed his eyes closed and tried desperately to make sense of everything. He actually felt light-headed. "I was down in the damned computer lab." Then he looked at Simon. "What do you mean, 'another excuse'?"

They were already striding along, Wyatt following Simon's lead to where, he presumed, Remy currently was.

"That so-called fire in the kitchen? I think it was a setup. To give her the chance to talk to Ian."

Without you knowing.

Simon didn't even have to say it.

Wyatt stopped. "To hell with it. If she wants to sneak away with Marck, who am I to stop her? God knows I've tried—to hell with it all. Let her fucking go."

He spun away, blinded by anger, and left Simon standing there watching. The pub was close by and Wyatt headed directly there, right into the bar he and his friends had gone into their very first night in Envy . . . just about a year ago.

It was fitting. This would be his last night in Envy.

He decided then and there he was going to go back to Glenway with David and Cat. There was no reason to stick around here, especially once Remington Truth surrendered herself to the Strangers.

He could be with his family—what left of it. The family the Strangers had nearly destroyed.

Wyatt growled out an order for a whiskey, vaguely noticing that he wasn't alone in seeking solace with drink. There were enough people in the pub he assumed were planning to drink their way into oblivion before the attack came . . . or maybe they'd been told there wouldn't be an attack any longer because Remington Truth had appeared and were celebrating.

When the glass was set in front of him, he stared down into the liquid gold. The smell rose to his nostrils, and he lifted the glass, tossing the entire shot down in one gulp. Fury, irrational and hot, blazed through him, coloring his vision.

He hadn't been able to do it.

When it came down to it, he hadn't been able to do it. At the last minute he brought the sledgehammer down on the table, purposely missing the crystal. Left a big fucking dent in the metal surface and the crystal untouched.

Then he'd picked up the damned stone and whipped it across the room. It slammed into the drywall like a bullet, embedded itself like a crystal in the flesh of a Stranger. He stared at it for a long moment, looking at its feeble orange glow, tempted . . . tempted once more to smash it and annihilate the people who'd taken it upon themselves to be God . . . to destroy and rebuild the earth. To decide who lived and died. To sell out immortality.

His vision swam and he'd dashed at his eyes with trembling fingers.

At last, defeated, he pried the stone out of the wall, trembling with rage and loathing. Those bastards had taken everything . . . and yet, he couldn't bring himself to destroy them. Even to save Remy.

For how could he ever look honestly into those

blue eyes if he did? She was willing to give herself up, one life for that of many.

As he'd done countless times himself.

Furious and yet defeated, he had shoved the crystal back in the file cabinet and left the computer lab, neglecting to give Dantès more than a brief goodbye pat.

And now here he was, staring down into his second whiskey, more confused and screwed up than he'd ever been in his life. At least when he'd come out of the cave he knew how to feel: dead.

Now he was just lost.

When someone slid onto the stool next to him, Wyatt assumed it was Simon. Instead of looking over, he sneered down at his hands cupping the glass, curling his lip in a threat to *leave me the fuck alone*.

"If I'd have given you that look when I was younger, you'd have swatted my ass."

Startled, he looked over into his son's eyes. "You're probably right," he said after the surprise passed.

David ordered a drink, too, and Wyatt took a sip of his own, contemplating the fact that his eight-year-old son was sitting next to him in an old man's body, having a whiskey. Beyond surreal.

"You haven't asked much about Cat's mother," David said when the bartender moved away.

Wyatt's mouth twitched up at one corner. "We've been a little distracted. I figured there'd be time enough later to get the details of your life for the past fifty years." A ripple of grief had him tightening his fingers around the glass.

"Cat's mother, Grace, was actually my second wife," David continued with hardly a pause. "I was married to Marie, the love of my life, for three years before she died."

"I'm sorry," Wyatt said. "Really sorry."

"Yeah. Well, we don't have very many fancy treatments for cancer in this world—unlike Dr. House. So," David said, continuing once again in a no-nonsense way, "I have a little empathy for the fact that you lost us all—your wife and children. Obviously what I went through was nothing compared to your hell—"

"What are you talking about? You *lived* through hell. You were a boy, a young boy . . . and you lost everything. Not just *your* world, but—" Wyatt's throat closed up and he pinched the bridge of his nose. Christ. He was going to lose it right here in the goddamn bar.

David put a hand on his arm and squeezed gently. "You're right. It was hell. It was so far beyond hell, you can't imagine. But here I am today. Relatively healthy for an old guy, not bad looking and with most of my hair—thanks to the great genes of my father. Hardly ever have the nightmares anymore—it's been a good three years since the last one. Still have a good portion of my faculties still in place, with two amazing daughters plus a darling granddaughter . . . *and* I found my father again. After fifty years. And he's such a stud my daughter can't hardly keep her eyes off him when he's not wearing a shirt. Jeez . . . could you invent a more awkward situation?"

In spite of his misery, Wyatt couldn't hold back a laugh. But the flash of absurd humor was short-lived and he glanced over at David. "It's a miracle we found each other. The greatest gift I've ever gotten."

His son swirled his whiskey and lifted it to drink. "I thought I'd never be happy again after I lost Marie. I felt like every time I allowed myself to smile or laugh, I was out of line. It was my duty to mourn her and miss her and keep myself for her. Forever. You know?"

Wyatt rolled his eyes. He knew where David was going with this. "Our situations are worlds different."

"How is that? Because you have guilt to add into the mix? Is that what makes you special, what makes you able to be more of an asshole and for longer than I was? You feel guilty for going on a vacation, so you can never be happy again? You can never allow yourself to live because of something that happened fifty years ago that you—nor anyone else—could never have foreseen or prevented?"

"What's your point?" he growled. "That I should be happy? That I should smile and forget what happened? I *can't*. The earth was destroyed. All of civilization—fucking *gone*. My family was murdered. You were left—"

"My point," David said, craning around in front of him so he could catch Wyatt's stubborn gaze, "is that Mom's been gone for fifty years. There's not a damn thing your guilt and grief and dickishness is going to do to bring her back or to change what happened. I'm not suggesting that you shouldn't feel any grief or sadness. Of course you should—in your mind, it's been only a year. But don't hold back on my account, Wyatt. Don't put it on me."

"I don't know what you're talking about."

"Bullshit. The minute you remembered Cat and I existed, back when you found Remy, you shut it all down. Cut it off." He settled back in his chair and took a big gulp of whiskey. "Whatever's going on with you and Remy is your business—but what it's *not* is a betrayal of Mom or her memory. That was a lesson I had to learn myself, after Marie died . . . when I met Grace, only a year later." He tilted his head. "Hm. You and I have a lot more in common than I realized, including superior taste in women."

Wyatt finished his whiskey, swishing the last bit around in his mouth before swallowing. The heat from the liquor had abated, his fury had leveled off. He remembered the pure white light of pleasure, the intense body and mind release he'd had with Remy last night. It was like nothing he'd ever experienced before . . . as if something had been dragged out from the darkest depths of his soul and then brought into white light. Cathartic.

"Oh, thank God, there you are!" The next thing he knew, Cat was there, pulling his arm to drag him off the bar stool. "You've got to come quick. Down to the computer lab—"

"Knock it off, Cat," Wyatt said, tempering his irritation because she was his granddaughter. But still. "I know what you're doing. You can tell Remy she doesn't need to distract me—"

"It's the lab, it's on fire, I swear to you," she said, pulling harder. "It's not like that. Dad, tell him!"

"I think we better go," David said, his attention going from Cat to Wyatt. His face was sober, even concerned.

"The lab?" Wyatt said, still reluctant, even though a little prickle of worry niggled at him. "Dantès?"

"He's out, but it's burning . . . it's weird. Come *on*."

By now Wyatt's hesitation had evaporated. He followed Cat at a full run, aware that David was behind him, keeping up as well as he could. The secret elevator doors were open when they got there, guarded by

Dantès, who whined and looked concerned when he saw Wyatt.

He bounded down the spiral stairs, sniffing but unable to scent smoke, and faltered, wondering if this was, indeed, another trick. But no, once he got to the bottom of the stairs, he saw something glowing in the room beyond the main computer room. Orange and flickering.

Still no smoke . . . which was odd. An uncomfortable prickling rushing over him, Wyatt bolted into the room. He was met by a wave of heat, blasting into him like a wall.

The place was melting. The metal table, the file cabinet . . . all had softened, the cabinet folded into little more than a silver puddle. The walls were dripping with moisture, shuddering from the temperature. He saw the orange crystal, blazing and shimmering with what could only be profound heat, sitting on the melted file cabinet next to the Jarrid stone.

His mind racing even as he rushed into the room, Wyatt wondered how the two stones had come to be next to each other . . . and then he remembered. He'd been so infuriated, he'd shoved the Mother crystal into the file cabinet without wrapping it in asbestos . . . and apparently into the wrong drawer. The one that contained the Jarrid stone.

He drew in burning air, felt it scorch through his lungs and seep into his skin, eyes, nostrils . . . just as it had during the fire. But there was no smoke, nothing to clog his lungs and vision, and he was moving. Miraculously, he was able to make his limbs work, and he stood over the two stones. They weren't fused together but were next to each other, and he could see the energy radiating between them.

Aware that no one was there, that no one could have followed him this far, Wyatt reached for the orange crystal. He saw his hand move through the undulating waves of heat, shimmering blue and orange and yellow, and when he touched the stone, he felt it sear into his flesh.

But he picked it up, enclosing it in his fist . . . and the room cooled.

Instantly.

Holy fucking shit.

CHAPTER 24

Remy swallowed hard. Her insides churned and sloshed and she could hardly draw a breath. The heat of the day was at its height, for it was just past noon—ten hours before the deadline.

She wanted to get it over with.

She wanted to know Envy was going to be safe.

She wanted to be gone before she had to see Wyatt again.

Ian glanced down at her as they walked out of the gates of Envy. His eyes appeared strained, and not simply because of the sun blazing down on them. She knew that for all his harsh comments and selfishness, he was concerned for her too. And, knowing Ian, concerned for himself as well.

The semicircle of five Humvees were in plain sight, less than a half mile from the city. Guards stood in front of them with rifles, halfway between the gate and their vehicles. Close enough that Remy could see their faces.

She hoped to hell they wouldn't shoot until they found out who she was.

Ian must have had the same thought, for he raised

his hand in greeting and called out the name of one of the bounty hunters who stood there. Although his wave was acknowledged, the firearms remained upright and at the ready.

Apparently his peers didn't trust Ian any more than she did, when it came down to it.

She walked across the thick green grass and felt the walls of Envy rise behind her. She was not going to think about what she was doing. What she was leaving behind.

It would do no good and it would only serve to weaken her resolve. Just one step after the other. Step. Step. Step.

She had to blink hard to hold back tears. A picklike sensation scraped her insides hollow as she forced her limbs into motion. She should be thinking about what to say and how to conduct herself with the Strangers, but instead she was thinking of everything behind her. Her new friends. Her beloved dog. The man she loved.

Leaving Wyatt to be with his family, to settle the battle within himself, was the hardest part . . . and yet, in some ways, it was the easiest. Life with him would never be easy. He was too prickly, too autocratic, too caught up in shoulds rather than coulds.

But what a man he was.

She lifted her chin as she and Ian approached the guards. He greeted two of them by name, and the rest edged closer. One of them looked familiar to Remy from her bounty hunting days with Ian.

"Tell Hegelson I'm here," her companion said.

"Hegelson? What the hell would he be doing here?" said a tall man with a shaved head. He sneered.

Apparently, Ian knew better. "He's here. Tell him Ian Marck has what he wants."

"I remember you," said one of the men. He looked at Remy with disinterest then turned his attention back to Ian. "Hegelson doesn't want to be disturbed. He's got other things on his mind. Until ten o'clock tonight, that is." His grin was unpleasant.

Another of the guards jostled against the man who'd recognized her. "That's the bitch Seattle had," he muttered, scratching his bald head. "Remember her? I don't think Hegelson'll want to tap that."

Ian tensed next to her, reaching for something, but Remy kept her eyes coolly on the bald man. "Oh he'll want to see me," she said. "I'm Remington Truth."

All the heads swiveled toward her, and Remy knew she'd crossed the point of no return. She might as well play it all the way. "Get Hegelson out here or he'll never get the Mother crystal."

Ian glanced down at her. She didn't bother to give him an apologetic look; she'd seen no need to give him a play by play of her intentions.

The men scrambled into action then, with several rushing off toward an old house—presumably to carry the message.

When the one who'd sneered at Ian aimed his rifle at them, Remy said, "Put it down. Did you not notice I came here of my own volition? If you hurt me or Ian, you'll never get the crystal."

"Oh, I have my ways of getting information I need . . . whether it's offered freely or not so freely." The sneering man's eyes were narrow and predatory.

"That might be the case, but Hegelson won't appreciate it if either of us are in no condition to give the information. Trust me. He's been looking for this for fifty years. You don't want to chance fucking it up."

He looked as if he wanted to say something else,

but a commotion behind him drew his attention. The group of guards parted to reveal a man whom Remy instantly realized was Liam Hegelson.

"Remington Truth," he said as he stepped forward. "And Ian Marck. How fascinating."

"I'd say it was a pleasure to meet you, but, well, it's not," Remy told him. She was damned proud of her strong, steady voice. "I have no respect for a man who would hold an entire city hostage in order to get what he wants."

Hegelson's blue eyes gleamed. "A man does what a man must do to gain his freedom."

"As does a woman." Remy scraped her attention over him, mustering up every bit of disdain she could. She even curled her lip—a move she'd learned from Wyatt. "Which is why I've brought you this."

As she reached into the pocket of her pretty blue sundress, Ian turned to her, shock and dismay on his face. "No, Remy," he said, reaching for her arm. "Don't—"

A rifle suddenly at his throat choked him off, and she looked at Sneering Man, who seemed altogether too trigger happy. "You're overreacting," she told him. "And you're being rude." She looked at Hegelson. "Tell them to back off. All of them. Or this discussion is over."

Hegelson shrugged. "If the discussion ends, the deadline is reinstated. Ten p.m. and Envy is toast."

Remy kept her smile cool. "Do you really think I came out here willingly without some contingency plan? I haven't evaded you and your goons for twenty years by being a fool. Now tell your minions to back off or I walk away."

She could feel Ian's confusion and tension next to

her, but didn't spare him a glance. He'd played his games. She could play hers.

Hegelson eyed her hand, which was still thrust in her pocket, then gestured for the guards to step back. "Disarm," he said.

Remy waited until the guards were a good distance away before removing her hand from her pocket. Her fingers were closed, and Hegelson's eyes went directly to her fist. She could feel hunger and greed vibrating from him, and it confused her.

Did he not realize the Mother crystal was deadly?

She held out her hand and opened it.

"What the hell is that?" Hegelson's face turned furious. "What is this?"

"This is the dead crystal from your bounty hunter Lacey," she said. She glanced down at the eerie object in her hand. It looked like a large gray sun fashioned from granite. The center was a stone, the stone that had protruded from Lacey's skin. But radiating from the stone were a multitude of tiny arms or rays that had grown like roots or veins through Lacey's body. When the crystal was alive, it brought life and immortality to the wearer.

But now . . . it was dead.

And Hegelson clearly recognized it.

"Consider this me doing you a favor," Remy said. "Lacey came in close proximity to the Mother crystal and this is what happened to her. She died within minutes. Marley Huvane—yes, she's been here in Envy all this time—did the same. If I give you the Mother crystal, Liam, you won't have it in your possession for more than ten minutes and you'll be dead."

"You expect me to believe this?" Hegelson choked. "You're even more foolish than I thought. I—"

"We've already established how foolish I'm not," Remy said. "I came out here in good faith to negotiate with you, and by doing so, Liam . . . I've saved your life. Now—"

A loud noise behind her drew his attention, and Ian's too. Remy looked over her shoulder and her insides dropped.

Striding toward them with smooth, purposeful steps was Wyatt. He was accompanied by Simon, Elliott, Quent, and Fence, two of them flanking him on either side.

For a moment Remy was struck by the sight of them. They looked like a group of superheroes or a team of warriors: the cluster of five men, powerful, filled with purpose and beautiful in their strength.

As they approached, she tried to catch Wyatt's eye, but he was looking at Ian, and then Hegelson.

"Who the hell are you?" demanded the latter, gesturing for his guards.

"I've come to give you what you want," Wyatt said, holding out a clenched fist. "The Mother crystal—"

"No!" Remy cried, shoving at his arm. "What the hell are you doing?" She spun on him. Why was he ruining everything?

"The Mother crystal." Hegelson fairly licked his chops . . . but then with a glance at Remy, he seemed to recall her warning and stepped back several yards. "You, Morris—you get it from him."

"No, Wyatt," Remy said again, trying to shove him out of the way. "I have this under control," she hissed between clenched teeth, glaring up at him as she tried not to cry. He was so solid, and warm, and familiar, and she was *furious* with him . . . and yet . . . he was *here*. "You're ruining everything!"

He looked down at her for the first time. His cold eyes softened. "Trust me," he said.

She drew in her breath to argue, but something in his expression . . . something *new* . . . stopped her. The clutch in her gut eased. And she stepped away. "Fine," she said, loud enough for the others to hear. "Give him what he wants."

"Morris!" Hegelson ordered. "Take the stone into custody." He edged back even more, the damn coward.

"Here it is," Wyatt said, and to Remy's surprise and shock, he flung the stone from his clenched fist.

As it arched through the air in a glittering orange blaze, Ian and Hegelson both gave involuntary cries and started toward it. At the same time, Wyatt grabbed Remy by the front of her dress and yanked her toward him.

"You aren't going anywhere," he said, his eyes dark and filled with an expression that made her insides flutter. "Stay with me, Remy." The next thing she knew, he was kissing the living hell out of her . . . and despite everything going on around them, she had her arms around his neck and was kissing him back. Someone—it had to be Fence—gave a gleeful whistle, and she heard the low rumble of his chuckle.

But then she remembered where they were and the situation they were in, and she struggled out of Wyatt's arms. "What the hell—"

She stopped talking when she saw what everyone around them was looking at.

Not more than a hundred yards away there was a column of . . . something. Something shimmering, like heat waves in the sun. Morris lay on the ground nearby, struggling to pull himself to his feet. Ian stood halfway between them and the shimmering column, and it wasn't until he shifted to the side that Remy saw the orange glow on the ground.

"Is that . . . the Mother crystal?" she murmured.

Wyatt nodded, sliding his arm around her. "I told them they could have it," he said, grinning. *Grinning*. Wyatt was grinning.

Remy felt her insides explode into a burst of warm, delicious butterflies. "So you *can* smile," she managed to say.

He looked down at her, that devastating smile enough to make her knees weak. Then it faded a little. "You weren't running away with Ian . . . you were leaving *me*," he said. "Weren't you?"

She frowned, uncertain what he was trying to say. Dimly, she realized the others had edged away, some toward the shimmering orange crystal and others toward the Humvees.

"I was setting you free," she said, not sure if it answered the question. Regardless, it was the truth.

"And if I realized I didn't want to be free . . . ?"

"Then I wouldn't be leaving."

"Ever?"

"Ever."

"Look," he said, and pointed. She saw the crowd of people around the stone, but none of them could get close enough to touch it. Even from where she and Wyatt stood, she could see the heat wavering, and fancied she could even feel it. It was a stalemate. A checkmate.

"How long has it been like that?" she asked.

"Since I tried to destroy it," he told her.

"What? Wyatt, *no*." Shocked and horrified, she pulled away, but he was shaking his head. "God, no, you *didn't*—"

"I said 'tried.'" He took her by the shoulders and looked down at her with sad brown eyes. "I thought I could do it for you—to save you. But then I realized . . . not only that I couldn't, but that you would never forgive me for doing it."

"No, no, I wouldn't want that," she said, her pounding heart settling. "Never."

"I know. And so I couldn't do it. So I got mad and threw it in the drawer next to the Jarrid stone . . . without thinking and without wrapping it in asbestos. I can only guess, but I think they must have reacted with each other and . . . wow."

"Wow is right."

He slid his arms around her and pulled her close, then, looking down at her, eased away. "Aw, Remy, I'm so sorry," he said, his brows furrowing with chagrin.

"It's all right," she said. "You've had a lot to work through. I knew—"

"No, no . . . no that." He was grinning again. It was as if once released, his smile could no longer be contained. "I'm sorry about that," he said, and gestured to the front of her darling new sundress . . . which was now black with soot where he'd grabbed her.

He brandished the hand that had been holding the crystal, and she saw that the blackened flesh was already peeling away, and that the skin on his wrist and arm was puckered.

Remy couldn't quite hide her cry of dismay. After all, it was her new dress. She'd worn it once. She shook her head.

Life with him would never be easy.

But . . . oh, life with him would be wonderful.

EPILOGUE

Once he'd made his point, Wyatt collected the crystal, fisting it in his phoenixlike hand as the spectators gawked.

He walked over to Liam Hegelson, who prudently backed away from the proximity of the stone, and said, "Here's how it's going to be. You remember M.A.D.—from your history lessons, wayyy back before you destroyed the fucking world? The Cold War?"

Hegelson, whose face had gone rigid and a little frightened, replied, "Yes, of course. Mutually Assured Destruction. The U.S. had the bomb, and so did the Soviet Union. So neither of them were going to use it, knowing that the other would do the same and both would be destroyed."

"Exactly. So this little gem," Wyatt said with a steely grin, "is going to be kept in a very special place inside Envy. If there is any breath of a threat from you or your . . . minions—living, immortal, or undead—the crystal gets annihilated. Instantly. And you know what happens then. Understand?"

Hegelson glared at him. "How do I know you won't just go ahead and destroy it anyway?"

"I already had the chance. Unlike you and yours, I'm not into genocide. Even to protect the ones I love. And as you can see . . . there's no one else who can get close enough to the stone but me. You'll just have to trust me." Wyatt bared his teeth in a very unfriendly smile.

"Very well," Hegelson said. And with that he turned and stalked away, calling his men to follow him.

"And that," murmured Wyatt, "is the end of that. At least for a while."

Amid the sound of Humvee engines starting up and the rumble as they drove away, Wyatt walked over to Ian. "I'm not certain whether I should thank you or beat the hell out of you. So maybe it's best if you be on your way. You'll never get the crystal, and you sure as hell won't get her."

Ian gave him a cool smile. "If I'd wanted her, I could have had her. But as it is, I wish you the best. Both of you."

He turned and walked away.

"It took me a long time to fall in love with you," Remy said, teasing her finger through the patch of hair on Wyatt's chest. "You were such a jerk."

"I believe the word you preferred was dickhead."

"Right. You wouldn't even tell me your name when you were trying to keep me from leaving Envy." She yanked gently at a few hairs for emphasis.

"I was pissed at you. The last time I'd seen you, you put a damned bullet in the wall above my shoulder."

"I told you not to move, and you did. I wanted you to know I wasn't playing around."

"I *breathed*."

"So you say. I think you were about to lunge at me and try to disarm me. You had that look in your eye."

His lips twitched. "I would have succeeded if you didn't have such a happy trigger finger."

"So I was *right*! You were testing me."

"Damn straight. I don't like anyone pointing a gun at me. Even you." He combed his fingers through her loose hair, then gave his own little yank.

"Ow." She smiled and kissed his jaw. Bliss. Absolute bliss. For the first time she could remember, Remy felt safe. Relaxed. And *home*.

"But it wasn't until you threw that damned snake at me that I realized what a piece of work you were," he said, still playing with her hair.

"Is that when you fell for me?"

He shook his head, seemingly distracted by the way her dark hair looked against the pale skin of her breast. He stroked his hand gently over skin and hair, making the two textures slide against each other. She gave a luscious shiver as he said, "Hell, no. You just made me more annoyed. I almost fell on my ass down those stairs. Could have broken my neck."

"So you've claimed. But it wasn't a very big snake, there were only a few stairs . . . and you're much more coordinated than that," she said, arching toward him a little. She smiled in gratification when his gaze shifted down to her breast and he leaned in toward her.

There was silence for a while, broken only by the soft sounds of gentle suction, the quiet, delicate smacks of mouth to mouth. A soft sigh, a low groan.

When he pulled back, using his tongue to take a quick swipe at the corner of her mouth, Wyatt said,

"When I found you . . . under the truck, I was still pretty pissed off at you. Especially when you took one look at me—through your puffy, black eyes in a battered face—and said 'You' through your cut and swollen mouth. Like you'd've been happier to see anyone else but me—when you couldn't even stand up."

"You just kept showing up—how could that be? The fact that you were the one to find me . . ."

"That was all Dantès."

"Well, he wouldn't have been there to find me if you hadn't had him with you. And besides, you didn't seem pissed. You were . . ."

"The word is horrified." All of the gentle teasing left his voice and he tightened his arms around her. "It's a wonder—a miracle—that you survived . . . both physically and emotionally. That you had room for . . . this. With me."

She buried her face in that warm section of his neck and throat, drawing in the familiar, comforting smell of him. "I love you," she said. "So much. But you were a dickhead for a long time."

The side of his face moved against her temple as he smiled. "And you were a pain in the ass."

"And then we fell in love."

Next month, don't miss these exciting new love stories only from Avon Books

Kiss of Temptation by Sandra Hill

Condemned to prison for the sin of lust, Viking vampire angel—or vangel—Ivak Sigurdsson is finding centuries of celibacy depressing. When temptation comes in the form of beautiful Gabrielle Sonnier—who needs help breaking her brother out of prison—Ivak can't help but give in. But as the two join forces, they both begin to wonder if their passionate bond is really only lust, or something more.

Stolen Charms by Adele Ashworth

Determined to wed the infamous thief, the Black Knight, Miss Natalie Haislett has no trouble approaching Jonathan Drake—reputed to be a friend of the Knight—for an introduction. This may be difficult as Drake is the Knight himself! While traveling together in France as a married couple in search of the Knight, passions bloom and the daring bandit sets his sights on the most priceless treasure of all . . . Natalie's heart.

Sins of a Ruthless Rogue by Anna Randol

When Clayton Campbell shows up on Olivia Swift's doorstep, she's stunned. No longer the boy who stole her heart, this hardened man has a lust for vengeance in his eyes. Clayton cannot deny that the sight of Olivia rouses in him a passion like never before. But as tensions between them rise, the hard-hearted agent will face his greatest battle yet . . . for his heart.

At Avon Books, we know your passion for romance—once you finish one of our novels, you find yourself wanting more.

May we tempt you with . . .

- **Excerpts** from our upcoming releases.

- Entertaining **extras**, including authors' personal photo albums and book lists.

- Behind-the-scenes **scoop** on your favorite characters and series.

- **Sweepstakes** for the chance to win free books, romantic getaways, and other fun prizes.

- Writing **tips** from our authors and editors.

- **Blog** with our authors and find out why they love to write romance.

- **Exclusive content** that's not contained within the pages of our novels.

Join us at
www.avonbooks.com

An Imprint of HarperCollins*Publishers*
www.avonromance.com

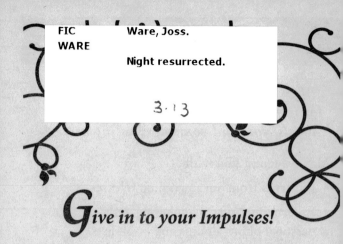